They were bound by love, hate and greed . . .

BETHANY NEWTON. Wrongly sentenced to an Australian penal colony, she dreamed that one day, she would be reunited with her beloved daughter—even when an infamous rogue helped her flee to America . . . and changed her heart, and life, forever.

"BLACK JACK" CUTLER. His reputation as a highwayman was surpassed only by his love for Bethany. Yet the secrets of his past drove a wedge between them.

SIR ADRIAN FIELDING. Bethany's father-in-law, he was a man whose greed and cruelty knew no bounds. When his eldest son rebelled against him, Sir Adrian swore that Bethany and her daughter would pay for his deed.

MARY FIELDING. Tormented by her husband's heartlessness, she hid away Bethany's child . . . and dreamed of finding happiness in the arms of a man she truly loved.

ALISON BANKS. Her generous heart held more than enough love for the baby girl who wasn't her own . . . and an undying passion for a man whose heart was beyond her reach.

FAR HORIZONS

Praise for A DIFFERENT EDEN by Katherine Sinclair:

"Absorbing . . . A pleasure to read!"

—Laurie McBain

"A page-turner . . . A fast-moving, exciting plot, and fine, truly living characters. I read the book all at one sitting."

—Roberta Gellis

Katherine Sinclair Books From The Berkley Publishing Group

A DIFFERENT EDEN
VISIONS OF TOMORROW
FAR HORIZONS

FAR HORIZONS

KATHERINE SINCLAIR

BERKLEY BOOKS, NEW YORK

FAR HORIZONS

A Berkley Book / published by arrangement with
the author

PRINTING HISTORY
Berkley edition / January 1991

For information address: The Berkley Publishing Group,
200 Madison Avenue, New York, New York 10016.

ISBN: 0-425-12482-7

A BERKLEY BOOK® TM 757,375
Berkley Books are published by The Berkley Publishing Group,
200 Madison Avenue, New York, New York 10016.

PRINTED IN THE UNITED STATES OF AMERICA

10 9 8 7 6 5 4 3 2 1

For Paul Michael Strahan

FAR HORIZONS

THE BEDROOM DOOR opened suddenly, and Bethany was caught in a yellow beam of lamplight. She froze, the lid of the jewel case slipping from her hand, landing softly upon its velvet-lined cocoon.

Two footmen were at her side before she could move. One of them seized her wrist and pried open her fingers. A gold ring bearing a crest studded with rubies and sapphires fell to the polished wood floor.

"Caught red-handed, I'd say," the first footman said with satisfaction. "Thought nobody saw you slip up here, with all the revelry going on downstairs, didn't you?"

The sound of music from the party taking place in the great hall was almost lost in the hollow roar of the sea crashing against the rocks below the moon-silvered windows.

"Please." Bethany found her voice at last. "I must speak with Sir Adrian."

The footman snorted derisively. "You'll talk to the constable, m'girl." He held the lamp higher, illuminating her face. "Why, you're a pretty little thing. You'd have done better to choose an easier livelihood. You're not cut out to be a thief."

"I'm not a thief. That ring belongs to my husband. I haven't touched anything else, I swear. Please believe me. At least let me talk to Sir Adrian—"

"I'll find the master," the second footman said to the first. "Maybe there'll be a reward for us for catching her. You keep an eye on her until I get back."

Waiting, Bethany told herself that perhaps the fates had arranged for her to confront Sir Adrian. Surely he would take pity on her now, when he realized how desperate she was.

Minutes later he strode into the room and ordered the footman to light the gas mantle. As the cold gaslight flooded the room, Bethany gazed up at Sir Adrian Fielding. He looked younger than she expected, although she knew he must be close to fifty. Tall, broad shouldered, darkly handsome, his features more Continental than English, he returned her gaze with hooded eyes that had a slightly sinister charm.

"Sir Adrian, I am Bethany Newton," she said breathlessly.

The footman bent to pick up the ring. "This was in her hand, sir. She was rifling your wife's jewel box."

"You may go," Sir Adrian said. "Let me know as soon as the constable arrives."

When they were alone, he scrutinized Bethany with clinical detachment. She wished she looked more presentable, but these past months of near-starvation had taken their toll. Her honey-colored hair had lost its sheen, and she knew her eyes must surely look like huge gray lakes, bottomless and empty, in her shrunken features.

She clutched her threadbare shawl, feeling engulfed by it, seeing herself as she must have looked in his disdainful eyes—a shapeless, shabby creature notable only for the audacity of her actions. She could expect no sympathy here, so there was little use in attempting to appeal to his better nature by divulging all of the facts of her predicament.

"You didn't respond to any of my letters, or I would not have resorted to this. Neil told me of the ring. I came straight to where it was kept. . . . I wouldn't have taken anything else. Neil said the ring was a gift from his maternal grandfather. That it belonged only to him and was not part of the estate. That even though you had cut him off, the ring was still his—"

"The ring is not the point here, miss."

"I am *Mrs.* Newton. Your son and I are legally married."

"I once had a son. . . . His name was Neil Fielding. Not Newton."

"He adopted the nom de plume because he did not want to embarrass you."

Sir Adrian paced a small circle around her. "If Neil Newton and Neil Fielding are one and the same, then he embarrassed me by marrying beneath him. Tell me, do you have any relatives?"

"A brother."

"Ah, so you are not alone in the world. Why did you not go to your brother for help?"

Bethany looked at her feet, imagining Sir Adrian's reaction if she were to tell him that her brother was an opportunist who was presently considering how he could best profit from the situation. "My brother and I . . . have been estranged since Neil's arrest. I haven't seen him since the trial."

"Trial?"

"Your son had heard that a group of discharged mill workers intended to break into the mill to destroy the machines that had replaced them. He went to appeal to them to try to get their jobs back by other means . . . but the police were waiting, and he was arrested with the workers. He was guilty only of being at the scene, but when the mill owner learned that he was the same Neil Newton who had been writing the news stories about the plight of the workers, he pressed vandalism charges against Neil, too."

Sir Adrian was silent, contemplative, for a moment. "I take it Neil married you after he left home and began to write his inflammatory articles for that yellow rag?"

"He wouldn't let me come to you for help, even when he was arrested. He never told anyone his true name, even though it might have saved him. Neil didn't condone the destruction of the machinery that was replacing the textile workers, but he did truly believe the workers were ill treated by the mill owners. That was only one of his concerns. He also wrote extensively about the disgrace of child labor."

"He was convicted?"

"Yes, and sentenced to transportation for ten years."

"I take it he was able to maintain his masquerade as Neil Newton throughout the trial?"

Bethany nodded.

"In your letters you asked for money. You stated that you wished me to provide you with the means to join your husband. Surely you don't expect me to believe you intend to go to a penal colony?"

"I begged to be allowed to accompany him in his banishment . . . but my request was denied. Sir Adrian, I must go to my husband. I did not ask you for charity, only for that ring, which was Neil's personal property. I know I should not have broken into your home, but you wouldn't respond to my letters. That ring would have bought me passage to the penal colony."

His eyes were cold, pitiless. "But don't you see, you will probably get your wish, at government expense—that is, if the magistrate doesn't decide to hang you instead."

"It is therefore ordered and adjudged by this court . . ."

Bethany gripped the wooden rail of the dock tightly, but although she listened intently to the judge's toneless voice, her eyes were fixed upon the man who lounged, as though relaxing in a drawing room, in the front row of the courtroom. Sir Adrian Fielding leaned forward slightly.

A pale woman with a heart-shaped face that might have been attractive had it not been for a downcast air and apologetic brown eyes had slipped into the seat next to him only seconds before the judge returned to pronounce sentence. Bethany knew she must be Mary Fielding, Sir Adrian's second wife. He'd given her one furious, incredulous glance that seemed to indicate her arrival was both unexpected and unwanted.

". . . that you be transported upon the seas, beyond the seas . . ."

A scream was trapped in Bethany's throat; her whole body seemed to have turned to ice. She looked again at Mary Fielding, who had not been present in the courtroom previously and who now cowered in her seat, shrinking away from her husband. Clearly she had defied him in order to be here for the sentencing.

". . . to such place as His Majesty, by the advice of his Privy Council, shall think fit to direct and appoint . . ."

Bethany had time only to wonder if she could possibly have seen sympathy in Mary Fielding's gaze before the judge pronounced her sentence.

". . . for a term of seven years."

She flinched. A hollow hopelessness engulfed her. Seven years! She bit her tongue to keep from crying out. As a free settler she might have been able to find Neil, but as a convict, how could she possibly seek her husband? She'd given Neil her word that she would never disclose their connection to the powerful Fieldings or bring disgrace to the family name. She had not told anyone, from the policeman who arrested her, to the barrister who defended her, that she was married to the son of the man who accused her. Only Sir Adrian knew her true identity, and she felt guilty that in asking for his help she had broken her promise to Neil. That promise, and Neil's pride, was about to destroy both of them.

"Take the prisoner away," the judge ordered.

In the instant before she was dragged from the dock, Bethany flung one frantic glance of appeal toward Mary Fielding.

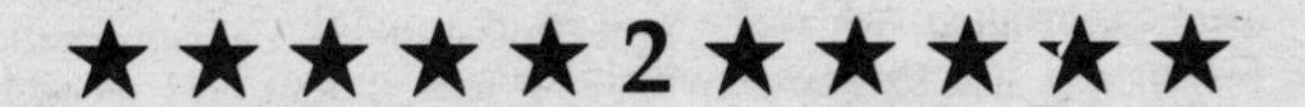

UNTIL THE MOMENT the haunted gray eyes of the prisoner in the dock met hers, Mary Fielding was unsure why she had defied her husband by coming to the court of the assizes.

Bethany Newton's lovely face was a mask, her eyes empty, and she swayed on her feet as sentence was pronounced. She appeared to be too stunned to speak. Then her gaze met Mary's in mute appeal.

It seemed in that split second there passed between Mary and the prisoner a message so powerful that it eclipsed everything else. Mary was vaguely aware of her husband rising to leave, of a baby beginning to wail up in the gallery, of the muted rattle of rain against the windows, of the shuffle of the bailiffs' feet—but only distantly. She was overwhelmed by an aching sense of injustice, of outrage so acute that she was immobilized by it. Her feelings were baffling because Bethany Newton had been proven guilty beyond a shadow of a doubt.

Mary blinked. Her husband's face, registering impatience, came into focus. The prisoner Bethany Newton—delicate, ethereal as a ghost, doomed—was gone.

"Did you hear me?" Adrian's voice at last penetrated Mary's numbed brain. "Come on, woman, for heaven's sake, move. If you sit there like a fool for another second we'll have to stay for the next case. I warned you not to come. I knew it would upset you."

Rising unsteadily to her feet, Mary stumbled as Adrian took her arm. They were caught up in the column of exiting spectators swarming down the aisle, apparently anxious to leave before the next prisoner, a Luddite, was tried. That poor soul evidently had not aroused the same curiosity as the beautiful Bethany Newton.

A shabbily dressed woman with a purple birthmark on her cheek jostled Mary in the crush, and Adrian snapped, "Look where you're going." He used his silver-knobbed ebony cane to prod a path through the crowd.

Outside, the rainswept street was a pewter ribbon that reflected yellow pools of gaslight and the colored lanterns shopkeepers had strung in their windows in the hope of attracting Christmas shoppers. Mary moved in a daze, heedless of her husband's reprimand when she walked in a puddle.

When at last they were inside a hackney cab Mary asked, "Where will she be sent?"

"New South Wales or Van Diemen's Land, I expect."

"Oh, dear heaven, Adrian! To be banished to the ends of the earth for such a trifling crime."

"Trifling? The theft of a valuable ring? And the Lord knows how many other pieces of jewelry she stole before we caught her red-handed. It wasn't so long ago, before the advent of liberals such as yourself, that the Newton woman would have been hanged for such a crime. She should consider herself fortunate indeed that she will merely be banished for seven years."

"But she's not a woman of the lower classes. How can she survive in a penal colony? Oh, how I wish you hadn't pressed charges. I had no idea she was a gentlewoman."

"A gentlewoman?" Adrian burst out laughing. "You little ninny, you think because she speaks grammatically she is a gentlewoman? She was the mistress of a wealthy man who saw fit to have her instructed in elocution. No doubt because her Cockney whine irritated him."

"However do you know that?"

"It came out after her arrest."

"Did this wealthy man come to her trial?"

"Of course not. The man in question is not only of high rank but also well known. Why should his name be dragged through the mud? Besides, their affair ended some time ago."

"Then . . . the man is known to us? Was he there that night, at the party? Who is he, Adrian? Please tell me."

Unexpectedly, Adrian reached over and patted the back of her gloved hand. "Why trouble yourself with such knowledge? Far better not to know. For one thing, you might betray the fact that you know of his association with her. After all, we do move in the same rather narrow social circles. Put her out of your mind. She is responsible for her own fate."

"But I can't help wondering why she was driven to such a desperate act. She seemed intelligent, yet you said her only defense was to deny that she had taken the ring, even though it was found in her possession. And why on earth did she choose a house as remote as Riverleigh to burglarize? Especially on the night of our party, with people wandering all over the house. Do you think she came to see her lover? I wish I could have spoken with her—"

"Enough of this nonsense! I forbid you to speak of that wretched woman again. The matter is closed."

Mary turned to peer through the steamy window of the carriage. A knot of carolers were clustered at the corner of the street, singing "Away in a Manger." The sweet voices of the ragged children rose against the clamor of the news vendors and din of the city. One frail little girl with enormous dark eyes looked directly at Mary as their carriage went by, sending a plume of dirty water spraying over her. Mary would have liked to stop the carriage, give the children a few coppers, and tell the little girl she was sorry her threadbare coat had been drenched by the carriage wheel, but she knew Adrian would never permit it.

Had Bethany Newton once been an innocent child like that? Mary had expected a hard-looking woman, but the prisoner in the dock had proved to be little more than a girl, with light honey-colored hair pulled back severely from her fragile features. Her huge dove-gray eyes, so desperate, so haunted, lingered in Mary's mind. Surely those eyes were incapable of lying? Mary had to remind herself that Bethany Newton was that most despicable of women, the mistress of one of Adrian's friends, therefore capable of deceit.

Turning to her husband, Mary drew a deep breath and said, "Adrian, would you mind if I stayed in town to finish my Christmas shopping? I could go to the station to meet the boys the day after tomorrow and travel home to Riverleigh with them."

"I shall be busy, you know. You'll have to entertain yourself."

"Yes, I know you have your business to run. I shan't get in your way."

"Very well, so long as you understand." He ordered the cabbie to take them to Victoria Gardens, where he maintained a town house. The office from which he ran his shipping company was situated at the Liverpool Pier Head, and Adrian spent most of his time in the sprawling seaport, crossing the River Mersey to their country house on the Wirral peninsula only for weekends and holidays. It was an arrangement Mary had accepted with something akin to relief, since during their three-year marriage Adrian had always made her feel inadequate. She felt a sense of relief when he departed, dread before he returned.

The house in Victoria Gardens was quite modest, a three-story terrace house on a square surrounding a small park. Early in their marriage Adrian had made it clear that the only visitors he expected there were business acquaintances and that his housekeeper could handle them without Mary's interference.

He had taken his bride to the brick and stone manor house that stood like a fortress at the windswept point where the Mersey met the Irish Sea. Even after three years, the rambling house Adrian called Riverleigh still seemed unwelcoming and filled with the presence of his first wife. At Riverleigh Mary felt a curious sense of affinity with the barren and gale-buffeted cliffs that withstood the fury of the raging sea and icy winds, remaining aloofly serene and untouched in their lonely splendor.

She hoped Adrian would not question her sudden desire to stay in town, since this close to Christmas he must know all of the shopping was finished. Fortunately he seemed preoccupied. With luck he would remain so while she attempted to find out why Bethany Newton had given her that imploring look just before she was taken away.

The rain came down in a solid sheet as they reached the house, and Adrian unfurled an umbrella to hold over her as they dashed up the steps and into the vestibule. They were admitted by the housekeeper, a rawboned woman with a faintly distrustful air, named Mrs. Creel. She looked disapprovingly at the wet imprints their feet left on the hall floor as she took Mary's cloak.

"I wasn't expecting you, Lady Fielding. Fortunately there'll be enough for dinner because Mr. Ivers is coming and he has a hearty appetite."

Adrian regarded Mary in the manner of one confronted with a wet puppy. "You're soaked to the skin. Perhaps Mrs. Creel should prepare a mustard bath for you to soak your feet. We don't want you coming down with one of your interminable bronchial attacks just before Christmas."

"I'd really prefer a cup of tea," Mary said. "And if you would light a fire in my bedroom . . ."

Mrs. Creel frowned. "I've lit one in the master's room. You could change in there."

Adrian promptly disappeared into his study, and Mrs. Creel compressed her lips into a resigned line and went to the kitchen. Mary wondered which of them had indicated more clearly that she was an intruder here. She supposed servants took their cues from their masters, because the situation at their country estate was no better.

Three years ago Adrian had made her his wife, but had not taken her into his life; she hovered uncertainly on the edges of it. Their marriage had taken place shortly after Adrian had quarreled with his eldest son Neil, cutting him off so completely from the family that no one had since been permitted to utter his name.

During the first two years of their marriage Mary had hoped to bear children of her own, but after four miscarriages she did not conceive again, and she hid her bitter disappointment from her husband who, having sired three sons with his first wife, was unconcerned that Mary remained childless. Then, too, Adrian's estrangement from his eldest son perhaps was another reason he did not desire more children.

She went up to the second floor guest bedroom and was relieved to find she had left some winter clothes in the wardrobe on her last visit.

A fire blazed cheerfully in the hearth of Adrian's room, and after changing her clothes she stood in front of it, warming her hands. A moment later the housekeeper knocked on the door.

"I'm sorry, Lady Fielding, I had no idea you'd left an unopened letter in the pocket of your cloak. I'm afraid I've crumpled it."

"Letter?" Mary asked, bewildered. She had definitely not placed an unopened letter in her cloak pocket.

Taking the rain-smeared envelope from the housekeeper, Mary looked at the name crudely printed on the cheap paper, and knew that no one of her acquaintance had addressed her as "Lady Mary." All at once she recalled being jostled as she and Adrian were leaving the court of the assizes. Had that shabbily dressed woman with the birthmark on her face slipped the letter into her pocket then?

"Thank you, Mrs. Creel." She waited until the housekeeper departed before tearing open the envelope.

The message inside was brief and unsigned: "If you've got any pity in you, come to the Rose and Crown on Castle Street tonight at nine. There's a lot that wasn't told at Bethany Newton's trial."

★★★★★ 3 ★★★★★

BETHANY FELT HER already defeated spirits drop still further at her first sight of the hulks at Portsmouth. As the longboat in which she and the other female prisoners bobbed on the heaving surface of the oily water, the hulks materialized in the mist, as forbidding as any medieval prison.

The hulks had once been warships, now out of commission and used to house convicts awaiting transportation. The ships lay bow to stern, gun ports barred with iron. Deckhouses and makeshift lean-tos jutted out at every angle, connected by lines of bedding strung between rotted masts.

"Cheer up, ducks," the woman to her left whispered. "We'll be a long time dead. Might as well enjoy life while we can."

Bethany tried to give a small smile in response.

Even before the fettered women reached the hulks they were assailed by the reek of them. No slum tenement ever smelled worse. Rotting lines trailed festoons of rancid seaweed, and the huge rusty chains that held the ships to their last anchorage groaned a chilling welcome as the new convicts were mustered on the quarterdeck.

"Here we go, then, lovey," murmured the flamboyantly dressed woman, who seemed determined to befriend her, as they formed lines.

In the longboat Bethany had learned only that the woman's name was Leona. She had tawny hair, eyes of rich amber shot with gold, and an impudent grin. A deep cleft in her chin seemed like a punctuation mark beneath extraordinarily full lips. Even without the brilliant green silk gown and velvet cloak she wore, she would have been a sight to behold. The fourteen-pound iron attached to her right ankle appeared to be merely a device to attract even more attention.

"Shut your mouths. No talking," a rough voice cautioned as a burly warder made his way down the ranks of new convicts. "You'll hand over your money and valuables for safekeeping."

Leona snorted loudly and was roughly pushed into line by the guard, whose practiced eye quickly found anything of value. Bethany watched numbly as her wedding ring disappeared into his pocket. Leona handed over earrings and a pendant and inquired cheekily, "What about my ankle bracelet? Don't you want it, too?" She lifted her skirts and rattled her leg iron at him.

The ultimate humiliation came next. While still on deck and with no privacy whatsoever, the women were forced to remove their outer clothing as well as their petticoats, unless they were too tattered to interest the guards, and don prison clothes, which appeared to be made of rough canvas.

Leona glanced with a knowing eye at the two damp patches on Bethany's shift in the region of her breasts. "Ah, you poor little thing . . . you were suckling a babe, were you?"

Blinking back a tear, Bethany nodded. "She was born in prison. They . . . tore her away from my arms . . ." She couldn't say more for fear of bringing forth another deluge of agonized tears.

An older woman nearby hissed at her, "Tell yerself the baby's dead, 'cause you won't never see 'er again. She'll go to a parish poorhouse, and infants hardly ever survive."

"Shut your trap, you old witch," Leona snapped. "Of course her baby will survive. And she'll be back to see her again, too." She gave Bethany a reassuring pat on her shoulder, which had the effect of causing her tears to well again.

"Quiet there! Shut up, you whores. You'll be told when you can talk. Come on now, hurry up."

"Please, sir," Bethany said, catching the guard's arm. "How long will we be here? Would . . . someone be able to visit me, or at least send a message to me?"

He turned to look at her, his eyes drawn first to the translucent perfection of her features and then dropping to her slender body. He ran his tongue slowly over his lower lip. "Well, now, that all depends. Favors don't come cheap 'ere in the 'ulks."

Bethany shivered and shrank from him. Leona whispered in her ear, "If you've got to pay that way, you might as well wait for bigger game, duckie."

The warder slapped Leona's cheek, a stinging blow that left a red imprint. She didn't wince or cry out, but simply regarded him with utter contempt.

"Come on, down to your cells, you lot, and quick about it,"

the man said, prodding Bethany with his fist. "You and me, we'll talk about messages later."

There proved to be no time for visitors or messages, because a departing transport had space for two more female convicts when two women died in the process of being transferred from the hulks. Leona and Bethany were selected to take their places.

Bethany begged to be allowed to remain where she was, but was curtly informed she didn't know when she was well off, since the voyage to Australia was far easier than life on the hulks.

She found herself aboard a ship flying the red and white pennant that proclaimed it to be a convict vessel. The prisoners' berths ranged in two rows with a passage between them, and Leona slept in the narrow bunk above her. Five women shared six square feet of berth space. Bethany estimated there were about fifty female prisoners aboard, the majority of the transportees being men. Some ships, she'd heard, carried only female convicts.

Their vessel, the *Peregrine,* was a converted merchantman, as were most of the transports except for a few naval ships. The only ventilation came from a hatchway over her head, which was heavily grilled and padlocked, and the air belowdecks was stifling, with the promise of worse to come as they drew closer to the equator.

Bethany's breasts ached as her milk stubbornly refused to dry up, and she wondered if her nightly crying for her lost baby could be causing her to continue to make milk. Her leg iron had rubbed an angry gouge into her ankle, but her physical distress paled before the agony of her mind.

Shortly after boarding the ship Leona disappeared for several hours, and when she returned to her berth it was immediately obvious that she now wore a smaller leg iron.

Leona returned Bethany's puzzled glance with a shrug, but there was a suspicious brightness to her amber eyes that suggested unshed tears. "I'm going to do what I have to do to survive this, duckie," she said defiantly, "and I suggest you do the same. There's a guard—"

"No," Bethany said quickly. "I couldn't."

"Suit yourself. But let me tell you a few things I found out. We'll be at sea well over a hundred days and we'll work our passage. The men will holystone the decks and swab and scrub the crew's quarters and mend sails, and the women . . . now, what do you think they'll do? The laundry? Maybe. But we'll warm the beds of the crew and the soldiers, too, I'll be bound. We're all whores to them. Might as well find a protector and service one man instead of many."

Bethany shivered. "I'll kill myself first."

"What, and never see your baby again? Where there's life there's hope, duckie, and don't you forget it."

A guard's face appeared at the grilled hatchway. "All right, you wenches. Up on deck."

"What for?" Leona called. "You've taken everything of value. 'Struth, I don't even have a comb left."

"Now we're on blue water you're to have your iron struck," came the rejoinder.

Leona's gaze dropped to her newly acquired small leg iron and then turned to Bethany in dumb outrage. "*What?* Why, that lying swine! He got a rise out of me, all right."

"I wondered why there were chains and basils on our bunks," Bethany answered. "I expect they use those if we don't behave."

The guard who struck the iron from Bethany's leg was a huge brute with a knife scar that ran from the corner of his mouth to his ear, giving him a ghastly parody of a permanent grin. He fingered the torn skin of her slender ankle and then ran his hand up to her knee, an expression of rampant lust written on his coarse features.

Bethany jerked her leg back out of reach, almost falling before she realized it was no longer necessary to compensate for a fourteen-pound ball chained to her ankle. The guard leered at her. "You're a pretty little thing and no mistake. I daresay I'll be seeing a lot more of you before this trip's done."

When it was Leona's turn to have her iron struck, she attempted to kick the squatting man in his groin, but apparently he expected this and promptly knocked Leona's other foot out from under her. She sprawled on the deck, showing a great deal of bare leg, to the amusement of the watching male convicts, crew, and guards.

"You mind what you're doing, you bitch, or I'll give you a taste of the lash for your pains," the soldier snarled at her, and Bethany shuddered at the look on his face.

Later, back in their berth, Leona gave Bethany a worried look. "Too bad that big bruiser took a fancy to you, duckie. His name is Lieutenant Ruben, and the captain gives him free reign with the convicts."

"I'm more worried about what he might do to you," Bethany said. "Why on earth did you try to kick him?"

"He's the swine that promised me the smaller iron if I'd be nice to him. He didn't say anything about *all* the irons coming off. Christ, I'm still sore from him. He's built like a bull."

Bethany looked away quickly, embarrassed.

Leona said, more softly, "I'm sorry. I shouldn't be so blunt. I'm not used to being around ladies. How'd you ever find yourself in this mess, a woman with your looks and education?"

Bethany was silent for a moment, wondering if Leona would believe her story if she confided in her. She decided to be evasive for now. "I was convicted of theft. What about yourself? You aren't like the other female convicts either."

"I was on the boards. An actress. Got caught with a trunk of theatrical costumes that didn't belong to me. I may sound a bit like a lady, but that's as far as it goes. You, now . . . Why, I wouldn't be surprised if you were from a good family."

Unwilling to discuss her past, Bethany said, "Tell me about some of the parts you played. Did you ever do any Shakespeare? That lovely contralto voice of yours—"

Leona interrupted her with shouts of laughter. "God's teeth! Shakespeare, she says. No, duckie, I did melodrama. Mostly in the provinces, but I played in London a few times, too."

The ship lurched, shuddering, and began to roll ominously. What little light penetrated the hatchway was soon lost beneath leaden skies as a squall tossed the vessel violently upon the heaving sea.

For the next two days the *Peregrine* battled the storms of the Bay of Biscay. Wind, rain, lightning, and huge whitecapped waves lashed the ship. Bethany realized that their leg irons had been struck in the nick of time, since even without them it was almost impossible to move about. The women clung to their berths to prevent being dashed against decks and bulkheads, and few would have had any appetite for food even if they could have found a way to transfer it from flying plates to their mouths.

At least, Bethany thought, the specter of the leering face of Lieutenant Ruben was temporarily pushed from her mind.

Then, abruptly, the skies cleared and the ship resumed an even course. Ravenous, the women ate the brined beef known as salt-horse and drank lime juice, sugar, and vinegar to guard against scurvy. All of the convicts, men and women alike, were put to work restoring order to the ship, swabbing decks, mend-ing sails, and washing the laundry. The men made fishing lines from strips of canvas, and the fish they caught by trolling hooks relieved the monotony of their diet.

Bethany was glad to be out on deck, despite the heavy work of rubbing canvas shirts against a corrugated washboard in a huge iron pot of water. Leona, working beside her, was rummaging through a duffel bag filled with soiled clothing, and she suddenly exclaimed, "Well, look at this!"

She pulled out a familiar-looking green silk gown, now stained and torn at the seams. "This is my dress," Leona said indignantly. "The one I was wearing when I arrived at the hulks."

"I heard someone say that all of our belongings were sold by the captain to a secondhand shop," Bethany answered.

"Not this dress, though. I'd know it anywhere. I designed it myself. Look at the state it's in. Whoever wore it was too fat for it. Look at the ripped seams. Sloppy eater, too. See the mess she made on the bodice?"

"You know what this means," Bethany murmured. "It means there are passengers aboard as well as convicts."

"Wives of the marines, I daresay. Well, if I get my hands on the slut who did this to my dress—"

A crooked shadow fell across Bethany's washboard. She looked up to see Ruben looming over her.

He held a knotted rope, which he slapped against his palm. She had seen him use it to beat convicts who didn't obey him with enough alacrity, but as she looked up at him he stopped swinging the rope and instead held it up with one hand and began to caress it with the other, his small crafty eyes fixed on Bethany as he ran huge callused fingers over the rough fibers.

"Well, now, if it isn't pretty little Bethany Newton looking like butter wouldn't melt in 'er mouth. But we all know she's just another felon like the rest of the scum aboard, don't we? A thief, and not a very good one at that. Well, you'll have your light-fingeredness cured Bayside, believe me."

Lowering her eyes, Bethany scrubbed furiously. Ruben bent over her and placed his fingertip under her chin to force her to look up into his face. Even with a fresh breeze coming across the deck she was aware of the sour smell of his breath.

"You need to learn a new skill, little lady. One better suited to your new life. Thieving wasn't your bent, anyway. You be nice to me and maybe I'll teach you a few tricks you can use."

His hand dropped to her breast, and she gasped with shock and outrage. Everyone in the vicinity turned to watch.

Before she could speak, a male convict who had been swabbing the deck nearby suddenly hit his bucket of soapy water with his mop, sending it spilling over the deck. The suds swirled over Ruben's feet, and he turned with an oath on his lips and lashed out with the knotted rope at the man.

Bethany winced as the knot caught the man full in the face. She had observed him earlier when she first came on deck and had wondered about him, because his features were more refined and he was taller, better nourished than the other prisoners. They were, for the most part, hardened criminals with many previous convictions, who would all later claim to be simple bumpkins convicted of stealing a loaf of bread, or innocent men exiled for their political beliefs. The truth was that virtually all were city dwellers rather than country people, and only one or two were political prisoners. This was also true of the female convicts, who were of a class of gin-soaked women Bethany had never formerly associated with. She was beginning to think that she and Leona had been particularly unfortunate to be transported for a first offense.

But the man who had distracted Ruben with his spilled bucket bore the unmistakable stamp of breeding, despite his rough canvas garments. Something about the way his brilliant blue eyes flashed defiance and the set of his jaw said this man was no murderer or thief. He stood his ground, arm raised to ward off the blows Ruben rained about his head and shoulders.

Infuriated that the man appeared to be impervious to the beating, Ruben screamed, "Damn your hide, but I'll teach you to spill slop on me."

Bethany clutched the washboard in disbelief as he ordered two of his marines to lash the man to the shrouds and fetch him a cat-o'-nine-tails.

Leona grabbed Bethany's arm and said, "Come on, let's get below."

"You women stay where you are," Ruben roared. "You'll witness this flogging and learn from it. I've been too easy on the lot of you. It's time you all learned who's in charge here."

He grabbed Bethany's arm and thrust her closer to the shrouds, where the two marines had torn the prisoner's shirt from his back.

A second later the cat whistled through the air, and its vicious tendrils struck the prisoner. Bethany squeezed her eyes shut, recoiling in horror from the sound of the knotted cords biting into flesh.

The blows fell repeatedly, and after a time she was showered with blood and bits of torn flesh. Her knees sagged and she might have slid to the deck in a dead faint had not the proceedings suddenly been interrupted by a quietly resonant voice.

"That's enough, Lieutenant Ruben."

Bethany opened her eyes and saw that the ship's surgeon had placed himself between Ruben and the flayed prisoner.

For a moment all of the prisoners on deck seemed to hold their breath. The surgeon surely had no authority over Ruben, whom no one aboard dared challenge. The doctor was a tall, gaunt man with a lantern jaw and melancholy dark eyes. A perpetual aura of sadness clung to him like a second skin, and on the rare occasions when Bethany had glimpsed him, she had thought he looked more suited to burying the dead than to healing the sick.

"The punishment isn't finished, Dr. Prentice," Ruben said, a frightening gleam in his eyes.

Ignoring him, Prentice turned to the nearest marine. "Cut that man down." There was a deathly calmness to his voice, but his tone brooked no refusal. It was a voice of command that even Ruben recognized. "Carefully, now. Carry him down to sick bay."

Bethany forced herself to look at the prisoner as he was freed from the shrouds. His thatch of black hair was wet with blood, and his back was a pulpy mass resembling raw meat. Bile rose in her throat. She clutched the air for a second, then slid to the deck.

In the instant before she fainted she felt strong arms catch her and lift her up, and her last thought was a silent, frantic plea to the Almighty that she was not being borne away by Lieutenant Ruben.

FOR ONCE MARY Fielding was glad that her husband's business partner had joined them for dinner at the town house, as his presence would ensure that she would be able to slip away for her mysterious rendezvous at the Rose and Crown while they discussed the movement of their ships and the acquisition of cargoes and crews.

Mrs. Creel served a hearty steak and kidney pie, fare that was rarely brought to the dinner table by the rigidly correct butler at Riverleigh, and Mary would have enjoyed the pie had not Tate Ivers been sitting opposite to her regarding her with a faint frown.

Her husband's partner had always reminded her of a rearing bear, about to tear someone limb from limb. She supposed he was handsome in a terrifying way, with fiery red hair and eyes the color of forest moss, but his bodily bulk and long gorillalike arms were at odds with his penchant for fancy shirts and embroidered waistcoats. He spoke in a deceptively soft tone, which seemed strange for one who dealt constantly with rough seamen.

Mary felt ill at ease in his presence as he managed to indicate with every glance that she was intruding by being in Liverpool rather than at her country home where she belonged. On the rare occasions when she visited either the town house or her husband's offices Tate Ivers conveyed his displeasure and Adrian dismissed her mild protests by saying that Ivers didn't care to be in the company of women; it was not personal.

The meal was consumed in almost complete silence after Ivers commented that the rain was cold enough to turn to snow.

Mary had barely touched the dessert of apple dumpling and custard before Tate took out his pocket watch, studied it for a second, and remarked, "Vareck said he'd be here about nine, Adrian. It's too late to postpone the meeting. I had no idea your wife would be here tonight."

"I'm sure Mary will wish to retire early," Adrian replied. "She had a rather trying day, didn't you, my dear?"

She excused herself and bade them good night, then hurried upstairs to change her clothes. In order to avoid the possibility of encountering the expected visitor, presumably a business acquaintance, she decided to leave by the back door and so went through the kitchen.

Mrs. Creel was washing the dishes, and as she looked up Mary said, "I'm going out for a little while. I shan't be long . . . so I shan't disturb my husband to tell him."

"Out? By yourself, Lady Fielding?"

"I'm not going far," Mary replied firmly. For once the housekeeper was not going to intimidate her. The woman had no right to question her actions.

Before she could reach the back door, however, there was a sharp knock. Mary hesitated. "Surely it's too late for a tradesman . . . ?"

Mrs. Creel dried her hands and opened the door, her expression somewhat fearful. She moved aside quickly as a man stepped into the room and, without a word, started to cross the kitchen. He was easily as big as Tate Ivers and wore the heavy melton cloth jacket of a seaman. He did not remove his woolen watch cap when he entered the house. Mary remained frozen to the spot as he looked at her with the coldest eyes she had ever seen. Set in an immobile, almost expressionless face, his eyes were of such a pale silvery gray that they appeared almost to be transparent.

It was apparent he had no intention of greeting either Mrs. Creel or Mary, and knew exactly where he was going. Ignoring the door leading to the coalhouse and the one to the pantry, he opened the hall door.

Finding her voice at last, Mary said, "Wait a moment, sir. Who are you and what do you want?"

"It's Mr. Vareck, Lady Fielding," Mrs. Creel said quickly. "He's here to see Sir Adrian and Mr. Ivers."

"And do you usually enter our house through the back door, Mr. Vareck?" Mary asked, although she felt herself shiver as he turned to look at her with his pitiless eyes.

"Mr. Vareck is the first mate on one of your husband's ships," the housekeeper began.

"Let him speak for himself," Mary said.

His eyes flickered insolently over her. "Yes."

"Yes? Yes, what?"

"Yes, I always come in the back way. The two waiting for

me don't want the neighbors seeing the likes of me come in the front door." He turned and disappeared into the hall, leaving the door swinging behind him.

"Such a frightening man," Mrs. Creel said, shivering. "He just comes in, goes straight to Sir Adrian's study. Usually comes just before one of the ships sails. Leaves the same way . . . never a word to say to me as he goes by."

"If he's the first officer aboard one of Sir Adrian's ships, doesn't he ever go to sea himself?"

"Well, he used to. But I don't think he goes far nowadays, because he's here about once a month."

"The Dublin or Belfast run, perhaps?" Mary suggested.

"I don't think the company's ships make those short runs anymore."

Mary realized she was gripping her reticule so tightly her fingers seemed welded to the handles. "I hope I never have to encounter him again. He left a cemetery chill in his wake."

The Rose and Crown public house was not the type of establishment a lady would enter, and as Mary made her way to the ladies' saloon bar she was the object of curious glances.

A burly barman wiped off a small table with his shirtsleeve and pulled out a chair for her, his eyes bulging with disbelief. She ordered a glass of port, not daring to look around at the rough crowd of seamen, dockers, and their women. She had worn her plainest navy blue serge coat, but felt conspicuously out of place among shabby shawl–wrapped women and a sprinkling of gaudily gowned ladies of pleasure.

A woman detached herself from a raucous group near the bar and slid into the chair opposite her. Mary recognized her immediately by the purple birthmark on her cheek.

"You slipped the note into my pocket?"

The woman nodded.

"You're a friend of Bethany Newton?"

"Me, a friend of 'ers? Go on! Nah, I was in the clink with 'er." The barman returned with a glass of port and she said, "Bring me one of them. And a pint of stout."

Mary said, "Have you come to tell me she is innocent?"

"Nah, she was guilty as sin. But 'er babe ain't."

"Baby?" Mary leaned forward. "Miss Newton has a child?"

"Born in prison while Bethany was waiting for 'er trial. A little girl only four weeks old, poor little mite."

Mary felt faint, whether from the stale malt-laden air of the public house or from this startling news she was not sure. She took a sip of port wine, hoping it would revive her. "Surely they will not transport the infant?"

"Nah, that's the 'ole point, see. Why I'm 'ere wiv you. Better she'd given birth on the voyage; then Bethany could've kept 'er baby a bit longer. The ones what's born in prison gets put in foundling 'omes."

"I'm very sorry to hear about the baby, but I didn't know Miss Newton; I never even met her. Our only . . . connection was that she broke into our home and stole some jewelry. Did she ask you to come to me? What does she expect me to do?"

The woman had finished her port wine and now picked up a brimming glass of stout and proceeded to empty it without pause. She replaced the glass on the table, wiped the froth from her mouth, and said, "You could do what was promised. Find out where 'er babe is and take care of 'er. Miss Bethany's got nobody on earth but 'er brother, and that young swine didn't even come to 'er trial. Too afraid of your 'usband, I daresay."

"My husband? What has he to do with Miss Newton's family? My husband knows nothing about her, other than that our servants caught her in the act of robbing us."

"Garn! What do you think she was doing there at your country place that night? Begging him for 'elp, that's what. Now, she didn't tell 'im about the baby, see, not then, but she sent him a letter when it got near 'er time. He went to see her, promised 'er that the baby would be took care of if she kept 'er mouth shut about who the father was."

Mary realized she had been holding her breath. She let it out slowly. "I take it the wretched man is someone of our acquaintance?"

"Well, yes, you might say that." The woman gave a hideous smirk that was probably intended to be a conspiratorial smile. Her hand snaked into a battered purse that hung from her wrist by fraying strings. She fished out two crumpled sheets of paper.

"She asked me to give you them letters and see your 'usband keeps his promise about the baby. Bethany kept 'er word and didn't say nothing at 'er trial on account of she didn't want your family name dragged through the mud, see. But that last letter came the day they sent her to the hulks down in Portsmouth. Too late for Bethany to do anything about it by then, see." She tossed the letters onto the damp surface of the table as she stood up.

Bending over the table, she leaned close to Mary's face and whispered, "Look, dearie, I know you're in the dark about all this, and you seem like a decent sort. I don't know what your 'usband told yer, but the truth of the matter is—"

She broke off, gasping, as a giant of a man materialized behind her. His huge fist closed around her arm and he pulled her viciously away from the table.

Mary felt her blood chill as the man's icy stare fixed on her. She recognized him instantly as the man who had visited the town house earlier that evening, the man called Vareck. "Your husband was worried about you, Lady Fielding. I'll take you home now."

Quickly Mary dropped her reticule onto the table, covering the two letters. The woman with the birthmark had vanished into the smoke-hazed public bar. Mary rose, her heart hammering, picked up the reticule and the letters, and tucked them under her arm, hoping Vareck had not seen them.

Mary faced Adrian in his study. He sat behind his desk while she stood in front of it, feeling more like a recalcitrant schoolgirl than ever. Vareck and Tate Ivers had both departed. It was nearly midnight and the rain had given way to a mournfully howling wind.

"I don't know who the woman was," Mary said. "She never told me her name. She said that . . . a promise had been made to Bethany Newton, but not what that promise was."

The letters were hidden up in her room, still unread, and Mary had decided to say as little as possible about her encounter with the woman at the Rose and Crown.

Adrian's eyes bored into her, and as the pause lengthened Mary's discomfort grew, but she was determined not to be the first to break the silence.

"It was stupid of you to go to such a disreputable place alone. What were you thinking of? You could have been robbed or attacked, or worse. It's a good thing my man Vareck noticed you were dressed to go out, or the Lord knows what the consequences of your foolhardy jaunt might have been."

She tilted her chin slightly, hoping the gesture would give her the courage she was not feeling. "Is there something I should know about Bethany Newton? If Vareck had not arrived when he did, I think perhaps I might have learned that her connection to our family was more complex than that of thief and victim. In fact, I have a distinct feeling that she, rather than we, was the victim."

Adrian came halfway out of his chair, his eyes blazing. "What utter nonsense is this? You are the most gullible woman I've ever known. Can't you recognize a confidence trickster when you meet one? The woman who enticed you to the public house saw you at the assizes and decided to try to play on your sympathies with some absurd story, the reason for which was to extort money from you."

"What absurd story?" Mary asked quietly.

He waved his hand. "The one Vareck interrupted. You'd better go to bed. Tomorrow morning you'll return to Riverleigh. You aren't to be trusted to remain here. You might decide to go wandering around the docks again by yourself."

Mary sat in front of her dressing table mirror, one long strand of brown hair still unplaited in her cold fingers. Her eyes, sable brown and fringed with thick lashes, which Adrian had proclaimed to be her best feature, were now underscored by dark smudges. Behind her the gray light of an icy dawn crept through the cracks in the shutters.

She had always known she was a rather ordinary looking woman, not pretty enough to be attractive to others, not ugly enough to be interesting. Everyone had been astonished when Adrian had chosen her from a horde of eager young women to be his second wife. Not for the first time she wondered if her timid nature had been the reason, because he never shared confidences with her and she had quickly learned never to ask questions—especially about his missing eldest son, whose name was never mentioned. Mary had met Neil Fielding on a few occasions before her marriage to Adrian and remembered him as a thoughtful, intelligent young man who bore a strong physical resemblance to his younger brother Stewart. They were both fairer in complexion and coloring than Adrian and Tom, the youngest, and more inclined toward gentler pursuits, Neil being interested in writing and Stewart in music. Tom, like his father, was given to more physical pastimes.

Mary had no idea what had caused the rift between Neil and his father, but whatever had transpired, surely Adrian would not punish an innocent infant? Could he really disown his own grandchild?

Mary had slept only fitfully and welcomed the end of the long night, the better part of which she had spent agonizing over the two letters her husband had written to Bethany Newton.

Picking up the first letter again, she stared at Adrian's familiar bold script.

"Madam," he had written, "I am at a loss to understand why you write to inform me of your troubles. Even if your husband is indeed my son, which seems unlikely in view of your surname, I have no interest in seeing him again. In fact, I decided some time ago that I now have only two sons, not three. You may inform him that I do not expect to hear from either of you again and that, in any event, he has sealed his own fate."

Mary picked up the second letter, which had been sent to Mrs. Bethany Newton at the prison. There was no salutation, just angry words poured like acid onto the paper: "Your brother had the gall to write me a threatening letter. Damn you both, I promise you will pay dearly for those threats. Nor will I ever acknowledge your misbegotten child as a grandchild of mine. . . ."

There was a knock on her bedroom door and Mrs. Creel entered the room carrying a tea tray. Mary folded the letters and slipped them into her dresser drawer, concealing them under a box of hairpins and a silver-backed brush.

"Mrs. Creel, tell me, if a woman bears a child in prison and then that woman is then transported to a penal colony, what do they do with the child?"

The housekeeper blinked and considered for a moment. "Put it in a parish home, I should think."

Mary swiveled around on her dressing stool to face the housekeeper. "Bethany Newton, the woman who stole from us, had a child in prison. A little girl who would be about four weeks old by now. I want to find out what became of the infant, but I don't want my husband, or anyone else, to know of my inquiries. I . . . I am willing to pay for the utmost secrecy."

Mrs. Creel's deep-set eyes gleamed with avarice. "I daresay I could find somebody to look into the matter . . . for a price."

"I wondered if you could do it yourself? The fewer people who know about the child the better."

"Why, yes, I suppose I could."

"I must return to Riverleigh this morning; Stewart and Tom will be arriving later today."

"And if I find the child, Lady Fielding? What shall I do about it?"

Mary pressed her fingers to the knot of tension between her brows. This was the second question she had been unable to answer during her long night's deliberations. There had even been moments of wildest fantasy when she wondered if there was a way for her to take the child herself.

The first unanswered question, of course, was what had become of Neil Fielding to cause him to abandon both his wife and his child? Then, too, where did Bethany's brother fit into the puzzle?

At length she said, "An infant of that age will need a wet nurse. Could you find one who would agree to look after the child if she was guaranteed a stipend?"

"Oh, yes indeed. Plenty of poor women would jump at the chance."

"I would like to interview the woman first. She could come out to Riverleigh on the pretext of looking for work. I believe we need a new parlor maid. No harlots, please. I want a respectable woman. When you find the baby, send the woman to me. I'll give you a letter of reference she can carry, so that I shall know her."

Mary noticed that Mrs. Creel wore a particularly crafty smile of satisfaction as she left the room. Would she tell Adrian? Probably not. She would keep her mouth shut in order to receive the promised financial reward. In any event, for once Mary didn't care what the consequences of her actions would be. The life of an innocent child was more important.

In a first-class compartment of a train thundering north through winter-bare countryside, Stewart Fielding regarded his two traveling companions with a puzzled frown.

His younger brother, Tom, had been unusually quiet since their reunion, and Stewart still wasn't sure exactly why Tom had invited his boarding school riding master to visit Riverleigh for Christmas, since Tom was well aware their father disapproved of socializing with anyone he considered beneath their class. Besides, Roland Montague had a slightly shifty air, evidenced in darting sideways glances and nervously restless hands, that Stewart didn't care for.

"Where is your home, Mr. Montague?" he asked.

"I spend most of my time at school nowadays. During the holidays there's always work at the local stables."

"But before you became riding master at Tom's school," Stewart persisted, "where were you from?"

"Liverpool," Montague muttered, and turned to look out of the window.

Tom flashed a warning glance in Stewart's direction, indicating that the questions were at best inappropriate and at worse impolite.

Stewart found himself reacting to Tom in the same way he reacted to his father, by instantly obeying even an implied command. In the past year Tom had grown to look even more like the old man. Stewart knew he took after his dead mother and his older brother, Neil, which had endeared neither of them to their father. Like Neil he had their mother's languorous eyes and luxurious mop of silky brown hair, accompanied by rather delicate features that he'd once heard described as too perfect to be masculine. Stewart secretly feared in his case it was true, since he knew he lacked Neil's courage and dedication to his ideals.

Their younger brother Tom had inherited their father's darkly handsome features and rugged physical build and, although a year younger, was already taller and broader in the shoulders than Stewart. Unlike their father, who with age had acquired a closed, secretive look, Tom had an honest and open face and a ready smile, which he bestowed equally upon everyone who crossed his path.

Tom had always been more proficient in riding and rugby than in academic studies, and when he and the riding master met Stewart at Crewe in order to finish the journey together, he had felt slightly puny in their unabashedly masculine presence, since Roland Montague was also tall and muscular, his skin tanned from long hours outdoors, and his hair was almost as dark as Tom's.

Montague abruptly turned to Stewart and said, "Just because your father acted like a swine to Neil didn't mean that you had to follow suit. I can understand Tom not doing anything, because he's convinced your father can do no wrong. But you . . . God, you're so like Neil—"

"Mr. Montague!" Tom interrupted swiftly. "You swore to me you wouldn't bring this subject up to Stewart. This is not his fault. Look, I promised to be at your side when you confronted Father, but I won't have you bullying Stewart in the meantime."

For a split second Stewart was astonished into silence. What did Montague know about Neil? Then he asked, "Just what are you two up to? I feel as if I've walked in on the second act of a play."

"We're coming into Lime Street," Tom said, rising to retrieve their luggage and coats from the overhead racks. Handing their bags to them, he pulled down an old Garrick overcoat. "Look at this, Stewart. Mr. Montague is always getting ragged at school about it. It's an absolute relic."

Recognizing that his brother was firmly changing the subject, Stewart murmured, "It looks nice and warm."

"Not to mention the fact that a poverty-stricken riding master can't afford anything else," Montague added in a self-pitying tone.

"Actually I've always admired this coat," Tom said, slipping his arms into the sleeves and fingering the cape. "I might make you a handsome offer for it."

The two of them began to banter back and forth about the Garrick overcoat while Stewart concentrated on collecting his luggage as the train ground to a halt.

A cloud of steam momentarily cloaked the disembarking passengers, as well as those who were there to meet them, in concealing mist. Stewart was too concerned with protecting a portmanteau filled with Christmas gifts to be aware that he had become separated from his traveling companions.

Clutching his precious bag as someone knocked his hat forward, further impeding his vision, he waited for the surging throng to pass him by.

"Tom!" he called, as the steam started to dissipate. "Where the devil are you?"

He broke off as he became aware of alarmed voices and what appeared to be a scuffle involving several men a little way down the platform. Stewart was about to detour around the argument when Montague's head suddenly arose above the melee, which now had the appearance of a rugby scuffle.

A crowd had gathered between Stewart and whatever was taking place on the platform, but Montague's voice, shrill with fear, reached him.

"For God's sake, come and help me. They've got Tom."

Stewart flung his portmanteau at a hovering porter and

plowed into the mob, but by the time he reached the spot where the scuffle had been taking place there was no sign of either his younger brother or his attackers.

"They just shoved me aside and went for Tom." Montague was panting and disheveled. "I tried to ward them off, and Tom was fighting like a fury, but there were at least four of them. . . . I think they may have hit him with a cosh. He was sagging at the knees as they dragged him away."

Stewart didn't linger to hear more. He dodged around two gaping passengers and raced toward the exit gate where a long queue of travelers waited to show their tickets. But although he scanned every face, he saw no sign of his brother.

He was still searching when Montague caught up with him. "Didn't you hear me? I yelled after you. They didn't come this way; they went the opposite direction, back along the railway lines. I chased after them, but they've vanished into thin air. They must have jumped down onto the lines and dodged between the trains."

They doubled back and ran to the end of the platform, then searched the tracks and every compartment of the halted train. Enlisting the aid of several railway men, they combed the waiting rooms and every inch of the station, then sent men to check the adjacent warehouses. But there was no sign of Tom.

Prowling the now-empty platform, Stewart said to the riding master, "Father will kill me. I can't believe they'd kidnap Tom from a crowded railway station."

"Actually the crowd of disembarking passengers and porters and all the baggage were an effective screen. Only a few people near us were aware of what was taking place."

"Did you get a good look at the kidnappers?" Stewart asked.

"Roughly dressed . . . They could have been dockers or seamen. It all happened so quickly, and the station was filled with steam. I was pushed flat on my face, and by the time I picked myself up, they were gone. Do you think someone has a grudge against your father and took Tom in revenge?"

"It's possible. God knows Father's ships have used their share of shanghaied crews and there's a couple of first mates who make the poor devils' lives miserable. But his business partner, Tate Ivers, handles the ships and crews. Father sees to the cargoes and port authorities, so surely a disgruntled seaman would want revenge against Tate, not Father. No, it's more likely there'll be a ransom demand. Father is fairly wealthy."

Stewart didn't add, thanks to the fortune Mary had brought to the marriage. Stewart had always felt sorry for his stepmother, since his father's interest in her seemed to have ended with the acquisition of her dowry. They were silent for a moment. The stationmaster had gone to summon the police. Stewart glanced behind them and said, "At least that porter had the presence of mind to stay with our bags. Let's go and give him something for his trouble, shall we?"

The portmanteau with the Christmas gifts was safe, and so were Montague's valise and Tom's suitcase. Stewart looked down at the luggage and saw that Tom's coat lay atop his suitcase, but Montague's Garrick overcoat with its distinctive caped shoulders was missing.

"Looks as if someone copped your coat. Can't imagine why anyone would want that tattered old antique."

Montague stared at him strangely. "Tom was always playing pranks with that coat. I can't tell you how many times I found it on a scarecrow or hanging from the rafters." He pursed his lips. "Don't you remember? Tom put on my Garrick before we got off the train."

"You mean he was wearing your coat when . . ."

"Yes," Montague answered grimly, and glanced about him warily.

5

BETHANY FELT THE gentle swaying of the ship first, then warm sunlight falling on her face. She opened her eyes to find herself lying on a bunk with an open porthole over her head. A fresh ocean breeze dissipated the sickening odor of blood and pus.

She was in the ship's sick bay, and directly in front of her the surgeon was lancing a boil on the neck of a seaman. On the other side of the cabin the prisoner who had been lashed with the cat-o'-nine-tails lay on his stomach, his flayed back exposed. He was so quiet, so still, that Bethany thought he surely must be dead.

Will Prentice, with some sixth sense that must have felt rather than heard her stir, glanced back over his shoulder. "You can stay where you are until you're feeling better. No one will trouble you here."

He finished draining the abscess and sent the sailor back to his duties. The flogged prisoner was his only other patient this early in the voyage.

"Is he . . . dead?" Bethany asked as the doctor wiped his hands on a grimy towel.

"Cutler? Dead? Good Lord, no. It would take more than a few lashes to send that devil to meet his Maker."

"That devil, as you call him, saved me from the unwelcome attentions of one of your officers. I am indebted to him, and I beg you to treat his wounds."

Prentice turned to look at her and she suppressed a shiver. His eyes, sunken among cadaverous features, seemed to bore right through her. "I have already treated him, with a bucket of salt water, which I assure you is the prescribed method of healing his back."

"But he's so quiet. He must be in dreadful pain, or perhaps unconscious."

"Not Cutler. He's lying there cursing his fate and plotting all manner of mischief, not least of which, I suspect, is mutiny. But Lieutenant Ruben informed me that this particular prisoner will spend the rest of the voyage chained in the hold, so we have nothing to fear."

"How can you be so callous? Are you not a physician?"

Prentice's face was expressionless. "Callous? I am not callous."

Then you are as unemotional as a stone, Bethany thought, and perhaps I despise that more.

Prentice went on, "My full title is surgeon superintendent, and I am aboard this vessel to try to prevent some of the abuse perpetrated upon transportees by the captains and crews of earlier hell-ships. Believe me, seamen would deal with the convicts much more harshly than do the soldiers. Most sea captains are hard, unlettered men who have come up from the fo'c'sle themselves. Aboard some ships convicts are lucky to survive the voyage. I am not only a healer but the closest thing to an advocate the convicts have."

It was the longest speech she had heard him make, and she was astonished that he felt the need to vindicate himself to her. She said quickly, "I didn't mean to criticize you. After all, you did stop the punishment."

"It was unjustified. A few hours in the cramping box would have served to set an example. Indeed, had it been any convict other than Cutler, I'm sure even Lieutenant Ruben would have been less harsh. But Cutler is a wild animal who has to be kept leashed."

"What on earth did he do that makes you speak of him so?"

"Where have you been that you never heard of Black Jack Cutler?"

"Black Jack? The highwayman? I didn't think he'd ever be taken alive."

"Jonathan Cutler, also known as Black Jack, was sentenced to life in the penal colony because the judges didn't want to turn him into a legend by hanging him, which is what he deserved."

Bethany was disappointed; she'd hoped Cutler would turn out to be that rarity on the transports, a political dissident. Although she had not heard him speak, his appearance suggested he did not belong to the lower classes, which spawned most English criminals.

Prentice cleared his throat. "Perhaps I should keep Cutler here in sick bay for a few days until his flesh begins to heal. Would you think me less heartless then, Bethany?"

"Thank you." She noted that he had used her first name instead of addressing her by her last, as did everyone else she had encountered since her arrest.

"Would you like a drink of water?"

"Yes, please."

He handed her a tin cup, and as she sipped the water he studied her in a somewhat clinical manner.

"I know the bare facts of your crime and sentencing, but I wonder how a woman of your charm and beauty, not to mention your obvious breeding, could have found herself in such a predicament?"

"My life before I boarded this ship is my own business."

"I didn't mean to intrude. Forgive my clumsiness. I merely wanted to find out if you can read and write. Can you?"

"Yes."

He was silent for a moment, and she had the strangest feeling that he was engaged in some silent argument with himself. At length he said, "I must keep a log of my activities on the voyage. It will be a record of lancing abscesses, sprinkling chloride of lime by the water closets, soaking blankets in urine tubs in the hope of killing the accursed lice, and various other distasteful tasks, not least of which is keeping the damned log itself, since I loathe recording each mundane detail on paper. If I could persuade you to write the log for me, at my direction, you would be assured of at least a couple of hours a day when you would not be at the mercy of soldiers and crew."

"I would be most happy to write your log for you."

"Good. We'll begin tomorrow afternoon. I'll send for you."

Uncertainly, since this seemed to be a dismissal, Bethany put the tin cup down on a long wooden table bolted to the deck. There were still bloodstains on both table and deck, and she looked away quickly.

She started for the door and in doing so had to pass by Cutler's inert form. He opened his eyes and looked at her, and, caught in the full force of the most vividly blue eyes she had ever encountered, for a second she paused. Although no words passed between them, she felt the power of that glance and wondered if perhaps some of the stories about Black Jack's mesmerizing effect on women could have been true.

As though reading her thoughts, the surgeon said sharply, "Don't be misled by the man's looks. He's a blackguard without conscience. His only concern is for himself. He's no Robin Hood. And more than one pretty young thing has lived to regret being dazzled by what she believed to be chivalry, which was in fact no more than a prelude to seduction."

Bethany looked back at Prentice, surprised that his rather hesitant manner of speaking had abruptly vanished.

She replied quietly, "Seduction is preferable to rape. The women aboard this ship fear forced cohabitation. Are their fears justified?"

Prentice looked away uncomfortably. "Most of the female prisoners are whores anyway."

"Even if that's true, it isn't the point, is it?"

"I expect most of them will either sell their favors for a pouch of tobacco or a swig of rum, or select one man to protect them from the rest."

"I will fling myself overboard first," Bethany said.

His melancholy eyes pinned her to the spot for an instant, as though striving to interpret the sincerity of her declaration. "If you were to choose death before dishonor, you would certainly be an exception among the female transportees."

Hating him and, even more, her own helplessness, she quickly left the sick bay.

* * *

As soon as it became known that Bethany was working for the surgeon superintendent, Lieutenant Ruben kept his distance, although she still felt his eyes follow her in a way that made her skin crawl.

Ruben claimed Leona as his woman, and Bethany was distressed to see that Leona often returned to her berth with bruises on her face and arms.

Prentice kept his word in regard to Cutler, who remained in sick bay for several days. The first day Prentice was present instructing Bethany on how to keep his log. He also said that if she cleaned the sick bay and helped with the patients who were sure to come knocking at the cabin door, she could spend most of her time away from her convict quarters.

On her second visit Prentice was called to the skipper's cabin and Bethany found herself alone with Cutler, although the surgeon manacled the prisoner to the bunk before leaving.

"Thank you for your plea to the doctor on my behalf," Cutler said the instant they were alone. He spoke in an astonishingly cultured voice.

Bethany dropped her quill in surprise. "I fear all I did was to delay your solitary confinement for a few days. Besides, it is I who should thank you."

The vividly blue eyes twinkled with amusement, although there was still pain in their depths. "You think I deliberately spilled my bucket on the lieutenant to distract him from your . . . charms?"

Bethany flushed. "Didn't you?"

"What, and risk a lashing? Lord, no. It was an accident. What incredibly vain creatures women are to imagine a man's every act is designed to impress them. Even, it seems, convict women."

Bethany picked up her pen and began to write furiously. "For your information, I am innocent of any crime."

"Of course," he agreed with mock gravity. "Aren't we all?"

"Not you. You're Black Jack the highwayman."

"Some people call me that."

"You are that most despicable of criminals, a man born to the upper classes who had no need to resort to highway robbery."

"Ah, but don't you see that we of the upper classes actually have much in common with the lower classes. Like them, we are tough and arrogant, not to mention resilient, masters in the art of survival; otherwise the aristocracy would long ago have disappeared due to sheer uselessness. But, like the lower classes, we are unprepared to support ourselves in a world of merchants and tradesmen should our fortunes fail—as mine did. What could I do? I possess no useful skills other than being a crack shot and excellent swordsman."

"You could have joined the army or the navy. Or entered the church," Bethany suggested.

"My God, the woman surely must be joking. In any of those endeavors I would have been required to take orders. I was never born for that."

"So you became a highwayman. In view of the result, don't you feel that was a grave error of judgment?"

He grinned. "I had a good run. Five years. And they wouldn't have caught me if I hadn't been betrayed."

"By a woman, no doubt."

"You show little loyalty or respect for your own sex, Miss Newton. No, I was not betrayed by a woman. The ladies have always been my staunchest supporters."

"So I've heard," Bethany murmured.

"I hope you give no credence to the more lurid rumors that were whispered about me, most of which were gross exaggerations."

"I doubt we'll ever see each other again after we reach our destination, so what does it matter what I think of you?"

"Oh, don't be too sure. Jack Cutler is a man of resourcefulness and daring. Particularly when it comes to a pretty woman, and I hear there aren't too many of those where we're bound."

"You speak of yourself in the third person, as though Jack Cutler were a separate being from yourself."

"You're ignoring my declaration of interest in you, Miss Bethany Newton. When I escape, shall I take you with me?"

"Escape? You're to be chained in the hold. And even if you freed yourself from your fetters, where would you go? Over the side to make a meal for the sharks?"

He gave an exaggerated grimace. "Must you say that with such relish? I shall find a way to escape when we reach the colony."

"You won't survive the voyage, Cutler." The voice that interrupted was soft but had the lethal edge of a stiletto. "Lieutenant Ruben has it in for you."

Bethany jumped as the surgeon appeared in the cabin doorway as suddenly and silently as a great bat. Her first thought was to wonder how much of their conversation he'd heard.

Prentice continued in the same deadly quiet voice: "And even, if by some wild imagining, you reach bayside, you won't last long enough to escape. Gentlemen never do. They aren't equipped for the ugly reality of convict life."

Turning abruptly to Bethany, he said, "You'd better get back to your quarters." She was surprised and dismayed to see cold fury in his eyes. Surely Cutler was not the first convict to talk of escape; it was the dream of every transportee aboard.

The *Peregrine* moved into warmer waters and the air below-decks became stifling. The sun blazed overhead causing hot pitch to drip from the seams through the barred hatches, and some of the women suffered burns. For several days the ship lay becalmed in the doldrums, and tempers frayed to breaking point.

One of the other women, a hard-faced Cockney named Doris, decided that life was too easy for Bethany since the surgeon excused her from laundry duty. Doris began to try to pick fights.

" 'Ere comes 'er ladyship," she taunted. " 'Ave you been enjoying the sea air, your grace? Is the passage to your liking, then?" She stuck out her foot, and Bethany tripped over it, falling heavily to the deck. Doris shrieked with laughter.

Knowing she was no match physically for the muscular woman, Bethany picked herself up and remained silent. If only the wind would return and the ship would move again, perhaps tempers would be stretched less taut.

Leona, who was lying on her bunk, raised herself up on one elbow. "Doris, you ever do that again and you're going to answer to me."

Doris spat in her face.

The next moment the two women were clawing and scratching each other while Bethany pleaded with them to stop. The other women squealed with delight and urged Doris to kill the bitch.

The melee ended when Ruben appeared and flung a bucket of seawater down the hatch, drenching not only the combatants but Bethany as well. The echo of Ruben's coarse laughter faded into the hot still air as Bethany shook the water from her hair and crawled dispiritedly into her bunk.

These were the people with whom she would spend the next seven years. Neil's sentence was ten years. Even if they found each other, after so much time wouldn't they be strangers? And after they served their sentences, what then? As far as she knew, no provision was made to return the transportees to England. Australia had few settlers, and most of them had originally been convicts. Oh, God, what kind of a society would be founded by people like these?

As desperately as she wanted her baby back in her arms, she thought perhaps her child was better off in England, being cared for by the Fieldings. She didn't believe that Sir Adrian would turn his back on his only grandchild despite what he had written in that last letter. Knowing her brother as she did, Bethany was sure that Roland had tried to blackmail Sir Adrian. Besides, perhaps the woman who had befriended her in prison had kept her promise to go to Mary Fielding and beg her to intercede with her husband. Bethany had assured herself so many times that her little girl was safe with the Fieldings that her mind had begun to accept it as being so.

Bethany's attention was snapped back to the present when all of the convicts were mustered on deck to witness a punishment. Two of the men had been caught filing spoons to make into weapons. They had been sentenced to be triced to a grating and given four dozen lashes.

Will Prentice came on deck to witness the punishment, and Bethany sent him frantic messages with her eyes that she could not bear to watch it, but she was not excused.

The surgeon seemed able to slip a mask into place and remove himself from that which he did not wish to see. Bethany had on several occasions noticed this ability of his to distance himself from others and had wondered about it, as it seemed to be a rather odd character trait for a healer. He stood on the sidelines, impassive, apparently untouched by what was happening to the unfortunate wretches whose backs were torn to ribbons by the cat.

Afterward he ordered seawater thrown on the men's flayed flesh and ordered them carried to sick bay for observation for a few hours.

Later Bethany sat at the doctor's desk writing in his log that the punishment had been carried out. Her hair hung heavy against her neck, and she was clammy with perspiration. The two flogged men moaned feebly, and from time to time she went to them to offer them water.

The ship's timbers creaked, the sea slapped the hull, the quill scratched the log. A shadow fell across the desk. Prentice had returned as silently as a ghost. His ability to move about without making a sound unnerved her, and the quill slipped from her fingers.

He stood looking down at her. "You feel I should not allow the floggings. But they are necessary, believe me. We are dealing with hardened felons, and to give them an inch would be to invite disaster."

"Why should I have an opinion? I'm one of the hardened felons you're dealing with."

"Ah, a flash of spirit. Good. I was afraid you'd been too gently bred to fight. You'll need all your courage to survive the next seven years."

"What will they do with the women in Australia?"

"Some of them will be assigned to settlers, to work as servants. The ones not selected for assignment will be sent to the female factory, a hellish place you should avoid at all costs. You'd be tossed in with the lowest female scum our society has been able to produce, at the mercy of brutish guards and equally brutish settlers, who would use and discard you at will."

He knitted his brows as his eyes flickered over her face. "In your case, unfortunately, I doubt any good wife is going to want you in her household. Too much temptation for the husband. And if a bachelor settler takes you . . ."

It was unnecessary for him to finish the thought.

The wind returned at last, billowing in the canvas, and the ship sailed on. The next time the convicts were assembled on deck it was for a ceremony of a more boisterous nature. They were "crossing the line," and "Neptune" had come aboard to initiate those who were crossing the equator for the first time.

Arrayed in a dolphin skin hung with shells and starfish and stinking under the tropical sun, the god of the sea and his "mermaids" wielded scissors and razors to shave the neophytes and then tossed buckets of salt water and soap slop over them.

The women were spared the scissors, but Neptune made sure they were thoroughly doused. Doris drew a cheer when she promptly discarded her sodden dress and paraded naked about the deck.

By this time every woman aboard was cohabiting with a seaman or a marine, and Bethany knew she had been spared only because it was believed she was Will Prentice's woman. She thanked the fates that the surgeon was a gentleman, albeit a rather frighteningly remote and cold one. On the rare occasions when his hands had brushed hers while handing her the log or taking it from her, she had been repulsed by how icy cold his fingers were. As cold and bony as a skeleton's.

After slipping away from the rowdy rite of passage on deck, she went to the sick bay to duly record the crossing of the line and to her surprise found the surgeon seated at his desk staring morosely at a half-empty whiskey glass.

"Oh . . . I thought you were on deck."

He turned to look at her, his eyes darkly empty, like the pitch black of bottomless caves. "I've crossed the line many times. The nonsense has long since lost any novelty value."

"I'll come back later to do the log."

"No. Stay. Sit down. Would you like a drink? A real one, I mean. Rum? Whiskey?"

There was something different about him, and she wasn't sure she was comfortable with it. The image of a corpse coming to life crossed her mind. "No, thank you. I've never cared for the taste of spirits."

She started to leave, but he snapped, "Sit down, I said."

Perching on the edge of a chair she forced herself to meet his ravaged gaze. Having worked with Will Prentice every day she knew he was a competent physician who did not differentiate between convicts, crew, and marines when it came to medical care. He urged the guards to treat the convicts humanely and was always ready to bring the voice of reason to any dispute.

But there was something missing from Will Prentice, and until this moment she had been unable to define what was lacking. Now it occurred to her that he had no friends aboard and she had never heard him mention family or friends at home in England. It was as if he had sprung, fully formed, onto this ship, with no past history, without even the most tenuous connection to another human being. It was eerie, rather like associating with an actor playing a part. Or perhaps the wandering spirit of one whose earthly body no longer served him.

Sometimes a slight North Country accent crept into his speech, which, along with an occasional grammatical slip of the tongue, indicated that like most of those in his profession, he was from the middle classes. But other than this, there was no clue to his origin or his past.

She cleared her throat. "Something is troubling you? I suppose you must miss your family in England. You've never spoken of them, but—"

"The biggest disgrace of the colony is what happens to the female convicts." He drained his glass. "You're bound for what is little better than a brothel. The women, if they aren't disorderly when they embark for that cursed shore, soon become so in order to survive."

Bethany waited, wondering where this was leading. No comment from her seemed necessary, since there was little she could do about her situation.

"You once said you'd throw yourself overboard before cohabiting with any of the men aboard this ship. Tell me, will you kill yourself before submitting to some brutish settler who probably only months ago was a convict himself?"

She swallowed a hard lump in her throat and decided to be honest with him. "No, sir. I shan't kill myself, no matter what happens to me. You see, I have a husband somewhere in the penal colony, and I left a child behind in England. I want to live to see both of them again."

6

THE WIND HOWLED in the chimney and the coals in the hearth flared brilliantly. The lamps had not yet been lit in the drawing room at Riverleigh although these mid-December days brought an early twilight.

Adrian paced back and forth, the firelight elongating his shadow on the brocade-covered walls until it assumed grotesque proportions.

Standing dejectedly before his father, Stewart watched that monstrous shadow, afraid to behold his father's anguish and rage. His stepmother sat quietly in a fireside chair, her expression tense, her fingers kneading the folds of her skirt.

When the silence had lengthened unbearably, Adrian suddenly growled, "Why couldn't it have been you they kidnapped?"

Mary gasped. Stewart felt his entire body stiffen with the pain of his father's rejection.

"Oh, Adrian, you are beside yourself," Mary protested. "You don't mean that—"

"Don't I? Look at him, standing there almost in tears. He's my son, but I swear I can scarcely comprehend that he is flesh of my flesh. He should have been born a girl, with his mincing manner and soft ways. A man would have defended his brother, to the death if necessary. But he stood meekly by and let them take Tom—" Adrian's voice broke.

"Tom's riding master was also present," Mary pointed out. "He is a grown man, but apparently he could not protect Tom."

"Ah, yes, Roland Montague," Adrian said in a deathly quiet voice. "Where is he now?"

"I don't know, sir," Stewart answered. "He must have left the station while I was still talking to the constable."

Adrian glanced at the mantelpiece clock. "I'm going back to Liverpool immediately. I can't do anything here."

"If I could go with you, sir, perhaps I could help—" Stewart began.

"Stay out of my sight," Adrian snapped. "And if, God forbid, they've harmed a hair on Tom's head, I never want to lay eyes on you again as long as I live."

He turned and strode from the room, slamming the door behind him. They heard him calling for Wentworth to have a carriage brought around for him.

Mary rose swiftly and crossed the room to Stewart's side. She placed her hand gently on his arm. "He's distraught. He doesn't mean it. It was his shock and fear speaking." She paused. "Stewart, I didn't dare suggest it in front of your father, but do you think it's possible Tom was playing another of his pranks? You know how he is."

Stewart sighed deeply. "No, I don't think this was a prank. Montague had a nasty bruise on his jaw, and he said he thought one of the men struck Tom on the back of his head with a cosh. I doubt Tom would arrange for either of them to be hurt just to play a joke. But, Mary, there is something that's lingering in my mind. You see, when we left the train, Tom was wearing an old relic of a Garrick overcoat that belongs to Montague, who seemed to think that perhaps the kidnappers had grabbed Tom by mistake; they are somewhat alike in height and build and coloring. I did tell Father this when I arrived, but he dismissed it immediately. He felt it was unlikely any kidnapper worth his salt would take a penniless boarding school riding master."

"I'm inclined to agree, Stewart," Mary replied.

They stood silently together for a moment; then Stewart said, "Christmastime seems always to bring disaster to our family. My mother died in December, and it was Christmas Eve when Father and Neil quarreled and Neil left home."

Mary squeezed his hand sympathetically.

There was a knock on the door and the butler appeared. "Excuse me, milady, but there is a young woman here in regard to the parlor maid's position we have open. Her name is Alison Banks. I wouldn't have troubled you at such a time, but she insists upon my showing you this reference. Apparently it's from an old school friend of yours. Forgive me, milady. I know you must be too worried about Master Tom to be bothered—"

Stewart was surprised when his stepmother immediately said, "It's all right, Wentworth, I'll see her. I've been expecting her. She is bringing me news of my old friend. But please, do come to me at once when Master Tom comes home."

The young woman who waited in the servants' sitting room had a high forehead and a level gaze that suggested intelligence, and she might even have been pretty had it not been for her pinched features and undernourished body. She seemed scrubbed clean, and her chestnut-colored hair was drawn into a neat bun at the nape of her neck, but her coat was threadbare and her shoes pitifully worn.

"Why, you're scarcely more than a child yourself," Mary exclaimed. "Surely Mrs. Creel could not have given you this letter to bring to me? She must have intended it for your mother or perhaps an older sister?"

"Mrs. Creel thought I would be suitable, Lady Fielding."

"Did she explain to you the nature of the position?"

"Yes, milady. You want someone to take care of an infant."

"I can't believe she would send you to me. You're far too young and inexperienced."

"I went to school and finished top of my class, Lady Fielding. Mrs. Creel knew my father and mother. She thought I'd suit you because I've a baby of my own that I'm still breast-feeding. He's six months old and thriving."

"And do you also have a husband?" Mary asked.

"No, milady, not now. My husband and my father were both lost at sea on the same ship a month before my son was born. I'm all alone in the world. I've been taking in laundry and doing a bit of sewing, but nobody will give me a steady job because I have a child. It would make all the difference to the boy and me if we could count on a few shillings coming in regularly."

There was desperation in the young woman's hazel eyes now, but Mary saw no change in her demeanor, which remained calm, composed. Alison Banks was not going to beg, and Mary respected her for that. She also felt a wave of compassion, since it was obvious the young woman had been feeding her baby at the expense of her own nutrition.

Alison added, "Mrs. Creel sent you a note. I didn't want to give it to your butler." She pulled a sealed envelope from her pocket and handed it to Mary.

"Alison is a good girl," Mrs. Creel had written. "She's a hard worker and too proud to take charity. Both her husband and her father were lost on the *Sea Venture.*"

Mary blinked. The *Sea Venture* was a Fielding vessel that had sunk in the Caribbean during a hurricane. She was impressed by the fact that Alison had not used this to plead her case. Mary had always felt shipowners had a moral, if not a legal, responsibility to provide for the widows and orphans of seamen who were lost while on a voyage. But apart from a pittance paid through a widows' and orphans' fund, there was no continuing financial support. The owners' attitude was that it was up to the men to provide for their families before and after their death.

The rest of Mrs. Creel's letter read: "Since I'm sending Alison to you, you will know that I have found the baby. She is in a home on the outskirts of Liverpool and was quite poorly when I saw her. When I told the matron that a benefactor would provide for her, she said we can take her any time. I think they believe the baby is dying, and she may well be. I must tell you this, but also I must tell you that I have never seen a more beautiful child. If you wish to proceed, send Alison back to see me and I will instruct her."

Mary looked up at Alison. "Where do you live?"

"I have a room in a boardinghouse." There was no need for her to elaborate, Mary could well imagine the lodgings she had.

"Mrs. Creel will find a flat for you. All of our dealings will be through her. I do not expect to see you again or ever to lay eyes on the infant."

"You mean I'm to take care of her?"

"Yes, I believe we can come to an understanding."

Alison's eyes lit up as she smiled for the first time, and in that instant Mary felt her only misgiving, for she saw now that Alison Banks would be a real beauty when those gaunt hollows in her cheeks had filled in. How long would such a lovely girl remain a widow, and would a new man in her life uncover the baby's connection to Adrian? But no, how could he? No one but Bethany Newton knew who the father of her child was, and she had been banished to the ends of the earth. Mary was unsure why she felt such an urgent need to care for the baby, but she wondered if perhaps it was motivated by her own need for some purpose in her empty life.

Mary said, more curtly than she intended, "I suggest you concoct a story of a friendship with the baby's mother, who died giving birth. You will never mention my connection to you or how you came to have the child, do you understand? Good day and good-bye, Mrs. Banks. We shan't meet again."

Adrian walked briskly toward the Pier Head, past the Goree Piazza where the iron rings attached to the wall recalled that only a few years earlier African slaves had been chained there awaiting transshipment to America.

He frowned as he went by. England's abolition of slavery had all but bankrupted him, since all of his ships had been engaged in the slave trade. Adrian had vowed never again to rely on only one type of cargo. Therefore despite the handsome fees he was paid to transport convicts, he had leased only the *Peregrine* to the government for that purpose. Thanks to Mary's dowry, he now had ships plying both the Atlantic and the Caribbean.

Atop Bidston Hill a yellow flag with a black ball in the center fluttered in an icy wind from Cropper & Benson's flagpole, signaling the arrival of one of the new Black Ball liners off the Bar Light fifteen miles down the river. Each of the more prominent merchants and shipping agents had his own flagpole, and the flags were hoisted so that preparations could be made at the Pier Head to receive the incoming ships.

Adrian's flag, a white hawk in flight emblazoned on a blue ground, was not flying today, but he glanced toward the hill out of force of habit as he strode toward his office.

Office boys darted in and out of the buildings on either side of the street, carrying rolled bills of lading under their arms and dodging one another on the crowded pavement. The business of sending cargoes around the world required a great deal of along-shore activity.

Adrian's anger had reached the boiling point by the time he pushed open the office door. The high-ceilinged room was heated only by a coal fire sputtering in a narrow fireplace, the effectiveness of which was further diminished by a brick placed on either side of the hearth to cut down on the consumption of coal. Most of the shipping clerks standing before high slanting desks covered with bills of lading, consular invoices, and letters ordering cargoes forward wore woolen gloves with the fingers cut out to allow them to hold their quills.

Ignoring his shivering clerks, Adrian went directly into one of the two private offices and slammed the door shut behind him. Tate Ivers was seated at his desk, and Vareck stood looking out of the window at the profusion of masts and furled sails etched against the gray expanse of the river.

"Well?" Adrian demanded.

Vareck turned slowly. "The crimps say they took the one wearing the Garrick overcoat, like they were told. How could they know your son would be wearing it?"

Adrian was sure a blood vessel would burst in his temple. His fists tightened at his sides. "My son is a boy, seventeen years old. Couldn't your damned crimps distinguish between a boy and a man?"

"Tom is big and muscular for his age, Adrian," Tate pointed out, "and he and Montague have the same coloring. I can see how the mistake was made. By God, I wish I'd known you were planning such a vicious act. I'd have found a way to stop you."

"Would you, now? Tell me, when did you become finicky about using Vareck to acquire crews?" Adrian asked sarcastically.

"I'll grant you that he persuades a few reluctant tars to sign on again, but I don't accept men who've never been to sea before, and I would never shanghai a man for spite."

"For spite? There was more to it than that," Adrian said shortly. He had no intention of telling his business partner that Roland Montague had tried to blackmail him, or that Montague was Bethany Newton's brother and had brotherly knowledge that could ruin Sir Adrian's good name. Tate had no idea that Bethany Newton was actually Bethany Fielding.

Turning to Vareck, Adrian asked, "Where is my son?"

"Aboard the *Circe.*"

Adrian's blood chilled. "Good God. She has McTrane for a master and Bullock for a mate."

Vareck's transparent eyes regarded him maliciously. "Well, you said you wanted Montague punished. In fact, your exact words were that you wouldn't care if he didn't survive the voyage."

Adrian drew a deep breath. "Where is she bound?"

There was a long silence. Tate finally said to Vareck, "You'd better tell him."

"Guinea," Vareck answered. "Then America. A southern port, of course."

The office spun for a second in a dizzying whirlwind. "A slaver? You've put my son aboard a *slaver?*"

Tate said, "The *Circe* was sold to new owners. Hindu traders who don't give a damn about British laws against transporting slaves."

"It's not much worse than transporting convicts anyway," Vareck remarked. "And you didn't think twice before you leased out the *Peregrine.*"

"Watch your tongue, you insolent swine," Adrian snapped.

"Speaking of the *Peregrine,*" Tate put in, "I have another startling bit of news for you, Adrian. If I were a religious man or a superstitious one, I'd give serious consideration to the belief that our worst deeds are turned back on us."

"Get to the point," Adrian growled.

"The *Peregrine* was short a couple of female transportees on sailing day. Bethany Newton was selected to sail on her. It's ironic, isn't it, that she's aboard one of your own ships, while your son—"

"Damn you both to hell for your bungling incompetence," Adrian shouted. He stood up and with one sweep of his arm sent everything on Tate's desk flying to the floor. Tate's bushy eyebrows twitched slightly, but he made no comment, although he had no control over the convicts assigned to the *Peregrine.*

"You, Vareck," Adrian said, "will sail for Africa on the first ship leaving port. Find my son and bring him home. There'll be a year's wages for you as a bonus when you return with him."

Vareck left without a word.

"What will you tell your wife?" Tate asked.

"Only that I have men searching for Tom."

"Is that fair to her? It will be months before Tom can get back."

"He isn't her son, is he?"

"No, but she's fond of him, Adrian."

Adrian stared at Tate, the seed of a sudden suspicion sprouting. "Why are you so concerned with my wife's feelings, may I ask? You've always appeared irritated by her presence, and you go to great lengths to be disagreeable whenever she's around."

Tate's craggy countenance flushed slightly. "I just think it would be cruel to keep her worrying and wondering about Tom for so long."

"When we were boys together, Tate, I recall that while the other boys teased the little girls they liked, you were always rude to the ones you were smitten with—"

"For Christ's sake shut up," Tate said, his face a dull red now, "before you say something that will cause me to do something I'll regret."

"Odd how we believe we know someone, isn't it? Your bachelorhood always gave me a different impression of your sexual preferences. Are you aware that from time to time there are whispers about some of the pretty young boys who find themselves taking unexpected ocean voyages after crossing your path?"

"Damn you and the whispers to hell, Adrian. I must see that our ships have crews to sail them, and if I have to use Vareck and his crimps from time to time, so does every other shipowner. The life of a seaman appeals to very few men. But unlike most of the other owners, I insist that every man Vareck brings to a ship of ours is a seasoned tar. It's a damn shame they got Tom by mistake, but that does seem to be judgment on you, Adrian."

Ignoring the outburst, Adrian continued, "We all misjudged you. Your fancy clothes and lack of female companionship distracted us, did it not? And to think all this time you've been harboring an unrequited love."

Tate rose to his feet, his eyes blazing. "I'm warning you, Adrian . . ."

Shrugging, Adrian turned to leave. "It's of little consequence to me if you're pining for my wife. Her fortune saved the company from bankruptcy when we lost the slave trade, and she runs my household efficiently. I never wanted her for more than that."

"You bastard," Tate said softly.

But Adrian wasn't listening. It had pleased him to taunt Tate, easing momentarily his misery about Tom, and he didn't seriously feel threatened by Tate's abruptly revealed interest in Mary for the simple reason that she was terrified of the man.

He thought it might even be amusing to throw them together more often and watch the big oaf squirm. Adrian needed Tate, because the Fielding ships sailed more efficiently nowadays, never lacking crews and provisions as they had in the past. But Adrian regretted that in the financial chaos that followed the prohibition of transporting black slaves to America and the Indies, he had taken Tate on as a partner . . . scant months before he met Mary, at which time the infusion of more capital into the company became unnecessary.

Tom Fielding came to his senses as a stream of ice-cold salt water doused him. He was lying on the gently swaying deck of a ship as it sailed past Bidston Hill. He could see the flags hanging limply in a gray drizzle of rain.

A man stood over him, feet astride, empty bucket dangling from one huge paw. He had a tangled beard, tiny eyes set deep in a pockmarked gargoyle's face. For an instant Tom thought the apparition must be a creature from his darkest nightmare, but then a vicious kick to his side convinced him that this was no dream.

"On your feet, Montague," the brute ordered.

Scrambling to obey before the man's foot again prompted him, Tom wondered why he was being called by the name of his boarding school riding master.

He had been shanghaied, he realized in astonished dismay. Was Roland Montague aboard, too? There was another inert figure on the deck, but it wasn't Montague. The man wore a salt-grimed jacket and a woolen watch cap and had surely been to sea before, although perhaps of his own free will, but he now seemed too old and frail for the rigors of seafaring. Like Tom, he was doused with seawater and kicked to consciousness.

When both men were on their feet, their tormentor surveyed them with exaggerated scorn. "God's blood, but you're a miserable-looking pair of buggers. An old man and boy still wet behind the ears. Christ, the crimps must have been hard up."

The old man drew himself up to his full height, bowed extravagantly from the waist, and then hiccupped. "Ned Morecambe, sir. Would I be addressing the first mate of this vessel, and if so may I inquire her name and whither she's bound?"

"Aye, I'm the mate and you can shut your blasted mouth and speak when I tell you."

A crewman approached and said, "Mr. Bullock, sir, I've

sailed with the old man before. He's a fair navigator when he's sober."

"Take him below and sober him up."

The beadlike eyes of the mate fixed ferociously on Tom. "And as for you, Montague—"

Since politeness hadn't prevailed, Tom decided to try upper-class disdain. "My name isn't Montague, you great lout. It's Fielding. Thomas Fielding. My father owns the Fielding Shipping Company, and God help you and the scurvy scoundrels who brought me aboard this stinking tub when my father finds out—"

A fist as big as a ham crashed into his jaw, and everything went dark again.

In her private room at the Fielding town house in Victoria Gardens Mrs. Creel surveyed Alison Banks with satisfaction. "You did well."

Alison bit her lip. "Lady Fielding seemed so nice. I didn't like lying to her about how I've been living since I was widowed."

"Oh? You'd rather be back in the gutter, would you? Starving and selling your body to put bread in your mouth and milk in your breasts for your babe?"

"I couldn't let Davey die, could I? There was no other way. I couldn't find work."

"You just remind yourself, my girl, that unless you do exactly as I tell you, you and your whelp will be back on the streets."

"You promised me that nothing would happen to that other baby, the one she wants me to take care of. You did mean that—"

"I said so, didn't I? Now you'd better get down to the parish home and get the baby."

"But . . . Lady Fielding said you'd find a flat for us first."

"You don't need a flat. I'm putting you and the two bairns up in the attic."

"But . . . the Fieldings will see us, hear us. The babies will cry and—"

"There's three stories to the house. They use the first two. Usually it's only Sir Adrian who stays overnight. My room's on the third floor and nobody but me goes up there. Nobody will see or hear you up in the attic. You'll be able to come downstairs when he's at Riverleigh and when he goes to his office. You'll be comfortable up there."

Alison looked down at her son, sleeping contentedly in a clothes basket beside her chair. She rose to her feet. Mrs. Creel was well aware that she would do anything to ensure her baby's survival.

Before she could pick Davey up, the housekeeper said, "You'd better leave him here with me. The matron of the home will think it odd that you want to adopt a baby when you already have one."

Alison was reluctant to do so, because she feared the woman, but she could hardly argue with her. Since Davey had just nursed at her breast, he probably would take a long nap, and perhaps she could get back before he awakened. Besides, she had little choice if she wanted a home for them. Alison just wished she knew exactly what Lady Fielding's housekeeper planned for them all.

7

BETHANY STOOD BESIDE Will Prentice at the ship's rail, staring at her first glimpse of what in England was thought of as another planet, a world of exile, desolately alone at the far end of the earth.

"That's North Head, at the upper part of the harbor," Prentice said. In the bright light his haggard features seemed more melancholy than ever, and when he spoke it was in the same unemotional tone he used to describe a gruesome injury for entry in his log or to point out to her a particularly impressive sunset.

He went on, "It looks a little like a broken shortbread, doesn't it? With huge crumbs jumbled below the sandstone cliffs. Battered by constant winds, pounded by boiling surf. . . . Look how high those plumes reach. The aborigines call this place Boree—the Enduring One. It's seven thousand miles to South America, and there's nothing below us but the Antarctic. We're at the bottom of the earth."

Bethany scanned the top of the cliffs with their sparse scrub and shivered, feeling the magnitude of her banishment overwhelm her. But Neil was here, she reminded herself, and somehow she would find him.

"You'll see some strange trees. Eucalypts and red gums, the likes of which no Englishman ever saw before coming here. They're not evergreens, more like evergrays, and are forever shedding their bark in an almost obscene manner."

"You've been here before?" Bethany asked.

"Yes." He paused. "However, this time I shall be staying for a while."

"You intend to make your home here?" Bethany asked in surprise.

"I had no choice in the matter. A surgeon was needed for the New South Wales Corps. So you see I, too, am an exile."

"Not in the same way I am."

"What if I could arrange for you to be assigned to my household as a servant? Would that be agreeable to you?"

She turned to him, hope flaring. He had treated her with respect throughout the long voyage, demanding no sexual favors. She was the only woman aboard who had been spared sexual bondage, and her gratitude was great. The surgeon, she decided, must respect the institution of marriage and, knowing she had a husband, had not forced himself upon her. "Oh, if only you could . . . I would work hard for you, I promise."

He stared at her for a long moment, as though unsatisfied with her reply. She had seen that look on his face before. It puzzled her because she had no idea what it meant and because it was so fleeting she wondered if she had imagined it. Most of the time his haggard features wore an impersonal expression that perhaps physicians cultivated of necessity, to hide their dismay at the horrible diseases and injuries they had to treat.

After a moment he said, "Very well. I'll see what I can do before we drop anchor. It's bedlam when a convict transport docks, a scene reminiscent of a slave auction. The settlers—many of whom were transportees themselves and have now served their sentences—fight over the convicts to be assigned to them, especially the women. Educated women such as you are particularly in demand as nannies and governesses to look after their children, but I'm afraid you can't hope for that. You'd be too much of a threat to the wife."

How many times he'd reminded her of that! Had his reason been that he wanted her to work for him all along? How very devious men could be. She said, "I'll go and finish packing your medical supplies."

The *Peregrine* glided past the dangerous reef, sailing along the wind-etched ledges of Vaucluse and Parsley Bay toward the wide harbor of Sydney. By ten in the morning the crew had dropped anchor in Botany Bay. The ship was soon surrounded by a bobbing flotilla of rowboats carrying settlers anxious to view the newly arrived labor force.

Leona dragged Bethany up on deck to watch the spectacle. She hung over the side, calling to the men in the boats, asking if they had any theaters or playhouses. Her questions were greeted with hoots of laughter.

Then all at once Leona clutched Bethany's arm. "Look . . . they just brought your champion up from the hold. I didn't think he'd live to see Sydney, did you?"

Bethany spun around just in time to see two marines lead Jack Cutler on deck. She was shocked at his appearance—ragged, dirty, pale as a priest and gauntly thin. Yet despite his long confinement in the dark hold belowdecks, he held his head high, blinking in the sudden unaccustomed sunlight as he dragged his fetters across the deck.

The moment Cutler appeared, Ruben pushed through a knot of marines who had clustered along the rail to drink in the sight of land after months at sea. "Well, look what the bilges coughed up. Black Jack Cutler himself, still alive, I see. But not for long. How long do you think you'll last as a government man, Gentleman Jack?"

"What does he mean?" Bethany whispered to Leona.

"Ruben told me that most of the convicts will be lent out to private settlers. But a few of them are kept by the government as laborers, building the roads and breakwaters and jails and courthouses and public works, making roads through the bush. It's the worst punishment, because they'll work on chain gangs."

In the instant before Cutler was flung into a waiting longboat, he turned and swept the deck with his eyes until he spotted Bethany. Despite his condition, he smiled and bowed.

Bethany was curiously moved by the gesture.

Crossing the sun-sparkled harbor with Will—he'd suggested that since they would be sharing living quarters she now call him by his given name—and several ship's officers, Bethany felt some of her despair evaporate under the clear southern skies. On shore she could see whitewashed cottages with verandas, their gardens bordered with bright geranium hedges.

Her surge of hope vanished the moment she stepped ashore

and encountered a long line of convicts marching in single file, leg irons rattling. Some wore gray and yellow jackets with duck overalls, others white woolen frocks and trousers, all daubed with broad arrows and numerals in black, white, and red. She learned later the different styles of dress denoted how long it had been since the men arrived. She forced herself to look at each man, but Neil was not one of them.

Worse than the sight of the men was the appearance on the quay of a group of women, who despite the early hour, openly solicited disembarking seamen. The lewdness of the prostitutes, their gutter language and actions, revolted her, while at the same time she felt an unwilling kinship with them. Would that be her ultimate fate? A ticket of leave to a hell worse than penal servitude? Were those women surviving in the only way open to them? Aboard the transport she'd heard that free settlers often took convict women to be their "wives," but since the ties were not legal, discarded them when they tired of them.

Will left her with his baggage while he went to report his arrival and readiness to take up his duties. She sat on a steamer trunk, feeling like a piece of baggage herself. A row of fruit stalls across from the quay swarmed with people who were not quite English and yet not recognizably foreign. Over the babble of voices she heard the shriek of cockatoos and saw that many were confined to cages hanging from the stalls. Caged birds, caged men and women . . .

She experienced a moment's panic, fought the urge to run, somewhere, anywhere. Neil, oh, my dear, my husband! Where are you?

"Bethany, are you ready?" Will appeared at her side so suddenly she jumped, startled. How like a great silent bat he was. She shivered in the sunlight, repulsed by him.

The house to which Will took her was built at the very edge of town, a last outpost upon whose fragile walls pressed the great empty Australian bush.

"I wanted to be as far away from the rest of the denizens of this accursed place as possible," Will said as he opened the door and walked inside. Silently Bethany followed.

"The house and furniture were built by convict labor," he continued, "so I suppose we shouldn't expect too much. I have to report to the barracks and have a look at the infirmary. You can stay here. I'm not sure when they'll unload my trunks from the *Peregrine,* but if they're delivered before I return, you can start unpacking. Here are the keys."

After he left she prowled the house, speculating on which of the three bedrooms he would give to her, and wondering uneasily if a house and furniture built by convicts had been deliberately jury-rigged and would suddenly tumble into ruins around them.

She felt disoriented by the fact that the Australian summer was ending at the time the English spring brought the promise of rebirth, and somehow the thought formed a sad analogy with her life. The memory of a tiny baby girl, so perfect, so beautiful, came back to haunt her and as she had learned to do on the long voyage, she kept her tears at bay by remembering Neil.

Was he somewhere nearby? Oh, please God, don't let him be on one of the chain gangs! Neil, my darling, if I could just see you, be with you, if for only a moment . . .

The intensity of her feelings awakened longings that tormented her. She loved him so. He had swept her away in a romantic daze. How could they have foreseen that tragedy awaited them?

Neil had arrived in her life when it was in turmoil and had taken command. Although he told her nothing about himself other than that he was a struggling journalist, it had seemed unnecessary at the time for her to know more. He exuded breeding and wealth the way a lantern gave off light and he had pursued her so single-mindedly, devoting so much time to her, that it had never occurred to her to wonder why she was never invited to meet his family.

Bethany's father had been vicar of a dockside parish, and she and her two brothers had led a sheltered life, tutored at home by a well-educated mother, doted upon by a gentle father. The parish was a poor one, but Bethany and her brothers never realized this, as there was so much love in their home. Her older brother, Roland, spoiled darling of his mother, had departed two years before her pleasant life at the vicarage came to an end.

Her uncle, reputedly the black sheep of the family, a seafaring man the family had not seen for years, had appeared on their doorstep one day. He had a duffel bag on his shoulder, a parrot in a cage, and a wooden stump where his lower right leg used to be.

After embracing her mother, he said, "If I could just stay with you for a bit, until I get back on my feet . . ." and had looked down at the stump and laughed.

He had spent several years on a whaler and lost his leg to a shark when a surfacing whale had capsized their harpoon boat. For a few days he regaled them with stories of the sea and the great mammals he'd hunted from a frail little craft. Then suddenly he had fallen ill. Only then did they learn there had been typhoid aboard the ship that brought him to Liverpool.

Despite Bethany's protests, her mother immediately sent Bethany and her younger brother to stay with their only other relative, an elderly aunt who lived across the river in a village on the Wirral peninsula. But it was already too late.

A month later Roland, safe at university, and Bethany were the only members of the family left. Bethany had clung precariously to life, racked with pain and fever, too weak to mourn the death of the others.

The landlord's agent had come to collect the rent and found Bethany barely alive, the bodies of her aunt and brother cold and stiff in their beds. The agent had shown compassion not usually associated with those in his profession and asked his employer that she be allowed to die there in the house in peace.

But she hadn't died, and one day the landlord lost patience and sent the eviction men. Neil Fielding, who called himself Neil Newton, had appeared at the same time.

Bethany had opened her eyes and looked into his compassionate gaze, and in that split second she had known that her life would never again be the same.

"Please don't be frightened. I would like to help you, if I can. I've been writing an article about the eviction practices of some landlords. Is it true you are being evicted because your aunt and brother died of typhoid?"

She nodded weakly.

"They say they have to burn everything in the cottage and board it up for a time. Have you anywhere to go?"

She shook her head. "I have a brother . . . but I can't go to him." Roland had written to her immediately following their father's death, telling her to stay away from him, since he didn't want the filthy disease, and bemoaning the fact that their father's solicitor had told him there was no inheritance, so he would be forced to leave the university and fend for himself.

As she remembered how cruel Roland's letter had been, her eyes filled with tears.

Neil said gently, "I know of an innkeeper who will give you work when you're stronger and a room until then."

Too weak to wonder at the kindness of a stranger, she found herself borne away in a hired coach to a Tudor-style inn called the Eight Bells on the outskirts of Birkenhead, where she was given a small room overlooking the river. The innkeeper's wife, a motherly woman named Nancy, cared for her. Neil visited her almost every day, always properly chaperoned by Nancy.

For the next several weeks Bethany existed in a misty world that was neither quite real nor yet a dream. Gradually her body recovered from the ravages of the illness and her mind began to question the circumstances of her stay at the inn. When she mentioned to the innkeeper's wife her concern over the enormity of the debt she was incurring, Nancy replied, "But your young man has paid for your board."

Her young man. Bethany liked the sound of that. When Neil came to visit again she asked Nancy shyly if they might speak privately somewhere other than in her room, and when they were alone, Bethany said, "I don't know how I shall ever be able to repay you. I am quite overwhelmed that you would do so much for a stranger."

"A stranger? I do not feel you are a stranger. Something happened the first time I saw you. . . . It was as if we were meeting again after a long separation. My heart seemed ready to burst from the joy of finding you again, even though logic told me we had never met before."

She smiled at him, all traces of shyness vanishing. "Oh yes," she breathed. "That's how it was. Magical, mysterious."

"Bethany . . . I make a somewhat precarious living writing pieces for various periodicals. If you had not been orphaned, I doubt your family would have taken kindly to my courting you, since I have so little to offer."

"You have your kind heart, your compassion," she protested.

"And my devotion, forever. But so little in the way of worldly goods that I'm ashamed. A miserable flat over a greengrocer's in the worst part of Liverpool and a hand-to-mouth existence at best."

She was puzzled, because his clothes were of such fine quality and she recognized in his speech that he must have attended a fine university. Nancy eventually told her that he was the first-born son of a wealthy and powerful man who had cut him off without a penny for taking up the cause of mistreated seamen aboard his ships and writing impassioned pleas for an end to child labor in the Lancashire mills.

Bethany resolved not to be a further burden to him and asked Nancy to put her to work. She served ale and washed glasses and most of the time was too exhausted to contemplate the change in her fortunes, the hard work, and the indignity of strange fingers pinching her bottom.

One afternoon she slipped away and went up to the inn's widow's walk and watched the ships sailing up the river. The fresh air brought a tingle to her cheeks and she was ravenously hungry, but she lingered, waiting for Neil, knowing he would come.

She always knew, almost to the exact moment, when he would appear, when every part of her would flare into brilliant life. Their meeting had been ordained; she knew that just as surely as she knew she loved him.

From the widow's walk she could see the promenade along the river, and almost as if she had conjured him out of her thoughts, she looked down to see Neil walking toward the inn.

The inn's cobbled courtyard ended at an iron rail at the river's edge, and Neil paused there for a moment, staring down the choppy surface of the Mersey toward the Irish Sea. The river was subject to the same tides as the ocean, and the incoming high tide surged toward him, swirling below the rail where he stood. He squared his shoulders, as though gathering courage from the churning water; then he turned and looked up to see her standing on the widow's walk, and his face lit up as he removed his hat and waved it.

She waved back and then ran to meet him, her heart fluttering as she made her way down the inn's oak staircase. Neil was in whispered conversation with Nancy at the foot of the stairs. She nodded, smiling, and disappeared as he took Bethany's hands in his and raised them to his lips. "I have a surprise for you. Come on."

He led her down the inn's central hall to a private dining room. A table was set for two, with a centerpiece of red roses and long red tapers in a handsome silver candelabrum. A log burned in the fireplace, and the room was fragrant with the scent of potpourri.

"Neil! Surely we are not going to dine in here? I can't allow such extravagance—" she began, but he led her to a velvet chaise longue beside the fire, and when she was seated, he dropped to one knee before her.

"Neil, what are you doing?"

His eyes were alight with mischief. "My dear Bethany, surely you must have guessed my fond feelings toward you? Dare I hope you return my love?" Despite his light tone, he was anxious; she could see it in the tense line of his jaw, in the way his hands trembled slightly as they held hers.

"Neil, darling," she whispered the word of endearment, thinking how wonderful it sounded. "Please get up. If this is to be a proposal, I want you to be very sure, very serious."

The next second he was beside her on the chaise, his arms around her. "I love you more than life. Bethany, dearest, I'm not worthy of you, I know, but I can't live without you. Marry me? Please."

She sighed happily and melted against him. Later, after Nancy had served them an elegant dinner of roast pheasant, he told her that he had acquired a position on a small weekly news sheet that was printed in Manchester. He'd found a flat, and if she would agree, they could be married immediately.

"Nothing would give me greater happiness," she assured him.

"Shall I go to see your brother first, to formally ask for your hand? I mean, since Roland is your only living relative . . ."

"No," she said sadly. "I haven't heard from Roland since our parents died. I don't even know where he is."

On the day of their wedding she pinched her cheeks to bring color to them and washed her hair in chamomile to make it shine. She bought some lace and sewed it to the neck and cuffs of her best gown, a light blue bombazine that had been reserved for church when she lived at home with her family.

Nancy lent her a lacy bonnet and gave her a small bunch of violets to carry. Nancy and her husband were their only witnesses, and because Neil had to complete an article for his paper before the following day, after the ceremony they departed by train for Manchester.

She was filled with joy, and it seemed her feet scarcely skimmed the stairs that night as they climbed the steps to their flat. Neil swept her up into his arms and carried her over the threshold. Very gently he put her back on her feet, closed the door on the rest of the world, and took her into his arms. His lips sought hers tenderly, then with growing ardor. Placing his hands on either side of her throat, he slid his fingers under the neckline of her gown and pulled it from her shoulders.

"You are so lovely, so delicate; I'm afraid I might hurt you," he whispered. He touched her breasts gently, tentatively, his caress so infinitely tender that, inexplicably, tears sprang to her eyes.

"I want to be your wife in every way," she responded. "Please . . . don't hold back." She flung her arms around his neck and rained kisses on his face until he picked her up in his arms again and carried her to the bed.

Her knowledge of what a man did to a woman was vague, but she had been warned to expect pain. If what she felt was pain, then pleasure had been misnamed. A coiled spring seemed to have formed at some inner core of her being, and with each kiss and embrace, it tightened until she could hardly breathe, wanting the tension to ease, yet wanting it to last forever.

When Neil removed his clothes she looked away, embarrassed to see his aroused nakedness, but he caught her chin with his forefinger. "Please don't turn away from me. Between a husband and wife there should be no secrets, no shame. I want you to know this part of me because it will express my passion for you. It is the physical extension of my mind, of all I feel for you—my love, my desire, my hunger to worship you. This is how we will join. This is how I will bring you pleasure. Feel him, Bethany, touch him, he's yours. . . . No, not gently. Firmly, like this."

Scarcely aware of what she was doing, knowing only that she was caught in some spell that she did not have the power to break, she did as she was told.

Slowly, wonderingly, he laid bare the rest of her body, touched, explored, kissed each new delight. "Your skin is like silk, Bethany. Your breasts are perfection."

A moment later he breathed against her skin, "Do you feel our fire, Bethany? Tell me you do. We're both about to be consumed in the flames."

Then he was above her, his handsome face alight with love, his body careful not to crush her as his hands gently parted her thighs.

"Bethany? Are you dreaming?" The voice that shattered the memory of her wedding night belonged to Will Prentice and dragged her so abruptly back to the reality of a Spartan little house in the Australian penal colony that she jumped.

She blinked as he came into the room, dropping his medical

bag on the scrubbed wood table and pulling his hat from his head. Silhouetted against the brilliant sunshine spilling in through the open doorway, his tall gaunt frame, stooped shoulders, and lantern jaw gave him the appearance of a specter, and she shrank imperceptibly away from him.

"I—I didn't hear you come in," she stammered.

He looked down at her for moment, his melancholy eyes studying her face. "You were thinking of home. Try not to. It is a torment that feeds upon itself."

Bethany looked away, feeling her cheeks burn with the knowledge of what she had been thinking about when he arrived. How happy those first days of marriage had been . . . until Roland appeared on the scene, bringing with him the same menace that Will Prentice now seemed to exude.

"I have brought some provisions," Will said. "I'll bring them in and perhaps you could cook a meal for us."

She watched him walk from the house, unaccountably disturbed by his silent and unobtrusive gait. He moved in a tentative, reticent manner, the same way he addressed her. A casual observer would have imagined that she was the master and he the servant, instead of the other way around. What an enigma he was, and how ambivalent her feelings were toward him. Sometimes while they were at sea she had observed him standing beside the rail, lost in thought. He seemed so alone, wrapped in a shroud of mystery and aloofness, that she felt a little sorry for him.

Soon, after she had made a comfortable home for Will Prentice, she would try to enlist his aid in her search for Neil.

By the time she had made some inroads into the ancient dust that coated the house, cleaned the pots and pans and stove, and prepared a meal, she was too weary to eat. She sat opposite Will at the plain but substantial table the convicts had built, her eyelids drooping.

The silence of the bush was oppressive, and despite her fatigue, she tried to make conversation simply to destroy the unnerving quiet; but Will had again retreated to that remote place in his mind from which everything else was shut out.

At last, aching with weariness, she rose and asked, "Would it be all right if I retired now?"

He blinked her back into focus. "Yes."

"Which room shall I take?"

"The front one, of course."

Of course? She nodded, bade him good night and went up the stairs. The front room was the largest of the three bedrooms and contained a double bed. There were single beds in the other rooms. It was kind of him to give her the best room.

Twitching with tiredness, she removed her clothes and, not even bothering to take down her hair, collapsed into bed.

Some time later she was abruptly aroused from deep sleep by the sound of the bedroom door closing with a dull thud.

Struggling to come awake, unsure where she was, she sat up in bed. The room was hot and still and filled with the scent of a giant gum that pressed against the window. "Who . . . what is it?"

"Who do you think? It's me, Will." His voice was slurred with drink, and for once his footsteps did not fall silently on the floor as he crossed the room toward the bed.

8

MRS. CREEL CLIMBED up the narrow wooden staircase leading to the attic and pushed open the door.

"It was made into a studio years ago, so there's a fireplace and an oven. The master keeps some old furniture up here. I put your Davey down in that trunk over there."

Alison quickly glanced at her sleeping son to reassure herself he was all right, then looked down at the tiny infant girl in her arms. "Have you ever seen a more beautiful baby? Look at her, she's like a little china doll. They called her Hope at the parish home. I think because they didn't believe there was much hope she'd survive."

Mrs. Creel gave the baby a cursory glance and said shortly, "If she doesn't, you go back to the streets, remember that."

Alison looked around the attic, which consisted of a long room with a sloping ceiling and dormer windows. They could be warm and comfortable up here, once the festoons of cobwebs were gone. Amid the clutter of dusty furniture she saw there was even an old perambulator, which no doubt had once been used for the Fielding infants.

"There's bread and cheese and sausages in that safe over there and tea and sugar on the shelf. You'll have to carry your own coal up, and you be sure the master and none of his visitors are about when you go down to the coal shed. You can see the front street and back entry from the windows up here, so you've no excuse for running into anybody but me."

"I'll be careful," Alison promised.

"Just now there's a terrible to-do in the family, because the youngest boy, Tom, has disappeared. Kidnapped or even done away with, I shouldn't wonder. Proper spoiled their Christmas for them, I can tell you. Then there was the business of Bethany Newton. You might as well know that's her baby you're holding."

Mrs. Creel told her briefly what had happened to the baby's mother. Alison decided that it was very kind of Lady Fielding to care for the baby of a woman who had robbed them, but the big question in her mind was still Mrs. Creel, and the vindictive gleam that came into her tiny deep-set eyes when she spoke of her employers.

The morning of Christmas Eve dawned bright and clear, although there was frost on the windowpanes. Seeing the pale winter sunshine spilling through the attic windows, Alison decided to bundle the babies up warmly and take them across the street to the park. They'd all been inside for two full weeks, and a little fresh air would do them good.

Baby Hope was thriving, clearly gaining weight. Alison felt great tenderness toward the tiny girl and was glad that with her own improved diet she had enough milk to nurse both babies. Davey regarded the new arrival with great solemn eyes and didn't seem to mind sharing his mother with her.

Alison eased the perambulator carefully down the stairs, then with a baby under each arm, crept past Mrs. Creel's closed bedroom door, knowing the housekeeper arose late when Sir Adrian wasn't in residence, and he certainly wouldn't be here on Christmas Eve.

Walking around the park with the parade of nannies out with their charges, Alison felt as if she had at last escaped the horror of the months when she'd been forced to take to the streets, although she still awakened in cold terror from her nightmares. This morning, however, she looked up at the clear pale sky and felt such a sense of rebirth that her eyes misted.

After spending a happy hour in the park she decided to return to the house and was walking along the street with the intention of circling to the back entry when a hackney cab drew to a halt at the front door and a young man jumped down, almost colliding with the pram.

"Oh, I say, I am sorry. I didn't mean to startle you," he said at once. "I hope I haven't awakened the babies."

"I . . . I . . . no. They were already awake," she stammered.

He smiled, the warmest smile she had ever seen. He was a very nice looking young man—about eighteen, she guessed, a year or so younger than she, although Alison felt a great deal older than that.

"You must be new to the neighborhood," he added. "I don't recognize your charges, either, although I haven't been here since summer and I suppose those babies weren't born then? I don't know an awful lot about babies, actually."

Bethany realized he had taken her to be a nanny and thought, Why not let him go on thinking that? "The little boy is six months old and the little girl just six weeks."

The young man knitted his brows in puzzlement. "Isn't that . . . unusual, for a brother and sister?" He flushed with embarrassment. "I mean . . ."

Alison laughed to cover her consternation and to give herself time to think. "Oh, they're not brother and sister. . . . Their mothers are . . . er . . . sisters."

"Lucky little boy to have both a pretty cousin and a pretty nanny. Here, let me help you up the steps with the pram. It looks too heavy for you. Which house?"

"Oh . . . no, thank you. I mean, I'm not going home. I was on my way to the park."

"Then I'll help you across the street. Allow me to introduce myself, I'm Stewart Fielding."

Alison stood rooted to the spot. Stewart . . . He was Adrian Fielding's second son.

"And your name?" he prompted gently, taking the pram from her and easing it carefully down over the curb.

"Alison Banks."

"I'm delighted to meet you, Miss Banks."

For a split second she considered telling him she was Mrs. Banks, but decided there was no point. She'd never see him again; she would take care of that.

They crossed the street to return to the park, and at the

wrought-iron gates she took the handle of the pram from him. "Thank you. I can manage now."

Stewart hesitated, then tipped his hat. "Perhaps we'll meet again? I'll look for you in the park." He sighed deeply. "I'd love to walk with you now, but I've been summoned here to meet my father, and I must be waiting when he arrives. Good day, Miss Banks."

"Good-bye, Mr. Fielding," Allison responded, her heart beginning to hammer. Sir Adrian was coming today! Oh, please don't let him discover us.

The minute Stewart disappeared into the house, she raced the pram back across the street at full speed, hurried around to the back entry, and hid the pram in the coal shed. She carried the babies up the stairs one under each arm, fearing with every step that a door would open and she would confront Stewart or, worse still, his father. What could possibly be the reason for their meeting here on this of all days?

Stewart paced nervously around his father's study. One wall was covered by a gigantic map of the world with various ports connected by inked-in shipping routes. Most of the Fielding vessels plied the Atlantic between Liverpool and the American eastern seaboard, and one or two went on to the Gulf ports of Galveston and New Orleans. There were also three ships that sailed between the Gulf and the Caribbean, returning to England only when extensive repairs were needed.

In the window alcove stood a large wooden globe, supported by carved teak legs, and he stopped and turned it slowly. Was it possible Tom was aboard a ship somewhere? The crimps were always more active at Christmastime, since few sailors wanted to be in mid-Atlantic in the December squalls. But surely no skipper would dare to set sail with Adrian Fielding's favorite son aboard? As soon as Tom revealed who he was they would put him ashore at the first port of call.

Stewart walked to the window and looked across the street at the winter-bare trees in the park. The memory of the pretty face of the young nanny, Alison, momentarily distracted him from his anguish over Tom's disappearance. Most of the young women of his acquaintance were the spoiled and pampered daughters of the upper classes or rich merchants, and he'd liked Alison's fresh-scrubbed appearance and her shy but unsimpering expression. He couldn't imagine her ever giggling or flirting or acting coy.

The study door opened abruptly, and his father came into the room. He still wore his overcoat and carried his cane. When he saw Stewart was waiting he stopped in the middle of the room and slapped the silver knob of his cane against his leather glove. Stewart had the distinct feeling his father would have liked to pound it against his head.

"I hear you've been hanging about some of the least savory public houses and waterfront taverns," Adrian said.

"I thought perhaps someone might have heard who kidnapped Tom. Father, I still think there's a possibility it was a case of mistaken identity. I've been trying to find Roland Montague, but it seems he's dropped out of sight, too."

"You young fool, do you want to end up the same way as your brother? Or worse, dead in some alley, knifed for your watch and pocket change? It's a miracle you've lasted this long."

"I'm sorry, Father. I couldn't think of anything else to do. We have so little to go on—no ransom demand, nothing."

"I told you to come here today because I wanted to be absolutely sure no one at Riverleigh overheard our conversation." His father paused, a pulse beating in his temple. Then he said heavily, "I know where Tom is."

Relief washed over Stewart. "You do? Oh, thank God!"

"He's not out of the woods, or perhaps I should say out of the tempest, yet. He's aboard a ship bound for Africa. I've sent a man to bring him home."

"But . . . why would you keep this a secret? Mary has been beside herself with worry."

"I don't want anyone to know where your brother is because the ship he's on is involved in illegal slave trading. I have enemies, Stewart, who would dearly love to see my name dragged through the mud. Would anyone believe my son had been taken aboard against his will? It's more than any skipper's life is worth. No, they'd believe Tom to be the supercargo, watching out for my interests. There's some doubt as to the owners of the slaver and they would claim the ship was mine. I've been something of a pariah among shipowners ever since I leased the *Peregrine* to the government to transport convicts."

"But if Tom was shanghaied by mistake, surely when the skipper learns who he is he'll put him ashore?"

The silver knob of the cane stopped pounding the leather-covered palm. His father's face suddenly looked gray. "I think perhaps . . . they didn't believe him."

"Could we at least tell Mary—"

"No. She's too much of a scatterbrain. She'd let it slip."

"I believe you misjudge her, Father." Stewart would have liked to add that, like him, Mary simply became tongue-tied and nervous in Adrian's overpowering presence, but his father's cold stare forestalled him.

Adrian peeled off his leather gauntlets and tossed them on the desk. He began to unbutton his overcoat. "While you're here, I thought we could spend a little time discussing the business. It's time you learned what you and Tom will inherit one day."

He turned his back to hang his coat on a wood and brass tree as he added, "I've made a new will, disowning Neil completely. Everything will go equally to you and Tom. I hope one day you two can run the business in the same way Tate Ivers and I now do."

For one split second Stewart considered telling his father that he didn't want to be a shipowner, that the idea of being a part of that brutal business was abhorrent to him. He shivered, imagining the thunderclouds that would claim his father's face. If only there was some other profession he could profess to want to follow, as Neil had declared he wished to write. But Stewart knew that his love of music would scarcely qualify, in his father's opinion, as an occupation fit for a man. The moment was already lost, as his father resumed speaking.

"Now, let me tell you of my plans for transatlantic packets. If we can beat the record of the Black Ball Line between Liverpool and New York, we can capture the majority of the emigrants as well as the wealthier passengers. I intend to provide luxurious accommodations on the new ships."

While stowing the emigrants between decks in the most primitive conditions, Stewart thought. His older brother Neil had insisted on sailing to New York aboard a Fielding vessel packed with emigrants and had returned to demand that his father improve their accommodations. That had been the first of many battles between the two of them.

Stewart recalled Neil's plea: "The emigrants have to take their own food, fight for a place at the stoves to cook it, and spend the nights on wooden shelves in a battened-down, heaving, pitching ship. Men, women, children. Father, it's inhuman. Yet they're better off than the miserable crewmen, who are sent aloft in screaming gales, flogged and beaten in order to coax the last bit of speed out of their ship. I won't work for you, Father, and by God if you don't do something I swear I'll write a scathing piece condemning you and every other shipowner . . ."

The argument had ended with Neil storming out of the house. He hadn't published the threatened article, probably because no newspaper would accept it.

After the final confrontation, when Neil left for good, their father had forbidden Tom and Stewart to have any contact with their older brother. Neil had visited Stewart at Cambridge and told him he was going to isolate himself completely from the family for a time; he would use a nom de plume in order not to embarrass his father. They had never learned what that pen name was, nor had they seen Neil since.

As his father discussed the new transatlantic packets, Stewart wondered why the fates had caused both of his brothers to vanish, leaving behind the one least able to cope—with their father or with his ships.

Something disturbed Mary's sleep shortly after midnight and she sat up in bed. There it was again, the sound that had awakened her. Someone was throwing gravel at her window. She slid out of bed, shivering in the unheated room, and pulled back the draperies.

Below on the terrace a shadowy figure beckoned her. A frosty beam of moonlight caught the face: Tate Ivers! What on earth was he doing at Riverleigh at this hour? Adrian had not yet returned from Liverpool despite the fact that it was Christmas, and surely Ivers must have met with him there.

Mary put on her slippers and pulled an overcoat over her nightgown, then went downstairs and out into the cold clear night.

"Mr. Ivers, what on earth—"

"Forgive the theatrics, but I didn't want to arouse the whole house."

"Please, come in."

"No," Ivers said quickly. "I'll only stay a moment. Could we talk somewhere less open?"

Mary was tempted to ask him to leave, but something in his manner stopped her. "The summerhouse," she said. "This way, quick before we freeze to death."

They walked across the lawn to the weathered wood summerhouse built at the highest point of the cliff to afford a view of the open sea and the ships entering the Mersey. It was only slightly less cold inside the octagonal wooden structure.

"I have news of Tom," Ivers said as soon as they were inside. "I couldn't bear to think of you worrying about him all through Christmas."

Mary caught her breath. "Is he safe?"

"Yes, as far as we know. He was shanghaied. We've sent a man to bring him home, although knowing young Tom, I suspect he'll probably make his own way back as soon as he has an opportunity to jump ship."

"Is my husband aware of this?"

"Yes. He's known from the day Tom was taken. If Adrian learns I've told you, there'll be trouble between us. But . . ."

Mary was saddened that Adrian had not told her, and she wondered why. She looked at Ivers, who hovered over her like a great bear, and saw that he was looking at her in the strangest way. "Is there something else I should know, Mr. Ivers?"

He turned to look out of the windows. Through the cold glass they could see the vast dark presence of the ocean, silvered by moonlight, and hear the waves breaking against the rocks below. "Neil has left the country also."

"He emigrated? You must be mistaken. Only the lower classes emigrate."

"Not necessarily. There are also those who believe our class system is evil, who dislike the government, or whose families want to be rid of them, and some are fugitives. In Neil's case, he . . . was arrested with the Luddites and transported."

So that explained why Bethany had been left alone. Mary murmured, "Dear Lord! Does Adrian know all this?"

"He didn't learn of Neil's arrest and trial until after he'd been transported, because Neil used a false name. But Adrian knows now. The young woman, Bethany Newton, was—is—Neil's wife."

"Mr. Ivers, I'm sure your reasons for coming to me at this odd hour with this information are, in your own mind at least, compassionate ones. But I do feel we are being disloyal to my husband in discussing the whereabouts of his sons behind his back."

He shuffled his feet uncomfortably, and unaccountably she felt as if she had chastised a large, clumsy, but faithful hound. Perhaps it was the lateness of the hour or the strange intimacy of the deserted summerhouse, but her previous fear and dislike of this man began to evaporate. She added quickly, "But thank you, most sincerely, for telling me about Tom. I've been so worried."

"Mary—Lady Fielding, if you ever need advice on anything at all, or if you need a friend . . . I want you to know that there is nothing I would not do to help you. All you have to do is send for me. Will you remember that?"

Too stunned to reply, Mary watched in amazed silence as Tate Ivers, his face contorted with embarrassment, turned and, stumbling over his feet, ran from the summerhouse.

THE BRANCH OF the big gum stirred outside, scraping the window, and Bethany slid from the bed in the same instant that Will Prentice fell heavily upon it.

She heard a muffled curse, then the sound of his hand slapping the sheet and pillow, searching for her.

In the sullen darkness she flattened herself against the wall, only half awake and unsure if she was caught in the grip of a nightmare. Along with the scent of eucalyptus creeping in through the window cracks, a faint odor of whiskey had invaded the room.

"Beth-an—ee . . ." His drunken voice slurred her name. His body moved on the bed, a deeper darkness surrounded by shadows. "Wh-where . . ."

He grunted, rolled off the bed, and crashed to the floor.

Holding her breath, clammy with fear, she waited.

Silence.

Then the gum branch muttered against the windowpane again. In the distance a long-drawn-out wailing began, a sound somewhere between the lament of a hound howling at the moon and the hunting cry of a pack of wolves. Bethany jammed her fist against her teeth, willing herself not to scream.

A minute passed and she dared not move. Then softly, rhythmically, the sound of deep breathing filled the room.

Thank God, he had fallen asleep. A drunken stupor, no doubt, but she was too grateful for the reprieve to stop to consider that this was only the first of many nights she would spend alone with him.

She tiptoed from the room, closed the door carefully behind her, and went to the back bedroom. For a long time she lay between musty-smelling sheets, too tense to sleep.

The following morning she heard him come down the stairs just as she finished carving slices from the side of bacon he'd brought the previous day. He went into the living room, which also served as a dining room.

Bethany had never had to cook at home at the vicarage, and she was glad now that she and Neil had been so poor that of necessity she had learned some household skills.

She carried the food from the kitchen, pausing for a moment on the threshold of the living room to silently observe Will reading one of his medical books. He had discarded the dark jacket he usually wore, and in a white linen shirt he seemed a little less specterlike, although the clear daylight did not play kindly on his cadaverous features.

Drawing a deep breath, she went into the room. "Good morning. Did you sleep well?" Oh, no! Why had she asked a question that would draw attention to last night?

For an interminable minute he didn't respond. She had always been uncomfortable with his long deliberation before answering a question, which seemed to indicate she had not asked the right one, but this morning his silence was full of lurking menace.

At length he said, "You slept in the back bedroom."

"Yes." She cleared her throat. "Did you hear that strange sound last night . . . a sort of howling, yelping?"

"Dingoes. Wild dogs. They probably won't come near the house."

"Shall I pour your tea?"

He regarded her with brooding bloodshot eyes, then nodded.

After sipping the tea for a few minutes he said, "Your friend Leona has moved into Lieutenant Ruben's quarters. He's to remain here to guard the chain gang that's building a road out into the bush."

Bethany was glad to hear the buoyant actress was somewhere nearby, but sorry she was still with the brutish Ruben. "Will I be able to see her?"

"Yes, of course. . . . Bethany?"

Another long pause. She willed him to speak. She wanted to

scream at him: Go on, say it. Tell me that I'm to be your common law wife and there isn't anything I can do to prevent it. When she could no longer stand the waiting, she asked, "Was there something else, sir?"

"Sir? I thought we agreed you'd call me Will."

"But you're my master, my keeper." Her voice had become shrill. "I'm your servant, your assigned convict servant. Surely we must keep that fact foremost in our relationship?"

For once he looked startled, perhaps even dismayed.

Bethany slammed his teacup down in front of him and fled to the kitchen. He didn't follow.

A little later he called to her that he was leaving. He did not return until late that night, and immediately after eating his evening meal he went to bed.

Bethany lingered over the dishes in the kitchen, crept up the stairs when she could no longer keep her eyes open. She went into the back bedroom. There was no lock on the door, but she put a chair under the knob and slept fitfully.

She reminded herself that throughout the long voyage she had seen Will Prentice drink only once. If he became drunk only rarely, and if he tried to sleep with her only when he was drunk . . .

Oh, God, she thought, if he touches me I'll die. How could I ever face my husband again? Neil. She had to find Neil. She couldn't think of anything but her reunion with her husband. Somehow he would save them both, if only they could find each other. At the moment her only hope of finding him lay with Will Prentice, if he chose to help her.

At dinner that evening she tried to be a little more pleasant to him, but after a while she noticed he was regarding her with a bemused expression. Her conversation faltered, then died.

"Please don't stop talking," he said, "I find your conversation pleasant after listening to the litany of ailments of the men of the corps all day."

She cleared her throat. "I wondered . . . if I could ask a favor of you."

"Of course. What is it?"

"You may remember that while we were at sea I told you my husband, Neil Newton, was transported several months before I was. If you could . . . use your influence . . . to find out where he is . . ."

The silence that fell seemed endless. His face was a mask. She waited, her eyes pleading. At last he said, "I'll see what I can do."

Since they lived so far from town, Will traveled by a horse-drawn cart to the barracks and brought back any provisions they needed. But after a few days alone in the house, Bethany decided she would walk into town and find the cluster of army housing that sprawled around the barracks, in the hope of seeing Leona.

After walking for half an hour along the dirt trail leading to the rapidly growing settlement, Bethany suddenly found herself confronted by a gang of chained convicts hacking brush and rocks under the watchful presence of armed members of the New South Wales Corps.

One of the guards saw her and shouted, "Over here, missy. I'm the one you're looking for."

Before she realized what was happening, several of the guards surrounded her, laughing and catcalling and reaching out to pluck at her skirts and touch her hair.

She tried to back away, but found herself in the arms of one of the men.

Afterward, she wasn't sure exactly what happened next. But there was a shouted warning to let her go, the rattle of chains, and a grunt from her tormentor as one of the convicts crashed into him from behind.

Wrenching free of his suddenly slack grip, Bethany ran. She knew without looking back who had again come to her aid. The cultured voice of Black Jack Cutler had risen above the other voices the way a pure note of music might emerge from a cacophony of shrill sounds.

Too shaken to seek out Leona, Bethany returned to Will's house. He was late returning that evening and instead of his usual soft approach burst through the door like an angry whirlwind. Terrified, she shrank back against the kitchen table.

"I've just finished treating Cutler," he announced. "He'll probably recover from the blow of a rifle butt to his head, but I doubt his back will be able to stand another flogging, and that's what he'll get as soon as I've patched up his skull."

Bethany sank into the nearest chair and buried her face in her hands.

"Perhaps if you were to stay away from Cutler, his lot might be easier," Will suggested coldly.

She raised her head and looked at him. "I had no idea when I took that path that he would be working there. I was looking for Lieutenant Ruben's quarters so that I might visit Leona. How could I know the soldiers would act so despicably toward me or that one of the convicts would dare intervene on my behalf?"

His eyes flickered over her. "You are fair game to them, just one of many transported convicts, most of whom have questionable morals. It appeared to the soldiers that you were deliberately enticing them. And it was not just one of the convicts who flew so chivalrously to your aid; it was Black Jack Cutler, the most dangerous convict in the colony."

"I am grateful to him," Bethany whispered. "And I'm sorry he was hurt."

"You're young, naive, despite your present circumstances. You have no conception of what a man like Cutler is. Confound it, but women can be so stupid! They believe the worst sinner can be redeemed. The truth of the matter is that some men are rotten at the core and all the surface polish in the world won't change that."

"I swear to you that I didn't deliberately seek him out. I was looking for Leona. Please believe me."

"Bethany, I've allowed you to come and go as you please, but now I must insist upon your remaining here."

She nodded wearily. "It was just that I longed to speak with another woman."

"I know how lonely you are," he said quietly. "I am lonely, too. We share this house, but we are both alone in it."

Fearing where that line of conversation might lead, Bethany jumped to her feet and said, "I'll serve supper now, if you're ready."

He called after her, "When I have time, I'll take you to see Leona."

The next day Bethany stirred a pot of stew, then turned her attention to the bread dough, rising aromatically in a yellow bowl beneath a clean tea towel.

As she pummeled the dough on a floured board a sudden gust of air, almost as searing as the breath of the oven in this last heat wave of the dying summer, whipped the window curtains. In the next second the window slid upward and she looked into the vivid blue eyes of Jack Cutler. A bloodstained bandage encircled his head.

"Dear God!"

"No. Dear Jack. Are you alone?"

"Yes, but how . . . Where—"

"The surgeon foolishly didn't shackle me to the bed in the infirmary. I pretended to be unconscious, of course. Now, don't stand there blathering, love. I need a file, a meal, and a kiss for luck."

She flung open the kitchen door before he reached it. He shuffled in, his movements hampered by his fettered ankles, and bowed extravagantly, then winced and clapped his hand briefly to his forehead.

"You'll never get away," she said.

"I've got this far. What about a file?"

"There are some tools out in the shed. The . . . men who built the house left them."

"The convicts he was assigned, last time he was here."

"I didn't know that. I'll go and look through the tools."

When she returned he was attacking the half-cooked stew, spooning it, still bubbling, into his mouth in ravenous gulps. Dropping the spoon, he took the file from her and immediately went to work on his leg iron.

"Does he ever come back during the day?"

"Not usually. But they'll be searching for you by now and are bound to come this way. Where will you go?"

"Out into the bush."

"But how can you survive? There are wild men—aborigines—and animals."

He looked up, sapphire eyes twinkling. "Don't worry, I won't be taking you with me. Not yet, anyway."

"Heaven help me if they find out I helped you escape."

"They? You mean Prentice. Has he threatened you with the female factory if you don't behave?"

"I have a husband. Here . . . somewhere." She hadn't known she was going to say that.

The file ground harder, whining against the iron links of the chain. "I gather he isn't a settler?"

"If I could only find out where he is."

"I'll keep a sharp lookout for him."

"Neil—my husband, Neil Newton—isn't in Sydney. Will . . . Dr. Prentice ascertained that much. He believes he may be in Van Diemen's Land."

"Will, is it? Tell me, does Will keep any firearms here?"

She shook her head. "He carries a rifle with him, but never leaves it here. He hides it at night. I think perhaps he's afraid I might shoot him while he sleeps."

The leg iron broke, clattering to the floor. Jack rose, and before she realized what he was about to do, his arm snaked around her waist and he pulled her close to him. She looked up into his handsome face and was surprised to see anger there.

"Does he mistreat you?"

"No. He's kind, in his way."

"But he uses you."

"No, not in the way you mean."

"Then he's a fool as well as a dead man."

She found it difficult to breathe in his tight embrace and could feel her breasts rising against his chest. She tried to slow her breathing and remain perfectly still. "What do you mean . . . a dead man?"

"No doubt when he finds I'm gone, he'll come rushing back here to protect you. I'll be forced to kill him."

"Please . . . don't. I'll get you some of his clothes, pack food for you; then you must go. If you stay, I'll shout a warning to him, I swear it."

He regarded her silently for a moment. "You mean it, don't you? Are you opposed to killing in general or to this killing in particular? I've heard of the phenomenon of captives becoming attached to their jailor. Is that what happened to you?"

"Why are you holding me like this?"

He bent and kissed her mouth. For an instant she resisted, but then his lips drew her into a vortex of molten feeling and her knees sagged, her body melting into his. Every thought flew from her head, and when he abruptly released her she feared for a second she might fall. The impact of his mouth on hers stunned her. She could only clutch the table for support and stare at him. Somewhere in the back of her mind she frantically searched her memory. Had Neil ever kissed her like that? A joining of lips that was almost an act of love in itself?

"Very well. I'll take you up on your offer," he said, pulling his convict shirt off over his head.

"My offer?"

His face, wearing a grin, emerged from beneath the coarse material. "Of clothes and food . . . or did you have something else in mind?"

Cheeks flaming, she turned and ran.

Fifteen minutes later he finished dressing in Will's clothes as she wrapped bread and cheese and boiled bacon in a cloth. She didn't look at him as she handed it to him.

"Perhaps I should bind you to a chair. Then you can tell him I forced you to help me."

"Just go. I won't tell him you were here. He never wears that suit, so he won't miss it. I'll bury your leg irons in the garden."

He cupped her cheek in his hand, forcing her to look at him. "Do you realize we've only been able to spend minutes together at a time . . . and yet . . . I feel I've known you forever. Perhaps it's because I think of you so often."

"I don't want you to think of me. I have a husband, and I love him dearly."

"What has that got to do with me? With us? We humans are all separate entities, Bethany. We're never whole creatures to one another. Only those parts of us that connect are important. Our connection, yours and mine, has nothing to do with any other place, time, or person. You won't have what you have with me with anyone else. Always remember that."

His lips brushed her forehead briefly; then he was gone.

She watched him run up the slight rise behind the house, dodge the clumps of prickly saltbush, and detour around a copse of eucalypts, their misty gray foliage ghostlike against the sky. At the top of the hill he paused, turned and waved, and then dropped out of sight.

Bethany went back to the kitchen and picked up his leg iron. She held it for a long time, her fingers counting the links of the chain. She had told him about Neil but not about their child, and she wondered why. Was it because the bonds between a man and woman were tenuous at best and the possibility of betrayal was embedded in any love relationship, while the bonds between a woman and her child were irrevocable and forever?

She felt bewildered by her feelings. Jack Cutler had come and gone so quickly that it didn't seem possible he could have caused such an upheaval of her emotions.

Shaking her head, as if to dismiss him from her mind, she started toward the door with the intention of burying the telltale leg iron. As the door yawned open she drew in her breath sharply.

Will Prentice stood on the threshold, his face contorted with anger and his eyes fixed on the iron chain dangling from her hand.

★★★★★ 10 ★★★★★

THE SOUND OF church bells calling the faithful to Christmas morning services echoed across the frosty rooftops. Alison stood at the attic window looking down on the street. A rosy-cheeked pair of children bowled their new hoops along the pavement, and a determined little boy tried to keep a shiny red top spinning.

Both of the babies were napping, and she felt isolated, abandoned.

A year ago on Christmas Day she'd had a father and a young husband who loved her and a baby on the way. There'd been a fat goose in the oven, plum duff ready to set afire with brandy, and holly on the mantelpiece.

Funny, but now she could remember clearly only the holly—polished green leaves, thorns, and berries as red as blood.

Before today, whenever she caught herself thinking about the past, especially how she'd survived this last year, she had blotted out the memories, good and bad, by filling her mind with images of her son. But on this Christmas morning that didn't work.

"God, forgive me," she whispered. "I sold my body, and I know I must pay for my sins. Show me the way, please."

It had been an act of desperation. She was starving, homeless, and her baby was ill. If both of them were to survive, her choices were few. She could have gone into a workhouse, but her baby could not have accompanied her and would have been put into an orphanage or, since he was sick, more likely into the charity ward of a hospital, where he would surely have perished. She had to have money for a doctor, for medicine. With a babe in her arms, no one would give her work. She had begged on street corners, but the few coppers dropped into her upturned bonnet had not been enough. Then she had pleaded with a pharmacist in the chemist's shop to give her something to help the infant breathe, since he was suffering from a vicious attack of croup. The pharmacist, a portly middle-aged man, had allowed his greedy eyes to devour her body, then suggested that he could dispense medicine if she in turn would provide certain services for him.

He had found her a room and visited her almost every day. Mercifully, his sexual demands were few and he was easily satisfied. She gritted her teeth, closed her eyes, and pretended he was her dead husband.

The pharmacist also unburdened himself in other ways, discussing his business problems with her. He was surprised to find that not only had she received schooling far beyond most girls of her class, but also that she was quick with figures and innately more intelligent than he was. Vaguely threatened by this, he had passed her along to a friend of his, who provided for her and the baby for a time. Then his wife learned of the arrangement, and Alison found herself on the street again. It was there that Mrs. Creel had found her.

Alison knew well the desperation of a mother without the means to care for her child, a fact that forged a mystical bond between herself and the distant mother of baby Hope. She prayed that if there was a God in heaven He would somehow let that poor woman know her daughter was being loved and cared for.

Baby Hope stirred and began to coo softly. Alison bent over the baby girl and stroked her petal-soft cheek with one finger. "It's hard being a woman, little one," she whispered. "But don't you worry, Davey and me, we'll protect you."

Across the river Mary and her stepson had just returned from early morning services. Adrian had not accompanied them, as he had returned from Liverpool so late the previous night.

"We could have a hot toddy," Mary said to Stewart. "To ward off the chill and toast the birthday of our Savior."

"No . . . thank you."

"We're a fine pair, aren't we, Stewart? I daresay that, left to our own devices, we'd both sneak off to our rooms and curl up with a book, even on this most special day. But I really think we should make an effort. Our . . . absent loved ones would want us to. Will you play some carols?"

"Why bother? Father was right. It's all meaningless this year."

"Please, Stewart. I love to hear you play."

"Would you like to hear me play something I wrote myself?"

"Why, yes, I'd love to. I had no idea you composed music. How very clever you are."

"Not clever, Mary, just . . . I don't know. It's something I seem unable to stop myself from doing."

"Why ever would you want to?"

"Father feels I devote far too much of my time and attention to what should be only a pastime. I'm supposed to be preparing myself for an active role in the company."

He crossed the room to the grand piano that stood in an alcove, and raised the lid. A moment later the room was filled with a haunting melody that, despite its beauty, disturbed Mary deeply.

As he played, Stewart said, "I keep thinking about Tom. I wrote this piece for him. I suppose you could say it's a sort of musical prayer to bring him home safely to us."

Ned had pushed a piece of whalebone between Tom's teeth to keep him from biting his tongue. But as the cat-o'-nine-tails ripped into his back and his body jerked violently, arching in protest, it was the pain in his wrists, held fast in the shrouds, that screamed in his brain.

Tom could no longer see anything but a red haze that he feared was his own blood. He cried out after the tenth blow, then lost count. Eventually he was unable to do anything but moan.

He came to his senses in the hold, lying face down in bilge water. Someone was trying to lift him, cursing his well-nourished weight and bemoaning his own weak and aging muscles. Tom struggled to his knees, and wiry arms went around him to help him.

"I've rigged up a rack for you to lie on, lad," Ned said. "At least you'll be dry on it. On your stomach, now. I must clean your back."

"Who . . ."

"Ned Morecambe. They call me Navigator Ned, lad. I was shanghaied at the same time as you, and I'm going to show you the ropes. A few quick lessons on how to stay alive. Mr. Bullock will let you cool your heels down here for a couple of days before he puts you to work. It's his way of breaking your spirit, see, so you'll obey without question. He needs an obedient crew for this ship's dirty business. You're aboard a slaver, lad, bound for Guinea to pick up a cargo of human misery and deliver it to Charleston."

Tom groaned as salt water splashed onto his flayed flesh. "By God, I'll be off this ship at the first port of call, Ned. They can't get away with this. My father is Sir Adrian Fielding."

"Well, I'll believe you, lad, but thousands wouldn't. Now, I'll try to get down to you with some grub, to keep up your strength, and if you'll listen I'll tell you how to climb aloft without falling into the sea or smashing yourself on the deck."

The master of the *Circe* watched the muscular, dark-haired young man climb the shrouds with more grace than most apprentice seamen displayed, and certainly with no sign of fear.

Turning to his first mate, who stood beside him on the bridge, Captain McTrane said, "What do you think? Is it possible he's telling the truth and he really is Adrian Fielding's son? He certainly looks enough like him."

Bullock's small callous eyes squinted up at the youth, who was now two hundred feet above the deck, clinging to the yard and unfurling canvas. The old man, Navigator Ned, was in the crow's nest, yelling instructions over a rising wind. "Well, he's damned arrogant enough, and he knows more about shipping lanes and foreign ports than any seasoned tar. He's telling every man jack aboard his father will rescue him and see we're sent up for slaving."

McTrane gave a small explosive laugh. "Oh, holier than thou Sir Adrian is now, is he? Him who made his money slaving in the old days. Him who's leased his *Peregrine* for transporting convicts to the penal colony."

"Aye, be that as it may, Sir Adrian could make a lot of trouble for us if that's his son up aloft. You can be sure his man Vareck will be aboard the next ship out of the 'Pool, coming to fetch the lad home."

He gave the skipper a sly grin. "We could toss him to the sharks, swear we never laid eyes on him."

"No, I think not," McTrane said slowly. "Somebody might loosen the tongues of the crimps who sold him to you. I believe we should see to the lad's education. He needs to know what kind of line his father runs."

"What do you mean by that, Cap'n?"

"Remember the trader that was preparing to sail the day after us? The *Southern Cross?* She's bound for Van Diemen's Land, carrying provisions to the penal colony. She'll be stopping in the Azores . . . and so will we."

"Ah," Bullock said, comprehension dawning. "We put him aboard the trader and ship him off to the Australias? I like that idea, skipper. It would serve that swine of a father of his right."

McTrane muttered, "Sooner or later the lad will find out about the *Peregrine.* He can sail home on her. By the time he gets back to England our voyage will be long over and our cargo sold on the slave blocks at Charleston. He'll have no evidence to present to his father, and besides, I doubt the lad will even remember us, after what he sees bayside."

★★★★★ 11 ★★★★★

THE BASIL CHAIN, which so recently had been attached to Jack Cutler's ankle, slid from Bethany's shaking fingers and clattered to the floor.

Will Prentice stared at the chain for a second, then took a step toward her, his hand raised to strike her.

In that one split second—which later she would find etched into her mind like a punctuation mark, dividing the life of the timid and fearful girl she had been from that of the determined woman she would become—Bethany decided she would not meekly submit to his punishment. She had seen women convicts publicly flogged, humiliated, brutalized, and now she recklessly decided she would rather die than endure such treatment.

Leaping backward out of reach, she moved behind the kitchen table, keeping it between them as a barrier. "If you beat me, I shall run away, I swear it. I'd rather die out in the bush than live like a whipped animal."

His fist, stayed in midair by her words, instead brushed across his own forehead. "Dear God, what have I become?" he muttered under his breath.

For a moment neither spoke. Then he said, "At least you didn't go with him." He looked down at the basil chain lying on the floor. "We'd better get rid of the evidence before the soldiers arrive."

He picked up the chain and went outside. A minute later she saw him digging a hole under the largest of the gums. When he returned he said brusquely, "Get busy with some task. It will help disguise that guilty look on your face when they come looking for him."

Half an hour later when Lieutenant Ruben and his men came swarming through the house, Bethany kneaded bread, pummeling the dough ferociously while Will assured the searchers that Black Jack Cutler could not have come this way. "I came straight home, the minute I heard he had regained consciousness and escaped. Fettered as he was, I would have caught up with him."

Ruben glared suspiciously from one to the other, then rode off.

When they were alone Will said, "Leave the dough alone now and sit down. I have to talk to you."

Bethany sat stiffly on the edge of a wooden chair as he walked to the window, where he stood staring at the bleak landscape.

With his back to her he said, "They're bound to catch him, you know. He's weak and wounded and on foot. When they do they'll know who helped him." In an almost conversational tone he added, "I suppose you exchanged his convict's clothes for some of mine?"

He spun around. "Well?"

She nodded.

"Where are his clothes?"

"Hidden in the laundry hamper. I didn't have time to get rid of them."

"We'll burn them later on, when we're sure Ruben won't come back."

All at once it occurred to her that he was fast becoming an accessory to the escape, and what a risk to his career that was.

As she fumbled for a way to express her gratitude, as if reading her thoughts, he said, "I'm not concerned for myself. They need doctors here too desperately to dismiss me. But I am very much afraid of what might happen to you when it's discovered that you aided and abetted an escaping convict. You'd be sent to the female factory at Parramatta for certain. There's only one way I can think of to prevent that. You must marry me immediately. When you are my wife I can protect you."

"But I am already married. You know that."

He stared at her, his eyes seeming to sink even farther into their sockets. When he spoke his lips barely moved. "Your husband is dead."

In the following moment it seemed to Bethany that everything was spinning away from her, that she was alone in the universe, crying out her anguish, but no one could hear. It was as if a giant bell had rung inside her head, and in the subsequent moment none of her senses functioned normally.

When at last his words truly registered, she was able only to whisper, "No!"

"I'm sorry. It's true. I learned of it only this morning. I had made inquiries as to his welfare, and the reply came that he died of pneumonia shortly after arriving in Van Diemen's land. You are alone in the world now, Bethany."

The pain had no end, it accompanied her through her daily chores; it kept her from sleep each night. Nothing beyond her grief had any meaning for her, and because no greater agony than the loss of her beloved husband could be inflicted upon her, she feared nothing else.

Will was a gaunt shadow who came and went, who ate the food she prepared and wore the clothes she washed. She responded to his conversation with monosyllables. Days drifted into weeks.

Jack Cutler was not recaptured, so the authorities never found out she had helped him escape. However, disturbing stories began to circulate about a band of bushrangers, escaped convicts who lived in the bush and raided outlying farms, often murdering the occupants. Even in the midst of her deepest grief over Neil, Bethany could not believe Jack Cutler was responsible for such atrocities.

A new hospital was built in Sydney and Will was offered the position of chief surgeon when his contract with the New South Wales Corps ended. She wondered vaguely if he was planning to remain in the colony permanently, but didn't really care one way or the other. He did not bring up the subject of marriage again.

One evening after Will returned from ministering to his patients he announced, "I saw Ruben with a new woman today; she just arrived from Ireland." He paused, his cadaverous face swiveling slowly toward her. "I hear he sent your friend Leona to the female factory."

Bethany was unable to shed any more tears for Leona; they had all been spent on Neil.

Several weeks later Will arose one morning and announced,

"You're coming with me today. Pack some sandwiches and put on your bonnet while I hitch the horse to the cart."

He didn't tell her where they were going, and still in her numb, grief-stricken trance, Bethany didn't question him. They left the horse and cart near the quay and boarded a barge that took them along the arm of Sydney Harbor then up the Parramatta River.

The destination of the barge became evident to Bethany when she saw that it carried female convicts. Although she and Will were separated from the barge's miserable cargo, she saw that these women were the old, the ugly, the diseased, the mad, and the maimed—all of whom had no doubt been rejected in the settler's market.

Had Will decided he was tired of her but didn't want her to go to one of the settlers, so was depositing her at the female factory? She was filled with cold dread and didn't dare question him, fearing what his answer might be. She silently chastised herself for not having run away when she had the chance and for having allowed her grief over Neil to blind her to her own peril.

The riverbanks were lined with eucalypts, those ghostly gray trees that looked as if they belonged on some distant haunted planet. The stillness was broken abruptly by a flock of bright green budgerigars that whirled overhead.

A little farther up the river white cockatoos perched on the peeling bark of the tree branches, shrieking like banshees at the passing barge, and Bethany's sense of unreality, of being caught in a nightmare, deepened.

The wind set was fair, but still the trip took all day, and they spent that night at a ramshackle inn run by a hard-eyed ex-convict. The barge's constable warned Will to watch his belongings carefully.

She spent a sleepless night sitting on a chair in a room she shared with Will, who slept soundly in the bed. Just before dawn he awoke and said, "Let me tell you about my first journey to Parramatta. The female factory in those days was a filthy loft above a jail with a leaking roof, stinking privies, a fireplace for a kitchen, and floorboards so warped that the cells of the prisoners below were visible. The women worked shoulder to shoulder, carding and spinning wool into coarse cloth, from which the convicts' winter clothes were made. If they didn't manage to bring their bedding from the ship, they slept on the floor on raw wool crawling with ticks and fleas. The government didn't believe in pampering female convicts with mattresses or blankets."

Bethany made no comment. She knew he could not be rushed into making his point.

"The factory had room for less than a third of the women prisoners," he went on. "The rest had to lodge with settlers and pay their own board, about four shillings a week. I'll leave you to imagine how they raised the money, since they're not paid by the government. The male convicts, as well as soldiers and settlers, all had free access to the women."

Her patience was at an end. "If you are trying to frighten me or disgust me, please don't waste your breath."

His melancholy gaze regarded her reproachfully. "I am merely attempting to forewarn you about what will be for you a glimpse into hell. You see, they eventually built a new female factory, a pretty three-story Georgian structure, complete with a security wall. At first glance it may seem to you to be quite pleasant. Which makes what goes on inside somehow even more shocking than conditions in that old loft over the jail. Because nothing has changed for the women prisoners, Bethany, *nothing.*"

"You are taking me there today, I presume?" Bethany asked. "Won't I be able to see for myself?"

"I am not finished explaining the system here," he said, frowning. "Please pay attention. The women are sorted into three classes, 'general,' 'merit,' and 'crime.' The third class consists of incorrigibles whose hair is cropped as a mark of their disgrace."

Bethany's fingers drifted, with a will of their own, to the thick plait of hair that hung over her shoulder, and she could not suppress a shudder.

Noting the gesture, he said brusquely, "Very well, come along. It's time to go into Parramatta and see for yourself the infamous female factory."

Afterward, every other horror she saw and heard that day faded from memory. All she recalled, in vivid detail, was being taken to a tiny dank punishment cell.

What appeared to be a pile of filthy rags lay on a rodent-infested floor, stirring and moaning feebly as the light from their lantern illuminated the tiny windowless cell.

Bethany felt as if a raw wound were being probed, as if *she* were the pathetic creature that rose up from the stench of her own excrement, clutching feverishly at her skirts and mumbling incoherently.

Several seconds passed before Bethany realized that the ravaged body groveling at her feet was Leona.

Oh, God! Surely that bruised and battered skeleton with the shaved head and wild eyes was not the formerly pert and elegantly gowned actress who defied anyone to humble her!

A small cry escaped Bethany's lips as she bent to try to gather Leona into her arms, but a viselike grip on her shoulder stopped her.

"Don't touch her," Will Prentice commanded, dragging her back. "She's covered with lice and probably infected with scabies and the Lord knows what else."

Bethany found herself being propelled back along a dank corridor without having had an opportunity to speak to her friend.

Outside in the bright sunshine she began to shiver and wrapped her arms around herself. Her legs felt weak, although every nerve in her body was urging her to run from this fearful place.

She could hear what sounded like the echo of Leona's whimpering and realized the faint sounds of fear were coming from her own lips. "What happened to her? What has been done to her? Oh, dear God in heaven, whatever it was, it's inhuman—"

"She was too defiant, she would not bend, so they broke her. The guards, the other prisoners. She is in hell, as you can plainly see."

Will Prentice stood motionless, watching Bethany as she shook and wept for Leona. Then he nodded as though satisfied he had made his point. "I can promise you that you will never have to endure what she has endured. I can guarantee you a ticket of leave, on one condition."

She didn't hear what he said after the magic words, "ticket of leave." A pardon! Oh, was it possible?

"Furthermore, I can promise that you will return to England—to your child—in two years."

"In two years?" she repeated blankly, not understanding yet where the conversation was leading.

"That is when I can go home if I choose."

When she still didn't respond, he said patiently, "If you will marry me, I will arrange your ticket of leave and take you home with me in two years."

★★★★★ 12 ★★★★★

IT WAS IMPORTANT to keep her goal in mind, Bethany decided. To look ahead to the realization of that goal and simply not think about anything else. In two years she would be able to return to her baby in England. Oh, please God, let her baby survive until then.

In the meantime she would write an account of the horrors inflicted upon female transportees in the penal colony and, when she was home again, attempt to have her article published. Back in England, she would continue Neil's work of exposing social injustice through the press. After all, could not a woman wield a pen as well as a man? Journalism was not a profession that required brute strength or training denied a woman. She would contact Neil's former editors and publishers; perhaps someone would help her.

But for now she had to endure being the wife of Dr. Will Prentice.

She developed the ability to remove her mind from the sights and sounds and sensations of her physical being, so that when she went through the brief civil ceremony of marriage to Will, she made no comparison to that other joyful occasion when she became Neil's much beloved wife.

That night she lay in Will's bed, and he covered her with his gaunt frame. For an instant she panicked, feeling as though she lay with a skeleton, all cold, fleshless bones, and she concentrated on transporting herself to treasured moments she had spent with Neil, reliving them, losing present awareness in the magic of memory, refusing to feel, to respond. She merely yielded.

Will didn't speak. He didn't make a sound. It was as though he mimed the act of love. When he finished, he rolled away and although she knew he was still awake, he said nothing. Bethany rose from the bed and went downstairs. She filled a bowl with water and scrubbed herself until she was raw.

He was still awake when she returned and crept into bed beside him. He didn't touch her again that night.

The next morning Bethany made herself a calendar, so that she could secretly mark off the days until they left the penal colony to return to England. She didn't stop to consider that even if in seven hundred and twenty-nine days her exile was to end, that she would still be married to the coldly uncommunicative Will Prentice.

As Mrs. Will Prentice, she had more freedom to come and go, but Will insisted that she not travel into Sydney alone, since she would be forced to pass the chain gangs of convicts clearing the bush and building roads. He took her into town once a week for supplies and was generous in allowing her to buy odd pieces of furniture, usually made locally by former convicts, in order to make their house more comfortable.

One afternoon he came home early, worry creasing his already melancholy features. "I want you to come to the barracks surgery with me tomorrow."

Since she had volunteered to help him several times and been curtly informed that he would not allow his wife to witness the disgusting illnesses and wounds of uncouth soldiers, she was surprised by this announcement.

Any idea that he required nursing help was quickly dispelled when he added, "It isn't safe for you to be out here alone. Cutler's band of cutthroats robbed some settlers traveling to Sydney only a few miles from here. We thought they'd moved deeper into the bush, but apparently they're back."

He gave her a reproachful look. "I hope you now realize your folly in helping him escape."

"The travelers who were robbed—were they hurt?"

"No. But they lost their horses, saddles, everything."

"Did they say it was Jack Cutler who robbed them?"

"Who else would it be? Until he escaped, few of the convicts remained at large for long. This is an organized band of robbers who strike and then vanish into the bush. They have even had the audacity to ambush patrols from the fort. They are now well armed, and there is going to be an all-out effort to recapture them. Until they're safely back in chains, you will not leave my side."

Leona scrambled up the brush-covered slope, her breath grinding in her chest, oblivious of the saltbrush thorns that ripped her legs and the stony ground that bit into the soles of her bare feet.

Behind her she heard the thud of hooves and the crack of a whip as Ruben drove his horse in pursuit. A minute earlier she'd heard him yell to his men to return to their barracks, that he could see his quarry ahead and he didn't need help to bring back one whore absconding from the female factory.

Despite the hopelessness of her flight, for a woman on foot could not outrun a horse, she forced herself to keep moving.

She had feigned death the previous evening, knowing that corpses would not be removed until morning. Lying completely still, not making a sound, she had stared unblinkingly as the guard delivering the evening meals prodded and kicked her to get her to respond. At length he'd moved on, leaving her cell door open.

Under the cover of darkness, she had crept along the deserted corridor, back toward the wards where more favored female convicts spent their nights. She knew there would be midnight assignations and women slipping into guards' quarters or even leaving to go into town to meet convicts. With luck she would appear to be just one more flitting shadow among many others.

Since the guards knew it was impossible for women to survive in the bush, no sentries were posted outside, and within minutes she had slipped out of the building and was running for her life.

In her weakened state she didn't get far before collapsing from exhaustion. Finding herself in a wooded area, she had crawled into a leafy hollow and slept. She had come to her senses and started to run again just before dawn, when she heard the sound of Ruben and his soldiers searching for her.

Now, having reached the top of the rise, she flung herself over the rim and tumbled down into a boulder-filled ravine.

For a few seconds she lay among the rocks, bruised, cut, and winded. Then she looked up and saw Ruben rein his horse and look down at her, a contemptuous grin on his face. Slowly, unhurriedly, he dismounted.

Leona tried to scramble to her feet but gasped with pain as her ankle refused to take her weight. When she tried to hop away on her other foot she lost her balance on the uneven ground and toppled down again, crying with frustration.

Rolling over onto her back she watched Ruben descend the slope toward her. He towered over her, one shiny black boot nudging her hip. "Cor, what a disgusting sight. Not even fit for a dingo's supper, are you, ducky?"

He crouched down beside her, grinning even more broadly. "I warned you what would happen to you if you didn't behave, now, didn't I? You've got nobody but yourself to blame for this sorry state of affairs."

Leona licked her dry lips. "Please . . . don't take me back. Just leave me to die in the bush, please, I'm begging you."

"Nah, I can't do that, can I, now? It's me duty to recapture escaping convicts."

"Shoot me, then," Leona muttered. "I'd rather be dead than go back to that place."

He looked with distaste at her shaved head, then down the length of her malnourished body, clad in filthy and torn rags. "Maybe I should do that. God knows I don't want to put you on my horse with me. Christ, I don't even want to touch you. You'll have to walk back, ducks. I'll tie a rope on you."

He went back to his horse and removed a coil of rope from the saddle. When he returned, he kicked her in the side. "On your feet, whore."

Leona struggled into a kneeling position, unsure whether she was capable of standing. "My ankle—I think I sprained it."

"You want to be dragged all the way back on your knees, that's up to you." He bent over and slipped the rope around her shoulders.

In that split second before her arms were pinioned, she saw his sheathed knife hanging from his belt. Scarcely aware of her own actions, she grabbed the hilt of the knife, yanked it free, and plunged it into his chest.

A look of surprise claimed his face. He looked down at his spurting blood, raised one hand as though to strike her, then collapsed in a heap on top of her.

Panting, terrified, she struggled to dislodge his dead weight. She could hear someone screaming and didn't at first realize it was she. His face, still wearing that shocked expression, lolled against her bosom as his body continued to twitch, settling even more heavily upon her, squeezing the breath from her lungs.

Then all at once the burden was lifted from her.

She blinked as the sun slipped over the rim of the ravine and momentarily blinded her. Then she looked up and saw a nearly naked black man standing over her. Despite Ruben's bulk, the aborigine had effortlessly tossed him aside.

Leona fainted.

13

MARY FELT LONELIER than ever after Stewart departed for university after the Christmas holidays, leaving her at Riverleigh to face the winter gales and the emptiness of her life.

Since Tom's disappearance her husband had become a haunted, driven man who spent most of his waking hours in his Liverpool shipping office and slept at the townhouse. It was as though his entire reason for being had been, at least temporarily, taken away from him. How she wished Adrian could find it in his heart to draw closer to his middle son, if not to her, but he never mentioned Stewart's name. It was as though he had slipped into the void that had claimed Neil.

Her husband's business partner, Tate Ivers, called on her one afternoon in mid-January. She had not seen him since his unexpected nocturnal visit and, flustered, ordered tea to be served in the west drawing room, which afforded a view of the sea.

The great bear of a man looked thoroughly out of place, seated on a delicate brocade sofa, balancing a fragile china cup and saucer on his lap as he nibbled a tiny triangular sandwich of fish paste. Yet his manners were impeccable and he seemed to be completely unaware of the contrast between his appearance and his surroundings.

"What brings you over the water in the middle of the week, Mr. Ivers?" Mary asked.

He cleared his throat. "I have been considering—for some time now, as a matter of fact—purchasing a country house. It so happens that a property in which I'm interested has recently become available. A pleasant house, fronting on the river, only a few miles down the peninsula."

"How nice. We shall be neighbors, then. If there is anything at all we can do to assist you, please do not hesitate to ask."

He gave a short self-deprecating laugh. "Adrian is less than delighted about my plans. He accuses me of wanting to have what he has. I'm sure he'll be furious when he learns that I came to see you today. I hope my visit won't cause any problems for you, Mary."

"Adrian is so distraught over Tom's disappearance," she replied carefully, "that he seems to have no time to think about anything else. In fact, he hasn't been home for several weeks."

Ivers nodded, as though well aware of this. He placed his cup and saucer on the table beside him and leaned forward. "Then I accept with pleasure your offer of help. The house I am buying is badly in need of restoration and refurnishing. It requires a woman's touch in order to make it into a home, and as you know, I have no woman in my life."

Mary had wondered how Bethany Newton's infant was faring, but she had purposely avoided going to the Liverpool house to question Mrs. Creel about the baby's welfare. Not only was Adrian spending most of his time there, but Mary also feared becoming too involved with the care of the baby. She reasoned that if she never saw the child, she would not try to draw yet another unwilling subject into her life and her affections. Had she not loved Adrian's sons and been unable to protect them?

Adrian came to Riverleigh occasionally but did not mention his partner's proposed purchase of a home on the Wirral peninsula. As the weeks went by and Vareck did not return with Tom, her husband's torment grew to the point where she was afraid to speak to him except in regard to the most mundane household matters. She did not tell him of her visits to furniture dealers and landscape gardeners on behalf of Tate Ivers. Or of her trips to his new house to recommend which repairs and renovations should take place next. Or that they now addressed each other by their first names and had become, in a manner of speaking, friends.

Tate crossed the river to check on the progress of the restoration once a week and invariably took Mary out to dinner after inspecting the work. She began to look forward to these visits and to select furniture for him. Her days had taken on a purpose, and she was grateful to him for that.

One afternoon in early spring when it was unseasonably warm, Tate arrived bearing a wicker basket. "It's such a lovely day, I thought we might take a picnic down to the beach. I stopped and bought pork pies and sliced ham, bread and cheese, and wine."

There was a pleasant sandy beach within easy walking distance of the house, and they spread a cloth in a sun trap created by rocks left exposed by the outgoing tide. Tate insisted upon smoothing the sand before folding a blanket for her to sit on, carefully checked the direction of the sun so that it would not blind her, and worried that he had not thought to bring an umbrella or parasol, since she was not wearing a sunbonnet.

She laughed, feeling young and carefree and protected. "The sunshine feels wonderful, and I'm sure it's not high enough in the sky this time of year to burn my face."

"But your complexion is so fair, so delicate."

"I shall be all right, really."

He looked at the rock formations surrounding them. "After lunch we can explore the tide pools. I haven't done that since I was a boy."

"Nor have I. I'm so glad you suggested we come."

The sharp tang of brine on the sea breeze honed their appetites to a fine edge, and the food tasted wonderful. They devoured everything in the basket, sipping a sparkling wine from crystal glasses. Afterward they leaned back against a cool rock, sated, so completely relaxed that there was no need for conversation.

Mary listened to the soft sigh of the retreating tide, the cry of the gulls wheeling overhead, felt the sun radiating from the sand, and was completely content.

After a time Tate said, "If I don't get up and walk I shall fall asleep. Would you mind if I took off my shoes and socks, so I may wade in the water?"

"Wonderful idea, and I shall go behind that big rock and take off my stockings," Mary declared recklessly.

They splashed through the tide pools, gleefully pointed out sea creatures to each other, found several shells, and strolled along the beach at water's edge as the cold water of the Mersey lapped at their ankles.

The hem of Mary's dress was damp, her hair had escaped its pins, and long strands blew from beneath her hat. The sun on her back was warm and comforting and, when an obstacle appeared in her path, a rock or clump of seaweed, Tate would hold her hand in his big warm grip and guide her carefully around it. She felt safe, protected, completely at ease with this man, and wondered why she had ever disliked him. She decided that she must have been awed by his size, by the suggestion of brute force in those powerful muscles, by the blatantly red hair that glowed like fire in the sunlight.

There was a little wine left, and they finished it off, sitting side by side watching the waves surge up the beach as the tide turned. The sun began to slip toward the horizon, and the air grew chill. Tate rose to his feet, offering his hand to help her up.

"I've enjoyed today so much, I'm sorry to see it end," Mary said with genuine regret.

Her hand lingered in his and slowly he drew it to his lips and kissed her wrist. The imprint of his warm mouth traveled up her arm and seemed to radiate throughout her body.

She caught her breath, startled by the impact of his touch.

He smiled at her sadly. "When Adrian finds out, he will probably kill me."

"For a chaste kiss on my wrist? Surely not." Her voice shook slightly despite her effort to sound sophisticated and offhand.

"No, my dear, for my feelings of affection for you. Ah, Mary, how I wish I had met you before he did."

Not daring to respond, she could only stand there, her hand cradled in his, and recall Adrian's whirlwind courtship. For a few brief weeks he had showered her with attention and had so impressed her elderly parents that even if she had not been overwhelmed by him, they certainly would have insisted she accept his proposal. She remembered her father saying, "You'll never have another opportunity like this one. He's handsome, titled, has a magnificent home, a fleet of ships, and . . . let's face it, Mary, you have a nice dowry, but you're a rather plain-looking woman unlikely to receive any other suitable marriage proposals."

Dazzled by her handsome suitor, she would later wonder if she had been in love, not with the man, but with the idea of being in love. Especially after Adrian showed his true colors.

Not wanting to think about her shameful reason for eventually having agreed to become Adrian's wife, she murmured, "You have become a dear friend, Tate. I have never had a male friend before."

Even as the tender feelings for Tate washed over her, she wondered if this moment of closeness with him would ever have occurred had she met him before her marriage to Adrian. Perhaps her husband's coldness and neglect and her own loneliness had made her vulnerable.

"I wish we could have more than friendship," he said.

"We must go." She withdrew her hand from his.

"Have I frightened you, Mary?"

"No. But you . . . you shouldn't say such things to me."

"You must have guessed that my feelings for you—"

"Stop!" she pleaded. "It isn't proper. I'm a married woman."

He looked at her strangely. "Are you? Really?"

She turned away, busied herself picking up the tablecloth and folding it, packing the glasses into the picnic hamper.

They were alone on the beach now; the few children who had come to play during the afternoon had gone home.

Tate took the hamper from her hands and put it down on the sand, then drew her slowly into his arms. She didn't resist. Nestling close to him she felt the warmth of his body, its strength, the power of his arms as they held her in an embrace that shut out the rest of the world. She closed her eyes and laid her cheek against the smooth cloth of his waistcoat. Gently, with one forefinger, he traced the line of her brow, pushed a strand of hair back behind her ear, then stroked her chin.

"It's going to be all right, Mary," he said softly. "I would never do anything to hurt you."

Sir Adrian had been spending so much time in Liverpool that Alison lived in fear that he would discover her and the babies in the attic. His visits to Riverleigh on weekends were intermittent, and he arrived at the town house at unexpected hours, forcing her to remain in the attic most of the time.

She had to make surreptitious trips to the coalhouse, and to pick up the food Mrs. Creel left for her, in the middle of the night. Some evenings Sir Adrian returned to the shipping office after dinner, but not always.

One particularly cold day Alison ran out of coal in the afternoon and had to make a quick dash down to the coalhouse. She stopped abruptly on the second landing as she heard a key turning in the front door.

Quickly she drew back against the wall, not daring to run back up the stairs for fear of being seen. She heard Mrs. Creel's thin whine, "You're home early, Sir Adrian. I wasn't expecting you."

There were sounds of his cane being placed in the hall stand and the shuffling of feet as the housekeeper helped him with his coat.

Evidently Mrs. Creel was feeling particularly peevish, because a moment later she said, "I shall be requiring more housekeeping money at this rate. You're here seven days a week now, and that wasn't our arrangement."

"You've been padding your household accounts for years, so don't try that nonsense with me," Sir Adrian snapped back.

"Yes, well, you weren't so tightfisted in the old days, were you? Oh, no, you were quite generous then. Why, I even had a maid to help me in the house."

Upstairs on the landing Alison prayed they would soon move into one of the rooms downstairs; the longer they stayed in the hall the more likely it became that one of the babies would cry and she wouldn't be there to comfort the child. For a moment she was so worried Sir Adrian might hear a baby that it didn't occur to her that Mrs. Creel's tone was hardly that of a servant.

Sir Adrian said, in a chillingly quiet voice, "What are you telling me, Hannah? That hell hath no fury like a woman scorned? If so, let me remind you that when you warmed my bed I was a widower, and society turns a blind eye to such indulgences, particularly when the woman involved is a servant."

Alison heard the sound of his footsteps going along the hall toward his study, followed a moment later by Mrs. Creel's lighter step and her whining voice: "If I'd known then what I know now, you'd never have seduced me. You should have told me you wouldn't want me when I wasn't young anymore. . . ."

Tiptoeing back up to the attic, Alison almost felt sorry for the housekeeper.

At least once a week Mrs. Creel came into the attic to look at baby Hope and inspect the premises. She burst into the room without knocking the following morning.

Alison had just finished feeding Hope, and Davey was lying on a blanket on the floor at her feet. Ignoring the baby boy, Mrs. Creel peered at Hope, nodded as though satisfied, then walked around the room, apparently searching for a stray speck of dust.

"He's gone down to Portsmouth. His ship, the *Peregrine,* is due back and he's gone to see about getting another cargo for it. So you'll be safe for a few days if you want to go to the park."

"Oh, good," Alison breathed. "I was beginning to feel I was in prison. The fresh air will be good for the babies, too."

Mrs. Creel had completed her circle of the small room and returned to look down at baby Hope, now contentedly lying on Alison's lap watching her face. The housekeeper's thin lips curled maliciously. "She's going to be a real beauty, isn't she?"

Unaccountably, Alison felt a chill. Mrs. Creel's words didn't sound like a compliment; they carried the menace of a veiled threat.

After she left, Alison lost no time in dressing the babies to go out. She took the perambulator down the back stairs, then ran back up to pick up the babies.

Reaching the first landing, she collided with a young man backing out of a storage room carrying a bundle of sheet music. He spun around to face her and she stared in numb disbelief at Sir Adrian's middle son, Stewart.

★★★★★ 14 ★★★★★

LEONA WAS SURPRISED to come to her senses and find that not only was she still alive, but someone had removed her stinking tattered clothes and bathed her. She glanced down at the faded but clean gingham gown she now wore, reached up to touch a cotton bonnet that hid her shaved head, and tried to remember how she got here.

She was lying on the ground with what felt like a blanket under her, in the shade of a venerable gray-green gum tree that whispered in a faint breeze, scenting the air with eucalyptus. A bandage was tightly bound around one of her ankles.

"Feeling better?" a voice over her head asked.

When she tried to swivel her neck in the direction of the voice, she found it difficult to raise her head.

"To answer your first question—albeit unspoken—an aborigine on a walkabout found you and brought you to us. He has no love for the soldiers and reasoned that you faced certain execution if they found you with Ruben's body, so he brought you here to us. We, by the way, are also absconders."

The educated voice was vaguely familiar, and she tried to bring the face into focus. A halo of blacker than midnight hair, brilliant blue eyes, devilishly handsome features . . . Now she remembered. "Black Jack Cutler," she whispered, her voice cracking horribly.

"Himself. In the flesh." He held a flask of water to her lips, and she drank thirstily.

"I thought they'd have hanged you by now."

"Not yet. But speaking of hanging, we'll have to take you a long way from here and soon. Every soldier in the colony will be after you when Ruben's body is discovered."

"That swine," she muttered, her eyes filling with tears as she recalled the degradation and cruelties she'd suffered at Ruben's hands.

"I'll get you some food," he said. "Don't try to get up. Your ankle is badly sprained."

She looked around her. Several horses were tethered nearby, and two men were skinning an animal beside a campfire. A couple of other men were cleaning their guns. As Jack Cutler went to get her something to eat, Leona wondered how long these escaped convicts could evade recapture, particularly if they were slowed down by a woman with a sprained ankle.

Every settler and soldier, every convict and seaman, the entire settlement, was stunned by the discovery of Ruben's body and the fact that, somehow, Leona seemed to have got away with murder.

At first everyone was certain she would be recaptured within hours, but as the days slipped away and word came from outlying farms that riders, one of them a woman, had been seen heading deep into the Outback, Bethany prayed that Leona would make good her escape.

Will no longer insisted that she accompany him to the hospital. The new road had now passed their house, and other settlers had built nearby, so she was not so isolated. However, since her convict status was known to their new neighbors, Bethany was not invited to socialize with them. This hurt, but she kept busy with her household chores and with her journal and every day marked off the hours until her return to England. *Home and my baby* became her rallying cry whenever despair besieged her.

Nor did her husband make any attempt to get to know his neighbors; he spoke derisively of "the Australian aristocracy" of free settlers.

"They have strict rules of conduct," he told her. "They do not allow the sun to tan their skin, since this might suggest convict labor. They never bathe in the sea, because convicts do. Most stupid of all, they will not eat fresh fish or salt meat—convicts' diet, you see—but they will eat fresh meat and salt fish, despite the wonderful fresh seafood so readily available!"

She would have accepted the Australians' strange mores in order to have social contact with them, and she suspected that Will would have found fault with any community in which he lived, in order to have an excuse for living like a hermit.

He was fond of quoting a saying popular among the convicts: "Australia is marked for glory, because its people were chosen by the finest judges in England."

Will usually picked up the mail and brought it home with him, mostly bills from tailors or copies of medical journals. Apparently he had no friends or relatives in England who wrote to him; therefore, she was surprised one day to see a letter from home, the envelope addressed to him in a distinctly feminine handwriting, especially since he had not opened the letter.

It lay on his desk all day, and several times she crept into the room and stared at it. Once she picked it up, imagining a faint fragrance that emanated from it, but of course after the months it had spent at sea, that was impossible. The handwriting, a delicate script, conjured up a vision of a frail old lady clad in lavender silk, a lacy cap on her silver hair, her feet resting upon a needlepoint footstool as she penned a letter to a prodigal son. . . .

But, of course, it could have come from a young woman. In fact, upon further scrutiny she wondered if perhaps there was a childishly backward slant to the writing. Who had written it? Who? *Who?* Her curiosity grew as the day wore on.

But Will came home, ate his dinner, then picked up the newly arrived medical journals to read. He ignored the letter.

It was still there the following morning, only now it seemed to fill the entire house. She could not stop looking at it, touching it, holding it up to the light.

When a voice spoke suddenly, at first she thought her own thoughts had burst from her lips: "You could steam it open."

The letter slipped from her fingers as she turned around. Jack Cutler leaned against the open back door, nonchalantly eating a chunk of fresh bread pulled from one of the newly baked loaves she had left to cool on the windowsill.

"What are you doing here? Oh, don't say something flippant. Don't you realize the danger you're putting us both in? Didn't you see the road, the new people? Oh, dear heaven, if you're caught, I'll be punished, too!"

He mumbled, spraying bread crumbs, something about not speaking with his mouth full.

"You're impossible," she fumed. "I should run outside and

shout for help. I never should have helped you in the first place. You're a highwayman and always will be. Why, all those people you robbed, not to mention murdered . . ." She had to pause for breath.

Picking up one of her tea towels, he patted his mouth, wiped his fingers fastidiously, and gave her an encouraging smile. "Go ahead, get it all out. Anything else? No? Well, first let me assure you that I stole only from other thieves and from our former guards, and I killed only in self-defense, no matter what you might have heard to the contrary. No innocent settlers were murdered by me or by my friends, although there are other gangs of escaped convicts roaming the bush who do not abide by our code of ethics."

"If that's true, then why have so many settlers said that you and your men robbed them?"

"Because, dear heart, it is so very much more exciting to be robbed by Black Jack Cutler than by some scurvy pockmarked felon from the London slums or the peat bogs of Ireland. It is, if you will, a case of the victim being elevated to the status of the perpetrator."

"What utter nonsense! I suppose you're going to tell me that you weren't guilty of all those crimes in England either?"

"No, I'm not going to tell you that because you've obviously already made up your mind about me."

She asked, "What do you want?"

Stepping into the kitchen, he closed the door. "A couple of things, actually. First and foremost, of course, to see you. You're as pretty as a picture, by the way. Second, I need some clothes—female clothes, that is."

"If you think I'm going to give you clothes for some . . . some woman of low morals who has joined your band—"

"Leona thought you'd be glad to help her, but—"

Bethany's hand flew to her mouth. "Is she all right?"

He nodded. "A sprained ankle, that's all. We've taken her a long way from here, but she needs food, pots and pans, clothes."

She was already gathering up all her spare pots, grabbing a handful of cutlery, wrapping two of her loaves in a tea towel. She sped across the kitchen to the door, paused, and said, "I'm going upstairs to get some clothes."

To her consternation, when she reached the bedroom he was hard on her heels. "You could have waited downstairs," she hissed between her teeth.

He gave her an innocent smile. "But I wanted to help."

"The last time I saw her, she was terribly thin," Bethany said, pulling several dresses from her wardrobe. "I think these will fit."

"Just give me two. You don't want your good doctor to ask why your wardrobe is suddenly depleted." He paused. "I notice he shares this room with you."

She was taking underwear from her chest of drawers, and she froze, a petticoat in her hands. "Your assumption is not correct—"

"On the double bed behind you," he said in a strangely unemotional tone, "I can see a man's nightshirt folded on one pillow and your nightgown on the other."

She felt her cheeks flame and for some utterly unknown reason couldn't look at him. "It's none of your business, but Dr. Prentice and I are married."

The silence lasted so long that eventually she was forced to turn around and look at him.

He wore an expression that seemed composed equally of anger and disappointment. "I see. You berate me for stealing a few horses and relieving a couple of soldiers of their weapons, but you think nothing of committing bigamy."

"My husband is dead. He died of pneumonia."

"My congratulations upon concluding your mourning period so swiftly and successfully."

She gripped the petticoat tightly, wanting to strangle him with it. How easy it would be to justify her marriage, to explain. But why should she? What did she care what he thought of her? She pushed dresses, petticoats, and pantalets into a pillowcase and handed it to him. "Take them and go. And for heaven's sake don't get caught with them, or I'll hang, too."

"Aren't you coming downstairs to be sure I don't steal anything?"

"Get out."

"No message for Leona? She told me that you and she were friends on the voyage out."

"Tell her . . . tell her I'm praying for her safety. Also that I regret she has fallen into even worse company than she was in before."

She had kept her back turned to him and had no warning when his hand slid under her hair, raising it to expose the back of her neck. His lips pressed a kiss to the nape of her neck. He laughed softly; then she heard the bedroom door close quietly.

After running to the window, she raised the curtain, but there was no sign of him. She went downstairs, nervously searching for any hint that he had been there. There was none, despite the fact that the room still seemed to be filled with his presence.

Having assured herself that all was in order, she sat down at the kitchen table and allowed herself to feel relief that Leona was, at least for the time being, safe. But a nagging question posed itself: What was the relationship between Jack Cutler and Leona? He had come looking for clothes for her. Did that mean . . . ? And even if it did, why should she care? Disturbingly, Bethany felt a twinge of jealousy.

Her mind was so filled with thoughts of Jack Cutler and Leona that she did not think about Will's mysterious letter until he returned that evening, gave her his usual perfunctory greeting, an icy-lipped peck on the cheek, then took his medical log to the desk, pushing aside the unopened letter as he did so.

"Would you like me to bring your log up to date for you?" Bethany asked. He often brought it home for this purpose, having merely listed names and symptoms, then dictated to her his diagnoses and treatments.

"Yes, thank you." He pulled out a chair for her and she sat down. "I believe Lance Corporal Higgins was the first patient—"

Bethany could stand the suspense no longer. "Will . . . you haven't opened this letter. Had you forgotton about it?" She held up the envelope.

He frowned. "You may burn it."

"Surely you should read it first?"

"I know what it contains. Here, give it to me." He snatched it from her hand, tore it into pieces and flung it into the grate where she had laid paper and kindling for a fire, but had not lit it because the evening was warm.

Late that evening after he had fallen asleep, she crept downstairs, retrieved the torn pieces of the letter, and pieced them together in the dim light of an oil lamp turned low. She blinked in surprise as she read the first words: "Dear Father, Nanny says I must not write to you any more. She says you don't want to be my father. But I don't want to be an orphan . . ."

Bethany shifted the remaining bits of paper, trying to arrange them in order, but the pieces were very small and she could decipher only fragments of sentences: ". . . so lonely. Nanny punished me . . . Please don't hate me . . ."

She had not heard the creak of the stairs and jumped when Will spoke. "If you were so curious about the letter, why didn't you ask me what it contained?"

★★★★★ 15 ★★★★★

FOR A MOMENT Stewart and Alison stared at each other speechlessly. Then Alison seized his arm and whispered urgently, "Please . . . come up to the attic. I'll explain."

Bewildered, Stewart followed her up the stairs. He remembered her, of course; she was the pretty young nanny who cared for two babies for one of the neighbors. But what on earth was she doing in his father's house?

The attic room was immaculately clean and tidy. The two babies, pink and healthy, lay on makeshift cots. The boy kicked and cooed while the baby girl held up her tiny hand, examining it with solemn concentration.

Stewart turned to Alison, who wore an expression of absolute panic. "Miss Banks—" he began.

"It's Mrs. Banks," she said quickly. "I'm a widow. The little boy, Davey, is my child. I'm taking care of the little girl; her name is Hope."

"I have a feeling," Stewart said, "that my father is unaware of your living arrangements."

"When Mrs. Creel sent me to your stepmother, I had no idea we would be deceiving Sir Adrian."

He sat down on what seemed to be a trunk comfortably disguised by chintz cushions and skirt. "Perhaps you'd better tell me the whole story."

As she hesitantly described the desperate straits in which she had found herself after the death of her father and husband, then told of Mrs. Creel's fortuitous offer, Stewart watched her closely. She was startlingly pretty, even prettier than he remembered from their previous meeting on the street. But there was a haunted desperation in her eyes that was dismaying in one so young, for it bespoke hardships beyond imagining.

When she finished speaking he said, "So Mary, my father's wife, is aware that you're here?"

"No, I don't think she is. I believe she asked Mrs. Creel to find a place for us, but Mrs. Creel—"

"No doubt decided to pocket the rent instead. But what connection is there between Mary—Lady Fielding—and the baby?"

"Hope is the baby daughter of Bethany Newton, the woman who was caught stealing from your father. The baby was born in prison and put in a parish home when Bethany was transported."

Stewart digested this silently for a moment, then nodded. "Yes, it would be like Mary to do something like that. But God help her if my father finds out."

"You won't tell him, will you, please, sir?" Alison dropped to her knees in front of him, laying her hand on the lapel of his jacket and looking up at him from beneath thick curling eyelashes.

Shocked by the open invitation in that glance, he jumped to his feet. "No, I won't tell him."

She buried her face in her hands and began to cry. Feeling helpless, he raised a hand to pat her head, but snatched it back, fearing the gesture might be misinterpreted.

He mumbled, "Please don't do that. I would never betray Mary, so your secret is safe with me. But, Mrs. Banks, we can't let this situation continue. My father would have a fit if he found out. I believe the first thing we should do is to insist that Mrs. Creel follow Mary's instructions. We must move you and the babies to your own place."

"She'll be angry that I let you discover us."

"You let me deal with her."

He found the housekeeper in the kitchen. She glanced at him over her bony shoulder. "Did you find the music books all right?"

"Yes, thank you. I also found Alison Banks and the babies."

Mrs. Creel let the silver platter she was polishing slip from her fingers and clatter to the scrubbed wood table. An expression of fear claimed her face. "It's just until I can find her a decent place. Your stepmother put me up to it. What could I do? I couldn't risk my position here by refusing . . . You won't tell your father, will you, Mr. Stewart?"

"My father has enough to worry him at the moment. Alison

tells me the baby girl is the child of the woman who was transported. Is that true?"

She nodded, her small eyes veiled and cunning, suggesting there was more to this than Alison was aware of, perhaps even more than a compassionate gesture on the part of Mary.

Stewart had often been accused, usually by his father, of having the intuition of a woman. It was meant to be an insult, but Stewart had learned to trust his instincts about people, and he was convinced there was a great deal more to this situation than met the eye.

He said, "We must find a place for her at once, before my father returns from Portsmouth. Don't I recall that they converted some of those old houses on River Street to flats?"

She frowned. "Yes, but they're far too grand for the likes of her."

"Oh? Did Lady Fielding suggest you find a hovel somewhere? Go upstairs and help her pack. I'm going to look at the flats."

At that moment the back door opened suddenly and a man entered the kitchen. Stewart felt himself draw back involuntarily, not only from the burly physique of the man, but from the coldest eyes he'd ever encountered.

Mrs. Creel also looked frightened. She said, "Why, Mr. Vareck, when did you get back?"

So this was the terrible Vareck, whispered about by Neil and Tom but never seen by any of them. But then, the Fielding sons did not often visit the kitchen of the Liverpool house.

"Is he here?" Vareck asked, his voice a low growl.

"No, he's in Portsmouth. This is Mr. Stewart."

The cold eyes flickered in Stewart's direction.

"Did you bring my brother home?" Stewart asked.

For a second he thought the man might ignore the question. Vareck turned as though to leave, then muttered, "He jumped ship in the Azores. Where he is now, nobody knows."

Stewart told himself that Tom was strong and resourceful, despite his youth, and would find his way home. But Stewart dreaded having to live with his father in the meantime.

He felt an even greater urgency to move Alison Banks and the babies out of the attic.

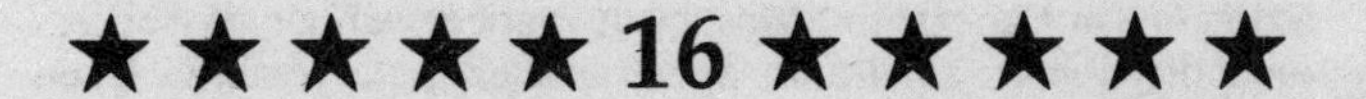

WILL PRENTICE TOOK two glasses from the cupboard and splashed rum into them. He handed one to Bethany and drained the other in a single swallow. She had seen him drink spirits only twice before, once on the voyage from England, and again on their first night together in this house.

He looked down at the torn pieces of his child's letter pieced together like a jigsaw puzzle on the floor in the circle of flickering yellow light cast by the oil lamp.

Bethany took one sip of the fiery rum, more out of politeness than from a need for false courage. "I'm your wife," she said quietly, "but I know nothing about you—where you came from, whom you may have left behind. I should not have read your letter, and for that I apologize. However, the letter reveals that you have a child—a child you have apparently cut off completely. How can you be so cruel? Do you not know the pain you are causing?"

How well she remembered how much Neil had suffered because of his estrangement from his father. How she longed to hold her own baby in her arms. It was incomprehensible to her that any parent could deliberately abandon a child.

Will poured himself another drink and tossed it down, but did not reply. He stared moodily into his empty glass as if it were some sort of crystal ball that could foretell the future, or perhaps explain the past.

She said, "I assume your first wife died?"

"No, she is very much alive, and I love her more than she realizes."

Bethany blinked, wondering if she had heard correctly. Had he become intoxicated so soon? Was the rum speaking? Surely he was not admitting to bigamy? Or was it that, like so many of the freemen in the colony, he did not consider his marriage to her, a convict, legal or binding? "If you love your wife, then why—"

"*You* are my wife, Bethany, my first and only wife."

"But the letter . . . your child . . ."

He stared at the lantern standing on the hearth and spoke in a halting voice unlike his usual briskly commanding tone. "I had a practice in Lancashire. Most of my patients were mill workers or colliers, poor as church mice, who came to me only when they'd been mangled by the machinery or couldn't breathe for black lung. I rarely treated women, they had their midwives for childbirth and endured their illnesses in stoic silence. . . ."

His voice trailed off. He picked up the rum bottle again, stared at it for a moment, then put it down. "But there was one wealthy family; they had a country home near the village where I practiced, and there was a daughter . . . an only daughter, who was consumptive. She spent the winters in Italy, came to Lancashire in the summer. I was called to see her one day . . . not that there was much I could do for her. But after my visit she felt so much stronger that she—and her parents—believed I had helped her."

Bethany listened in silence, watching the shadows play across Will's gaunt features.

He continued, "I have never been the kind of man women are drawn to. I'm well aware of that. They find my looks, my manner, disturbing, perhaps even sinister."

Perhaps hoping for a denial of this, he paused, but Bethany remained silent. With his towering height, cadaverous features, and habit of moving about on silent feet, he could well have been mistaken for the specter of death personified.

"So you see, Bethany, when this consumptive young woman begged me to visit her, spoke so warmly to me, when indeed her wasting disease seemed to go into remission and she blossomed like a delicate flower in my presence . . . well, I was overwhelmed, humbled, almost convinced that I was curing her, although of course there is no cure for tuberculosis. I should have known that. I did know that. I began to neglect my practice and spend every moment with her. But all at once her parents, who had welcomed me as a physician, became alarmed at the prospect of having me as a son-in-law. A humble doctor was not of sufficient rank for their precious only child. They forbade me to see her, insisted she was well and no longer needed my professional help."

He fell silent again, and Bethany knew he was remembering the pain he had felt. "Summer was ending and I knew she would be returning to Italy. I had steeled myself to forget her. I knew

I would have lost her anyway, since she was dying of her disease. But then one evening when I was alone in my house she suddenly appeared on my doorstep. She was distraught, sobbing that if she left England without me she would die. I brought her in, tried to calm her, and . . ."

His hand went to his forehead, covering his eyes as though to blot out the memory of what happened next. There was no need for him to elaborate; Bethany could well imagine him holding the sickly young girl in his arms, trying to comfort her, both of them knowing that their parting was imminent, inevitable, and perhaps final.

"You made love to her?" Bethany prompted gently.

A sound, something akin to a strangled sob, escaped from Will. "The next day her parents took her to Italy, and I never saw her again. They didn't bring her home the following summer, and it was winter again before I learned what had happened to her. Her father burst in upon me during my surgery hours one morning, ranting and raving that I had killed his daughter . . ."

For a moment he was too overcome to go on. Then he drew a deep breath, and when he spoke there was heartbreak in his voice. "She had died giving birth to a child."

"Your child?"

He whispered, "I was a doctor; I should have known she could not possibly withstand the rigors of carrying and bearing a child. I . . . I should have taken precautions. But I did not. My irresponsibility killed her."

"No! She would have died anyway, of consumption. Will, I'm a woman, and I would a thousand times rather die bringing a new life into the world than wasting away from disease. Don't blame yourself; she had fulfilled her destiny as a woman. Surely that thought gave her comfort in her last hours? She had ensured her own immortality and she had given you the ultimate gift a woman can give a man—a child. How could you turn your back on that child?"

"That child," he replied grimly, "caused the death of her mother."

"*Tuberculosis* killed her mother."

"She might have lived a little longer had she not had the baby. I might have seen her again. Perhaps we could have married, and she would not have died giving birth to an illegitimate child, disgraced in front of her family and the world."

Bethany rose to her feet. "Ah, so we get finally to both self-recrimination and self-pity. Such useless emotions. Tell me, have you ever seen your daughter?"

"No."

"She's with her grandparents?"

"I assume so. She mentions only a nanny when she writes."

"Then there have been other letters. Did you reply?"

"No! Nor shall I ever respond. No more questions, Bethany. This is none of your business."

He went back to bed, and Bethany gathered up the torn pieces of his daughter's letter. If only there had been a return address. . . .

She remained downstairs for a long time, thinking about what he'd told her. Several questions posed themselves, not only about Will and his daughter, but about how his tragic early love affair had affected his relationship with her. Had she been safe from his sexual advances on the voyage because he cared for her and had not wanted history to repeat itself? And was the death of his first love in childbirth the real reason he practiced contraception now they were married, rather than his stated reason of not wanting a child to be born in this desolate spot?

Not that Bethany wanted to bear a child. She had a child, a beautiful baby daughter, waiting for her in England. Since the midnight hour had passed, she went to her hidden calendar and marked off another day that brought her closer to being reunited with her own beloved daughter, born out of the love she had shared with Neil, her true husband.

They did not speak of Will's daughter again. Bethany wondered whether his exile was self-imposed or if the wealthy and influential parents of the mother of his child had forced it upon him. Her heart went out to that nameless little girl who so longed to be connected to her father, but she could not help feeling that perhaps Will Prentice might be better as an imagined parent than as a father in the flesh, especially if he took it upon himself to punish the child for her mother's death, which in view of his statements, seemed possible.

On the days when Bethany did not grieve for Neil, she gave in to anger, against Sir Adrian for not helping his son, against Will for denying his daughter, even against Neil for dying and leaving her alone in the world.

Then one morning shortly after Will left for the barracks hospital, Jack Cutler again tapped on her kitchen window.

She quickly opened the door and let him in. For once there was no teasing glint in his vivid blue eyes, no bantering tone. His expression was serious. He took her hand and led her to a chair, motioned for her to sit down.

"We're leaving. I came to ask you to go with us."

"Leaving? I don't understand."

"Leaving the colony. We have enough men now to take over one of the ships in the harbor. We can't go back to England, of course, but God willing, we'll start new lives in America."

"No! You can't; you mustn't risk it. It's far too dangerous. Even if you took a merchantman, the navy would run you down."

"How much longer do you think we can evade capture here? We've been living off the land, and a damn poor life it is. I for one have no intention of spending the rest of my life as a fugitive. We'll escape or die in the attempt."

His hands gripped her shoulders painfully. "Come with us. Leona is going. If by some chance we're caught, I'll say I forced you two women to join us. You've nothing to lose."

"I don't understand . . . why you want me to go with you."

For a second the mocking gleam appeared in his eyes. "Don't you? Can you be oblivious of your own allure?"

"I'm a married woman," she murmured, hoisting the old warning flag even though she knew he would disregard it.

"Will you come?"

"No, I can't risk being sent to the female factory. In less than two years I can return to England with a ticket of leave; I can go home not as a fugitive but with a pardon. Why should I risk that for the opportunity either to perish at sea or to live the rest of my life in exile?"

His hands fell away from her. He stared at her for a long intense moment. At length he said, "What if your good doctor lied to you about taking you home as a free woman in two years? What if he is considering taking over a vast sheep station and remaining in Australia? The lure of a baronial estate must be great to a man accustomed to a sick bay aboard a ship or a convict-built house such as this. Especially in view of the isolation of the sheep stations, which would surely appeal to one as antisocial as your doctor."

"But . . . he promised me that we would go home as soon as his contract with the New South Wales Corps ended."

"What if he told you that in order to get you to go through a form of marriage with him here, even though he knew that so-called marriage was neither legal nor binding?"

"What are you saying? Have you proof of that?"

"No. And you shouldn't put any more stock in my word than in his. But there is a good chance my assumption about Prentice is correct, and I *can* offer proof he is a liar. In any event, I believe my other news will persuade you to come with us."

"What do you mean?"

"A new man has joined us. His name is Albert Harrow. He was transferred here from Van Diemen's Land and assigned to a farmer who flogged him nearly to death the first day. He managed to escape and we found him. He knows your husband. They were together in Van Diemen's Land."

Bethany's breath stopped somewhere short of her throat. "You mean he *knew* Neil, before he died."

"Neil Newton—who told Albert his real name is Neil Fielding—was alive and reasonably well a week ago."

Bethany wasn't sure what happened next. The room spun, his face blurred, sounds receded, time lost meaning and catapulted her backward, then forward. Hope flared, then faltered. Could it possibly be true? She couldn't live through the agony of grief again, not after beginning to come to terms with it.

A moment later she found herself in Jack's arms, clinging to him for dear life. "Are you sure? Oh, can you be certain?"

"Listen to me, Bethany; we don't have much time. Your husband will be in the next batch of prisoners being transferred here to work on the chain gangs. There's a slim chance that we can help him escape—I'm not promising anything except that we'll try—but only if you will come with me now and take your chances with us."

"Will lied to me. He said Neil was dead."

"Yes, yes," Jack said impatiently, "but we don't have time to agonize over that now. Suffice to say that I'm worried about what will happen to you if the doctor discards you. You've seen the pathetic prostitutes hawking themselves on the waterfront. Do you want to end up like them? Are you coming or not?"

"To be with my beloved Neil, my true love? Of course I'm coming. Quickly, let's hurry."

Jack grinned. "Hadn't we better pack your belongings first?"

MARY LOOKED AT the enormous bouquet of daffodils Tate handed her and smiled, her spirits lifting. How could anyone be downcast when confronted by these golden harbingers of spring?

Tate said, "I must hasten to assure you that these are from the local greengrocer, not picked from among the thousands bordering your driveway"—he smiled ruefully—"which weren't blooming the last time I came to Riverleigh. In fact, I don't believe I've ever been here at this time of year before. I suppose it was a foolish purchase, in view of the fact that you're already surrounded by daffodils. But I've always loved them for their unpretentious cheerfulness."

She gestured for him to take a chair. "I love them, too, for their promise of spring, and I'm touched that you would bring me a bouquet." She rang for a maid and asked her to bring a vase filled with water.

"Have you finished moving in?" she asked.

"Yes. I didn't bring much from my flat. I'll probably stay in Liverpool during the week and just come to the house on weekends, as Adrian does . . ." He broke off.

They were both aware that Adrian rarely came to Riverleigh these days; he stayed in Liverpool, meeting every ship, questioning every master docking in the port, in a desperate attempt to learn what had become of Tom.

Mary said, "You'll stay for lunch?"

"I thought perhaps you'd like to go out. It's such a lovely day. I found an inn tucked away on a quiet lane winding through the woods. Lord knows how they stay in business, I doubt anyone but wandering poachers even know of its existence. We could have lunch there."

Now the restoration and furnishing of Tate's house was complete, Mary knew that in accepting invitations from him she was allowing their relationship to progress beyond the point of propriety. But the prospect of seeing him only on those rare occasions when Adrian invited him to Riverleigh was too dismaying to contemplate. She hesitated before replying, gazing at the daffodils in her arms. "It's been dreadful since Vareck came back without Tom. I keep thinking of him, picturing him in terrible circumstances. I feel guilty taking even the simplest of pleasures."

"Nonsense," Tate said gruffly. "Why should you punish yourself? What good would that do young Tom? Besides, I have every confidence he'll make his own way home. He's the most capable of Adrian's sons when it comes to taking care of himself. He's probably having the time of his life; he never cared much for school, did he? He spent every school holiday hanging around the office, begging me to take him down to the docks with me. He probably knows as much about running a shipping company as I do. He's been wanting to go to sea since he was a small boy."

Mary nodded in agreement, although she recalled with a shiver that Adrian had tried to dissuade Tom with horror stories about the treatment of common seamen, pointing out that ships' officers came up through the fo'c'sle and he'd have to endure the hardships of life as an ordinary seaman. Far better to learn the shipping trade ashore and then, when his education was complete, sail as supercargo aboard one of the Fielding ships.

Tate added, "He'll certainly have enough sense to jump ship at the first port of call and sign on a homeward-bound vessel."

Knowing that he was trying to assuage her fears for Tom, she replied, "Yes, I'm sure you're right. And thank you, I'd love to have lunch at the inn. What's it called?"

"The Mucky Duck," Tate answered with a mischievous grin.

The Tudor-style inn, half-timbered, with diamond-pane windows and a cobbled courtyard, set against a background of dense woods, was actually called the Black Swan.

They ate freshly baked barm cakes, thick slices of cold ham and cheddar cheese, and crisp apples, washed down with sparkling cider. Afterward Tate suggested they go for a walk to help their digestion, and they set off along a narrow path that wound through the woods.

Great oaks towered over them, dark and mysterious, and songbirds filled the air with sweet melodies. Mary felt, unaccountably, both happy and sad—sad, she supposed, because the time was at hand for her to tell Tate that they could not be alone together again.

Before she could bring herself to say this, however, Tate said, "I have a favor to ask of you, Mary. But first let me explain . . ."

They had come to a clearing through which a brook meandered, trickling over smooth pebbles. There was a fallen log, and Tate brushed away dead leaves and spread his large handkerchief for her to sit on.

As always, he was immaculately dressed, although perhaps a little too flamboyantly for a gentleman. His flame-red hair glowed like a beacon whenever a stray beam of sunlight penetrated the canopy of leaves, and his eyes, green as forest moss, could twinkle like a leprechaun's or flash with warning fire. She had become accustomed to his formidable size and stern, craggy features, knowing the gentleness that lay behind his fearsome facade.

"Did Adrian ever tell you how we met?" he asked as he sat down beside her.

"You were schoolboys together, weren't you?"

"For a short time, yes. Then we met again years later. I became a full partner in the company just before he met you, as a matter of fact, although we retained the Fielding name.

"I spent my early years in an orphanage," he said, speaking more quickly than he usually did, as though afraid if he slowed down he might not have the courage to continue. "I was adopted at the age of nine by an elderly bachelor. He sent me to the same boarding school that Adrian attended. However, when I was twelve my adoptive father died without making provision for me in his will. I went to sea as a cabin boy and didn't live ashore again for nearly twenty years."

He stirred a drift of dead leaves with a well-polished shoe. "I suppose that might explain my longing for a home of my own. I can remember sailing into the Mersey and seeing the houses along the river, lit up, warm and welcoming, and thinking about the families in them."

He paused, obviously embarrassed at having revealed his loneliness. "I thought when I eventually settled ashore, I would have a home and a family, but . . . Well, let's not talk about that. I'm telling you this to explain why I bought the house, why I would now like to have a housewarming party in order to meet my neighbors. I want to become part of a community; I want to end my isolation from society."

"Tate, I understand perfectly, and a housewarming is a wonderful idea. You certainly don't have to justify it to me."

"Well, as a matter of fact, I do," he said cautiously, "because I am about to ask if you will be my hostess. I will, of course, be inviting some of our business acquaintances also, and if Adrian wouldn't mind—"

"I'm sure he wouldn't mind," Mary said, delighted at the prospect of a party. It had been so long since they had given one, or even attended one, since her husband had refused to socialize until Tom returned. Still, surely he would make an exception for his partner's housewarming. "I'd be happy to be your hostess."

A slow smile appeared on Tate's face, and impulsively he leaned over and kissed her cheek. Startled, she turned toward him and found his lips touching hers. His mouth was warm, his lips firm, yet surprisingly tender. She felt his breath mingle with hers, and she was overcome with longing. There was a sweetness to the kiss that she had never experienced with Adrian, but then, her physical connection to her husband had always been tainted.

She turned away quickly, hoping Tate did not see the tears that sprang to her eyes.

"No," Adrian said coldly. "I have no intention of going to his housewarming party, and you will not act as his hostess. I forbid it."

He looked down again at the documents on his desk, wordlessly dismissing her.

It was his first visit to Riverleigh in weeks, but still he had brought work home with him. She had tried to talk to him during dinner, but he curtly informed her that he was well aware of Tate Ivers's foolishness in acquiring that white elephant of a house and he didn't want to hear any more about it.

Mary had waited for him to leave his study, but as midnight approached she had decided to beard the lion in his den.

Now she stood in front of his desk, watching his nib scratch his signature on the heavy parchment of a legal paper, trying to grasp that he had forbidden her even to attend Tate's party.

"But why? He's your business partner, your friend . . ."

He looked up at her, his eyes narrowed. "I'm well aware that you've been buying furniture for him, hiring carpenters and gardeners. Wasting your time restoring a house he will seldom use, too stupid to see it was all a ploy to spend time with you."

Her mouth was dry. "What . . . what are you implying?"

"That Tate Ivers thinks he is in love with you."

"No, no, you're mistaken! His behavior toward me has always been most proper."

"I've known other men like him," Adrian continued. "They seek out only unattainable women. It's a safeguard against being trapped into marriage. Then there are the discontented wives—like you, my dear—who crave drama in their dreary lives."

Mary gripped the edge of his desk, wishing there was a chair near as she feared her knees might give way. "You're quite wrong, Adrian."

"I've been preoccupied with my concern for Tom, perhaps not as vigilant as I might have been in forestalling Tate's clandestine courtship of you. But all that is now over. In future, Tate Ivers will not be a part of our lives." He tapped the legal documents on the desk in front of him. "I am in the process of dissolving our partnership."

"Surely not because I've helped him with his house?"

He gave her a disdainful glance. "Don't flatter yourself. Tate and I are not in agreement about the future of the company. He's too blind to see that speed is the essence of a successful shipping line, and I'm sick and tired of him allowing masters to coddle their crews—"

Adrian broke off, as though suddenly deciding she could not possibly comprehend what he was talking about. He waved his hand, dismissing her. "Go to bed, Mary. I'm busy."

Mary hesitated for a moment, wishing she had the courage to argue, then murmured, "Good night, Adrian."

In her bedroom she paced the floor, unhappier than she had been since that dreadful night when Adrian had bound her to him forever.

A tragic accident had taken both of Mary's parents from her scant months after she met Adrian.

The constable had come to tell her that her mother and father had been killed instantly when their carriage overturned. She was alone in the world, heiress to a considerable fortune, racked with grief, bewildered, not knowing which way to turn.

Her father's solicitor, a kindly man, had arranged the funeral. The following day he told her, "Mary, we'll have a formal reading of the will when you're up to it. I can tell you that except for a few bequests to servants and so on, the bulk of the estate is yours. Because you have no knowledge of your father's business and holdings, he appointed me to handle the estate, which represents a considerable fortune, on your behalf."

"I should be most grateful not to have to worry about the business and my father's holdings," Mary answered, still trying to comprehend the enormity of her loss.

"Of course, should you marry," the solicitor added, "you would become your husband's chattel, and he would acquire your inheritance and do with it whatever he wished."

He paused, his brows knit in a worried frown. "Your father hoped that when you married you would bear a son to whom the business would eventually pass. He wanted the company to continue, bearing his name. I believe he made this clear to Sir Adrian, and there was a mutual agreement, although not in writing as I suggested, and that concerns me. You see, it's my personal belief that Sir Adrian's shipping company is in dire financial straits. His ships were used almost exclusively to transport slaves to America, and our abolition of that vile trade has caused him severe financial losses."

Mary said, "But I shan't marry Sir Adrian or anyone else until my mourning period ends. I don't even want to think about marriage now. I can't think of anything but Mama and Papa and how much I miss them. My sadness is too deep . . ." She dissolved into tears again.

The solicitor seemed very relieved to hear this.

Adrian had been in Portsmouth on the day of the funeral, but he returned the next day and came to see her at once. "I'm so very sorry, Mary. What a shock you've had."

She had been comforted by his embrace, but his next words shocked her. "We shall get married at once. I'll make the arrangements."

No declaration of love, no formal proposal of marriage!

"But I can't—not so soon! It would be most improper."

"Under other circumstances," he said, "you could indulge the busybodies who insist the bereaved shut themselves away for a mourning period, although in my opinion such rituals merely perpetuate grief. But you are the sole heir to a considerable estate. You need a husband to take care of it for you."

"My father's solicitor—" she began.

"Lawyers!" Adrian spat out the word. "Thieves and liars, most of them. He'd steal you blind and you'd never know what was happening. No, we shall have a quiet wedding at once, and then you won't need to concern yourself with business matters."

"Adrian, I think I could learn to care for you, and be a good wife . . . in time. But not now, not while I am still beside myself with grief. I still can't believe my dear mother and father are gone. I feel as if my whole world has collapsed in ruins."

"I see. How long do you think you will need to mourn?"

"I don't know. At least a year . . . perhaps longer."

He frowned slightly, but said no more then.

At that time he was living in the Liverpool house, having closed Riverleigh after his first wife died, and Mary had never seen either of his residences. The weekend after the funeral he came to see her again. She wore deep mourning and had ordered all of the curtains and draperies closed. A somber wreath hung on the front door.

"Come on. We're going out," Adrian said.

"I can't go out. I am bereaved, in mourning."

"Nonsense. We aren't going to a social affair. I want to take you to Riverleigh. Get your bonnet. It will do you good to get out, and you've never seen my house. It's been in the family for generations, and it's where we'll live after we're married."

They had never been alone before, except for brief periods in her parents' drawing room when a maid might pop in at any second. But she expected that there would be caretakers at Riverleigh, so did not consider the invitation improper.

Her first sight of Riverleigh, perched like a fortress on the bleak cliffs, had been far from reassuring. It was obviously run-down, in a poor state of repair. The grounds were overgrown with weeds, and there was a desolate, abandoned air about the place, evidenced by crumbling mortar and tendrils of dead ivy clinging to age-darkened walls. Broken slates that had blown from the roof in the constant wind littered the dying lawns.

But she was even more dismayed when Adrian unlocked the massive brass-studded front door and they went inside. It was immediately obvious that no one had lived in the house for some time. Dust sheets were draped over all of the furniture, there were cobwebs everywhere, soot from the chimneys blackened the hearths, and the stench of mouse droppings and mildew permeated the air.

Adrian said unnecessarily, "I'm afraid I've let the place go since my wife died. But we'll soon get it put to rights. I had Mrs. Creel come over and clean the butler's quarters, so we can go there and talk after I've shown you the rest of the house."

Mary followed him through the drafty halls, shivering from

the damp and cold, forcing herself to comment favorably on one dreary room after another. She had felt less melancholy in her own home, despite the closed curtains and mourning wreath.

They came eventually to the butler's quarters—a bedroom, adjoining sitting room, and small kitchen where the butler in residence could make himself a cup of tea or a light meal to eat in private, away from his staff. A fire had been laid in the grate and Adrian lit it, then produced a bottle of wine. He had clearly anticipated that she would come to Riverleigh with him and had prepared accordingly.

It was only then that it occurred to her that they were alone in the house. There were no caretakers. She began to feel uncomfortable.

She sipped from the glass of wine he handed her, then said anxiously, "I think perhaps you should take me home now, Adrian."

He regarded her from beneath hooded eyes and for once his darkly Continental good looks seemed more threatening than appealing. "There's plenty of time. Enjoy your wine."

For the next hour he talked, mostly about himself and his ships, about his sons, especially Tom, and about his plans to build the largest, fastest fleet of merchant ships in the world.

She told herself he was merely trying to distract her from her grief, but there was something about the way he looked at her that made her nervous.

When an early twilight began to fall, she jumped to her feet and said, "Adrian, I really think we should be going now. I expect the cliff road is quite treacherous after dark."

It was then that he stood up, removed his coat, and pulled her into a rough embrace. He kissed her, a hard, bruising kiss that took her breath away. For an instant she was frightened and struggled in his arms. But she was powerless to withstand the force of his passion. He held her firmly, and his mouth explored hers in a way she could never have imagined.

More astonishing was her own reaction. She seemed to be melting, flowing like warm honey into an unknown vessel that nevertheless promised untold delights.

Like virtually all of the women of her time, she had been taught to fear and be repulsed by the prospect of physical intimacy, assured that decent women permitted it only within the boundaries of marriage and then only for the purpose of procreation. It was drilled into every unmarried girl that only depraved women of the streets enjoyed such a loathsome activity and that even after marriage a wife should take every precaution to ward off her husband's lust. Wives were cautioned to undress in private and never, under any circumstances, to respond by returning kisses or moving or twitching during the act, lest it encourage the perpetration of further indignities upon her reluctant flesh.

But Adrian was now caressing her tenderly, in a most intimate manner, and Mary was engrossed in pleasure and did not seem to have the will to stop him. Her feebly whispered protest that what they were doing was sinful was lost in the compelling warmth of his mouth against hers. Before she realized what he was about to do he picked her up and carried her into the butler's bedroom.

He placed her on a hard, narrow bed and swiftly dealt with the buttons of her black silk mourning gown, laying bare her small breasts, which he caressed so tenderly that she held her breath, wanting him to continue.

"Your body is so delicate, Mary," he murmured. "Your skin is like alabaster. Do not fear what we are about to do. The pain will be momentary."

"Adrian, please stop," she begged, the plea wrenched from the last rational part of her mind. "We are not married."

"But we *will* be married, and as your husband I will expect conjugal rights. Do not resist me. Think how much more pleasurable our wedding night will be after we have dispensed with the tiresome matter of your virginity."

"No, I can't marry you," she whispered, desperately casting about for a way to tether her own raging desire. "I'm in mourning."

"Oh, for pity's sake, what does that have to do with us? With you and me?" There was a touch of impatience in his tone. "Everyone dies sooner or later. Your parents are gone; accept it. But we, my dear, are alive."

He slid her gown and petticoats down over her narrow hips, and moments later she lay naked before him. She closed her eyes in shame at her own wantonness, for she was trembling with need. His hands explored her body; then she felt his lips touch the exquisitely tender peaks of her nipples, causing her entire body to arch toward him. He chuckled softly then and withdrew from her. She lay shivering, her eyes still tightly shut, all thoughts of flight vanishing.

She heard his boots strike the floor one by one, then the sound of his clothes being removed. His hands went to her thighs, parting them; then the hard weight of his body covered her, his manhood urgent and demanding. Her eyes flew open and she gasped as he penetrated her.

A sharp, knifelike pain brought a cry from her lips, but Adrian smothered it with his own lips, his tongue forcing her teeth apart, ravaging her mouth as that other part of him ravaged her body, and she, depraved creature that she had become, gloried in it.

In some wild, distant part of her mind a voice cried out that she was being ravished; yet she wanted the ravishment to go on forever, and she was disappointed when it ended swiftly in a scalding explosion.

Then, to her bewilderment, he gathered her gently into his arms and held her, stroking her brow, kissing her forehead. "It was necessary, Mary. I had to rid you of the burden of your spinsterhood. It came between us. It prevented our marriage, the start of our life together. You wore it like a suit of armor, a shield to keep me at bay. I know this was distressing for you, painful, perhaps. But now we can move on, go forward, to a better understanding of each other. I am going to teach you the pleasures of the flesh, my dear. I have never believed a man should have a wife to run his household and a mistress to give him pleasure. Two women when one will do? A foolish extravagance."

He held her in his arms for a long time, and now his touch was gentle, soothing. He massaged her back, her shoulders, he stroked her hair, pressed warm kisses to her face, the hollow of her throat, her breasts. He made no attempt to enter her again, but used his fingers and tongue and lips to find every sensual nerve she possessed until at last, her body aflame, she was ready to beg him to consummate the act again.

Sensing this, he took her again, and this time he swept her along with him in his passion, carrying them both to a fever pitch of physical pleasure so that when she cried out again it was an involuntary sound of joy, composed equally of release, fulfillment, and emotional bonding.

During the hours that followed, Adrian taught her every way the bodies of a man and woman might join. With each new sensation she marveled at the comfort and pleasure men and women were able to give one another. She became a creature of the flesh only—mindless, shameless, as eager to give as to receive. It was, she thought much later, a tribute to Adrian's skill as a lover that he had so quickly transformed a shy virgin into a wanton.

Just before dawn he kissed her, deeply and lingeringly, and then he said, "There have been women in my life since my first wife died, but now I pledge lifelong fidelity to you, Mary. I will never violate my marriage vows, and neither will you. We are bound together until death us do part. Never forget that."

"I love you, Adrian," she whispered. It was true; during that long night of lovemaking he had captured her heart.

He said, "Now, undoubtedly we have conceived a child this night, so I'll hear no nonsense about delaying our wedding for a mourning period. I've arranged for a civil ceremony to take place this afternoon."

Nestling in his arms, every sensual nerve in her body awakened, she was too sated to argue or even make a feeble protest. She was no longer sure there was any valid reason why she should not become Adrian's wife. In fact, were they not already husband and wife in the eyes of God and nature?

He kissed her again, caressed her breasts, picked up her hand and guided it to where he wanted her to caress him.

She felt like some long-unused instrument brought to life by the touch of a master musician. Passion stirred between them again, and there was no reality beyond the bed upon which they lay, limbs entwined, mouths joined. She no longer felt shame; his body was known to her, and her shyness about her own nakedness had vanished hours ago. She was astonished that the physical joining of a man and a woman could bring such ecstasy, when she had been taught to expect only pain and shame in the marriage bed.

As the sun rose she was surprised to find she was ravenously hungry, she who previously had regarded food merely as a necessary fuel now had an appetite worthy of a navvy.

"Adrian," she whispered, her lips close to his, "I will gladly marry you immediately, if you will first provide me with a very large breakfast."

He laughed. "There's a ham hanging in the pantry, and we have eggs and bread and marmalade. Will that do?"

"If you will light the range, I will cook." She rose from the bed, stretching her arms languorously over her head, oblivious of her nudity.

"Good gracious, you know how to cook?"

"Necessity is the mother of invention, is it not? We are alone here."

He looked at her, his eyes moving slowly over her body. "What a pity you have to cover yourself with clothes, Mary. Your body is really quite beautiful."

She blushed, pleased by the compliment, although the early morning chill caused her to shiver. He jumped from the bed and wrapped a blanket around her. "Get back into bed. I'll come for you when I've got the range going and the kitchen is warm."

How easy it was to obey him when all of his commands seemed to be for her own good! She allowed him to take charge, to direct her every movement. When her conscience stirred, protesting that she was wicked to indulge in the pleasures of the flesh with her parents not yet cold in their graves, she stilled the accusing voice by assuring herself that a love such as theirs could not be bound by society's conventions; it was too great, too overwhelming for that. Besides, as Adrian pointed out, mourning periods certainly did not benefit the dead but merely prolonged the suffering of the living.

They made love repeatedly that morning, then crossed the river to Liverpool and were married in a registry office. They dined at a café, returned to Riverleigh, and made love the rest of the day and far into the night.

The next day Adrian sent for some of the staff who had previously worked at Riverleigh, hired new servants, and began to put his house in order. She missed him when he left to attend to his shipping business in Liverpool and flew to him when he returned, greeting him at the front door with wild hugs in front of the astonished butler.

"Oh, my darling, I'm so happy you're home," she exclaimed. "I missed you so, I was so lonely while you were gone."

"Go up to your room, Mary," Adrian said. He kept his arms stiffly at his sides, making no attempt to touch her. "I'll join you in a moment." His expression was frighteningly blank.

Waiting for him in her room, Mary chastised herself for making such a scene in front of a servant. She had undoubtedly embarrassed her husband, but surely he would understand that she was still in a highly emotional state—bereaved, a new bride, dealing with both loss and love, grief and sexuality—and he was the only person on earth able to comfort her.

When he walked into the room her heart sank. Cold rage was written on his face. "You will never, ever, put on such a display again, do you understand? You are not to touch me or to speak to me in an intimate manner in front of anyone else, least of all a servant. You will conduct yourself like a lady, as my wife, with all the decorum that position demands. If you ever behave like a harlot in public, I will lock you in your room and keep you there."

Sick with shame, she saw all too clearly why unmarried girls were warned that only depraved women enjoyed sex.

It was soon only too clear that, when he had said he wanted her to be both wife and mistress to him, he had meant those two roles were to be kept quite separate. He acted with cold indifference toward her outside the bedroom, but still made love to her with an ardor that thrilled her even while she puzzled over his swift changes of mood.

Within a few weeks, however, she awakened one morning feeling nauseated and faint. A fearful lethargy gripped her, and no matter how long she slept, she was always exhausted. The tingling in her breasts and lack of monthly cycle confirmed that she was with child. Overjoyed, she immediately told Adrian.

He kissed her gently, in an almost reverent manner, and assured her, "I will, of course, respect your condition, so have no fear in that regard."

She missed his visits to her bed, despite her fatigue, and hoped he would spend more time with her outside the bedroom, but this did not happen. As time went by she realized that her husband's world revolved around his sons and his ships. Her father's company was sold, all of the assets going into the Fielding Shipping Company, giving Adrian the capital to expand.

Then one morning as she was walking downstairs a sharp pain doubled her over and she felt a warm trickle down her leg. Looking down she saw blood on the step. She clutched the banister and called feebly for her maid.

There were three more miscarriages in rapid succession. At the same time she suffered frequent colds and bronchitis. She lost weight, became a gaunt shadow, too weak to do more than drag herself out of bed to lie on a chaise lounge downstairs.

Adrian began to stay overnight at the Liverpool house more and more frequently. When she tried to tell him of her loneliness, he told her curtly that she was hardly well enough to entertain; therefore of necessity he had to invite business acquaintances to Victoria Gardens where Mrs. Creel was better able to deal with guests.

As the Fielding fleet of ships grew, Adrian became obsessed with dissolving his partnership with Tate Ivers, with acquiring more ships, better crews, more profitable cargoes. At the same time, his passion for Mary diminished. Lovemaking became perfunctory, sporadic, until it stopped altogether.

She recovered her health slowly, and they began to entertain at Riverleigh occasionally, but Adrian still avoided her bed. When she could no longer bear his coldness, she hesitantly approached him to ask what she had done to displease him.

It was close to midnight, and he was working in his study. He continued to write in a shipping ledger and answered without looking up. "Nothing. You are handling the household very efficiently. I am well pleased with you, Mary."

Gazing at the floor, her cheeks flaming, she whispered, "But . . . you no longer come to my bed."

He looked up, frowning. "Surely the reason for that is obvious? You are too frail to bear a child. I should have thought you would appreciate my concern for your health."

How could she tell him that although she did long for a child, to her their lovemaking had been complete unto itself, not needing the tangible evidence of a child as a result, but being simply an expression of their love for each other. While she faltered, searching for words, he sounded the death knell of her hope for a return to physical intimacy.

"Although some men practice various forms of contraception, these are unreliable at best, perhaps even dangerous, and I will not risk your life by taking such chances."

He added, in a more kindly tone, "There is no need to be downcast. I am quite content with our marriage, and since I already have sons, it is of no great concern to me that you are barren."

Why did he have to use that word?

"Furthermore, Mary, I am no longer young, with a young man's obsessive need for a woman. My energies now will go into building a great fleet of ships, which one day will go to my sons."

Now she understood. His passion for her had been transitory, unlike his passion for his ships, while his love had always been for his sons, not for her. She had merely provided the means of fulfilling her husband's ambitions, by bringing her fortune to the marriage. She had served her purpose and now would be allowed to exist in the shadows of Riverleigh, unheeded, unneeded.

Head bowed in mortification, she turned to leave. He stopped her at the door with a chilling pronouncement: "Occupy your mind with other matters, Mary. Remind yourself constantly that you are too frail to risk childbirth and therefore must forgo marital relations. And if the danger to your life is insufficient to deter you from inappropriate thoughts, then remember our vow of fidelity to each other. I will never allow you to break it. I will see you dead first."

18

BETHANY WAS EXHAUSTED by the time she and Jack Cutler had ridden deep into the bush to the hideout used by his men, but fatigue vanished the moment she dismounted and Leona came running across a moonlit clearing to fling her arms around her.

"Bethany! God's teeth, but I'm glad you're here. I wanted to ride in with Jack to get you, but he wouldn't let me. Let me look at you! You're a sight for sore eyes, I can tell you. I haven't seen another woman since . . ." She broke off, shuddering, undoubtedly remembering the horrors of the female factory.

Her hair was beginning to grow back, although it was still very short, and some of her former curves had returned. Bethany was particularly glad that the old bravado had returned to her friend's voice. "You look well, too, Leona."

"I've a pot of tea brewing in my tent. We'll stay up all night and talk."

"Come on, ladies," Jack said, taking the reins from Bethany.

She looked around in bewilderment. They had stopped before what appeared to be a sheer wall of giant boulders sheltered by tall gums. "Where is the encampment?"

"Follow me," Jack said, leading the horses through a rocky gateway into a narrow gully.

Leona slipped her arm around Bethany's waist. "There are twenty men hidden in these hills. We have horses, tents; we grow some of our own food and hunt for the rest."

"Jack said he'd been living off the land, but I didn't believe him," Bethany whispered.

"Well, he did help himself to some horses and guns, mostly compliments of the New South Wales Corps, but neither he nor his men have robbed any settlers since I've been with them."

They came to a narrow opening between two towering rocks, only wide enough to allow one horse to pass through, and Leona took the reins of Bethany's mount to lead him. Jack called to a shadowy sentry watching the entrance to their hideout and then led the way.

The rocks not only hid the encampment but also muffled all sounds. Bethany was surprised to see men sitting around a campfire, a corral containing horses, and several tents.

Leona said, "You must be tired; you can meet the others in the morning. Come on. My tent's over there in the trees."

Inside the tent, Leona wrapped a blanket around Bethany to ward off the chill of the night, then poured tea from a billy can into a tin cup. Bethany sipped the hot sweet tea, hoping it would drive away some of the fear that had accompanied her on the mad ride from Will Prentice's house.

Sensing this, Leona said, "We're safe here. Nobody knows about this place. And if all goes well, we won't be here much longer. Jack told you about their plans?"

She nodded. "Leona, is it true . . . what he told me about my husband, Neil? I don't know who or what to believe anymore, but I had to come to find out."

"A man joined up with us just a few days ago, and he overheard Jack talking to me about you. I mentioned your full name—I said something like 'Oh, you wouldn't know what to do with Bethany Newton if you had her' or something like that—and this man, his name is Albert, he says, 'I was in Van Diemen's Land with a man named Neil Newton, and he talked all the time about his wife Bethany.' "

Bethany clasped her hands in silent thanks. "Jack said he would try to help Neil escape."

Leona knitted her brows thoughtfully. "Albert did say your Neil was coming to work on the chain gangs, but, Bethany . . . don't count on Jack Cutler helping him escape. Black Jack has his eye on you, duckie. Why would he want to restore you to the arms of your loving husband?"

"I shan't leave Australia without Neil," Bethany said simply.

The young lieutenant shifted his feet uneasily as Will Prentice stood staring at him, his eyes like black coals in their sunken sockets. "I want her found, do you understand? And I want her brought back to me intact. *Intact.* Do I make myself clear?"

"I'll see to her safety personally, Dr. Prentice. I won't let any of my men manhandle her."

The doctor walked to the back door and pointed to the tallest of the gums lining the ridge behind his house. "There are tracks of two horses over there. I followed them for a while, but lost them at the river."

"They can't have gone far. We'll find her, Doctor."

"I have reason to believe Black Jack Cutler took her away. I want him caught, and I don't care what condition he's in when you bring him in. In fact, if he's dead it will save us the bother of a hanging, won't it?"

"Yes, sir. And don't worry, we'll find him. He can't hide out forever."

"I want him found *immediately,* Lieutenant. You are to ride day and night until you find him."

As the lieutenant went outside to rejoin his men he saw the doctor pick up a woman's apron that hung on the back of a chair, and clasp it to his heart.

Leona came upon Jack as he stood watching Bethany wash clothes in a stream that tumbled down the rocks into a small pool. Jack was standing near the top of the waterfall, some thirty feet above her, but she was unaware of his presence.

"Caught you!" Leona whispered in his ear, her approach having been covered by the sound of the falling water.

"What are you doing up here, Leona?"

"Looking for you, ducks. Were you hoping to catch her bathing?"

He ignored the taunt. He and Leona had taken each other's measure and decided friction between them was inevitable so why not relish it.

"Men!" Leona spat out the word contemptuously. "Why don't you try thinking with your brain instead of that other part of your body?"

"I assume there's a point to this conversation somewhere?"

"When are you going to get us a ship? Your lady love is here now, so what are we waiting for?"

He fixed her with a tolerant stare. "This may come as a surprise to you, but before we can undertake a voyage such as the one we're planning, we need men capable of handling a ship.

Now, a few of our men have been to sea, mostly as ordinary seamen, but we need a navigator. This is the reason we're still here, and this is the reason we continue to help convicts escape—in the hope of finding one who knows something about navigation."

Leona gave an exasperated sigh. "For cripe's sake, Jack—there'll be a crew on the ship, won't there? You can throw the officers to the sharks and—"

"No," he interrupted swiftly. "I won't force a crew to sail with us. They'd hang for mutiny. The men who come to America with us will do so of their own free will."

"So you're telling me we're stuck here indefinitely?"

"Maybe not. We heard on the grapevine that there's a man with some knowledge of navigation in the batch of convicts coming over from Van Diemen's Land today."

"Ah," Leona said knowingly. "That's the batch Bethany's husband will be with, isn't it? You wasted your chances, Black Jack—you should've seduced her before he got here."

"Why don't you go and wash out your mouth, Leona?"

Bethany was awakened by Leona shaking her. It was not yet light, but in the faint glow of a waning moon, spilling in through the open tent flap, she could see Leona's expression was both excited and concerned.

"They're here. . . . They just got back from the raid, and they brought four new men."

Struggling to come fully awake, Bethany clutched Leona's arm. "Is Neil one of them?"

Leona hesitated a second. "Yes, but . . ."

A cry of joy escaped from Bethany's lips, almost drowning Leona's next words: "But he's hurt, Beth. He was wounded in the escape."

Scrambling out of the tent, Bethany ran toward the group of men clustered about the dying campfire. Someone had lit a lantern, and as she drew closer she saw three men, still wearing their ankle chains, sitting on the ground gulping water. A fourth man lay on a blanket as Jack held a flask to his lips.

Pushing him aside, Bethany flung herself upon the man on the ground, crying, laughing, whispering his name over and over again. "Neil, oh, my darling, my dearest husband. Neil, Neil, I was afraid I'd never see you again."

Her husband's eyes, glazed with pain, turned wonderingly toward her. "Bethany? Oh, God, is it really you? If by some miracle I'm back in England with you, then I'll die happy. But if you have come to this accursed shore, then I shan't be able to bear it."

For answer she kissed his lips, wrapped her arms around him, and held him to her. He felt painfully thin and she realized he was having trouble breathing, so she gently laid his head down again. She looked down the length of his body and caught her breath. He was soaked with blood.

A hand closed over her shoulder and Jack said, "We need to cut off his shirt, see how bad it is."

She held Neil's head, cradling it in her lap, as Jack and Albert cut away the rough canvas clothing, revealing a cruel gunshot wound in Neil's side. He had also been shot in the leg, and bones protruded through the flesh of his calf. Bethany gasped. How could he have traveled in this condition?

Jack took charge of the situation. "Albert, get hot water—and a knife. We'll have to probe for gunshot. Leona, we need bandages and something to use for splints. Does anyone have any whiskey or rum?"

They worked feverishly, barely speaking to one another. Neil bore their fumbling ministrations stoically, not uttering a sound as Jack dug a pistol ball from his side. But when he and Albert forced the bones of Neil's leg back into place, mercifully he fainted.

When dawn broke Bethany still sat holding her husband's head in her lap. He slept now, warmly wrapped in blankets, with the campfire burning nearby. She looked down at his dear face, so pale, so lined with suffering, and her tears came in an uncontrollable flood.

"Get up," Jack's voice ordered from somewhere over her head.

She looked up at him through a veil of tears. "No, I'm staying with him. I want to be the first one he sees when he wakes up."

"We're going to put him inside one of the tents. We don't want to leave him out in the open when the sun comes up. And you need some rest."

Reluctantly she rose to her feet, aching muscles screaming in protest. She followed as Jack and one of the other men carried Neil to a tent. When she tried to enter, Jack barred her way.

"Go to your own tent and get some sleep. He's not going to come to his senses for hours."

"You won't keep me from my husband's side—"

"Yes, I will. I'll carry you to your tent if you don't go. You're ready to drop from exhaustion." In a gentler tone he added, "I'll have one of the men sit with Neil and wake you if he needs you."

When Leona came to awaken her several hours later, Neil had a raging fever. Bethany sat at his side, bathing him with cool water. Leona brought her some food and then sat in the cramped tent on the other side of Neil's pallet. She took the cloth from Bethany and wiped his face. "You eat that or we'll have another patient to take care of."

Neil mumbled deliriously, but quieted down when Bethany laid her hand on his forehead. She stuffed some cold meat into her mouth with her other hand.

Leona watched them with worried eyes. "You think he'll be able to travel?" she whispered. "Jack's talking about going in a couple of days. He's got a man who studied navigation now."

Bethany looked down at her husband. He would have to be carried, and he surely could not withstand rough handling.

Later that day, when he slept, she crept out of the tent and went to find Jack.

He stood apart from the others, a tall shadow against the rock, and he turned as she approached. "How is Neil?"

"He has a fever and is in terrible pain. Oh, how I wish we had something to relieve it. But he's so brave; he doesn't complain. He was horribly mistreated in Van Diemen's Land. Did you see the marks of the cat on his body?"

"Yes, they're almost as impressive as mine," Jack responded dryly.

Bethany didn't hear him; her mind was filled with thoughts of her husband. "He's so thin, so drawn. I wish you could have known him as I did. So handsome, so intelligent and compassionate. He was a journalist, you know. His great passion in life was exposing social injustice, and he did so at enormous personal risk—in fact, that's how he came to be transported . . ."

She had not realized how her adoration of Neil was pouring from her lips, and she continued to talk about him until Jack, exasperated, interrupted her. "You may rest your case. I concede. The man is a saint, perhaps even a god descended to earth."

"Please don't be sarcastic. I'm just so happy to be reunited with my husband," Bethany said. "And I'll be forever grateful to you for helping him escape."

"Will you, now? How grateful? Grateful enough to let me take you into my arms and kiss you?"

She stepped backward. "When I . . . allowed you certain liberties . . . I believed my husband was dead. Please behave like a gentleman from now on—and that includes watching what you say to me."

"Perhaps I can get the saintly Neil to give me some lessons in acting like a gentleman?"

"I'm going back to my husband—" Bethany began, but Jack caught her by the arm. "*Is* he your husband? Are you sure of that?"

"What do you mean? Of course I'm sure."

"In his delirium he mumbled several times that he wanted his father notified of his death. He repeated the name: Sir Adrian Fielding. Your paragon of virtue apparently married you under a false name. I'm not sure that your marriage, therefore, was legal."

"Fielding is Neil's real name, but I assure you our marriage is perfectly legal, and it's really none of your business why we call ourselves Newton."

Bethany turned to leave, and Jack said, "We'll be leaving in two days. He'll have to be ready to travel by then, or we'll leave him behind."

"If he isn't strong enough, I'll stay here with him," she answered.

"Do you want to fall into Will Prentice's hands? He's organized an exhaustive search for you. We saw marines and guards fanning out in every direction."

"I won't leave Australia without my husband," Bethany said. "I'd rather die with him than go on living without him."

MARY SAT ALONE in the gazebo, watching the late afternoon sunlight dapple the lawn, enjoying her solitude, and wondering again what Adrian would do when he learned she had defied him.

She had decided to be Tate's hostess at his housewarming.

The party was to take place the following evening, and Tate would pick her up early in the day to take her to his house.

She looked up, somewhat dismayed to see Stewart walking across the grass toward her. He had been coming home from university much more frequently of late, and Mary put this down to his anxiety about his brother, but his presence at Riverleigh this particular weekend might complicate her plans.

"Hello, Stewart. I wasn't expecting you . . ." She broke off, noticing his expression was more troubled than usual. "Is something wrong?"

He sat on the gazebo steps, his long legs stretched out in front of him, his beautiful hands spread on the wood beside him as though finding octaves on a keyboard. "Mary . . . I accidentally stumbled upon Alison Banks and the babies."

She drew a deep breath. "I see. Have you told your father?"

"No. Nor do I intend to. But I think you should know that Mrs. Creel was keeping them in the attic at Victoria Gardens."

"What? But I've been paying for a flat for them. Oh, that dreadful woman! Thank heaven it was you and not your father who discovered them."

"I found a little flat for them, and they're all settled in. Bethany Newton's baby girl is thriving. I . . . I suppose I'm wondering why you haven't gone to see them."

Mary said slowly, "I was afraid to—in case your father found out. You see, the baby is his granddaughter."

Stewart's mouth fell open. "Not . . ."

She nodded. "Neil was using the name Newton; he and Bethany were married. He was working for a newspaper in Manchester, reporting on the Luddites. It seems he attempted to prevent a raid on the mill machinery and was caught at the scene. He was transported to the penal colony."

"Good God almighty," Stewart said quietly. "Why didn't he let us know?"

Alison looked around with pride at her living room. Freshly ironed lace curtains fluttered at the bay window, the wooden floor was polished to a fine sheen with beeswax, a vase of narcissus stood on a rosewood table. Behind the clean chintz curtain that concealed the kitchen area of her flat, a batch of scones—baked earlier that day in the oven beside the fireplace—awaited the arrival of her visitor. Both babies were napping.

She looked forward to Stewart's visits and always wished he

would stay longer. He stopped by to see she had everything she needed and would play with the babies for a little while. Alison felt comfortable with him and loved to hear him talk about the music that was the passion of his life. Knowing nothing of the great composers and musicians herself, Alison found herself carried away to a world of sound and sensation that gave her curious comfort, considering that she experienced it only through the medium of Stewart's voice, since there was no piano.

Alison had no illusions about their friendship; she didn't even consider the possibility it could lead to romance. How could it, since their stations in life were poles apart? What she did worry about was losing his friendship and respect, not to mention baby Hope and her nice flat, if he found out about her past.

He called to her—softly, so as not to wake the babies—through the letter slot in her door, and she ran to let him in.

"Something smells wonderful." He handed her a bulky parcel.

"Scones, fresh from the oven. What's this?" The parcel was large but quite light.

"Open it and see." Taking off his coat, he tiptoed into the adjacent bedroom where the two babies slept in their cots. Alison had never known a young man so sweet and gentle or so at ease with infants. Most men either ignored babies or acted afraid of them.

When he returned she had peeled away the wrapping paper and was staring in amazement at a pile of baby clothes—tiny knitted matinee jackets, leggings, shawls, pram covers, bonnets, mittens.

"Stewart, I don't know what to say."

"It's all from Mary, my stepmother."

Alison sat down abruptly, clutching a down-soft woolen shawl. "Lady Fielding knows you found us? Oh, Stewart, I swore to her . . . a solemn oath."

"It's all right, Alison, honestly. We had a long talk, and Mary told me everything. Lord, if I'd known little Hope was my brother's daughter—"

"Your *brother's* daughter?"

"You didn't know?"

Bethany shook her head. "I wonder if Mrs. Creel knew. I always felt she was up to something in regard to Hope."

They stared at each other for a moment. Then Stewart said, "Let's put the kettle on and share all we know."

* * *

Stewart hesitated before entering his father's office, trying to gather his courage. If, as he suspected, he had been summoned because his father had found out about Alison, then he needed to decide exactly what to say about Neil's daughter, and about his own and Mary's involvement with her and with Alison.

Pushing open the door, he went inside. His father's clerks greeted him respectfully, although they were more accustomed to seeing Tom here than him.

The senior shipping clerk said, "If you wouldn't mind waiting a moment, Mr. Vareck is with Sir Adrian."

Stewart paced in front of the windows, thinking about Alison. He had grown to care for her and for the two babies. They seemed to him to be a ready-made family that enclosed him with a warmth and joy he did not find in his own family. He knew Alison listened for his footstep outside her door with eagerness and was always sorry to see him leave. No one had ever made him feel so important before, nor had a pretty young woman ever shown the slightest interest in him. With Alison he was never tongue-tied or shy. In fact, she was so eager to hear his ideas and views on life that she made him feel wise and sophisticated.

The door to his father's office burst open suddenly and Vareck, his face flushed and angry, came into the outer office calling back over his shoulder, "Damn you to hell, you'll pay me one way or another."

Sir Adrian appeared in the doorway, his expression cold. "How dare you threaten me, you misbegotten bastard? You came back without my son. I owe you nothing. I suggest you stay out of my way if you know what's good for you."

Vareck strode across the office, knocking a hapless office boy out of his path, and went through the outer door, slamming it behind him so hard the wall shook.

Stewart stood rooted to the spot until his father's gaze found him and he said shortly, "Come into my office."

Sir Adrian got right to the point: "I intend to dissolve my partnership with Tate Ivers. He and I no longer see eye to eye on the running of the ships. He wants to coddle the crews with more time in port than they need. He even allows the masters to shorten sail at night and practically go to sleep. Speed is what we're after. European emigrants are pouring across the Atlantic to America, and the ships that carry the most passengers in the shortest time with quick turnarounds in port will dominate the trade. The emigrants will provide the most profit, and we can jam them in between decks. We'll put in wooden shelves for them to sleep on and a few stoves. They'll have to bring their own food."

The vision of packed emigrants fighting for a place at a stove or a shelf upon which to sleep in a battened-down, heaving ship was a daunting one. But before Stewart could comment, his father continued, "We'll divide the ships and assets. I'll keep the transatlantic ships, and Tate can take the Caribbean."

Although Stewart was not very knowledgeable about the business, he did know that the transatlantic traffic was worth far more than the Caribbean traders. "Surely Tate won't agree to this?"

"Oh, I think he will." His father gave a thin enigmatic smile. "Now, after his departure, I shall need someone I can trust to help me run the line. Until Tom returns, that someone, of necessity, will be you."

Stewart felt his spirits sink. "I . . . won't have my degree until next year."

"You don't need a degree in this business. There's no need for you to return to university. I shall need you almost immediately. Report here to this office first thing Monday morning. By then I'll have settled things with Tate."

Stewart found himself out on the street. A thickening mist swirled inland from the river, and a fog horn wailed its warning to approaching ships. The air had turned damp and unseasonably cold.

Mary regarded herself in her dressing table mirror with some astonishment. Tate had recommended a new dressmaker and begged to be allowed to help select the material and pattern for the dress she would wear at his housewarming.

"Forgive me, Mary, but you dress like an old lady instead of the vibrant woman in her prime that you are. Please, no dreary dark colors and cold satins! Something to show off that tiny waist, perhaps a floating crepe de chine in a color to set off your lovely hair and expressive eyes."

She marveled again that this great bear of a man loved fine things, from clothes to furnishings, and was so knowledgeable about them.

So here she was, looking at a stranger in the mirror wearing a soft rose gown sprinkled with tiny white daisies, a woman whose hair was dressed with flowers and whose eyes sparkled. She picked up her white wool cape and beaded bag and went downstairs.

Tate stood at the foot of the staircase watching her. His eyes lit up and he took a step toward her, his hand outstretched. "You look utterly lovely, Mary."

She felt excited, invincible, in charge of her own destiny at last. She was almost disappointed that Adrian hadn't come home for the weekend; she would have relished telling him to his face that she was going to the party.

During the short ride to Tate's house in his new carriage he told her about his guests, most of whom were his new neighbors. He'd also invited several business acquaintances and their wives, but they had all declined. "I think perhaps they know Adrian and I are at each other's throats at the moment, and they don't want to take sides."

"You didn't tell me you and he had quarreled."

"He wants to end our partnership, but his terms are ridiculous. He wants me to take a few schooners plying the Caribbean with low-profit cargoes while he gets the Liverpool to New York ships carrying passengers as well as freight. Not a very equitable division of assets. But let's not worry about business now. Tonight is for music and laughter."

The caterers had arrived when they reached the house, and the musicians were due any minute. Mary flew about—putting last-minute touches to the dining table, arranging flowers, checking place cards—while Tate selected wines and brandy and instructed the footmen he'd hired for the evening.

At last everything was ready and the first guests arrived. Mary stood beside Tate, receiving his guests, feeling completely at ease. Everything was going so splendidly, and Tate had been lucky enough to invite neighbors who knew one another well and who mingled happily. The meal proved to be excellent: a tasty clear broth, followed by fillet of sole, tender leg of lamb with mint sauce, new potatoes, and garden peas. Conversation flowed smoothly.

Later they moved into the drawing room where a pianist and a harpist were waiting to play.

Flushed from the wine, happy to be surrounded by convivial people, Mary had just signaled the musicians to begin playing when the double doors of the drawing room burst open and Adrian stood on the threshold.

A hush fell at his abrupt appearance. He stood for a moment, slapping the silver knob of his ebony cane against his gloved hand as if it were a weapon. He had not removed his hat or coat.

Mary half rose from her chair, feeling icy fear creep along her veins. Her husband's expression left no doubt about his rage. He walked slowly toward her, his eyes fixed on her face.

Tate, who was at the opposite end of the room, had started to make his way toward her when Adrian grabbed her hand and yanked her toward him. "Where is your wrap?"

"Adrian, please . . ."

"Let go of her, Adrian." Tate stepped in front of him. The other guests stared in disbelief, shifting their feet in embarrassment.

Adrian's eyes flickered contemptuously over Tate. "We can discuss the situation here in front of your newfound friends, or we can go somewhere private. It's immaterial to me."

Tate looked around at his guests. "If you'll excuse us for a moment. Please, enjoy the music. This is merely a business disagreement."

"Is it indeed?" Adrian glanced at Mary.

She cleared her throat nervously, all of her earlier bravado fading. "Perhaps we could go into the study?"

Her heart thumped painfully as she led the way to the study, and once inside, she had to clutch the back of a chair for support.

"Was it necessary to create such a scene?" Tate asked Adrian. "You knew Mary would be here. I practically begged you to come, too."

Mary suddenly felt small and frightened in the presence of these two very masculine men, who appeared ready to tear each other limb from limb. The enormity of her folly in allowing her friendship with Tate to bring about this crisis struck her like a whip. How she had underestimated her husband! He'd known all along and yet had said nothing to her. Why?

"I'll be brief," Adrian said smoothly. "I want you out of my company, Tate. You'll agree to the division of assets or I will name you as corespondent in my divorce suit against Mary."

The room spun out of focus. The mere mention of the dread word "divorce" made her feel faint. A woman dragged through the divorce courts was ruined, a pariah, left without support or reputation. Tate, too, would be an object of scorn if he was named corespondent. But it was so unfair. They had not committed adultery. Surely a stolen kiss was not grounds for divorce!

As if in response to her thought, Adrian went on, "I have a parade of witnesses to testify that you visited a rather remote inn together, not to mention the times you were alone in this house."

"Adrian, please don't do this to us," Mary begged.

Tate, to her surprise, remained calm. He asked quietly, "What exactly are your terms for dropping this suit, Adrian?"

"I want you out of my company."

"Very well. I will agree to dissolve our partnership and take the Caribbean schooners. In return you will not file for divorce."

Adrian smiled faintly. "One other thing. Obviously I must insist upon you putting distance between yourself and my wife. The role of cuckold is not one I care to continue to play. I suggest, since you'll be operating in the Caribbean, you remove yourself to the Indies."

"This is so unfair." Mary found her voice at last. "We have done nothing wrong, I swear it."

"It wouldn't make any difference, Mary," Tate said. "We'd still have our names dragged through the mud. No, I won't allow that to happen to you. I will leave the country."

"But your lovely house—"

"Please don't concern yourself. I would appreciate your returning to our guests, however. Adrian?"

"Go ahead. In fact, I'll join you. We need to establish just whose wife she is, don't we?"

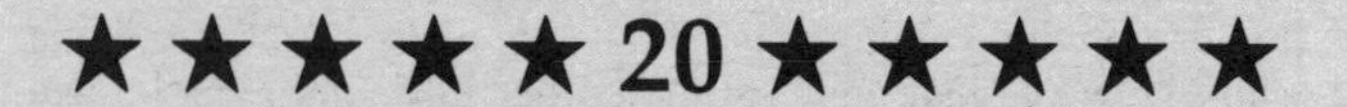

20

LATE ONE SATURDAY night the Pacific trader *Southern Cross* lay at anchor in Farm Cove in Sydney Harbor while most of her crew caroused ashore. Her skipper was also ashore, and her first mate and skeleton crew slept in their hammocks, confident that their ship was safe under the watchful eyes of the crew of a navy brig anchored nearby.

Just after midnight a boat glided alongside the *Southern Cross,* and a group of shadowy figures swarmed over the rail.

Moments later the trader's first officer was awakened by the movement of the ship. Before he could rise, he found himself looking into the bore of a pistol held by Jack Cutler.

"Every man on board is already pinioned. We've cut your anchor cables, and our rowboats are towing us down the harbor to the Heads."

The first mate, fully aware that he was in the hands of escaping convicts, cleared his throat nervously. "What are you going to do with us?"

"Put you and the others over the side, into the boats. You can row back. It will probably take you eight or nine hours to get back to Sydney. By then we'll be well out to sea."

Vastly relieved that he was not to be killed, the first mate nodded. Their ship had just been provisioned for a voyage to the Sandwich Islands, but he doubted there was a convict capable of navigation among the absconders, so he was sure they would soon be back in Sydney dangling from ropes. "I won't give you any trouble."

When dawn broke, the sailors were taken on deck. The first mate then faced a coldly angry Jack Cutler, who jerked his head toward a grating. Dark stains, obviously blood, soaked the grating and surrounding deck. "I see you're a believer in the cat. Perhaps I should take the time to give you a taste of it before you go over the side."

"No . . . no, it was the skipper's orders . . ." The mate's voice faltered.

One young crewman stepped forward. "The first mate is just as brutal as the skipper. They both enjoyed flogging men. We lost one man when he was keelhauled a few days out of Fiji. We've been beaten and starved, and I for one would like to offer my services to you. I've no desire to row back to Sydney and face the skipper after losing his damn ship."

Jack looked carefully at the young man. For all his tar's clothing and tanned skin, there was something about him that set him apart from his shipmates; it was more than his educated voice and air of breeding. And Jack knew that more than one hapless young university blade who had dared to go slumming in a waterfront tavern had found himself shanghaied. This young man—he was scarcely more than a boy, for all his well-muscled height—had a look in his eyes that Jack recognized. He'd worn it himself once, years ago, when he still thought justice always prevailed.

"What's your name?"
"Tom Fielding, sir."
"Fielding . . ." Jack repeated. Surely it was a coincidence? It was not, after all, an uncommon name. "You're welcome to join us, Tom. But you'll hang along with the rest of us if we're caught."
"Sir, there's a man manacled and chained in a rat's hole below. He's been down there for over three weeks, and God knows if he's still alive, but if he is, well, he's studied navigation."
The first mate, who had been silent, now burst out, "You'll be guilty of piracy, Fielding, if you take this ship."
Tom shrugged. "They can only hang me once, whether as a pirate or for helping convicts escape. Either way, I'll be rid of you, you black-hearted swine."
"Go and fetch your navigator up from below," Jack said. "The rest of you, put these men into the boats and let's be on our way."
He waited until they were safely out of sight of land before sending for Tom Fielding and then, in the captain's cabin, invited the young man to sit down and drink some of the skipper's finest rum.
"You sound educated, Tom. Tell me about yourself."
"My father is Sir Adrian Fielding of the Fielding Shipping Company." A shadow crossed Tom's eyes. "I always idolized him; I wanted to be like him. All my life I looked forward to the time when I could send ships all over the world—aye, and travel on them myself as supercargo. I didn't know he'd been involved in the slave trade or that he now leases ships to bring convicts to the penal colony."
Jack listened as Tom told of being shanghaied, of being sold from one ship to another, and of how his idealized vision of his family's business had been shattered by the sight of his father's convict transport, the *Peregrine,* in Sydney Harbor.
When he finished speaking Jack refilled their glasses. "Believe it or not, Tom, I came from a religious background. One of the refrains of my childhood was 'God moves in mysterious ways, his wonders to perform.' I think it's particularly mysterious and wondrous that we find ourselves together on this ship. You see, there's a relative of yours aboard."
Tom looked blank. "Forgive me, sir, but I assume you are

all escaped convicts. No member of my family has been transported."

"You didn't know that your brother Neil was here in Australia?"

"I do have a brother named Neil, but he's in England."

"He was transported while trying to prevent a Luddite raid on a mill. He was using the name Newton so as not to embarrass your father."

"Luddite? Neil? It's impossible. He's a journalist."

Jack looked at the young man thoughtfully. "Have you ever met Neil's wife?"

"No, but her brother was my riding master at boarding school. I think he took the position to get close to a Fielding. Roland, her brother, wanted to meet my father, and I agreed to take him home for the Christmas holidays. In fact we were on our way to plead with my father to reconcile with Neil and welcome Bethany into the family when I was shanghaied."

"You'd better come with me," Jack said. He led the way to the only other private cabin aboard the ship, formerly used by the first mate, and knocked on the door.

Tom saw a woman sitting beside the narrow bunk, upon which a man lay, his hand clasped by the woman, who held his fingers to her lips.

She turned to look at them as they entered the small dark cabin, and in the meager light from a porthole he could see that she was beautiful in an ethereal way despite her expression of intense worry. Her soft honey-colored hair was drawn back from her delicate face, and her large gray eyes, fringed with lustrous lashes, regarded him hopefully. "I pray you're someone with medical experience."

Tom looked at the face of the man on the bunk then and dropped to his knees on the deck beside him. "Neil . . . Neil, it's really you. Dear Lord, what happened to you?"

Jack said, "Bethany, this is Neil's youngest brother, Tom. Tom, meet your sister-in-law."

On the bunk Neil moaned softly and writhed in pain, turning his head from side to side, oblivious of all of them.

Later that morning Tom found Jack on the bridge in conversation with Ned Morecambe, who had quickly established that the convict who professed a knowledge of navigation had done so only to ensure himself a place on the ship. Without Ned, the voyage would have been doomed from the start.

Ned was saying, "I can plot a course and get us there, but you'd best talk to young Tom about whether that's our best route and whether we've enough water and provisions aboard. We were bound for the Sandwich Isles—"

"We can't take this ship to the Sandwich Isles, we'd be seized the minute we got into port. We'll take on water and provisions in the Marquesas." Jack, who could not see Tom approach, added, "And what makes you think some young fool who got himself shanghaied should decide our route?"

Grinning at Tom over Jack's shoulder, Ned replied, "Because that young fool is Sir Adrian Fielding's son, of the Fielding Shipping Company, and if anybody knows how to get us to America, Tom does."

Following the direction of Ned's gaze, Jack turned to look at Tom, whose footsteps had been lost in the flapping of canvas overhead and in the rising wind that snapped the shrouds. The sea had darkened under a leaden sky, whitecaps foamed and churned, and spray was flung by the wind into their faces.

"We can argue about the best course to plot later," Tom said. "For now I'm more worried about my brother."

Ned clasped Tom's shoulder in wordless sympathy as he left the bridge, leaning into the wind on the slanting deck.

"I believe gangrene is setting in," Jack said. "If it is, his leg will have to come off."

"But we've no doctor aboard," Tom said, horrified. "Who would do it?"

"I saw an amputation once," Jack said. "The surgeon left a flap of skin and folded it over the stump. Bethany worked with a doctor on the *Peregrine;* she could help. But first we'll have to convince her of the necessity of doing it, and soon."

"The *Peregrine?*" Tom's expression was hard. "You mean Neil's wife was transported on my father's ship?"

"She didn't tell you?"

"We've a long voyage ahead of us," Tom said, staring out at the roiling sea. "I daresay we'll learn a lot about one another before it's over."

"Do you think you can persuade Bethany to let us amputate Neil's leg before this weather gets any worse?"

"When I tell her he'll die otherwise? Of course she'll agree."

"I'll get a couple of the brawniest of the men to hold him down," Jack said. "You go and talk to her."

Tom looked up at the sky. "We can't do it now. There's a big blow coming."

No sooner were the words out of his mouth than the ship was hit by a tremendous gust of wind and heeled to starboard. Minutes later rain came at them almost vertically in a solid sheet. The squall was upon them.

"We'll need every man aloft to shorten sail," Tom yelled aboard the mournful howl of the wind. "Then we must batten down the hatches. All hands on deck!"

Jack was grateful to Tom for taking charge, since few of the convicts had any knowledge of how to reef and furl sail, and all of them were frightened at the prospect of clinging to wet and slippery yardarms a hundred and thirty feet above a swaying deck. One man slipped and fell overboard and disappeared immediately in the huge waves that crashed over the bow. Another slipped from the shrouds and broke his leg.

By the time they had battened down the hatches and prepared to ride out the storm, the vessel was pitching and rolling too severely for Jack Cutler to attempt surgery on Neil's leg. It was all the inexperienced crew could do to keep the ship afloat, and Tom wondered what would have become of them had he and Ned not remained aboard.

Tom sniffed the wind and gazed at the purple-black clouds billowing over the angry sea and the hard dark line along the horizon and knew that this was not a passing squall but a full-blown storm that might last for days. He prayed that Neil could survive that long with his gangrenous leg.

Neil had brief periods of coherence. Bethany gently wiped his feverish brow and was always at his side when he opened his eyes and looked at her.

At the height of the storm she had to tie him to the bunk with a sheet, and she clung to the wooden posts to try to protect him from being tossed against the bulkhead. When the huge waves broke over them, the bulkhead was where the deck should have been, and she feared they were about to capsize. The oil lanterns swung wildly, and objects that were not tied down flew about the cabin.

When they were able, they talked. Neil would not speak of the horrors he'd endured in the penal colony, and neither would she. They spoke softly of better times, of their enduring love for each other, of the day when they would be reunited with their daughter. Wanting to spare him further worry, Bethany assured him that their baby was being cared for by his stepmother. She warned Tom not to say otherwise when he stuck his head around the cabin door to see if they needed anything. She did not mention that she had gone through a form of marriage with Dr. Will Prentice.

Leona kept her distance, and when Bethany asked Jack about her he said he thought she was seasick. Since Leona had never shown a tendency toward *mal de mer* on the outward-bound voyage, this seemed odd, but Bethany was too concerned with Neil to worry about Leona's absence.

Neil occasionally became bewildered about the presence of his wife and brother on the ship, at times thinking his father had sent them after him, then recalling in sudden horror that Bethany had also been transported and Tom shanghaied.

"The crimps took me by mistake," Tom told him one day when they were alone. "They were after Roland Montague."

Neil said, "I know Bethany's brother. He was always short of cash and unwilling to work for it. He tried to borrow from me many times. If he saw an opportunity to beg, borrow, or steal from Father, or even blackmail him, he'd take it. And if he had tried anything with Father . . . well, you know the old man wouldn't have hesitated to send Vareck's crimps to solve the problem."

"I thought you exaggerated when you wrote about the brutality of life at sea," Tom said bitterly. "I sided with Father, more's my shame. I idolized him, wanted to be like him. But I swear to God I'll never forgive him for letting this happen to you and Bethany."

"You probably won't get a chance," Neil replied, his voice weak and pain-racked. "We're all fugitives now, for the rest of our lives. Piracy is a hanging offense. None of us can ever go back to England. Bethany speaks of being reunited with our daughter, and I haven't the heart to tell her it can never be. Tom . . ." He clutched his brother's hand in a surprisingly firm grip. "Promise me . . . if anything happens to me . . . you won't let Bethany return to England."

"Nothing's going to happen to you, Neil," Tom replied, trying to keep the fear for his brother from his voice.

"Take care of her, Tom," Neil said. "She's the whole world to me. Swear you will."

"I swear it, Neil."

By the third day of the violent storm Bethany existed in a dream world of exhaustion, not unlike the fever delirium into which Neil slipped more and more frequently.

Sometimes it seemed they left their bodies in the dark and cramped cabin and strolled together through misty green meadows, and Bethany felt his arm about her waist and laid her head on his shoulder, and he murmured, "How blessed I am to have your love, my dear wife. How can I tell you how I worship you? I, who make my living with the words I write, cannot find a way to express my love because it is too great for mere words; it is my whole reason for being."

"When I'm with you," she whispered, "the sun shines brighter, the world is kinder, the flowers smell sweeter, and there is a God in heaven. Dearest Neil, I love you more each day."

The ship's timbers groaned as a giant wave struck the ship. The cabin rocked so hard that she was flung to the deck, rudely breaking the spell.

Crawling back to the bunk she looked into his glazed eyes and ravaged features, and fear clutched her. His leg was now so blackened and swollen that she knew they could delay the amputation no longer, despite the pitching of the ship. She thought of going to fetch Jack and Tom, but didn't want to leave Neil alone. One of them would come soon and she'd tell them they must operate at once.

She eased herself into the bunk beside her husband and wrapped her arms around him, holding him close to her heart.

He sighed, almost contentedly, and had it not been for the death rattle in his throat, she might not have known that he had slipped away from her forever.

Leona finally came to her that night. "I'm sorry I stayed away from you, Bethany, but I knew Neil would die. I've got this terrible fear of being with somebody when they die. It's superstitious, I know, but I'm afraid they'll somehow take me with them."

The following day the *Southern Cross* sailed into calm waters, and Neil was buried at sea under brilliant blue skies. Bethany stood with Tom's arm around her shoulders and did not cry as the canvas-wrapped body slipped beneath the glittering surface of the sea.

Her physical self was here on the ship, but her spirit was far away, sitting in an English meadow surrounded by buttercups and daisies while Neil lay on his back in the soft grass and spoke to her of the wonder of their love and all the hours and weeks and years to come when they would be together and their love would grow, shutting out the rest of the world.

She could not yet accept that she would never see his dear face or his smile again, or feel his touch. That agony would come later.

MRS. CREEL WALKED into Alison's flat and looked around. "Hmph, you've come a long way from that alley I found you in, haven't you?"

The two babies, playing happily together on the floor with brightly colored wooden blocks, looked up at her expectantly. Visiting big people usually swept them up into their arms for hugs and kisses, but this one did not.

Alison felt her throat constrict. She had not seen Sir Adrian's housekeeper since she left Victoria Gardens, as Stewart and Mary now took care of her and the babies. This unexpected visit by Mrs. Creel came like a thundercloud in the midst of a summer day.

"Is . . . something wrong?" Alison asked. "Oh, I do hope Lady Fielding isn't ill?"

The housekeeper's thin lips curled slightly. "I'm sure you do." She walked around, peering at the furniture, opening cupboards and drawers.

"Are you looking for something?" Alison asked, her hackles rising.

"You really landed on your feet, didn't you?" Mrs. Creel peeled off her gloves and sat down. Davey tottered over to her on fat little legs and tried to climb into her lap. She pushed him away, and he began to cry.

Alison picked him up and held him. "What exactly do you want, Mrs. Creel?" She kept her voice level because she didn't want to frighten the babies, but she knew her eyes were blazing.

"Get the girl ready. I'm taking her with me."

"What?"

"Are you deaf? Get Hope Fielding dressed to go out. She's coming with me. I'm going to take her to meet her grandfather. It's time."

Alison's mouth was dry. "You can't do that."

"Oh? Who's to stop me? One word from you, m'girl, and I'll tell young Mr. Stewart and his stepmother they've got a streetwalker taking care of the child."

Alison held her son close and kissed his silky hair. Her mind raced, wondering how to deal with this horrible woman. There was no use protesting that allowing two men to provide for her and Davey in return for sexual favors hardly made her a streetwalker. A kept woman, briefly, yes—and that was bad enough. Alison was deeply ashamed of that episode in her life.

"I don't understand why you want to take her to Sir Adrian. You must know how angry he'll be with his wife and son." *And what have you to gain, you old witch?*

Mrs. Creel sniffed. "They should have thought of that before they deceived him."

"I can't let you take her anywhere today," Alison said. "The doctor will be here soon to examine her."

"What's wrong with her?" Mrs. Creel asked suspiciously. The baby was the picture of good health.

"She's just getting over a bad cough," Alison lied, "and he wants to be sure the congestion's all gone."

The housekeeper rose to her feet instantly. "Very well. But you have her ready first thing tomorrow morning. I'll be coming for her early."

Even after the woman left the room, her insidious presence seemed to linger. Alison put Davey down and picked up a cretonne-covered cushion that had been crushed by Mrs. Creel's weight. She shook it to get rid of the housekeeper's impression, then went to open the windows.

She walked around the room, straightening objects, wiping away imaginary dust, wondering what on earth to do. One thing was certain: She was not meekly going to hand over Hope to Sir Adrian's housekeeper.

Rain pattered against the windows of the offices of the Fielding Shipping Company, overlooking the Liverpool Pier Head and Princes dock. Stewart stood up, stretching his aching muscles, and walked to the window to look out at the storm clouds moving up the river.

He hated his work. He hated this dismal room that was his prison. He hated having to deal with disgruntled crews and pathetic emigrants, with overworked clerks and undernourished office boys. Even worse were irate importers and exporters, who constantly complained about their shipments, and the customs and excise men who moved at a snail's pace. Everything in his working day was as gray and bleak as the rain-swept street below the window.

The one bright spot in his life was Alison and the babies. Stewart looked forward to his visits to them, feeling warm and secure within his surrogate family. He had been spending more and more time with Alison, even after Mary decided she wanted to see baby Hope and also began to visit the flat regularly. He'd been present the first time his stepmother called and had watched fondly as Mary, smiling although her eyes were filled with tears, picked up the beautiful baby girl and held her.

"Oh, my little darling," Mary had said softly, "how your mother must miss you and long for you."

The tender moment had been concluded on a sad and somber note as Mary told them of being present in court when Bethany was sentenced to be transported to the penal colony.

The three of them had solemnly vowed to keep baby Hope safe until Bethany and Neil returned.

Stewart went back to his desk and surveyed the paper clutter of bills of lading, manifests, letters ordering cargoes forward, passenger lists, orders for provisions and repairs, ships' logs. He was drowning in a sea of paper, and the music he'd heard inside his head all his life was beginning to fade away like a half-remembered refrain.

A knock on his office door was a welcome relief from staring at columns of figures that refused to balance. He called, "Come in," and his senior clerk's head appeared.

"There's a young lady to see you, sir. She says she's a friend of yours. It's possible she might be an emigrant wanting passage, but she insists on seeing you." He paused and added, "She's got two children with her—babies."

Stewart jumped to his feet and rushed to the outer office. Alison stood there holding Hope; little Davey was at her side, attached to her wrist by a harness. Stewart knew her well enough to see that she was desperately worried about something.

She began to apologize for interrupting him, but he took Hope from her and said, "Come into my office."

"I wouldn't have come if there was any chance your father might be here," she said as he closed the door behind her. "But you said he was going to Portsmouth, so I thought it would be all right."

Pulling out a chair for her, Stewart ruffled Davey's hair and said, "Hello, young chap."

The toddler smiled in recognition and responded, " 'Elloo."

"Mrs. Creel came to see me," Alison said. She told him of the housekeeper's visit that morning, and concluded, "She said she was going to take Hope to meet her grandfather, but I knew Sir Adrian was in Portsmouth."

"He's due back this evening," Stewart said thoughtfully.

"I always felt Mrs. Creel was up to something," Alison said.

"According to my older brother, Mrs. Creel used to be more than just a housekeeper to my father. Neil said he once visited the Liverpool house and found the two of them in a rather compromising position. That was the reason none of us were supposed to go there, although Father said it was because he used the town house for business purposes."

"I wasn't sure if you knew," Alison said. "I overheard a conversation between them that suggested something like that, and Mrs. Creel sounded bitter about the affair having come to an end. You don't think she plans to use Hope in some twisted scheme for revenge, do you?"

"Whatever her plan, from what Mary told us, I fear that Father's reaction will be to deny that the baby is his granddaughter and return her to the parish home. I think I'd better go straight over to Victoria Gardens and talk to Mrs. Creel. Perhaps I can persuade her not to tell Father about Hope."

"Stewart . . . before you go, there's something you should know about me. I'm afraid when I tell you what it is you'll hate me and Lady Fielding won't want me looking after Hope."

Her lovely face was strained, her eyes too bright, and he could see, even from across the room, that she was trembling. She turned to look at Davey, who was playing with the globe, spinning it on its stand.

"I could never hate you," Stewart said gently. "Whatever it is you want to tell me, let's not discuss it here. I have a flat not far from here; we'll go there."

* * *

Mrs. Creel sat in her favorite armchair in the drawing room at Victoria Gardens, her long thin feet propped on a footstool, a glass of Sir Adrian's best sherry in her hand, contemplating with malicious pleasure what might happen when she presented Sir Adrian's granddaughter to him.

He would bluster, of course, but she knew he'd do anything to keep his society friends from learning the circumstances of the child's birth and the present whereabouts of her parents.

She decided to keep quiet about the part Stewart and Lady Fielding had played in concealing the infant. They might be willing to pay her a little something on the side to avoid Sir Adrian's wrath. She would simply spring the baby on him and refuse to say who had been caring for it. This would also ensure her own protection, since the old sod wouldn't know who else was involved.

Lost in thought, she didn't hear a key turn in the front door and almost jumped out of her skin when Stewart suddenly strode into the living room.

"Why, Mr. Stewart—"

For once the rather shy and self-effacing middle son did not greet her apologetically, but stared her down, his usually gentle eyes blazing. "You will stay away from Alison and the children, Mrs. Creel, or you will answer to me."

Her small cunning eyes flickered over his face. "Will I, now? Your father is my master, not you. I'll do whatever I please, about the baby or Alison or anything else."

"I intend to ask Alison to be my wife, Mrs. Creel. I further intend to adopt my brother's child, to keep her safe from you until such time as Neil and Bethany come home."

She put the glass down and stood up, peering up at him with an evil smile. "Your *wife,* Mr. Stewart? You must be joking! You'd marry a streetwalker?"

He swallowed a dry lump in his throat. "I know all about Alison's past; she told me everything. It makes no difference to me."

"Maybe not, but it certainly will to your father, won't it?"

"Only if you tell him. Look, Mrs. Creel, let's get down to business. How much do you want to keep quiet about Hope's parentage and Alison's past?"

Mary reached Riverleigh just before the rain began. She took her precious letter into her bedroom and locked the door to make sure she would not be interrupted by her maid or the butler.

The letters were addressed to her in care of poste restante, and she always picked them up herself at the local post office.

Eagerly she tore open the envelope and began to read Tate's letter.

My Dear Mary,

Your letter came today and suddenly my exile is bearable, my surroundings less foreign, my difficulties surmountable. The months of waiting are over. You see, my dear, I feared that once I left England you would put me out of your mind. Oh, I know we promised to write, but I had convinced myself that you would never go to the post office and my poor letters would languish there unread. Oh, how brightly the sun shines on New Orleans today! The miserable schooner presently unloading its cargo of rum and spices suddenly seems as sleek and beautiful as any ship of the line!

There are, by the way, four other schooners, all equally decrepit, with drunken masters and reluctant crews. They were all surprised when I appeared on the scene, and will be even more so when they learn I intend to sail back to the Indies with them. By the time I'm finished with them they will have been transformed from seagoing scum to disciplined seamen the Royal Navy would welcome aboard the finest ships in Her Majesty's fleet.

You asked about New Orleans. How can I convey to you the essence of the city in a mere letter? There is a veritable orgy of new building going on, but the core of the city is still the Vieux Carré—the French Quarter—with its narrow streets, iron-trellised balconies, trailing vines, and bright flowers in large pots, quite exotically beautiful.

I was astounded at the commerce on the Mississippi. There are even steamboats plying the river, paddle wheelers (I wonder if steam will ever replace sail on ocean voyages? I feel it is a distinct possibility for the future).

New Orleans seems to be a center for adventurers and soldiers of fortune, who appear to have designs on the American West, Mexico, and the South American countries. Since this is an important port, with barges and paddle wheelers sailing up the river, merchant ships going out across the Gulf of Mexico (not to mention the occasional privateer, even in these modern times), and so many possible cargoes, it seems Adrian and I were foolish to let a rather lackadaisical agent here handle the schooners for us. I'm convinced I will soon build up my newly formed Ivers Shipping Company to the point where Adrian might regret the bargain he struck with me.

You said in your letter that he has made no further mention of me or of the events leading up to my leaving England, that he has not thrown that dreadful housewarming party in your face or mentioned our friendship, and for that I am grateful. Mary, you would tell me if he mistreated you in any way, wouldn't you? One word from you and I will return to your side with all speed. Always remember that. I pledge to you my enduring devotion.

I must close now, dearest Mary, and prepare to set sail for Jamaica. More soon.

Your devoted friend,

Tate

Mary clasped the letter to her breast, almost able to feel Tate's presence, hear his voice speaking to her. They were thousands of miles apart, but she felt closer to him than to any other human being on earth.

She went to her desk, eager to begin to write her reply, but as she dipped her pen into the inkwell there was a tap at her door. Quickly she pushed Tate's letter under the blotter and called, "Come in."

Wentworth, the butler, appeared. "Mr. Stewart is here, milady, and would like to see you. Shall I send him up?"

"No, I'll come downstairs. Where is he?"

"In the library, milady."

Glancing at the china clock on her mantel she saw that it was midafternoon; Stewart should have been at work in the Liverpool office. Poor Stewart, how he hated his new position in life! He had confided that he worked from early morning until late at night and still could not keep up. He simply was not cut out to be a businessman. He was an artist, a pianist and composer, and Mary was sorry that he no longer had time even to play the piano. She might have attempted to intercede on his behalf with his father, but Adrian no longer either talked to her or listened to her.

His silence had begun the day after Tate's housewarming. In front of others Adrian would respond briefly if she spoke to him, but he never addressed her directly, communicating only through the servants: "Tell your mistress I have invited a dozen guests for dinner on Saturday" or "Suggest to Lady Fielding that the gallery paintings are in need of cleaning." On the rare occasions when they found themselves alone together, he behaved as though she did not exist, looking right through her.

She recognized this shunning for what it was, punishment for disobeying him by serving as hostess at the housewarming, punishment for her friendship with Tate. Since Adrian's treatment of her was not too far removed from his attitude toward her earlier in their marriage, she tried not to let it worry her. Perhaps in time he would relent. And in the meantime, she had Tate's letters. She had not been allowed to say good-bye to Tate, but as she and Adrian left Tate's house that last evening Tate had managed to whisper to her, "I'll write in care of poste restante."

After being sure his latest letter was safely hidden in a hatbox in her wardrobe, she went downstairs.

Stewart, still wearing his overcoat, paced a worried circle around the library. He gave her a nervous smile.

"My dear, what has happened?" Mary asked.

"Nothing. Well . . . I came to tell you that I intend to ask Alison to be my wife."

"Oh, Stewart, I'm so happy for you," she said, but even as she congratulated him, she worried about Adrian's reaction to such a match. "Do you think your father will approve? Especially in view of the ready-made family you'd be taking on. Of course, when Neil and Bethany come home they will take their child, but in the meantime . . ."

"Mary, do you think perhaps we should tell Father about baby Hope—that she's Neil's daughter?"

Mary thought of the letters Adrian had sent to Bethany, and shivered. "Your father knew Bethany was with child when she was sentenced, but he refused to accept the baby as his grandchild. If he learns that you and I and Alison—yes, and Mrs. Creel, too—conspired to deceive him . . . well, I fear the consequences for all of us. It will be difficult enough for you to get your father's blessing for your marriage. Alison is a lovely girl, but hardly of your class, even apart from the fact that she's a widow with a child."

"Alison is not only sweet and kind; she's the most intelligent young woman I've ever met," Stewart declared with unaccustomed firmness. "Her mind is quick and inquisitive, and she absorbs knowledge faster than I ever could, despite my university education. I shall be damn lucky—oh, forgive my language—if she says yes."

"Do you love her?" Mary asked gently, and watched conflicting expressions cross his face.

He colored slightly. "Not . . . not perhaps in the way you mean. But I love her compassion, her goodness, her spirit."

"Forgive me for saying this, but are you sure you are not being tricked into marriage with her? Stewart, you are quite a catch for any young woman, you know."

He looked at the floor. "Most young women find me excruciatingly dull, which I suppose is all right, since I find most of them empty-headed. Alison is different. Besides, she has no idea of my intentions."

"Would you consider waiting a little longer before springing this surprise on your father? He's had so much to contend with lately."

"I really would like to have the wedding take place immediately."

"Oh, Stewart! She isn't . . . in the family way?"

Now his cheeks flamed. "Of course not! I merely want her to have the protection of my name."

"Wait just a few days, then, please, before you tell him? Let's try to think of a way to present Alison to him properly."

Mary asked herself silently what a delay could possibly accomplish, since Adrian would explode when he heard the news. Then what would become of Alison and the children? In wanting to protect them, Stewart might unwittingly be placing them in even greater jeopardy.

THEY HAD RENAMED the stolen ship *Liberty,* and on the long voyage from Australia at Tom's direction the escaping convicts made other changes in the vessel's appearance. Carpenters built a new wheelhouse, replaced some of the masts and spars, rigged the canvas differently.

"Why bother?" had been Jack's initial reaction. "If we can reach a civilized shore, we'll abandon her and set off overland."

"That would be a waste. Why not see that she's returned to her original owners?" Tom asked.

Jack laughed. "You think that will cause the Crown to drop piracy charges against you? Face it, lad, we're all bound for the hangman's noose if we're caught. I say, get rid of the evidence. Let's scuttle her as soon as we're safe."

"Tell me, have you given any thought to how you'll make a living in America?" Tom asked.

Listening to the conversation, Leona snorted indelicately. "You must be jesting, Tom. Black Jack Cutler was a highwayman in England. That's all he knows how to do, never mind his education and posh accent."

"Then we'll be parting company the minute we reach America," Tom replied, a determined gleam in his eye, "because I'm going to be a shipowner, and if you don't want her, I'd like to use this ship to give me my start."

"And what about giving her back to her owners?" Jack asked.

"I'm thinking that in a few months we could make enough by coastal trading either to return her or to make suitable restitution. The *Liberty* could be the first of many ships. I've decided what I'm going to do in America. I'm going into business for myself, in competition with my father eventually."

Leona looked from one to the other. "If Black Jack goes back to robbing the rich and if you stay on the ship, who's going to take care of Bethany?"

"I am," they both said simultaneously.

Tom glared. "Bethany is my responsibility. She was my brother's wife. I'll not see her further degraded by keeping company with an outlaw, if that's your intention. Besides, she doesn't even like you."

"She's grieving for her dead husband," Jack said. "But her sorrow will pass with time. And who said I intend to become a road agent in America? I might decide to be respectable."

"I will take care of my sister-in-law," Tom said firmly.

"Then start off by being honest with her. Tell her that her chances of going home to England are less than none."

"Oh, God's teeth, *men!*" Leona exclaimed. "Will you both just shut your mouths? She might hear."

She looked to the stern of the ship, where Bethany sat watching the wake cut a silver path to the horizon. She spent most of her time in that same spot, gazing at the sea, as if that phosphorescent wake were a thread connecting her to Neil's watery grave. She seldom spoke and Leona had noticed that even the roughest of the convicts treated Bethany with respect.

But Leona suspected that no matter where Bethany was, even in the highest ranks of society, her beauty would eclipse everything around her. The fine-grained lightness, the sheer delicacy of her ethereal presence, rendered other mortals clumsily ugly and coarse. Leona herself nurtured a fierce desire to protect and care for her friend and secretly had no intention of leaving her to the tender mercies of either Jack or Tom. Jack, Leona was convinced, was too much of a daredevil and would come to a bad end, while Tom was too ambitious for his own good.

They sailed into what Tom called the horse latitudes, and eventually put in to a pleasant harbor. They could see cattle roaming the cliffs above the beach, and several horsemen waved excitedly as they dropped anchor.

Leona hurried out on deck, and even Bethany seemed eager for a glimpse of land after so long at sea, asking, "Is it America?"

Tom ordered the anchor dropped, then turned to Bethany and replied, "No, this is Mexican territory. It's called Alta California. The Spanish built a mission here, I believe, and a road called El Camino Real—the King's Highway—that goes north up the coastline. There used to be Spanish settlers here, who were given land grants by the king of Spain. They raised beef and traded in hides. I'm not sure what happened to them after Mexico gained independence, but obviously there are some settlers here."

"Mexican? Spanish?" Leona said, disappointed. "We won't be able to talk to them. Can't we sail on to an American port?"

"To the north is the Oregon Territory," Tom said. "Which is jointly occupied by the Americans and British. I don't have to point out that we can't risk falling into British hands."

"I have a smattering of Spanish, and my French is good. I might be able to make myself understood," Bethany put in.

"Ned has been here before," Tom said, "and speaks the language."

"Good, we three will go ashore first, then." Jack ordered the longboat launched.

Albert Harrow glared at them over his shoulder as he turned the winch to lower the boat. "Why can't we all go? God knows we've been stuck on this miserable tub for long enough. It's a wonder we've not killed one another."

"Patience, man," Jack said evenly, although his blue eyes flashed a warning that was not lost on anyone within range. "We need to get the lay of the land first, make sure it's safe. No sense in blundering ashore into worse trouble than we left behind."

Leona, standing close to Bethany at the rail, said, "Isn't it a lovely sight? Oh, I can't wait to set foot on dry land again. I swear to God I'll never sail on another damn boat as long as I live."

Bethany gave her a sad smile. "I must sail to England at the earliest opportunity. My baby girl is all I have in the world now."

They watched the longboat skim over the sparkling water until it was caught by the surf and rushed to a sandy beach with such swiftness that it seemed almost to fly. Up on the cliff top the horsemen waved and yelled encouragement as the three men climbed toward them. Their greeting seemed friendly, and they appeared to be engaged in a lively exchange of conversation as they all disappeared from view.

"Come on," Leona said. "Let's tidy ourselves up a bit, ready to go ashore." She pulled at her short curls, a frequent habit since the shaving of her head. "Has it grown any more, do you think?"

"Yes, it's grown a lot on the voyage. It will soon be down to your shoulders."

By the time the longboat returned, the convict crew had grown restless and milled about the deck muttering their displeasure. The moment Jack and Tom stepped aboard, an uproar broke out as the long-confined men demanded places on the longboat. The two women stood in the background, straining to hear Jack's response.

"Hold your horses. We've a few things to vote on first."

"Are we going ashore or not?" Albert shouted.

"In good time, yes. The *patrón* of the largest rancho has invited all of us to a fiesta. The people we met were friendly, courteous, and young Tom here has already struck a bargain to take a cargo of hides north to Yerba Buena."

"Oh, he has, has he?" Albert said. "And what's he going to use for a crew? We're all sick of the sea."

Tom stepped forward and held up his hand. "Listen to me. There are a few haciendas here, Spanish families still living on the land granted them by the king. This part of the territory is so far north that apparently the Mexican government hasn't bothered them yet. There's no town, no village, even. If you men want to stay ashore here you'll live as beachcombers, or you'll work for the Spaniards. Any of you know anything about raising cattle? Skinning hides? This is arid country, not much rainfall. I doubt any other kind of farming, or even trapping, would provide you with a livelihood."

"My young friend seems to have forgotten just what your former professions were," Jack put in with a grin. "These men were thieves and pickpockets and cutthroats, Tom. The scum of London. Hardly qualified for any occupation that would require them to live off the land."

"I for one am going to strike out overland and keep going until I get to an American settlement," Albert said. "At least we speak the same language."

There was a murmur of agreement among some of the men. Tom said, "Surely some of you will sail on with Jack and me to Yerba Buena?"

"We'll decide what we want to do after we've been ashore, lad," one of the men said.

"So be it," Jack said. "We'll be loading the hides first thing tomorrow and sailing as soon as we're loaded. If you're aboard you'll go with us and share the profits from the cargo. The rest of you will be on your own. If you decide to go with Albert, be warned that there's a thousand miles of raw territory filled with hostile Indians between you and the nearest American settlement."

"Let's be getting ashore," Albert said impatiently.

The rest of the men swarmed forward, but Jack stopped them with a voice that cracked like a whip. "While you're ashore, you behave yourselves, you hear me? I'll kill any man who harms these people. They're offering hospitality and help and not asking questions about who we are or where we came from. I'll not tolerate drunkenness ashore, or bothering their women, or stealing from them."

A cheer went up as the longboat began the first of many journeys between ship and shore. Ned went with the first batch, to act as interpreter, and Jack appointed the biggest and burliest of the convicts, a man named Bourke who had been with him since the first days of his escape and whose loyalty was legendary, to keep the others in order.

Tom watched with a worried frown. "We should have called for a volunteer crew. Unless we get enough hands we can't take on a cargo of hides."

"By morning most of them will be too drunk to care. We'll have Bourke load them into the longboat," Jack answered.

"I'll not shanghai a crew—" Tom began.

"Think of it as saving their scalps," Jack replied. "I hear the North American Indians are fierce and warlike. The men wouldn't be dealing with Australian aborigines here."

He pushed through the eager men to where Bethany and Leona stood. "After we get some of the men ashore we'll take you. The cliff is steep, but there's a trail we can take. I believe you'll be able to manage."

"To get off this ship? Of course we'll manage," Leona said. "But what's all this about taking hides north?"

"There's nothing here for us," Jack answered. "And the overland journey Albert speaks of is too hazardous to take women along. Tom believes we can put into the dog holes up and down the California coast, picking up cargoes and trading. From what we've learned, Yerba Buena might be a good place to put you ashore. There are more settlers there, and a presidio—a fort. There's a customs house and even a couple of American families."

"But I can't stay—I must go on to England," Bethany said.

"Listen to me," Jack said harshly. "It's time to face facts. By now every one of us is notorious. There's a price on your head. You can't go to England. You'd be hanged for piracy."

"But my baby—"

"First we have to make a life for ourselves here. Then we'll find someone you trust to go to England and bring your daughter to you. But you, Bethany Newton Fielding, have to accept that you can never take the chance of going back yourself. And don't suggest traveling incognito—someone might recognize you. You're an escapee from the penal colony, and you're a pirate—"

"Don't keep calling me that!" Bethany cried, with more spirit than she'd shown since Neil's death.

Leona laid a hand on her arm. "He's right, Bethany. We're not out of the woods yet." She turned to Jack. "But surely you don't intend to stay in the Mexican territory forever?"

"Tom's father owns some ships that trade in the Caribbean. An agent in New Orleans handles them. Tom reckons they'll belong to him one day anyway, and he knows the markets well enough to start his own trading company. When we've acquired some capital and a good crew we'll sail for New Orleans—a fascinating city, I've heard, where I'm sure we'll all make our fortunes."

"You're throwing in your lot with Tom, then?" Leona asked.

"As my sainted father used to say, 'Sufficient unto the day is the trouble thereof,' or words to that effect." He looked toward the land, shading his eyes with his hand against the hot glare of the sun. "Come on, the longboat is coming back. Let's present you to the *patrón* and his family."

The chapel bell tolled a welcome, and smiling faces greeted them as they entered the hacienda through a wrought-iron gate and found themselves in an inner courtyard where olive trees and vividly blossoming vines filtered the sunlight. Water flowing from a tiled fountain in the center of the courtyard added to both the tranquillity and the coolness. The hacienda was an oasis, its thick walls concealing from view the sparsely vegetated and sun-scorched hills beyond.

Directly in front of them a long row of arches enclosed the terrace of the single-story *casa grande,* the main house, which Tom said was made of adobe, a hardened clay.

The *patrón* and his wife, a distinguished looking silver-haired man and a lovely dark-eyed woman, waited for them on the arched terrace. Neither Luis nor Carlotta del Castillo spoke English, but the warmth of their smiles was greeting enough. They were obviously sympathetic too, when they realized Bethany was a widow in mourning. She had donned her only black gown for the occasion, despite Leona's objections.

Bethany felt her eyes sting with tears as the senora embraced her and gently patted her shoulder, as if soothing an unhappy child. An elusive scent, not unlike lilacs, emanated from the *patrón*'s wife, and her gown was an elegant burgundy silk, trimmed with ecru lace. Bethany thought of her own dear mother, and her sadness deepened. She allowed the senora to lead her into the house, noting with some concern that the convicts were swarming all over the place as Indian servants hurried to set up tables on the long terrace and bring out food and drinks.

Tom, Jack, Ned, Leona, and Bethany were conducted through spacious rooms connected by wide arches to a private dining room where a dark mahogany table, elaborately carved and surrounded by high-backed chairs, was set for at least fifty guests. The *patrón* spoke to Ned, who translated for them.

"He says he has invited his friends and neighbors for the fiesta and that our crew will be served separately because the dining room can't accommodate so many." Ned grinned and added, "Probably afraid their table manners won't measure up and he's right. He says if there are other ships' officers he'll send for them, but I told him the other officers stayed on the ship."

They were quickly joined by two handsome young men and a rather sullen-faced young woman, who glared at Bethany and Leona over the top of a black lace fan. They were introduced as Eduardo, Felipe, and Teresa del Castillo. A moment later several other guests arrived, including a hawk-faced man wearing the gold-braided uniform of an officer in the Mexican army, who was presented as Colonel Alvarez.

Jack eyed the colonel thoughtfully and murmured to Ned, "Excuse yourself and go outside. Tell Bourke to inform the men that there are soldiers here. I doubt this officer traveled alone; he probably has a patrol with him. And even if he doesn't, it wouldn't hurt to let the crew think he has."

As the guests assembled, they took their places at the table. Over their heads two giant wooden wheels blazed with candlelight, and the damask cloth was covered with gold and silver dishes filled with abalone, roast pigeon, and spicy beef with red beans. Crystal bowls held an unfamiliar golden fruit, and when Ned returned he said these were mangoes. The subtle scent of the fruit blended appealingly with the aroma of all the other delicacies.

Tall-stemmed goblets were filled with sparkling wine, and toasts were made. Despite the language differences, conversation flowed. Bethany noted that Jack understood more Spanish than he spoke and often began to answer a question before Ned finished translating it. But halfway through the meal the inevitable question was asked.

Glancing sideways at Colonel Alvarez, Ned said hesitantly, "They want to know our home port."

Jack and Tom exchanged glances. Tom said quickly, "They know we don't have a cargo aboard, and with the exception of Bethany and Leona, none of us look like paying passengers. Let's take a chance and tell them the truth. That we escaped from the Australian penal colony. We can claim you were political prisoners."

"No," Jack said sharply. "If we're to begin a new life, let's not bring the old one into it. Ned, tell them the two women are passengers and that we discharged a cargo in the Sandwich Isles and came here with the intention of trading along the California coast. Our home port is New Orleans."

As Ned translated, Bethany's gaze met Jack's and he said, "If you continue to give me that disapproving look they'll suspect something is wrong."

"I was just thinking of the difference between you and Tom. Neil was honest, too. I don't believe he told even the smallest lie in his whole life, but lies come easily to your lips. I believe it is a serious character flaw."

"Oh, you do, do you? Tell me, are we speaking of that same blazingly honest husband who used an alias?"

"A pen name!" she protested. "And only out of concern for his father's feelings. Many writers and journalists use noms de plume."

Perhaps sensing a brewing argument, the *patrón* suggested they all move into the *sala* where a mariachi waited to play for them.

Señora del Castillo immediately rose and went to Bethany's side to lead her to a velvet-cushioned bench set in an alcove in the *sala,* an impressively large room adjacent to the dining room, the center of which was obviously used for dancing. The senora gestured for Ned to join them.

"She understands you are in mourning and will not dance," Ned translated. "But hopes you will enjoy the music."

As the musicians began to play a lively fandango, the senora spoke at length to Ned, who then turned to Bethany.

He concentrated for a moment. "I'll try to put it into English as near as I can to what she said. She says she is saddened to hear your husband died on the voyage, and she's worried that you have been left alone in the world without the means to support yourself. She's concerned that you do not mention a destination or relatives you might be journeying to. She thinks you might intend to return to the ship with your brother-in-law and feels it would not be proper for you to live aboard a trading vessel with so many men."

"Tell her that it has been decided that Leona and I will go ashore in Yerba Buena, where there are some Americans. We hope to find positions there, perhaps caring for children or as housekeepers."

Bethany knew that Leona had no intention of doing any such thing, but it sounded more respectable than saying her friend hoped to continue her career as an actress.

When this was translated, the senora leaned forward and patted the back of Bethany's hand sympathetically. She spoke rapidly to Ned.

He said, "She wonders if you would consider staying here for as long as you wish. She would like her sons and daughter to learn to speak English and would be grateful if you would teach them."

Bethany looked into the kind dark eyes and knew she would accept, but asked first, "Would her offer include Leona?"

"Would what include Leona?" Leona herself asked, appearing suddenly beside them. Bethany explained.

"Don't translate that," Leona told Ned. "I'd rather take my chances in Yerba Buena. I'd go mad stuck here. I need to find a nice little theater and feel the boards under my feet again."

"Then I'll go with you," Bethany said at once. She looked around regretfully. The hacienda seemed so peaceful, so far from turmoil. What a wonderful place to bring up a child! If she could persuade someone to go to England and bring back her daughter . . .

"No, you stay here," Leona said. "Better a bird in the hand than two in the bush. Besides, if there's nothing for me up in Yerba Buena, I can come back to you. From what Tom says, he and Jack will be sailing up and down the coast regularly until they can get the ship ready to go to New Orleans. We can keep in touch through them."

Bethany nodded regretfully. She would miss Leona, but saw the wisdom of her suggestion. Bethany said to Ned, "Thank the senora and tell her I would be happy to stay for a while."

Colonel Alvarez strode toward them and bowed to Leona, gesturing toward the dancers in the center of the *sala.* Leona gave Bethany a sly wink and said, "Why, certainly, Colonel. I'd be happy to dance with you."

Bethany could see, over Ned's shoulder, that Teresa del Castillo, who certainly had inherited neither her mother's graciousness nor her looks, was far from pleased that the colonel had selected Leona for a partner.

They made a striking couple on the floor. The musicians had switched from the fandango to a waltz, in honor of the foreign guests, and the colonel whirled Leona around in dizzying circles. Bethany could see that even as they danced their eyes were locked together in some unspoken challenge that seemed a bewildering blend of both sensuality and hostility. The watching Teresa snapped her fan and refused to dance with any of the caballeros who approached her.

Jack walked over and extended his hand to Bethany. "I'm quite accomplished at the waltz."

"And I'm in mourning," she replied icily.

"You'll never see these people again anyway. What does it matter?"

"It matters to me." She turned to Ned. "Would you please ask the senora if I may go to my room now?"

"I'll take you back to the ship," Jack said.

"I'm staying here. Please don't make a scene. It's all settled. I've been invited to stay here at the hacienda, and I've accepted."

"What?" Jack was obviously stunned by this announcement. "You can't be serious. You don't know these people."

Bethany gave him a tired smile. "You mean in the way I knew the convicts and soldiers bayside?"

Señora del Castillo rose to her feet and took Bethany's hand. Ned said, "She's going to take you to your room."

They went along a corridor and the sounds of the party soon faded behind stout adobe walls. At length Bethany found herself in a spacious room, furnished with heavy mahogany furniture, intricately carved, and illuminated by wall sconces in which candles flickered. The senora again embraced her and murmured, "*Buenas noches,* Bethany. *Hasta mañana.*"

The bed had already been turned back, warm water waited in a pitcher on a marble washstand, and there was a cool cotton nightgown and a warm velvet dressing gown. Tomorrow, Bethany thought sleepily, I must ask Jack or Tom to bring my things from the ship.

She fell into a deep sleep almost immediately, only to awaken abruptly, unsure if she had been asleep for hours or only minutes. Someone was patting her cheek and shaking her arm.

Jack Cutler sat on the edge of the bed, speaking to her in a low, urgent voice. "Listen to me. Don't be deceived by the apparent peacefulness here. I talked to the *patrón.* He's Spanish, not a *criollo* born in the New World. This rancho was granted to him upon his retirement from the army of occupation. He's never dared to look into the *expedientes* to see if the title to his land is honored by the present Mexican government."

Half asleep and confused by the strange surroundings, Bethany said, "How dare you come into my room—"

"I'm trying to warn you that at any moment the *patrón* might find himself stripped of all of his possessions. There's already talk of wiping the last vestiges of Spanish rule from Mexican soil. He's been saved so far because Alta California is so far from Mexico City."

"I still intend to stay here. Please leave my room at once."

"If the prospect of a raid by Mexican soldiers doesn't deter you, then consider this: The del Castillos' nearest neighbor's hacienda was recently attacked and burned by hostile Indians."

"You're trying to frighten me."

"I'm trying to open your eyes to the danger you'll be in if you stay here."

She sat up, drawing the covers around her neck. "I must make my own way in the world, Jack. I've relied on you and Tom, and before you came along, to my everlasting shame, there was Dr. Prentice. Now I must find out how to manage on my own. The del Castillos are offering me a position; I shan't be living on their charity."

"Dammit, woman, I'm worried about your safety, your life. To hell with your independence."

"Please go," Bethany said coldly. "It is totally improper for you to be here, and if my hosts learn you are, my reputation here will be ruined. Aren't you the one who said we should make new lives for ourselves in this country?"

"Yes," Jack said heavily, "I did. But I didn't mean for you to be the only gringa among Spaniards and Mexicans."

"Good night, Jack," Bethany said firmly. "I'll see you in the morning before you leave."

But he didn't move and his closeness in the shadowed room was dangerous, threatening in a way Bethany had never experienced, not even with Will Prentice. Her heart thumped madly, and she was unsure if that tattoo against her ribs was caused by fear or anticipation. She was appalled to realize that she was actually hoping he might kiss her good night.

But he stood up and murmured, "Perhaps you'll see reason after you sleep on it."

After the door closed softly behind him, Bethany hugged her pillow to her breast and tried to conjure up the image of her dead husband. She had to think about Neil, about the kind, gentle man who was everything that Black Jack Cutler was not. But that heart-stopping tension Jack Cutler had brought with him remained long after he was gone.

23

STEWART TOOK ALISON'S hands in his and repeated, "I said I want you to be my wife. I want you to marry me. I want to take care of you and the children forever."

Tears spilled down Alison's cheeks. She hung her head in shame. "Please don't joke with me, Stewart, I can't bear it."

"I mean it, Alison. Please take me seriously. It's taken all my courage to make this declaration. I want you to have the protection of my name; I never want you to be left to the mercy of someone like Mrs. Creel again."

She raised her tearstained face to gaze at him in wonder. "But I told you . . . what I had to do after my husband died."

"Don't speak of it again, Alison. Don't think about it. It's in the past, over and done with."

"But Mrs. Creel will tell your father—"

"No. She won't. I have her promise. No one ever need know.

I give you my word that I will never bring the matter up to you again."

Alison could hardly speak for happiness. She had grown to love Stewart deeply and could not believe her impossible dream of staying with him forever might actually come true. Impulsively she flung her arms around his neck, pressed herself close to him, and kissed his mouth passionately.

In her own excitement she did not at first realize that he was not responding. His lips were cool, dry, unmoving; he kept his arms at his sides, his body rigid, tensed for flight.

She drew back, puzzled.

He was flushed and his expression was guarded. "Alison, I . . . perhaps I did not make myself clear. As I said, I want you to have the protection of my name. I want to care for you and the children. . . . I especially do not want to see my brother's child returned to the parish home . . . but naturally I would not expect the marriage to be . . . to be consummated."

Alison turned away quickly, to hide her mortification. A marriage in name only. Of course, what else had she expected? She was damaged goods. A man of his position, a man as good and pure as Stewart, would never accept her as a real wife. He was making a great sacrifice for her and the babies as it was. She bit her lip so hard she tasted blood. She would have the protection of his name, but undoubtedly some other woman would receive his most intimate caresses. What a bittersweet gift this was!

His hands fell lightly on her shoulders. "I haven't told my father about you yet. I wanted to have your answer first. Mary asked me to wait until we could all get together at Riverleigh. Perhaps next weekend. Then I'll take out a special license, and we can be married right away. I feel the sooner the better, don't you?"

She nodded without looking around, feeling more like a prospective business partner than a bride-to-be.

Fog crept up the river and swirled, wraithlike, about the masts of the ships, the waterfront buildings, and the gaslit streets. From the public houses came raucous laughter and tipsily loud conversation, the tinkle of glasses, overlaid with piano renditions of ballads and chanteys, accompanied by voices raised in song.

With the concealing fog, it was a perfect night for Vareck's crimps to knock a few reluctant sailors over the head and drag them down to the docks. But Vareck had been drinking for a couple of hours, and supplying ships with crews was the last thing on his mind. He had grown increasingly angry that, after he had served Sir Adrian Fielding faithfully for years, done his every bidding, the old swine had simply tossed him out on the street.

Vareck grew maudlin, filled with self-pity, as he downed another brimming glass of ale. It wasn't his fault his crimps had grabbed young Tom, was it? Vareck himself hadn't been present at the railway station, because he knew that sooner or later he'd meet the Fielding brothers, and he didn't want them to remember him as the man who had shanghaied Bethany's brother. But he had described Roland Montague very carefully to the crimps, especially the fact that he wore that Garrick overcoat. How could he have known that Tom Fielding had put on the blasted coat?

Besides, hadn't he gone trailing all over Africa looking for the boy? Surely he deserved to be paid for that, at least. He hadn't been able to get anywhere near Adrian Fielding since the day he'd thrown him out of his office. Ah, but tonight was going to be different.

He opened his pocket watch and saw it was time to leave. There'd be no cabs in this fog; he'd have to walk to the station. He lurched out into the street, shoving a young sailor out of his way.

The walk to the railway station took longer than he expected, but the trains were all running late anyway. He stopped at the ticket office and inquired about trains coming from Portsmouth. He was told that several changes would be necessary, and no doubt the passenger would eventually come from Crewe; there was a train due in from Crewe within the hour. Vareck went into the railway saloon bar and downed another ale, then went to the platform to wait in the misty shadows.

The train arrived with a squeal of brakes and a burst of steam, and as it cleared he saw Sir Adrian alighting from a first-class compartment.

Two porters rushed to help him with his baggage, and since he was the first to leave the train Vareck assumed the other passengers had stepped aside to allow this. Arrogant bastard. He took it as his due that he'd be first, best, deferred to, groveled before. He looked down his aristocratic nose and, without uttering a word, created fear and submission in everyone who crossed his path. Well, Vareck was one man his lordship wouldn't best.

Vareck kept his distance, following after several other disembarking passengers, but keeping Fielding in sight.

Outside the station there were few cabs available for hire. A couple of hackneys had already been taken. The rest of the carriages were privately owned, there to meet family members, and as they rolled slowly away they were obliged to follow walking servants holding lanterns that did little to penetrate the pea souper. Vareck knew that Sir Adrian did not keep a coach at the house in Victoria Gardens, and as he had foreseen, Sir Adrian waited only a minute or two before setting off to walk to his town house.

He was quickly swallowed by the fog, but Vareck knew the route he would take. He followed.

There were few other pedestrians this time of night as the fog thickened. The yellow glow of the street lamps blurred overhead, and by the time they reached the entrance to Victoria Gardens it was necessary to walk close to the wall in order to keep from falling over the curb.

Vareck could hear Sir Adrian's footsteps ahead, but could no longer see the shadowy outline in the mist. It was time to act, before Sir Adrian realized he was being followed. Vareck felt inside his coat, his fingers closing around a leather sheath hanging from his belt.

Long ago he'd taken the knife from a Norwegian whaler in a fight, a lethal blade that could slice blubber as easily as butter, and with it he had dispatched more than one unfortunate wretch who'd challenged him. The instant the knife was in his hand, he lunged forward.

At the last second Sir Adrian must have heard him coming, and he turned. Instead of sinking into his back, the blade was deflected by his shoulderblade. Vareck growled in frustration, yanked it free, and raised it again. But Sir Adrian caught his wrist in a powerful grip and held his arm aloft.

They struggled, crashing against the wrought-iron railing enclosing Victoria Gardens, swaying back and forth, grunting, cursing. Although the wound in his back was bleeding severely, it didn't seem to have weakened Sir Adrian.

Vareck kicked, attempted to gouge, used every method of street brawling he'd ever learned, and still his opponent was gradually loosening his grip on the knife.

Then suddenly Sir Adrian stepped in a puddle, slipped, and lost his balance. Vareck leapt on top of him and drove the knife toward his heart. He felt the blade plunge into flesh, then hit bone. Damn! Fielding had raised his arm, and the knife was imbedded in it up to the hilt.

To Vareck's horror, Sir Adrian's other hand closed around his throat and tightened. Frantically Vareck tried to pull the knife free to stab him again, but it would not come. He could hear himself gurgling, fighting for breath.

After a moment Sir Adrian's grip slackened as loss of blood weakened him. Sobbing with relief, Vareck was able to pry the choking fingers from around his neck.

Gasping for breath, he struggled to his feet. A whisper of wind briefly stirred the fog, and he looked down to see Sir Adrian staring at him, golden lamplight reflected in his eyes. The knife protruded from his upper arm and the pavement around him was dark and slippery with blood.

At the same instant he heard voices, coming closer. Two men, laughing, talking, feeling their way through the mist. It sounded as though they were walking in the middle of the street. With luck they wouldn't see Fielding lying there, and the swine would bleed to death.

Vareck turned and ran blindly into the fog.

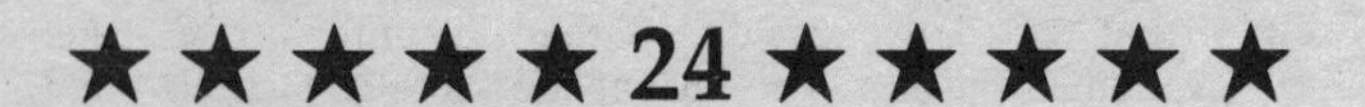

24

MARY CLOSED THE sickroom door and stood outside on the landing for a moment, breathing unevenly. She felt guilty that she hated to go into the room. It was, after all, her duty as a wife to attend to her husband's needs.

Difficult to deal with at the best of times, Adrian was an impossible invalid. She went downstairs to await the doctor, who had asked her to leave the room while he changed the dressings on Adrian's wounds.

He had been near death when he was found lying in the street, and the doctor had at first held out little hope. But the knife had missed vital organs, and despite severe loss of blood, Adrian clung stubbornly to life. His right arm had been cut to the bone and the wound in his back had punctured a lung. Convalescence would be a long, slow process, and Mary saw a bleak future stretching ahead of her while her husband remained at Riverleigh.

The doctor joined her in the library as he usually did after his visit and gratefully accepted a glass of sherry. "Thank you, Lady Fielding, I don't usually indulge while on my rounds, but your husband is not an easy patient to deal with."

"How is he today, Doctor?"

"I'm still worried about septicemia. Both wounds are infected, and I do wish he'd allow me to use maggots to get rid of the puss. But he refuses. He's very weak. He insisted upon trying to get out of bed, and as I warned him he would, he passed out."

"Oh, no!"

"Only briefly. He's back in bed and sleeping now. He's troubled about his ships, about how well his son is managing the business without him."

Mary studied the shelves of leather-bound volumes on the library shelves, wondering what Adrian would say if he knew of Stewart's marriage to Alison, wondering how well Stewart actually was running the company. "Stewart will be visiting him this evening; I'm sure he'll put his mind to rest then."

"Your husband is also frustrated by the fact that the man who attacked him has apparently slipped out of the country."

"Frustrated" was too mild a word, Mary thought. Adrian was enraged.

"Try to keep Sir Adrian as quiet as possible," the doctor instructed before he left.

She went back upstairs to her own room and opened her wardrobe. Several hatboxes were stacked inside, and the one on the bottom contained her treasures. Mary lifted out a summer bonnet she never wore, a frothy confection of feathers and flowers, then withdrew a ribbon-tied bundle of letters.

Tate's last letter had arrived, ironically, on the very day Vareck had attacked Sir Adrian. Mary had not yet answered the letter, but she had read it every day since.

My dearest Mary,

I just tore up a letter I had started, telling you about my voyage to the Indies, about my plans for my ships, about how pleased I am with the progress of my shipping company . . . because I realized that these things were not what I wanted to say to you. What is foremost in my mind, during my every wak-

ing minute, is how much I miss your gentle presence, how I long to have you near, to hear your voice, to see your smile. I curse myself for a fool for not telling you all that was in my heart while I was still in England.

Written words on a page cannot convey the love I feel for you, which courses through my veins, inflames my blood, causing me both incredible joy and deepest sadness. You are in my every thought. I find myself wondering what you would think of this or that, wanting to show you each new wonder I discover, to share with you the small pleasures of my day—a beautiful sunrise, starlit evenings when the scent of jasmine hangs in the warm still air, the joyous sound of a calliope as a cheeky little paddle wheeler pulls away from the levee, taking passengers up the river to their plantations.

Last night I walked by myself along the narrow streets of the French Quarter, and I heard piano music coming from an open window. The unseen pianist suddenly began to play a melody that evoked another time, another place, when we were together, and . . . for a little while . . . we were happy.

Mary, I truly believe the love that comes to us in our maturity is sweeter, more tender, more lasting, than any schoolboy passion. I spent my youth on the high seas, never staying long enough in one place to form an attachment of any meaning, but even if this had not been so, I know that as a young man I was not ready to love a woman as I now love you . . . enough to gladly die for you.

Sometimes I even find myself talking to you. Telling you all that I could not bring myself to say to you before. I loved you from almost the first moment I met you, and would have been content to love you chastely, without ever letting you know how I felt, had I been convinced that you were happy with Adrian. But you were not. He treated you abominably. Oh, you put on a brave face, but I knew you were desperately unhappy. Had we been able to spend more time together I believe I might have gradually found a way through your wall of reserve and got you to confide in me that your marriage to Adrian was a sham, perhaps even have persuaded you to defy convention and leave him.

But he forced a confrontation before we had reached that stage of confidentiality. Mary, what I am trying to say is this. I know that in our society divorce is the ultimate disgrace. I know also that since you have no grounds for divorce, you would have to leave your husband and be divorced by him for desertion. Oh, how I wish it could be I who had to suffer the stigma instead of you! I have told myself over and over again that this is too much to ask of you . . . yet that is exactly what I am now asking.

Leave him, Mary. Come to this young, new country and start a new life with me. I love you; I will love you forever. I swear to protect and care for you until the day I die. Say the word and I will come for you, or if you would prefer to leave the country alone, then I will send your passage money. Mary, we have only one life. Let us not squander it.

This is a serious decision for you to make, I realize that. Please take all the time you need to consider, although I am anxiously awaiting your reply.

Your devoted friend,

Tate

The words blurred as Mary's eyes filled with tears. Oh, how she longed to go to him! With every passing day her yearning for him grew stronger. If absence was the true test of one's feelings for another person, then her love for Tate surpassed even her love for God, and she worried that this was blasphemous and she was risking the wrath of the Almighty even to think such thoughts. Still, no matter what God's punishment proved to be, she would have been more than willing to give up everything to go to Tate, even living in sin with him if Adrian refused to grant a divorce.

But Vareck's cowardly attack on Adrian dashed all hope that this could be. At least until Adrian was well again. She simply could not leave her husband while he was so helpless.

She hid the letters in the hatbox and went to her desk to begin a reply. Briefly she described Vareck's attack and Adrian's present condition. She mentioned Stewart's difficulty in taking over the running of the company:

Poor Stewart, not only does he not have the right temperament to become a businessman, but he has been forced to try to fill both Adrian's and your shoes, a monumental task for even an experienced shipowner, and one I fear Stewart is ill equipped to handle. The clerks all but ignore him and have be-

come lax in their duties, so that on top of everything else Stewart has to check every single thing they do, and I'm sure you can imagine the attitude of the dockers and crews toward such a gentle and soft-spoken young man. He confides in me, but there is little I can do to help, other than to lend a sympathetic ear. . . .

Pausing, she wondered whether to tell Tate of Stewart's marriage. No, she would save that for later, since it involved a great deal of explanation about Alison and the babies, and she could not keep Tate in suspense about her decision whether or not to join him.

Tate, my dearest, she wrote, *I cannot express the joy your declaration of love brought to me. Know that your love is reciprocated a hundredfold and I long for the day we can be together again. But alas, this cannot be until Adrian has recovered from his wounds. You will understand, I know. As soon as he is well, I will—*

There was a knock on her bedroom door, and she hastily pushed the sheet of paper under her blotter and called, "Come in."

Stewart came into the room, and she was shocked by his appearance. His shoulders drooped dejectedly, and his gait was that of a tired old man. His handsome young face was creased with worry, and he was as pale as a ghost.

Mary's heart went out to him. He was far too young to be saddled with such responsibility, not only for the company but for a ready-made family as well. At this time of his life he should be carefree, enjoying a well-earned holiday between school and career, free to pursue hobbies and pastimes, to travel, and especially, to have time for his music. Mary was glad that baby Hope was in her uncle's care, and Alison was a likable enough young woman, but she was a working-class girl and totally unsuitable to be Stewart's wife. More than once Mary wondered what Alison had said or done to get Stewart to marry her.

Stewart kissed Mary's cheek. His lips were ice-cold. "Hello, Mary. I wondered if we could have a private chat before I face Father. I need your advice as to how much to tell him. Oh, God, I'm making such a mess of things."

She returned his kiss. "He's sleeping. The doctor just left.

Let's go for a walk so we can talk things over. I need the fresh air and so do you. The sea breeze will blow away the cobwebs."

A stiff breeze coming directly off the Irish Sea was invigorating, and they walked along the cliff top listening to the cries of wheeling gulls and the muted sigh of the ebb tide as it retreated from the rocks below.

"How are Alison and the children?" Mary asked.

Stewart's smile momentarily erased the lines of tension from his face. "Very well. Davey's vocabulary is growing by leaps and bounds, and Hope pulled herself to her feet yesterday. I think she's ready to begin walking. Alison is hoping you'll have time to come and see them soon."

"It's very difficult for me to leave Riverleigh just now. Your father needs constant attention." She paused. "He loathes the inactivity. He'll be anxious to hear all your news."

Stewart stopped walking and turned to look out across the water. "I fear my news will not relieve his mind. Our ships depart half empty because I cannot convince merchants and forwarding agents that I'll have the crews to sail on time, and our foreign collections are getting so far behind that I suspect the overseas agents are deliberately withholding payments and know they can get away with it because Father and Tate are no longer at the helm. But even worse than this, I hired incompetent masters for two of our vessels, and they both ran aground—total losses of ships and cargoes. Father will have a fit when he hears."

"Oh, Stewart, how dreadful! Was there loss of life?"

"Yes, I'm afraid so. I . . . I took it upon myself to give cash grants to the families of the men who were lost—just to tide them over, you know."

"I think that was commendable."

"Our solicitor doesn't agree. He says it was unnecessary and I'm going to bankrupt the company with such foolishness."

"But the marine insurance will pay for the lost ships and cargoes. We can surely spare a little something for the bereaved families?"

Stewart's face was ashen in the brooding light of an approaching storm. "I'm afraid . . . I somehow neglected to pay the insurance premiums. The loss is complete. I'll have to tell Father before the solicitor does."

"Oh, dear, must you give him all this bad news today? It really would be kinder to keep it from him. He's so ill. Could you pretend all is well until he's stronger?"

Stewart sighed. "I suppose so. If you can keep the solicitor away from him."

"You mustn't blame yourself for the difficulties with the ships," Mary said. "This was to have been an apprenticeship period for you, guided by your father. Certainly he never anticipated that you would be forced to deal with every aspect of the running of the company alone and unaided."

He turned his head to listen to the cry of the gulls, then looked down at the sea lapping about the rocks. "I hear a melody inside my head—the lonely song of the sea and the men who brave her whims. How I wish I could write it, play it, but there's never any time."

Giving her an apologetic glance, as though he had brought up a trivial subject, he added quickly, "But I don't hear the phantom music inside my head so much nowadays. Those are rain clouds moving in, perhaps we should go back to the house?"

Mary wanted to say, Go and write your music. Don't let anything stop you! Run away if you must!

But that would only have made him feel worse. She herself knew only too well that one had to put duty before personal desire. If there had been any other way to live with her conscience, she would at this very moment have been on her way to join Tate.

Alison covered the two sleeping babies and tiptoed out of the room. In the dining room the table was set, with candles waiting to be lit, fresh flowers in a china vase, the cutlery polished to a fine sheen. She had a joint of beef roasting in the oven, while on the stove an apple dumpling swathed in cheesecloth steamed in a large iron pot. The vegetables were prepared. A bottle of wine awaited transfer to the decanter.

Assuring herself that all was in readiness, she went into her bedroom to change into a becoming gown of pale blue, supported by several well-starched petticoats. After running a cologne-sprinkled hairbrush through her hair, she threaded a dark blue velvet ribbon through her shining locks.

Peering into the mirror, she pinched her cheeks to bring up the color. She was blessed with naturally red lips and so did not have to resort to dabbing them with cochineal, and her large widely spaced eyes had no need for kohl. Not that she would have hesitated to use any means, artificial or otherwise, to attract Stewart's attention. How she wished he would see her as a woman, a wife.

She loved Stewart to distraction, longed to be a real wife to him, wanted it so much it was torture to be near him and force herself to act like a sister. Surely he must see her love shining in her eyes? Could he not feel it?

But he was always so tired, so overworked, so worried. Perhaps when his father was back on his feet there would be more time to spend together and Stewart would notice the care she took with her appearance, the invitation in her glance, the softness that came over her when he was with her.

He had spent the previous day, a Sunday, at Riverleigh visiting his father. Alison knew Stewart had been dreading the ordeal, and she hoped that now it was over they would be able to spend a quiet evening relaxing over dinner, then talking together in front of the fire. Fortunately there was plenty to talk about.

Alison was learning a great deal about the shipping business simply by listening to Stewart talk about all of the problems he faced. He had brought a number of books home, as well as a large wall map of the world marked with the shipping lanes Fielding vessels plied, and she had studied these in order to be a more intelligent listener.

After he got all the problems of the day off his chest, they could have a nice glass of port. Alison was learning the upper-class habit of relaxing with a glass of wine, and she was also careful to emulate Stewart's table manners, even his accent. When his father recovered from his wounds and she was taken to be presented to him, she didn't want Stewart to be ashamed of her.

She was sure they were growing closer together. They were so at ease with each other, the best of friends really, able to talk about anything under the sun. Perhaps tonight when it came time to go to bed . . .

But she didn't let herself think of that. She had been disappointed too many times. If she smiled at him in a certain way or allowed her hand to brush against him, or even if she stood too close to him, he would acquire a dismayed, apologetic look that devastated her. Then he would move unobtrusively away, keeping his distance. It was as if he had drawn an invisible wall around himself and she was not allowed inside it.

This evening Stewart was even later than usual, and she knew the beef would be dry, the vegetables overcooked, and the dumpling soggy, but it was his expression of utter exhaustion and hopelessness that dismayed her the most.

"Oh, Stewart, you look so tired." She helped him off with his coat. "I hoped having a day off yesterday would do you good."

"A day with Father? You're joking!" He attempted a smile and kissed her cheek. He always managed a chaste peck on her cheek without touching any other part of her body.

She closed her eyes and drew a deep breath, inhaling his essence, wanting to turn her face so that their mouths might come together. But he had already moved away.

"I hope your dinner isn't ruined. I suppose the children are asleep by now? I so rarely see them nowadays. I'll just tiptoe into the nursery and tuck them in."

When he returned she was slicing the beef and reheating the gravy. "How was your father?"

"Angry, impatient, ranting and raving about everything, especially my incompetence."

"Oh, dear. I suppose he was angry about the two ships that were lost?"

"No, Mary advised me not to tell him about them. Father berated me on general principles, assuming—correctly—that I'm making a shambles of the company. I think perhaps part of his anger is directed at his own present weakness—and the fact that Vareck got away."

Stewart made a valiant effort to eat, but she could see he was simply too bone-weary. She suggested gently, "Perhaps you should go to bed early? Things won't look so hopeless in the morning."

"I can't. I have a valise full of work out in the hall. I must go over the accounts to try to determine which bills must be paid and which can wait. I must check the letters of credit and our cash receipts. I'm hopeless at arithmetic, but I can't rely on the clerks any longer; they've become lax because they know I'm such a dunce. I know they all stop working the moment I leave the office."

Alison considered for a moment, then reached a decision regarding something she had been thinking about for some time. She cleared her throat. "Stewart, when I was a little girl we lived over a grocery shop for a while. While my dad was away at sea, my mother used to help out in the shop, and sometimes I did, too, after I got home from school. The grocer had a terrible time keeping his books, so my mother used to help him. She was clever with figures. But she was expecting another baby and was very ill. . . . She died when the baby was born, and the poor little mite died a few days later."

She paused to blink away a tear, and Stewart reached across the table to squeeze her hand sympathetically.

"While she was ill she taught me to keep books. I can add and subtract and multiply and divide. I know my times tables, and I can balance a ledger. Stewart, why don't you go to bed and let me look at your accounts?"

He looked doubtful. "I appreciate the offer, Alison, but grocery shop receipts are hardly comparable to the kind of accounting necessary for a shipping line."

"Numbers are just numbers, whether they're in the tens or the hundreds or even the thousands. It's just a case of not being frightened of them, my mother used to say."

He smiled. "She must have been a remarkable woman, to have a daughter like you. I am very tired. . . . Perhaps I can make some sense of the figures in the morning. I will go to bed, and you're certainly welcome to look over the papers in my valise."

Alison quickly cleared away the dishes, took the cloth from the table, and spread the contents of the valise in front of her. She was so engrossed in her task that she didn't notice when the clock struck midnight, and continued to work into the early hours of the morning.

When Stewart awoke the next day, the sun was already high in the sky. He stumbled from his bedroom, half asleep and disoriented. "Why didn't you wake me? I should have been at the office hours ago!"

"You needed your rest," Alison said calmly. "Sit down and have your breakfast. I want to talk to you."

"But—"

She pointed to the kitchen table and gave him a stern glance. It was a look that brooked no nonsense, and had dealt with a pack of brothers before she used it on her first husband.

Stewart obediently pulled out a chair and sat down. After their marriage he had used a trust fund left by his grandfather to buy a house in Princes Park, a quiet suburb of tree-lined streets. The house had a tiny back garden for the children to play in, three bedrooms, and a box room upstairs, living and dining rooms downstairs, along with a spacious kitchen.

Alison tossed a couple of thick slices of ham into a cast-iron frying pan and reached for a bowl of eggs. "I went over the ledgers you brought home, and the balance sheets. I've marked the mistakes I found and made up a list of the invoices that have been outstanding the longest and should be paid. I've also written a letter to your debtors; you can have a clerk make as many copies as you need. If they don't pay up right away, we should have the company solicitor threaten them with debtors' court. More important, we've got to reassure your exporters that your ships will sail on time, so I've drafted a letter to the biggest agents and merchants."

She fried two eggs as she spoke, and Stewart blinked as he listened to her making plans to put the company in order.

"Now, I noticed on one of the invoices the exporter scribbled a note that his cargo didn't get to the ship on time because your clerk's letter ordering the goods forward didn't arrive soon enough for him to get his cargo packed and delivered to the docks before the sailing date. Even worse than that, one cargo was already in a warehouse on the Goree Piazza, but the warehouse manager wasn't notified to haul it down to the docks."

As she placed his breakfast plate of sizzling ham and eggs in front of him she said, "You didn't eat much dinner last night. Please try to finish this." She sat down with him and poured two cups of tea.

Stewart now saw that the contents of his valise were neatly stacked on one side of the kitchen table. A furtive glance at the sheet of paper lying on top of the pile revealed that it was a list of things to do, arranged in diminishing order from the most critical tasks to those that could safely wait.

"I want to go into the office and talk to your clerks, Stewart," she said.

He had a mouthful of ham and couldn't respond, but knew his eyes were bulging.

She went on quickly, "Please let me. I think I could talk to the men more on their own level than you can. You're . . . too much of a gentleman, Stewart. You never raise your voice. It's . . ." She'd been about to say it was one of the things she loved most about him, but stopped herself. "I've never met your father, but from what I've been told, under his gentlemanly skin there beats the heart of a brute and a bully. That's what his employees are used to and probably need."

Stewart smiled in spite of his alarm. "Alison, even if I agreed to such an unheard-of thing, which I shan't, I hardly see you as a brute and a bully!"

"Oh, you'd be surprised. I grew up in a houseful of lads—brothers that the sea scattered across the face of the earth, all gone, dead, or emigrated now—and I was the only girl. I've been dealing with bruisers and ruffians most of my life. Oh, after I was widowed and left alone to take care of Davey, I suppose I might have appeared a bit browbeaten, but it was just on the surface. Now that I'm Mrs. Stewart Fielding I'm going to fly my true colors again."

Stewart listened silently, undoubtedly wondering what had become of the soft-spoken servant he'd married, but Alison was too worried about him to be concerned about the impression she was making. She went on, "You see, Stewart, what you haven't grasped is that the clerks in your office need their jobs desperately. There are plenty of bright young men waiting to take their places."

She took a long-handled fork down from the wall beside the fireplace, speared a slice of bread, and held it toward the glowing coals in the fireplace. "Now, the way I look at it, you've got the right idea with the crews of the ships. If you treat them better than the other owners do, you won't have to use crimps—sailors will fight to get on your ships. But you'll need good officers, especially the first mates; they can make or break a crew, my dad used to say."

She buttered his toast and placed a dish of ginger marmalade on the table. He munched silently, digesting all she had said. Her hand slid across the table and rested on his arm. "Just give me a chance. Let me go into the city with you today. Just from talking to you I feel I know how your office is run. I can almost see what each of the clerks looks like. At least let me be there to help you. I won't open my mouth if you don't want me to."

He was weakening; she could sense it. He said hesitantly, "But what about the children?"

Alison hid her triumphant smile. "I've already talked to Mrs. Hughes next door. She's lonely since she lost her husband, and she says she'd be glad to watch them for me."

"Lord, what would Father say, if he knew?"

"He's not really in a position to say anything, one way or the other, is he? It sounds to me as if he and Mr. Ivers ran the company without giving much responsibility or authority to anybody else. Now they're both out of the picture and it's up to you."

Placing his knife and fork side by side in the center of his plate, Stewart rose to his feet. "I'd appreciate your help, Alison, although I wish I didn't need it."

She flung her arms around him and hugged him. It seemed to her that perhaps he didn't pull away as quickly as he usually did. But perhaps she held him too tightly to allow him to escape.

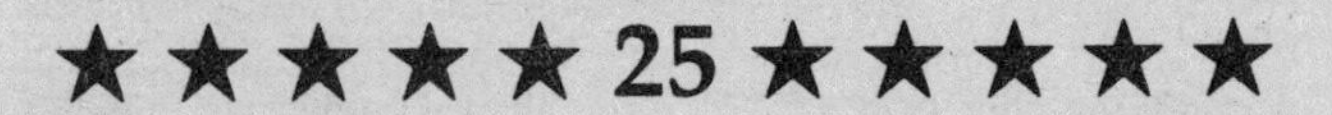

25

THE DEL CASTILLO sons, Eduardo and Felipe, prowled restlessly about the interior courtyard of the hacienda, dark eyes regarding Bethany with the resentment of active young men who longed to be following more exciting pursuits than memorizing English words they never expected to have to use. Their sister Teresa, knowing that her parents were calling on the padre at the mission, had already rudely departed.

"*Por favor, señores, escúcheme!*" Bethany said, not believing for a moment that they would listen to her. Still, she repeated the English question slowly: "What is the name of this town?"

The younger of the two sons, Felipe, dutifully repeated the question. His brother glared at him and muttered, "*Quiero irme.*"

Bethany sighed. She was learning more Spanish than they were learning English. "Very well, both of you may go," she said. She noticed that they had no problem understanding this particular English phrase, so perhaps some of her patient teaching was having the desired effect. They raced off, calling to their personal servants to have their horses saddled immediately.

She sat on the tiled edge of the fountain, content for a moment to enjoy the solitude. A whisper of a breeze stirred the bougainvillea vines, sending a shower of brilliant orange and purple petals swirling about her head. The sound of running water provided a cooling background melody to the singing of a pair of vivid yellow birds who serenaded each other on a gnarled olive branch. How languidly the months had drifted by since she came to the del Castillo hacienda. She never tired of the endless days of sunshine, and when she wasn't trying to teach English to the reluctant offspring of her hosts, she also enjoyed the warmth of the Californios, as she learned the Spanish settlers were called.

The moment of tranquillity was interrupted by the tolling of the chapel bell, and she recognized the signal that a ship was approaching the bay. The *Liberty* must have been sighted coming around the point, since she was due back any time. Bethany stood up and walked to the wrought-iron gate leading to the cliff top.

She looked forward to being able to converse wholly in English again, although she and Jack Cutler argued more often than they actually conversed. He and Tom had been back twice to pick up hides, and both times Jack had demanded that she leave with them. The last time she'd been afraid he might throw her over his shoulder and haul her forcibly aboard the ship.

As she walked along the cliff toward the point overlooking the bay, she considered again how different Jack was from her beloved Neil, who had surely spoiled her for every other man on earth. Not even his brother Tom possessed Neil's kindness and compassion, his gentleness and understanding. A tear welled up and she brushed it away. Would the pain never end?

The longboat was already skimming toward the beach by the time she reached the point. Several vaqueros had already ridden over to watch the arrival of the sailors, and Bethany heard the labored breathing of Rosa as she came lumbering up the slope behind her. Rosa, who was Teresa's personal maid, was undoubtedly outraged that Bethany had taken it upon herself to go to meet the sailors without a chaperone.

Bethany slowed her pace to allow the plump and aging Rosa to catch up. She muttered disapprovingly in Spanish, and Bethany pretended not to understand.

She stood on the point, the breeze billowing her skirts and ruffling her hair. Below on the beach the men had pulled the boat onto the sand, and Jack paused to look up at her. His hair was blue-black in the sunlight, his face darkly tanned. He and Tom both seemed bigger, more muscular, undoubtedly as a result of their months of seafaring. They made their way up the cliff by way of a narrow trail, moving with the surefooted ease of men accustomed to the heaving deck of a ship and the precarious footholds of shrouds and yardarms.

Tom reached her first and seized her hands in his, drawing

her close to kiss her cheek. "Hello, Bethany. You look wonderfully well, thank God. We have some news for you."

"My daughter!" she exclaimed, feeling herself turn numb with anticipation. "You've learned something about my daughter?"

Jack had now reached them, and she looked from one to the other, suddenly apprehensive at the expression on his face.

"Dammit, Tom," Jack exclaimed, "I thought we agreed not to blurt it out the second we saw her."

"I was just going to tell her about our next voyage," Tom protested. "I haven't said anything about her child."

Bethany almost screamed, "*What* about my child? Tell me!"

"We don't know anything yet," Jack said quickly. "But we may have news for you in a few months. We met an old friend of Tom's in Monterey. He was aboard a British ship that had sailed from the Sandwich Isles and is now on her way home to England."

"We've asked him to find out what happened to your baby, where she is now," Tom put in. "We can trust him, Bethany. I'm sure he'll learn her whereabouts for you."

Her heart had begun to race. If only it could be true! "How long will it be before we hear from him?"

"I told you not to get her all excited prematurely," Jack said. "Bethany, it could be months, even years. Who can tell? We don't know how long it will take him to find out what became of her, and even after he has some news, there'll be a long wait for a letter to reach New Orleans."

"New Orleans? Why can't his letter come here, to me?"

Jack took her arm and slipped it through his. "Let's walk back to the hacienda. We've too much to talk about to stand here in the open and settle matters."

They walked back toward the *casa grande,* with Ned following and Rosa grumbling along beside him. Tom fell into step beside Bethany, and unlike Jack he couldn't wait to tell her that they had now effected all necessary repairs to the *Liberty* and would sail her around the Horn, eventually taking her to New Orleans. No longer content with the random trading of the Mexican territory, and unable to trade in Oregon because of the British presence there, Tom was eager to move on to the American ports of the Gulf with its Caribbean trading and the East Coast's transatlantic trade, markets he'd learned about from his father's shipping company.

As they reached the gates of the hacienda Tom said, "You

must come with us, Bethany. We won't be coming back again. We're going to take one more cargo of hides up to Yerba Buena, and then we'll provision for the long voyage around the Horn."

"Leona has decided to come with us," Jack put in. "She found Yerba Buena too tame for her taste."

Bethany stopped walking and turned to face them. "No, I'm sorry. I won't come with you. How could I possibly support myself in New Orleans? Here I have gainful employment and a pleasant place to live."

"*Temporary* employment and a temporary place to live," Jack pointed out.

"Not at all. Even after my tutorial duties are completed, the senora has invited me to remain for as long as I wish, as her companion. She knows about my little girl in England and will welcome her also. When my daughter joins me, my life will be as perfect as it can be without my dear Neil."

Jack made an exasperated sound. "How can we make you understand that you're even less safe here than you were in the penal colony? The days of the Californios are numbered. If Mexico doesn't kick them out of the territory, and if the Indians don't slaughter them, the Americans will eventually cast covetous eyes toward the Pacific, and the Mexicans will fight. In any event, you will be in terrible danger."

They had now reached the portico of the *casa grande,* and Bethany felt the tranquillity of the hacienda surround her. Surely these stout walls could withstand any danger. The Indians who worked on the rancho were all gentle people, and although she had heard of the wild tribes of nomads who wandered the territory, surely the del Castillo vaqueros with their muskets could hold off arrow-wielding Indians?

Jack was surely exaggerating the possibility of war between the Americans and Mexicans, and the *patrón* had assured her that the Mexican government would honor his land grant from Spain. She decided that Jack would say anything to persuade her to leave, because he wanted her to accompany them to New Orleans. He was simply trying to frighten her. Well, she had endured too much to give up the peace she now enjoyed.

Just before they went inside to be greeted by the del Castillos she whispered, "Nothing you can say will make me change my mind. But I do hope you will stop here on your way to New Orleans, so that I can see Leona again."

"Be ready to leave with us when we return," Jack said grimly. "Because we're not leaving you behind."

The day after the *Liberty* sailed on her last voyage to Yerba Buena, Teresa was unaccustomedly polite and eager to please Bethany during her English lesson. The reason for this soon became apparent.

"There is to be a fiesta at the hacienda of my aunt and uncle, which is a day's journey from here. My parents and brothers cannot attend because some men are coming from Mexico City to talk about our land grant. Rosa complains that she is too old and her bones ache too much for the journey. I must have a chaperone, or I cannot go. I want you to come with me."

"When is the fiesta to take place?" Bethany asked, wondering if she might not even be here when the *Liberty* returned, which would spare her an argument with Jack and Tom, but deprive her of a chance to see Leona again. The prospect of spending time alone with the petulant Teresa was not terribly appealing, but she could hardly refuse the request if the senora also asked her to act as chaperone.

Teresa's dark eyes flashed in triumph, now that she felt certain she would not miss the party. "We shall leave next week, and good manners demand that we stay several days."

When the senora expressed her wish that Bethany accompany her daughter, Bethany wondered if either the del Castillos or fate had decreed that she would return to the hacienda a few days after the departure of the *Liberty* for New Orleans.

They set off for the hacienda of Señor del Castillo's brother the following week, traveling in a covered wagon loaded with a formidable amount of baggage.

With a driver and a guard in the wagon and three vaqueros, one of whom rode ahead to scout their route through the rough terrain, Bethany felt quite safe. Teresa, however, expected the feared *Indios* to appear over every ridge and did not relax until they arrived at her uncle's hacienda.

Bethany was greeted warmly, but here no one spoke English and with her limited Spanish she felt very foreign and isolated. Dutifully staying close to Teresa, who seemed to have forgotten every English word she'd ever learned, Bethany was glad when the day of the fiesta at last arrived.

Friends, neighbors, and relatives had journeyed for many miles, and the festivities lasted all day and night and continued the following day, leaving Bethany exhausted, her smile pasted to her face. Since she still wore her mourning gown she was not asked to join in the dancing, but keeping track of Teresa meant chasing her outside frequently when she slipped away with one of the handsome young caballeros who flocked about her.

Teresa then slept for two days and a night, and Bethany whiled away the hours feeling out of place and useless.

Bethany was greatly relieved when eventually the visit came to an end and they loaded clothes and gifts into the wagon and set off on the return journey.

The weather had become unbearably hot and a fierce dry wind blew from the inland deserts, carrying the pungent scent of sagebrush, stirring dust clouds, and slowing the progress of their horses on the unprotected higher ridges.

Just before they reached the hills separating the inland valley from the coastal plain where the del Castillo rancho was situated, a whirling cloud of dust swept through the canyons and engulfed them.

Their driver reined in the horses, and the two outriders came galloping back toward them, yelling to the men in the wagon to take shelter from a sandstorm blowing up from a nearby canyon.

"*Ah! No me gusta. Es malo!*" Teresa exclaimed tearfully as a gust of wind lifted the canvas covering the wagon and she was peppered with stinging sand. Bethany grabbed the flapping canvas and tied it down.

For the next few minutes the vaqueros were busy tying up the horses and covering the heads of the animals with blankets to protect them from the wind-driven sand. They then turned their attention to the wagon, pulling it into the shelter of a cluster of boulders. After that there was nothing to do but wait for the wind to drop and the cloud of sand to subside.

Teresa fingered her rosary beads and prayed. When Bethany attempted to reassure her that the sandstorm would soon pass, the young girl screamed a torrent of Spanish into the howling wind and Bethany caught the gist of her fears. Apparently it was not uncommon when the "devil wind" blew for a single spark, from a gunshot or a flash of lightning or a carelessly extinguished campfire, to ignite the summer-dry chapparal and send a brushfire raging down the hillsides, burning everything in its path.

The whirling sand had now blocked out most of the sunlight

and in the eerie amber light within the wagon Bethany saw that the four men and Teresa were huddled under serapes despite the heat. She realized then that a choking pall of dust was seeping in through the canvas, and she held her handkerchief over her mouth and nose.

Teresa shrieked again as the wagon rocked violently under the assault of the wind. Bethany reached for her hand and held it tightly, feeling the rosary clutched in Teresa's fingers.

Minutes dragged by, then hours. To Bethany's surprise, after a time Teresa lay down on the floor of the wagon and slept. Bethany covered her with a serape, making a tent over her face to allow her to breathe while keeping out the dust.

Bethany knew they were on the del Castillo rancho, not more than a few miles from the hacienda, where the stout adobe walls would offer protection. But to reach the hacienda they would first have to climb to the top of the hill and then travel through the pass, which would serve as a funnel for the blowing sand. So near and yet so far, Bethany reflected.

It suddenly occurred to her that only four of the men were present. The scout had not returned. She assumed he had taken shelter somewhere when the sandstorm caught up with him, but with the howling of the wind it was impossible to question the other men about the missing vaquero.

After a time she had to cover her eyes to protect them from the dust. She felt isolated, helpless.

Late that afternoon the wind dropped and gradually the blowing dust and sand settled. Bethany's throat was sore, her mouth dry, her lips cracked. Teresa awoke, groaning. Bethany found the water flasks and they drank thirstily. The men climbed out of the wagon to tend to the horses.

Bethany wet her handkerchief and wiped the dust from her face. She could see that Teresa's hair appeared brown rather than black, as it was so thickly filmed with sand.

As the howling of the wind faded to a low moan, a different sound made itself heard. Teresa clutched Bethany's arm and the two women listened. They could hear the tolling of the chapel bell in the del Castillo hacienda.

Feeling the fear communicated by Teresa's clutching hand, Bethany tried to find the Spanish words to reassure her, to tell her that perhaps the bell was merely moving in the wind, but she knew the steady toll was a signal that terrified Teresa.

One of the vaqueros appeared, his dust-filmed face tight with worry beneath his sombrero. He spoke rapidly in Spanish.

"Señor, más despacio, por favor," Bethany begged. She had to know what the signal meant. He repeated what he had said, more slowly, and she understood that not only was there trouble at the hacienda, but unfortunately their own horses had broken loose during the storm and run away. The vaqueros were going to try to find them and the women should remain where they were.

Bethany watched as the men set off on foot to find the horses. A prickly warning sensation plucked at her spine and she could not bear to be enclosed in the confining wagon.

"Let's get out," she said to Teresa, whose head was bent over her rosary as she prayed frantically for deliverance, but from what Bethany did not know. They had come through the storm and surely the horses could not have got far with blankets tied over their heads.

"Come on," she said firmly. "We need some air and we can climb up on those rocks and perhaps see where the men are."

She had to force Teresa to leave the sanctuary of the wagon, but once outside immediately felt better, although in the arid heat her flesh felt as if it were burning. She scrambled up the rocky side of the canyon to a ridge that afforded a view of the pass leading through the hills to the hacienda.

The moment she reached the ridge she saw the plume of black smoke that rose against the yellow sky, and there was no mistaking what that ominous column meant. Fire. Bethany felt her throat constrict still further.

Teresa, who had followed her up the slope, saw it, too. Her hand flew to her mouth and her eyes were wide with terror. "Madre de Dios!"

For one second Bethany hoped that perhaps a spark-induced brush fire had caused the smoke, but she knew that it rose from the cultivated fields near the hacienda, not from the wild hills, and from the concentration and density of the smoke she knew it could only mean that a building was on fire. Now the frantic tolling of the chapel bell became clear. It had been a distress signal.

A flurry of dust in the valley below caught Bethany's attention and as it drew closer she saw that their scout was returning. There was no sign of the other men, who were searching for the horses.

Teresa's sobbing was now becoming hysterical. Bethany seized her arm and shook her. "Teresa, calm down, please. Look—the scout is coming back. Let's go to meet him. He'll know how close to the hacienda the fire is."

Gripping Teresa's hand firmly, Bethany pulled her down the rocky slope. The scout thundered toward them, his horse lathered, his face grim.

"*Indios!* They have burned the hacienda!" he yelled before he reached them.

Teresa slid to the ground in a dead faint.

26

STEWART WAS BOTH awed and dismayed when Alison marched into the offices of the Fielding Shipping Company and accomplished more in a matter of days than he had been able to achieve in weeks.

At first the clerks had not taken seriously the presence of a woman within their all-male ranks. Stewart knew, too, that his own already tenuous grip on the reins of the company was further weakened by allowing his wife to peer over shoulders, rifle files, and ask penetrating questions. Why, she even went to the docks and warehouses to look at waiting cargoes, demanded that he take her on a tour of one of the packets, probed to learn every aspect of the business of sending ships laden with cargoes and passengers all over the world.

"They're whispering about us," Stewart told Alison miserably. "It just isn't proper for you to show such an interest in the ships. They think I'm a weakling and a fool for allowing it."

"Then let them know who is the boss," Alison said. "Dismiss your chief clerk, who should have been taking better care of your interests, and send a couple of the others packing, too. Inform the lot of them that I'm going to be looking over their shoulders for as long as is necessary and that you won't tolerate a word of disapproval from any of them."

Stewart was aghast. "Dismiss Tunstall? He's been with Father forever."

"Then he should have shown greater loyalty to you and to

the company," Alison said shortly. "The two young fellows in the corner spend most of their time talking to each other. Get rid of them, too."

She opened his valise. "I've roughed out some letters I want written and hand-delivered today. As soon as we sort out the office, you and I are going to call on all the importers and exporters on Water Street. Then we're going to the warehouses. . . ." She rattled off plans for a day's work that would have daunted even his father.

Stewart expected the men they called on that day to laugh him out of their offices, but Alison briefed him on what to say before they arrived, then remained silent and sedate during the visit. He presented her, and she sat in a corner of the office, hands folded demurely on her lap, smiling in a distant, patient sort of way, apparently not listening to what was said. Afterward she analyzed the conversation and told him precisely how to obtain business from that particular shipper.

On repeat visits it was clear that some of them were enchanted by her. Stewart noticed that their eyes would drift in her direction even as he was obtaining from them promises of cargoes at outrageously high freight rates.

After a while he began to see her as the import-export merchants saw her. Her chestnut hair gleamed in a smooth coil beneath a pretty forest green bonnet, her hazel eyes expressed an appealing shyness and were quickly lowered when confronted by a direct male gaze. Her figure was womanly, with a tiny waist and a swelling bosom that her braid-trimmed jacket modestly covered but did not quite conceal. Her complexion was flawless, as clear and lovely as lily petals, and her mouth was full-lipped, soft, and vulnerable. Since she allowed him to do all the talking, no one noticed that her pronunciation of certain words was unabashedly working class, although she strove conscientiously to eliminate that telltale clue to her origins. But at first glance she appeared to be a perfect lady, impeccably dressed and groomed, her demeanor befitting her new station in life.

False colors, Stewart thought. She looked feminine and sweet, but in business at least, she was as hard as nails.

As the days passed he learned that her presence at his side was taken by the merchants and shipping agents as a sign that as newlyweds they couldn't bear to be apart and the pretty Mrs. Fielding merely accompanied her husband in order to spend more time with him. She certainly didn't make a nuisance of herself, sitting quietly while Stewart Fielding conducted his business with a lot more shrewdness than anyone had previously given him credit for. Only the Fielding clerks knew the truth of the situation, and they kept their mouths shut about who was running the business, for fear they might otherwise find themselves without a job, like Tunstall and the others.

After Alison insisted upon seeing for herself the warehouses where the various shippers fought for space for their incoming and outgoing cargoes, she further astonished him by announcing, "You need your own warehouse and a good manager to run it. It would be an investment that would make shipments easier to handle and in the long run not only save money but give you an advantage over your competitors. Speed of handling, speed in getting cargoes and passengers to their destinations—that's what people want, and that's what we must give them."

"I'm not sure Father would agree to lay out more capital just now," Stewart said nervously.

"Your father is incapacitated," Alison said briskly. "He's given you free rein. We'll find a warehouse that perhaps needs fixing up a bit. I saw one on the Goree that needs a new roof, and the back wall could do with being painted. We'll offer them a small amount down and pay the rest in installments."

"Well, we'll see . . ." Stewart said, thunderstruck by the transformation that had taken place in his wife. Was this hardheaded businesswoman that same gentle nanny who had so lovingly cared for two babies, and whom he'd rescued from the clutches of Mrs. Creel?

Alison actually seemed to revel in the world of ships and crews and cargoes. If it had not been for the children, he doubted he would ever have been able to get her to go home. She seemed possessed of unlimited energy and stamina, welcomed problems and challenges that threw him into a panic. He had a mental image of her rolling up her sleeves and plunging willingly into the daily grind of work that had crushed his spirit.

Among the Fielding Company clerks, there was no doubt that Alison was now in charge of the office; yet miraculously no one outside the company became aware of this. Stewart supposed his clerks were too ashamed to admit they answered to a woman. The lovely Mrs. Fielding was considered a little eccentric in that she liked to visit her husband at work and frequently was seen about town with him, calling on merchants, riding with him in his carriage to the warehouse he'd bought on the Goree Piazza.

But the men smiled indulgently because she was a woman in love, and Stewart Fielding was a lucky young man to have a beautiful woman adore him so, even if she did intrude upon his working day.

Gradually Stewart accepted his wife's participation in the company, was grateful that she relieved him of so many decisions and burdens, and found that he again had time for his music. This fact alone prevented him from requesting that she go home where she belonged.

He admired Alison and was proud of her; indeed he was extremely fond of her; but he was very, very glad that their marriage was in name only, since surely no man could compete with her when it came to running a business. And, feeling inferior in that regard, how could any man ever have made love to her?

Shortly after they acquired the new warehouse Stewart began to interview prospective managers and Alison insisted upon being present, although she let him ask the questions. Toward the end of a long and tedious day of interviews, their new head clerk, an earnest young man named Formby, announced that another candidate for the position had arrived, but perhaps they would prefer not to see this one.

"Why? What's wrong with him?" Stewart asked.

"Well, sir, he's a former seaman and, well . . ." Formby broke off, clearing his throat in an embarrassed way. "He is missing uh . . . one of his limbs."

"Send him in," Alison said. "None of the others were capable of doing the work."

They heard the distinctive sound of a wooden peg striking the floor, along with a heavy footfall; then the man was shown into the private office.

He'd lost his leg at the knee, but after one embarrassed glance at the wooden peg protruding from beneath his trouser leg Stewart was more daunted by the man's immense height, brawny arms that looked quite capable of crushing a man to death, and glowering countenance that seemed to defy anyone to cross him. He could have been any age from thirty to fifty, with a darkly tanned skin and faded blue eyes that seemed to emit steel sparks. Somewhere at the back of Stewart's mind hovered the thought that in the unlikely event he were to hire this man, he would have acquired his own Vareck.

"Please take a seat, Mr. . . ." Stewart said, wishing Alison wasn't in the room. She sat near the window, idly turning the large wooden globe on its axis, and seemed less distressed by the man's appearance than most women would have been.

"Rudd," the man responded, taking the chair in front of Stewart's desk and lowering himself into it carefully as though afraid it might break under his weight. "Hagen Rudd."

Stewart cleared his throat. "Tell me about yourself."

"I was master of my own ship, a whaler. Lost her on a coral reef in the South Pacific. Lost my leg to a shark. The owner wouldn't give me another ship; he thought a one-legged skipper couldn't command men. So I sailed as an ordinary seaman, and three ships went down under me. One caught fire, another ran aground, and the third capsized in a gale. I got the reputation of being a Jonah, and nobody wanted to sail with me. The owner, God bless him, felt sorry for me, and found me work in a warehouse in the port of London. I can read and write and keep books, and I was soon managing the warehouse. Until it burned to the ground. Since then I've not been able to find work because superstitious men believe I'm cursed."

Rudd paused. "If you'll give me a chance, I'll work for nothing but a meal a day and a place in the warehouse to sleep until I've proved myself to you."

Stewart had listened in growing dismay to Rudd's recital of disasters and was about to decline the man's offer when Alison rose to her feet and said, "Done. You're hired. We'll give you a three-month trial. Can you start right away?"

"Alison, I don't think—" Stewart began.

Rudd turned to look at Alison and for a moment they stared, each taking the measure of the other. Then Rudd said, "I can start right away. But after a month I'll need to be paid wages. If I haven't proved my worth by then, there'll be no point in my hanging around for another two months, will there?"

"Very well. But in view of your history, my husband will wait until the month's trial is over to discuss your wages," Alison replied. She turned to Stewart. "Perhaps one of the clerks could take Mr. Rudd to the warehouse?"

Stewart, flushed with mortification, rang the bell on his desk to summon a clerk. Alison had gone too far this time, but he was too much of a gentleman to argue with her in front of the man. He instructed the clerk to provide a pallet for the man to sleep on and buy him a meal from the pie shop.

"We have a man clearing the warehouse in readiness for our first cargo," he told Rudd. "He can show you around."

After Rudd departed, his wooden leg thumping across the floor in the wake of a wide-eyed clerk, Stewart regarded Alison with a pained expression. "I wish you hadn't done that. We should at least have checked the truth of his story and obtained references from his previous employers."

"I believe what he said. No one would make up such a story. You surely don't believe in that nonsense about bad luck following some people, do you?"

"No, of course not, but we can't simply entrust valuable cargoes to a man we know so little about."

"With his past, he'll be so grateful to get a job he'll work twice as hard as anyone else and be four times as loyal. You'll see. Besides, we can use a month's grace before we have to pay his wages. By then we'll have collected some old debts."

"That's another thing I don't like. Gentlemen don't make threats in order to collect debts."

"Perhaps gentlemen would rather be bankrupt?" Alison asked with unexpected sarcasm.

An awkward silence fell. Stewart was too stunned to speak, and Alison's mouth was set in a tight, angry line. She picked up the manifest of a newly arrived vessel and walked over to a table set against a wall, which she had been using as a desk. He saw her finger move swiftly down the page as she checked the items with a speed that astonished him. She then flipped quickly through a number of invoices, checking totals. Whereas he had to struggle with figures, Alison seemed to have a natural mathematic ability. She also had an extremely good memory and an orderliness to her thoughts and actions that permitted her to organize the work and get it done. Before she began to accompany him to the office Stewart had wasted a great deal of time agonizing over what to tackle first.

He stared at the back of her head, at the shining coil of chestnut hair, the erect posture, the immaculate white collar of her dark blue gown. Her worktable was tidy, but stacked high with papers. His own desk was almost bare. He felt useless, helpless, and more than a little demeaned.

"Why am I even here?" he asked at length, his tone despairing, even to him.

But she misunderstood his meaning and replied absently, without looking up. "You don't have to stay. I can take care of the office if you have to go somewhere."

Stewart wanted to tell her that her attitude was not feminine, that she belonged at home with the children, that she was saving the company but destroying him. But of course he could say none of these things. All he could do was take his leave, knowing that she was perfectly capable of running the business without any assistance from him.

At the door he paused and looked back at her as she set aside the invoices and picked up a provision list for a long voyage to China.

"Why don't you move all of that to my desk?" he said wearily. "You'll have more space in which to work."

Alison dropped to her knees to hug Davey and Hope. The two children clung to her, pressing sticky kisses all over her face. Davey chattered about his day while Hope tried to turn her baby babble into real words. Alison looked up at Mrs. Hughes, who stood in the hall watching the children greet her. They were already in their night attire.

"I'm sorry I'm so late," Alison said. She sat on the floor and took the pins from her hat, which was borne triumphantly to the hall stand by Davey. "We had to interview managers for the warehouse. It put us behind all day. But you should have gone home as soon as Stewart arrived. He loves to take care of the children. Is he in his study?"

Mrs. Hughes, a motherly woman who should have had a large family of her own but who was a childless widow, looked embarrassed. "Your husband isn't home yet, Alison. I thought he'd come with you."

"Oh," Alison said, nonplussed. She began to unbutton her coat while still sitting on the floor with Hope climbing into her lap. "Did the charwoman come today?"

"Yes. She finished early, so I told her to clean the silver."

"I've been thinking I should hire somebody full time."

"Not to take care of the bairns, please!" Mrs. Hughes had been a McDougall before marriage, and hints of the Highlands still crept into her speech occasionally, especially when she was excited or upset.

Alison stood up and swung Hope up into her arms. "As long as you want to take care of them, I'm more than happy to have you do so; they're so fond of you. But I feel guilty that I asked you to come in for a few days and here we are almost two months later—"

"This has been the best time of my life, at least since my husband died," Mrs. Hughes assured her. "They're little angels, both of them. No trouble at all."

"But I'm gone so much I do need a full-time maid. It would be easier for you, too, as she could help with the children."

Mrs. Hughes gave her a worried frown. "It's none of my business, but . . . are you doing the right thing, do you think?"

"I have no other choice just now," Alison said shortly. She didn't feel inclined to defend her actions to Mrs. Hughes, too. What a blessing it was that Stewart, at least, was grateful for her help. Nor had he questioned her too closely about how she had learned so much about business matters. Her explanation that she had picked up the rudiments of arithmetic when her mother helped out the grocer was true, but Alison had neglected to mention a more recent apprenticeship to the world of commerce. The pharmacist who had taken care of her and Davey after she was widowed had often brought his books and records with him and liked to grumble at length about his employees and customers and the means he used to deal with them. It was from him that she learned most of what she knew. She had often wondered if in exhibiting such a knack for figures, as well as making several comments about what to her were obvious errors on the part of the pharmacist in his business dealings, she had frightened him into discarding her. But fortunately Stewart wasn't like that.

She glanced at the grandfather clock in the hall. Almost nine o'clock. Where could he be?

Stewart leaned back in his seat, closed his eyes, and lost himself in the soaring strains of Beethoven's Fifth Symphony, feeling an exultation that seemed to restore and renew his spirit, which he was sure had begun to atrophy for need of musical nourishment. He felt like a starving man gorging himself on an unexpected feast, wanting to grab the melody out of the very air around him, and hold it reverently in his hands.

After leaving the office he had dined alone at a small café on Castle Street, then strolled through the city. He didn't want to go home and face Alison because he felt the time had come to tell her that she could no longer participate in his business, that she should return to her duties as wife and mother. But how could he possibly tell her this?

Finding himself in front of the concert hall as carriages arrived to discharge patrons, on a whim he had decided to buy a ticket.

Now the music built to a crescendo, along with his euphoria. The symphony resonated in his head, a memory of intense pleasure, even after it ended and the orchestra left the stage for the interval.

In a pleasant haze, Stewart wandered out into the foyer and ordered a brandy. He was so completely relaxed that several minutes passed before he felt a twinge of conscience. In the last hectic months there had been time for nothing but work, for Alison as well as himself. Why hadn't he suggested they ask Mrs. Hughes to stay one evening so that the two of them could go out to dinner and attend a concert? How nice it would be now to have a late supper together and discuss the music. But would Alison have agreed? He doubted it. On the rare occasions when she was not engrossed in shipping business, she wanted to be with the children. There simply wasn't time for anything else.

"Stewart—Stewart Fielding?" a woman's voice beside him said.

He looked around to see a vaguely familiar face. The young woman was about his age and she was pretty with a vivacious smile and sparkling green eyes that regarded him flirtatiously from beneath long, lustrous eyelashes. She wore a magnificent white satin gown, the bodice of which was decorated with sparkling crystal beads that echoed the glitter of the diamonds encircling her throat and highlighting her platinum-pale hair. The full sleeves and bell skirt of her gown showed off a tiny waist, and, with her diminutive size, she was like a lovely, fragile porcelain doll.

"You don't remember me, do you?" she asked, dimpling. "Perhaps I've changed too much? The Oxford and Cambridge boat race? My brother was on the crew, and he introduced us. I'm Arthur Holloway's sister, Iris."

"Good gracious! Little Iris who fell into the river?"

They both chuckled, remembering the boat race four years earlier. Stewart said, "You've certainly grown up since then, Miss Holloway."

"Oh, please call me Iris. We can hardly be formal after you saw me in my wet drawers, can we?" Her laughter was like the pealing of bells, joyous, infectious.

Stewart smiled, although he had never heard a properly

brought up young lady mention her drawers before. "What are you doing in Liverpool?"

Iris gave a comical scowl. "Staying with the most dreadful aunt! Arthur's in the army, you know, and he's abroad. I'm not sure if you recall that Daddy's with the East India Company and we lost Mother many years ago. After Arthur left the country too, I was packed off to Aunt Elspeth." She glanced over her shoulder. "I must be careful; she's here with me but had to answer the call of nature."

Blinking, Stewart cast about for something to say. Not only did this outspoken young woman speak of her drawers, but she went so far as to mention bodily functions that no one even hinted about in polite society.

"The old harridan will have a purple fit if she sees me talking to you." Iris opened a beaded purse dangling from her wrist and pulled out a folded pamphlet. "I'm giving a piano recital for charity on Sunday afternoon. Please come. I have some wild tales to tell you about Arthur's adventures in the army."

"You're a pianist?" Stewart was intrigued.

"Quite a good one, as a matter of fact. I studied in London and Vienna . . . Oops! There's Aunt Elspeth. Must run. Please come on Sunday."

She was gone, disappearing into a procession of people making their way back into the auditorium for the rest of the concert. Stewart looked down at the pamphlet in his hand: "Miss Iris Holloway will play a selection of Chopin's sonatas, etudes, and nocturnes, Sunday afternoon at three o'clock at the home of Mr. and Mrs. . . ."

Chopin, Stewart thought longingly, in the moment before he asked himself why he had not announced immediately that he was now married.

27

MARY HANDED HER husband's doctor a glass of sherry, then glanced over her shoulder to be sure the library door was closed. "Doctor, I must talk to you about the problem I mentioned a few weeks ago, because it's becoming worse."

He nodded. "Yes, I noticed. He couldn't remember your name. And he became confused when I asked about his ships, as though he couldn't remember owning ships."

"Stewart came to see him to discuss business, bringing good news—the company is financially solvent, even expanding. He wanted to ask his father about buying a new vessel to replace one that was lost. But Adrian looked at him blankly and, after he left, asked me, 'Who was that young man?' I'm so worried, Doctor. What is happening to my husband? Is this memory loss a result of the infection of his wounds and that terrible fever he had?"

"The condition does sometimes come on following a lung infection such as the one Sir Adrian had," the doctor answered carefully, clearly uncomfortable discussing the matter with her. For several weeks he'd pleaded urgent appointments to keep, and hurried away immediately after seeing Adrian. But today Mary was determined to get to the bottom of the mysterious malady that seemed to have destroyed much of Adrian's memory.

"And how long will this condition last?"

"That's difficult to say."

"My husband is certainly not old enough for us to worry about senility, is he?"

The doctor studied his wineglass with ferocious concentration. "There is a condition called *pre*senile dementia, which seems to advance more rapidly and be more severe than the dementia that comes on in old age. I very much regret that there are some indications that this may be the case with your husband."

"But he seems to be all right sometimes. He spoke at length of his first wife the other day and remembered incidents when his sons were young."

"That is not uncommon, Lady Fielding; the memory of recent events seems to disappear first. I've noticed, too, on my visits that his moods swing between violent aggression and complete apathy."

Mary felt a prick of fear. "His table manners have become atrocious. He insisted on eating in the dining room last evening, but . . ." She didn't describe the mess Adrian had made, flinging food on the floor and smashing dishes without any provocation whatsoever.

"Have you noticed any impairment in his hearing or vision, in addition to his mental confusion?"

She shook her head. "No. But . . . his personal hygiene . . ."

"Quite so. I'm afraid we can't rule out the possibility that presenile dementia exists. I strongly recommend that you hire a nurse immediately—a good strong young man who has, if possible, had some experience with such patients."

"But you must cure him!" Mary protested.

"I'm sorry, Lady Fielding. There is no cure. The condition will become progressively worse."

"Dear God! What must we expect?"

The doctor squirmed before her pleading gaze. "Let us not cross our bridges before we come to them."

"You must answer my question. I have a right to know what the future holds in store for my husband—and for me."

He drained his glass. "There will be increased stiffness of his muscles; his movements will become slow and awkward. His intellectual capacities will deteriorate until he loses all ability to think, speak, and move."

Mary collapsed against the back of her chair, the room spinning. The next thing she knew 'he doctor was standing beside her, holding her hand and patting her wrist. "You need a strong young man to look after him," he repeated. "Sir Adrian might well live ten years or longer in the most advanced state of dependency."

The doctor's voice droned on, a recital of contradictions. This might or might not happen. This might help, but possibly would not. Mary was no longer listening. Her fingers slid into the pocket concealed in the side seam of her skirt, closing around the folded envelope that contained Tate's latest letter.

In it he had jokingly suggested that if Adrian didn't get back on his feet soon, when next Mary and Tate met they might well be silver-haired old dodderers rolling toward each other in bath chairs in some old-age home.

The doctor took his leave and Mary locked herself in her room and wept—for Adrian, for his sons, for herself, and above all, for her lost chance of happiness with Tate.

28

Bethany and Teresa together rode the scout's horse as he led them in somber silence through the burned fields of the del Castillo rancho, which were littered with the bodies of vaqueros. Eerily, the chapel bell still tolled its grim warning as they approached the *casa grande.*

The diminishing wind must be ringing the bell, Bethany decided. They had waited until sunset to approach the hacienda, as their scout believed if the hostile Indians were still nearby they would not attack after dark.

In the rapidly fading light they could not tell if anyone was still alive. But the empty silence was filled with foreboding.

Bethany could hear the hooves of the horse crunching the burned cornstalks, Teresa's sobbing breathing behind her, and, faintly, the thudding of her own heart. Other than the mournful tolling of the chapel bell, there was no other sound.

Still, they had to know for certain that no one was left alive, and they could not determine this while hiding in the hills. She had insisted that the scout bring Teresa and her to check for survivors when it became apparent that the other vaqueros had either been waylaid by Indians or decided not to return to be burdened with the task of protecting two helpless women.

The scout, a small wiry man named Miguel, stopped suddenly.

"What is it, Miguel?" Bethany called softly in Spanish, reluctant to raise her voice and break the awful silence.

But in the same instant she saw what had stopped him in his tracks. The *casa grande* loomed ahead, a gaunt shell charred down to its adobe walls, silhouetted against the scarlet-streaked sky. The pungent odor of burned wood permeated the air.

She slid to the ground and stood uncertainly beside the horse. Teresa sat motionless, staring in frozen silence at the ruins of her home.

Bethany said quickly, "Thank God your parents and your brothers were away in Mexico City."

Miguel handed Bethany the horse's reins, and she didn't need to be told to wait until he had searched the burned house for possible survivors.

While they waited, Bethany anxiously scanned the shadowed hills. Were the savages who had done this still there? Miguel had indicated that he believed the attack had taken place several days earlier, perhaps before the devil wind blew, since the fires in the fields had burned themselves out. Also—and this caused a shiver of horror—because of the state of the corpses. The *casa grande* fire had burned out, too, but smoke still rose from some of the outbuildings, which continued to smolder.

A few minutes later Miguel returned, shaking his head.

No one was left alive. The loss was too terrible to comprehend. Bethany murmured a prayer for the dead and forced herself to think of their own survival. She squeezed Teresa's limp fingers reassuringly. "We must get away from here. There's nothing we can do. We'll have to return to your uncle's hacienda."

"I'm hungry," Teresa said.

Bethany considered. They had carried cold roast pigeon and fruit for the journey between ranchos, but most of it had already been consumed. Bethany turned to Miguel. "Is there any food in the *casa grande?*"

Miguel shrugged and seemed disinclined to go back inside to look. When Bethany asked him to go back and search for food he pretended not to understand.

"Stay with Señorita de Castillo." She handed him the reins.

She picked her way through the burned debris into the *casa grande.* The stout adobe walls that had always made her feel so safe were still standing, although they had been blackened by the flames. What had once been graciously furnished rooms were unrecognizable. The destruction appeared to be complete, and she averted her eyes from the charred bodies of servants as she found her way to the kitchens. Little wonder Miguel had not wanted to see them again. She supposed the dead ought to be buried, but there were too many for one man and two women to handle. Besides, there was the danger that the Indians might return.

There was nothing left to salvage. What had not been taken had been smashed and burned. The attackers had spared no one. She hoped the servants had mercifully been dead before the flames reached them. Holding her skirts above the burned rubble, Bethany hurried back outside.

Teresa seemed to be frozen in shock, her eyes staring unseeingly ahead. At least she appeared to have forgotten her hunger.

Bethany said to Miguel, "We will go back into the hills to the wagon." Unwilling to fumble for the Spanish words she pointed to the hills. He nodded and helped her up onto the horse.

At least there was water in the wagon, and when the other vaqueros returned with the horses they would be able to go back to the hacienda of Teresa's uncle.

But the vaqueros did not return that night or the following day, and when the two young women awoke on the morning of the third day, Miguel was harnessing his horse to the wagon. He told them tensely that they must leave immediately. He had ridden out at dawn to search for the others and had seen a war party of *Indios* riding through the pass.

When he began to remove most of their baggage from the wagon Teresa became angry and ordered him to put everything back.

"He's right," Bethany said. "With only one horse to pull the wagon, we must lighten the load. Unpack your trunk, quickly. We'll just keep one change of clothes each. A cotton skirt or a gingham dress would be coolest."

"I will *not* leave my ball gown behind," Teresa declared tearfully.

Eventually Bethany gave in and allowed her to keep the dress if she agreed to leave nearly everything else behind. They hid the heavy trunks under some brush, along with all but one of the water barrels and everything else not essential for the journey back to the rancho of Teresa's uncle.

Miguel took the reins and guided the horse into a narrow canyon, hoping that if they stayed on the lower ground they would not be seen by the war party.

The rancho of the *patrón*'s brother lay to the east, in high desert country, and by midafternoon they felt safe from pursuit, but were feeling the effects of the arid heat as they left the cooler coastal plain behind.

When Miguel stopped the horse, Teresa immediately began to berate him. "Keep going! I must be safe with my uncle before dark."

"We must rest the horse," Miguel said. "I drove him hard.

He is tired. He needs water. He cannot pull the wagon any more today. We will go on at first light tomorrow."

He was adamant, despite Teresa's arguments.

"When my father returns I will have you whipped for disobeying me," Teresa screamed at Miguel.

Bethany said, "We're hot and tired. The poor horse has been pulling the wagon for hours. Imagine how hot and tired he is. Miguel is right. We must spend the night here."

Teresa ranted and raved and Miguel tried to explain that it would soon be dusk and because of the detour he had taken to avoid the *Indios,* they were less than halfway to their destination.

Eventually they prevailed over the furious Teresa. When night fell they settled down to an uneasy sleep.

At dawn the following day Bethany awoke suddenly, feeling apprehensive. Teresa, who had been sleeping beside her in the wagon, was gone.

Flinging open the flap of canvas at the front of the wagon, Bethany was vaguely aware of something missing, but before she could collect her wits Teresa appeared, running around the side of the wagon. "This is all your fault, gringa! How dared you interfere? What do you know about handling peons? They must be made to obey and whipped if they do not, or they lose respect for you."

Now Bethany realized what was missing: Miguel and his horse.

Teresa began to sob loudly. "We should have made him take us to my uncle last night. Now what can we do? We have no horse, no food, no water, and still much distance to travel."

"Water!" Bethany exclaimed. "That's where Miguel has gone—to find water for us. The barrel is empty, we have only our canteens. He'll come back, I'm sure."

But Miguel did not return, and after waiting for several hours they faced the grim reality that they were alone in the wilderness.

The *Liberty* sailed southward on smooth seas. To portside, the peninsula of Baja California thrust rugged cliffs from white sand beaches, and overhead the sky was a sun-hazed canopy of palest blue. Jack Cutler paced restlessly about the deck, oblivious of the vividly etched panorama of sea, land, and sky.

More than a week had passed since they dropped anchor in

the bay near the del Castillo hacienda. They had been disappointed to learn that all of the family were away, including Bethany who was chaperoning Teresa at a relative's rancho to the east. None of the *patrón*'s peons had been able to say how long the visits would last and so reluctantly, at Tom's insistence, they had set sail. Tom had argued that they had carefully provisioned their ship for the long voyage and could not afford to while away days, or perhaps weeks, awaiting Bethany's return.

Leona had been disappointed but philosophical. "Sounds as if she's made herself a home here," she'd said, "visiting relatives with the family and all. She knew we were coming back—maybe she was fed up with your attentions, Black Jack. Let's leave her with her Californios where she's happy. God knows the poor little thing hasn't had much happiness in her life."

But Jack's growing uneasiness about leaving Bethany behind did not diminish with the passing days, and as they approached the tip of the peninsula he made a decision.

Tom, who by mutual agreement had assumed the position of skipper, looked up as Jack opened his cabin door. "I'm not going with you. I want you to put me ashore."

"What?"

"I'm going back for Bethany."

Tom closed the ship's log in which he was making an entry. "Do you realize that you'll have an overland journey of nearly a thousand miles? How will you get back to her?"

"I'll take my share of the profits from the last cargo and trade for a couple of horses and supplies."

"Jack, she refused to come with us. She told us definitely that she wanted to stay with the del Castillos. In fact, I wonder if she deliberately arranged to be gone when we got back. She's still in love with my dead brother. You don't stand a chance with her, Jack. Face it."

"It hasn't anything to do with how she feels about me. I'm not leaving her alone among foreigners. Give the order to put into the nearest safe harbor and put me ashore."

Tom stared at him for a long moment. "You're determined to do this?"

Jack nodded.

Tom was silent. He looked at the log in front of him, chewed his lip thoughtfully. At length he said, "We'd none of us be alive to tell the tale if it hadn't been for you. I'll give the order to put about. We'll take the *Liberty* back for her."

* * *

"I can't go on," Teresa protested tearfully. "My feet hurt."

"Very well, we'll rest under those trees," Bethany replied.

They conversed in a mixture of Spanish and English and part of the time did not understand what the other was saying. But Bethany needed no translation of Teresa's constant complaints. As the pampered only daughter of the *patrón,* she had never had to lift a finger to do anything for herself, not even to comb her own hair, let alone prick her fingers on brambles as they searched for edible berries or compete with swarms of bees for the brackish water in a tiny spring. Her dainty slippers were designed for dancing, not for walking over rough terrain and scrambling up rocky slopes.

Bethany dropped her bundle, which was twice the size of the one Teresa carried, on the ground beside the tree. Teresa followed suit. They sat in the shade of a cottonwood, but the heat still rose from the ground, shimmering against the rock-strewn hills that lay between them and their destination. Bethany estimated that they had hiked no more than a few miles.

"*Tengo calor! Tengo sed,*" Teresa muttered from between sunburned lips.

"I'm hot and thirsty, too," Bethany responded. "But we drank only minutes ago, and we don't know how long it will be before we find water again."

Before she could stop her, however, Teresa had removed her canteen from her bundle of belongings and gulped thirstily.

"I suppose it will do you more good inside you than carried on your back," Bethany said, fanning herself with her hat.

Teresa drained her canteen and leaned back against the cottonwood, which whispered overhead in a hot breeze. She closed her eyes, and a moment later her even breathing indicated she was asleep. Bethany envied her the ability to nap, no matter what.

What a sight we both look, Bethany thought. Their skirts were in tatters; their hair straggled damply over their shoulders from beneath sombreros left behind by the vaqueros, which Bethany felt would afford greater protection from the sun than their own bonnets. Their bodices were stained with the juice of berries they'd harvested to supplement the stale tortillas, which were all that was left of the food they'd carried in the wagon.

Teresa had said that she believed some of the cacti were edible and would provide moisture for their dehydrated bodies, but after laboriously removing lethal spines from several different types of cactus, they were disappointed by the bitter taste, which left them thirstier than before.

Bethany surveyed the bulky bundle she had been carrying and Teresa's smaller one. They contained clothing, toilet articles, a pistol that had been left behind by the wagon driver, and several gifts from her aunt and uncle that Teresa had refused to leave behind in the wagon.

When Teresa awoke a little while later Bethany had opened the two bundles, which were wrapped in silk shawls, and was heaving items relentlessly out onto the ground.

Teresa gave a small scream. "What are you doing?"

"We have a long journey ahead of us. We'll travel faster if we're not carrying so much. We'll take just the flasks, the food, and the pistol. We can both sleep under one blanket."

"My ball gown!" Teresa cried. "I won't leave it for some *Indio* squaw to find."

There had been an earlier battle over the gown, which Teresa expected Bethany to carry, along with all of her other belongings. When Bethany refused, suggesting the gown could remain in the wagon and perhaps be picked up later, Teresa had stuffed it into the bundle Bethany insisted she carry for herself.

"Don't you dare touch my beautiful gown. I won't abandon it," Teresa screamed.

Ignoring her, Bethany tossed the brilliant red satin gown with its heavy jet embroidery and many petticoats, onto the ground. "We have to travel faster. We can't carry all this stuff. I've been thinking, too, that we're foolish to sleep at night when it's cool. We'll rest during the heat of the day and walk at night."

Indignantly Teresa jumped to her feet and snatched up her ball gown, then dropped it, screaming, as a scorpion scurried out from between the folds.

When they resumed their trek late that afternoon they carried only the essentials. Bethany was not sure how they would find the rancho on foot. She knew they had traveled inland and then turned north, so as the sun began to descend into the western sky she tried to keep the vermilion glow just behind her left shoulder. Teresa, accustomed to having others make her every decision for her, did not question that Bethany would lead her to safety. Their only real hope, Bethany knew, was to eventually run into some of the vaqueros from Teresa's uncle's rancho.

But as darkness claimed the earth she became disoriented, unsure of her direction. The hills all looked the same in the shadows. Although it was more comfortable walking in the cool of the evening, it was obviously not going to work. They curled up together under the blanket within a cluster of boulders, which Bethany hoped would provide a barrier between them and any wandering nocturnal animals.

As the sun rose the following morning Bethany awoke to a terrifying sound—a loud rattling noise on the rock over their heads.

Teresa was awake, staring in fascinated horror at the snake coiled on a boulder not more than six feet above them, its tail twitching furiously as it rattled its rage at the intruders in its territory.

"Get the pistol, quick! Shoot it," Teresa whimpered, rigid with fear. "Hurry! Its bite means death."

The bundle containing the pistol was under Bethany's head. She slid her hand into it and felt the comforting hardness of the barrel of the gun. When it was in her hand she whispered, "Start sliding back toward me. Don't make any sudden movements."

"No! I can't! Shoot it now."

"We have only three pistol balls," Bethany hissed between clenched teeth. "We may need them for a more deadly menace."

When Teresa still didn't budge, Bethany muttered, "Start inching away now, or I'll drag you by your hair."

Teresa did as she was told.

When she drew level with Bethany, both women began to slide backward. Bethany kept her eyes fixed on the snake, which immediately struck in their direction, but was mercifully out of range.

The reptile's furious rattle followed them as they scrambled to their feet and, slipping and sliding, stumbled back down the trail. When they were in a dry wash devoid of rocks and plants that might hide any other snakes, they stopped running and sank to the ground to catch their breath. Then Teresa gave a sharp cry.

Bethany jumped. "What is it?"

"I left my things up there in the rocks."

"You'd finished all of your water anyway, and I've got the pistol and the blanket. We can manage without the rest." She fixed the girl with what she hoped was a ferocious stare. "Don't even think of asking me to go back to those rocks."

"I'm hungry and thirsty."

"So am I. Keep your eyes open for any fresh-looking green bushes or trees; perhaps there will be water nearby."

They followed the wash, keeping the sun over their right shoulders, heading north. With the rising sun came insects, buzzing around their heads and flying into their eyes. The blisters on their feet broke open and bled, and had it not been for the fiery sand on which they walked, Bethany would have suggested discarding their shoes.

When the wash veered off in the wrong direction Bethany reluctantly decided to climb to the highest ridge and look around to try to determine their best route, or at least find a green oasis that might offer water and shade from the midday heat.

"Wait here," she told Teresa, "I'll climb up to that mesa and see if I can find a trail."

The slope was steeper than she estimated, and she had to cling with fingers and toes, fearing at any moment she might disturb another rattlesnake.

At last she stood on the highest point and looked around. The chaparral-covered hills rolled endlessly toward the horizon, each one identical to the last and all as devoid of humanity as an alien moon.

She turned to look in the opposite direction. Directly in front of her was a flock of circling birds—huge, ugly creatures that even as she watched began to settle on the ground around what was clearly the sprawled figure of a man.

He lay in a small clearing just below where she stood. She started down the slope toward him, sliding on the unstable gravel, shouting to drive off the buzzards.

Before she reached him she knew it was too late. He lay on his back, swarms of flies covering his face and the shaft of an arrow protruding from his chest.

There was no mistaking the striped serape slung over his shoulder. No wonder Miguel had not returned to them. The canteens he had filled with water lay on the ground beside him, but there was no sign of his horse, which undoubtedly had been taken by the Indians who killed him.

With her hand over her mouth and nostrils, Bethany cautiously approached Miguel's body, wondering if there was a way to bury him. But she had no tool with which to dig in the sunbaked ground, and there were no rocks nearby small enough to carry. Besides, she knew the Indians might return. It was more urgent to get herself and Teresa to safety.

She snatched up the canteens of water and hurried back to where her charge waited.

The young woman displayed no emotion when Bethany told her Miguel was dead. Perhaps she had simply had too many shocks lately to react. They drank from one canteen, ate the last of the stale and rock-hard tortillas, and started walking again.

The heat rose up from the ground, reflected from sand and rocks, and beat down from the cloudless sky, baking every drop of moisture from their bodies. After a time they merely placed one foot in front of the other and plodded on, unthinking, drained.

Teresa suddenly stopped and pointed. Bethany caught a glimpse of the green tops of trees above the next rise.

Please, let there be a spring there, Bethany prayed as they quickened their pace.

Maddened by thirst, Teresa found the strength to break into a run as they drew nearer the trees and she reached the copse of cottonwoods first. The next second she began to scream, a hoarse wail that stopped Bethany's breath in her throat.

Flying to Teresa's side, she saw instantly the reason for her anguish.

Scattered on the ground beneath the cottonwoods were several petticoats, silver-backed hairbrushes, mantilla combs, and a brilliant red gown—all of the articles they had discarded in order to lighten their loads. They had traveled in a circle, making no progress whatsoever.

Teresa continued to scream hysterically, and Bethany seized her by the shoulders and shook her. "Stop it! Stop—"

A cold hand closed around Bethany's heart as in the split-second interval between Teresa's screams another sound intruded. Bethany slapped her hand over the girl's mouth to silence her.

"*Listen!* Someone is coming!"

They could hear the snapping of brush and the sound of pebbles and small rocks being dislodged by the hooves of several horses that were coming down the trail from the hill toward the cottonwood copse.

All the color drained from Teresa's face. She pulled Bethany's hand from her mouth and whispered, "*Madre de Dios! Indios!*"

Bethany looked around quickly for a place to hide. "Over there—under those bushes."

She pushed Teresa ahead of her and they flung themselves on

the ground to crawl into a clump of manzanita, dragging their bundle of belongings behind them.

The surrounding scrub might conceal them, Bethany thought, trying to ignore a small voice that reminded her of what she had heard at the hacienda about the legendary tracking ability of the Indians. If they had indeed tracked them here . . . then there was nowhere to hide.

She found the pistol and loaded it, then rolled onto her stomach, holding the gun out in front of her with both hands. She could feel Teresa trembling beside her.

The blood pounded in Bethany's ears as she considered her alternatives. After firing the flintlock pistol there would be no time to reload before the Indians were upon them. If they were captured . . . there was little doubt what their fate would be.

With a hammering heart, Bethany wondered if she would have the courage to use her one shot to kill Teresa in order to keep her from falling into the hands of the savages.

★★★★★ 29 ★★★★★

THE YEARS FELL away as Dr. Will Prentice walked slowly up a long gravel drive toward a rather ugly brick house that sat forbiddingly behind a high wall. The home of one of the richest mill owners in Lancashire had changed little since he saw it last.

Lost in memories, he turned onto a narrow path that wound through the kitchen garden to the tradesmen's entrance. Just before he reached the back of the house he paused, wondering if he would be stopped by a passing gardener or gamekeeper if he were to detour into the rose garden. From there he could observe the lawns and croquet court. On a fine afternoon such as this, it was just possible his daughter would be out taking the air.

"Are you lost, sir?" a voice behind him asked, taking the decision out of his hands.

Turning, he was confronted by a man wearing a leather apron carrying garden shears.

"No. I can find my way. I just stopped for a moment to admire your roses. I haven't seen roses . . . for a long time."

Will walked on, quickening his pace. At the tradesmen's entrance he again paused. Would they let him see his daughter? Would the years have eased their pain? Perhaps Emma's grandparents were no longer alive? They would be well into their seventies by now. And Emma herself . . . what would she think about his sudden appearance in her life? She would be fifteen now, a young lady. What had she been told about her birth, about her missing father? Should he have written that he was coming? He had decided against sending word of his arrival for fear he would be told not to come.

He had never deluded himself that he had embarked upon this quest to meet his daughter out of any latent parental love and need for the child. He still felt, as he had years ago, that Emma's birth had been a tragic mistake. Even now, as he raised the brass door knocker and let it fall, his thoughts turned, not to Emma, but to his beloved wife, Bethany.

Bethany had berated him for abandoning his child, but this visit was not the result of an attack of conscience. His reason for being here was much more self-serving. Thwarted in his efforts to find his wife and determined that he *would* find her, he knew of only one slender chance of being reunited with her. Sooner or later Bethany would return to England to seek out her own daughter. If he could prove to her that he was a good man, a good father, not the cold and heartless creature Bethany had accused him of being, perhaps she would come back to him.

He didn't give much credence to the reports that, if indeed Bethany had been with the band of absconders who stole the ship, she, too, would hang for piracy. In any case, he would not allow the law to have her. They would go away somewhere with their two daughters, and he would keep her safe.

The tradesmen's door opened and a woman wearing a starched apron and mobcap stood on the threshold. He was thankful that she had not been on the staff years ago, therefore did not recognize him.

"Good afternoon. Forgive me for troubling you, but I wondered if your employers are in residence, and if so, if they would receive me?"

She blinked in surprise. "If you wanted to see the master, why didn't you go to the front door?"

Why indeed? Because in the old days he had been instructed to come into the house by way of the tradesmen's entrance, and it had not occurred to him to do otherwise.

The woman continued, "Well, anyway, to answer your question, Mr. Jennings doesn't see any visitors these days. He's in mourning. If you'd gone to the front of the house, you'd have seen the closed curtains and the wreath on the door."

"I had no idea he was bereaved. I'm sorry to hear of his loss, and under ordinary circumstances I wouldn't trouble him at such a time. But I have traveled a considerable distance to see his granddaughter. I assumed she was still away at boarding school, but when I went to the last school she mentioned in her letters I was told that she left last year to go to finishing school. If you would be so kind as to tell me which school Miss Emma is currently attending—"

The woman's face flushed bright red, her eyes glittered with anger, and her mouth opened in outrage. She seemed to quiver from head to toe, attempted to speak, sputtered, then drew a deep, indignant breath and slammed the door in his face.

Bewildered, he stepped backward, stumbling over the doorstep.

"You'd best not go to the front door, sir," a male voice said softly behind him.

Turning, Will saw the leather-aproned gardener straighten up behind a privet hedge, clippers in hand. "Excuse me, sir. I couldn't help but overhear. The housekeeper should've known you didn't mean no harm, but it was very upsetting, what happened—for everybody on the staff, too, you see. We were all very fond of Miss Emma. She was such a lonely little girl. We thought when she went off to school, but . . ."

Will thought he could hear a distant drumming sound, growing louder, and told himself it was simply a pulse beat. His instincts told him to walk quickly away, not to hear any more. Emma—not her grandmother, as he'd assumed—was dead. He didn't need to know more than that. He was simply too late; that was all.

But even as he started to walk away the gardener continued in a heavy voice, "So young she was. Such a shame. Only a child herself."

Will stopped and asked the question he knew he shouldn't ask. "What was the cause of Emma's death?"

The gardener, so ready to talk a moment earlier, now flushed and mumbled evasively.

"I am Emma's father," Will said, fixing him with a stare that he knew intimidated most men. "I have a right to know."

The gardener blinked disbelievingly, but it was obvious he was bursting to divulge more details, no matter who Will was. "She . . . died in childbirth, sir. I'm sorry. The baby died, too."

The pounding in Will's head was now deafening. "She was married?"

"No, sir. Try to understand . . . she was so lonely. The master and the mistress ignored her. Governesses came and went. I think it happened out of her need to have somebody of her very own."

Will stumbled back along the gravel drive, feeling angry, betrayed. His daughter had no right to cause history to repeat itself, no right to spoil all of his plans.

At first Mrs. Creel was not going to open the door to the man who stood outside. Peering around the lace curtain at the window she could see a tall, gaunt man dressed in a black frock coat and dark trousers. The skin on his face seemed stretched so tight that it revealed the skull beneath.

She shivered as the hollow eyes swiveled in her direction, acknowledging that he knew she was observing him. Even so, she would have left him standing there, had it not been for the fact that her neighbors on the street of terraced houses were gathering in a curious knot nearby. How she hated living in this little four-room house in a run-down neighborhood near the docks among these shawl-wrapped women, but it was all she could afford after Stewart Fielding issued her marching orders and shut down his father's town house.

Opening the door a crack, she snapped, "If you're trying to sell me insurance, I don't need any—"

The walking corpse's lips barely moved. "Bethany Newton's baby. Where is she?"

It took a moment for her to recover; then she opened the door wider. "Come in."

She ushered him into the musty-smelling parlor, which she rarely used. Gray bloom misted the furniture, and the tiny fireplace was draped with cobwebs, but she hadn't had company since she moved in, so hadn't bothered to dust or clean. "And just who are you, and what's your business with the baby—supposing I know anything about such a baby?"

"There's no need for you to know my name. I know who you are, and I know that you went to the parish home to which the baby was taken shortly before Bethany Newton was transported.

You went there to arrange the adoption of the baby, who was shortly thereafter picked up by a nursemaid you'd hired."

"I've done nothing wrong—"

"I'm not saying you have. I'm here to offer you a reward, in fact, for information leading to my ascertaining the baby's present whereabouts."

"How much of a reward?"

"That depends."

"On what?"

"On how helpful you are to me . . . and how discreet."

She gestured for him to sit down. "You're going to have to tell me what you're up to before I answer any of your questions."

"Suffice to say that I wish to reunite the child with her mother. Since her mother is an escaped felon, it is necessary to accomplish this secretly. I cannot approach the child's present guardians openly."

Mrs. Creel considered this for a moment. It would serve Stewart and Alison right if she helped this man kidnap the baby. "Well, now, supposing I could help you, I'd need some reassurance that I wouldn't get into trouble myself, wouldn't I?"

"It was not easy to track you down, Mrs. Creel. I learned you were a housekeeper in Victoria Gardens at the time the baby was adopted, but left that position later. I inquired of numerous neighbors and shopkeepers before I found one who remembered you'd moved to this neighborhood. Then I repeated the process to find your present address. I would say you have distanced yourself sufficiently from the child that you would not be suspected of complicity in any abduction. Apparently you were an intermediary in the adoption, acting for a third party. All I am asking is that you now help me in the same capacity, on behalf of the child's real mother."

He paused, glancing about the miserable parlor and no doubt assessing her reduced circumstances, then added, "Apart from the financial remuneration for your help, consider the humanitarian aspect. You would be reuniting a mother and child."

"Well, yes, there is that to it, isn't there?"

Will shifted his gaunt body slightly in the lumpy armchair and watched the greedy glitter intensify in Mrs. Creel's deep-set eyes. Offering her salve for her conscience probably hadn't been necessary. The right price would buy her help. He felt a stab of distaste for the woman. In a moment she would begin to haggle over the amount of the payment for her information.

She began a whining litany of her financial woes, which he tuned out by thinking of Bethany. If only he could have found her first, but she had vanished without a trace and with each passing month the trail became colder. There was only one certainty: Eventually she, too, would come looking for her daughter. Indeed, she would move heaven and earth to find the infant.

The child was the link that would join him to Bethany again. Once the little girl was in his custody they would travel together along every possible route the penal colony absconders might have taken. Either he would find Bethany or she would hear that Dr. Will Prentice was caring for her daughter and she would come to them, in joy and gratitude, bringing the love he craved.

30

STEWART HAD NEVER known anyone like Iris Holloway. In the scant weeks that had elapsed since he met her at the Beethoven concert he had vowed a dozen times to stop seeing her, but she had become as necessary to his well-being as air or food.

She was laughter and joy; she brought into his life a lightness that had never existed for him before. At the same time she was a receptacle into which he could pour all of his feelings, about music, about life itself.

Iris understood and responded in kind. She was a remarkably talented pianist whose ambition, he was surprised to learn, was to be a concert pianist. When he played his compositions for her, she gave honest opinions, constructive criticism, and often provided keen insight into ways to transform his pieces from the mediocre to the refreshingly original.

Yet at the same time she was playful, irreverent, even bawdy. Iris lifted from his shoulders the heavy burden of responsibility that he felt he had carried all of his life. She taught him how to laugh. How had he ever managed without her? She was indispensable to him.

Stewart had never felt the attraction for the opposite sex that seemed to occupy every waking thought of most young men his age; indeed, he had secretly feared he was asexual. But now he found to his astonishment that he was mesmerized by this exquisite young woman. More than that, he was suddenly aware of his own manhood in a way he had never been before. He had admired Alison, felt protective toward her and the children, been comfortable with her, enjoyed her company, before she became obsessed with his father's ships, but they had never entered the exhilarating arena of flirtatious tension in which he parried with Iris.

He had told Iris, when he went to hear her first piano recital, that he was married. She had shrugged, unconcerned. "What has that to do with me?"

"I . . . just felt I should tell you. My wife is very busy. There are two children. She couldn't come with me today."

"I'm glad. I don't care for women, especially wives. As a rule they're excruciatingly dull."

Unsure how to respond to such a statement, Stewart stammered, "Alison . . . wanted to take the children to the park."

Iris rolled her green eyes, which had taken on a catlike opacity at his mention of Alison. "Mothers are even duller than wives."

Feeling a compelling need to change the subject, Stewart had said, "While you were playing the sonatas I had a sudden longing to hear you play one of my pieces. Not that they're worthy of your talent, but I think I might hear them differently if I were not playing them myself."

They had stepped outside after refreshments were served and were standing on the terrace of the country home where the charity event was being held. Iris looked enchanting in white muslin patterned with tiny violets and twining green leaves. Green velvet ribbon and fresh violets were woven into her platinum-pale hair. She was a vision of carefree youth, unblemished, untouched by hardship or by the troubles that beset ordinary mortals.

She smiled, her dimples like mischievous punctuation marks in her vivacious features. "I would love to play your compositions, Stewart. When may I?"

"This evening?" he asked hopefully.

"We must be alone," she responded in a conspiratorial whisper. "I have a friend who will swear to Aunt Elspeth I'm with her, if you can get away by yourself. But where could we meet?"

"My father owns a house in Victoria Gardens. It's been closed for a while, but there's a fairly decent piano there."

And so it had begun. That evening they met at the town house and removed the dust sheets from the piano and bench only.

They sat side by side sharing music, dreams, memories. A rapturous couple of hours passed too swiftly, and Stewart later thought of that first meeting as an aperitif, whetting his appetite for much more.

Soon they were meeting whenever they could get away. There was never enough time, to talk, to listen, to play. Before long Stewart found himself confessing to her his shame that he had allowed his wife to take over his father's business.

Iris wrinkled her retroussé nose. "She sounds like such a stick!"

"No, no, she's a wonderful woman."

"What feeble praise! Does she share your love of music? Does she understand it? Does she understand *you?*"

"She used to listen to me talk about music, but she's so busy with the children and the business nowadays that we scarcely have a chance to exchange the time of day."

"But, my dear," Iris said softly, "don't you see how lucky you are? *Let* her spend hours at the office. Let her do all the work. Then we shall have more time to spend together. I have a wonderful idea: Why don't we have dinner together tomorrow night at Victoria Gardens? I shall cook for us."

They removed the dust sheets from the dining table and lit a fire in the drawing room. Iris cooked a delicious curry. Stewart opened a bottle of wine. They discussed Mozart. Iris played Stewart's newest composition; he told her he called it "Wildflowers," but didn't add that it was dedicated to her, that her effervescent personality reminded him more of wildflowers in a sunny meadow than of the sedate irises of a tamed garden.

When he was not with Iris he found himself thinking about her all the time. The only other thought that intruded was a brief stab of conscience that his relationship with her was improper. He quickly stifled his guilt by reminding himself that Alison was his wife in name only, that in fact marriage had elevated her far beyond her original station in life. Furthermore, it was obvious she preferred to spend her time in the world of business or with the children, rather than with him; therefore he was not depriving her of his company by seeing Iris.

But what about Iris? Should she not be seeing eligible bachelors? He brought up the subject the second time they dined together at the house. It was a warm summer evening, and he had brought cold roast chicken, fresh fruit, and crusty bread.

Iris had brought a bottle of champagne. "To celebrate our one month anniversary," she told him gaily. "We met a month ago today!"

"Has it really been a month? Iris, I feel guilty about keeping you from spending time with your other friends."

"Keeping me from spending time with all those dreary men Aunt Elspeth drags in for me to marry, you mean? Lord, I can't imagine *ever* wanting to marry. What a dreadful bore! One might as well lock oneself up in a tomb. And I can't stand children. Besides, if I didn't want to be with you, I wouldn't be here."

Greatly relieved, Stewart opened the champagne.

The food and champagne were consumed to the accompaniment of much laughter and several ribald jokes. Iris's rather risqué sense of humor never failed to amaze him.

When they finished eating, they repaired to the drawing room with the intention of playing "Wildflowers" as a duet, but the moment they were seated side by side on the piano bench, Iris took the wineglass from his hand and placed it deliberately on the top of the piano, oblivious of the damp ring that promptly formed on the rosewood surface.

"I can't wait any longer for you to kiss me, Stewart. So I'm going to kiss you. I've been wondering what it would be like. You have the most devastatingly appealing mouth, did you know that?"

Before he could say a word, she pressed her mouth to his and her lips parted slightly. Her kiss was cool and warm at the same time, her breath sweet. The blood pounded in his ears, and he was instantly aroused.

But she withdrew her mouth almost at once, smiled prettily, and said, "Your mouth is wonderful. It tastes as nice as it looks."

She cocked her head to one side, as though giving careful consideration to a matter of great importance. "You taste a little like peppermints and nasturtiums . . . cool and invigorating, yet spicy and mysterious, too."

"You like to eat nasturtiums?" Stewart asked faintly.

"Indeed I do. They liven up a dull salad. Now let's play 'Wildflowers' before I do something completely outrageous."

He wanted to say, Oh, please continue to be outrageous! But he was so physically aroused by her kiss he was afraid to do anything other than turn to the keys.

She gave him another quick kiss when they parted, and that night he was unable to sleep for thinking about her.

On subsequent nights he dreamed about her, and during the day he wandered about in a pleasant haze, his mind filled with images of her. At the same time inspiration for new melodies crowded one another in his head, begging for expression on the keys. The music and memories of Iris, her laughter, the silver halo of her hair, became interchangeable, one a part of the other, combining to create an irresistible siren song.

A week later they attended another concert and, moved almost to tears by the beauty of the music, afterward by unspoken agreement they went to Victoria Gardens.

They walked into the darkened house, and it seemed to Stewart they were accompanied by an unseen force that surrounded them, holding them in thrall. Was it their mutual joy in the music they'd heard this evening? The euphoria of finding a soul mate?

Ignoring the lamps, he bent to light the fire he had instructed a newly hired charwoman to lay in the drawing room fireplace that morning. When a flickering golden glow filled the room he turned to face Iris.

Neither spoke. For a moment they simply stared at each other. His heart was beating so loudly he thought the sound must fill the room.

Then Iris placed her hands on his cheeks and looked up at him with her sparkling green eyes, her dimples showing impishly. "You feel the same way I do, don't you? Admit it, you wretch! The music has moved you. . . . More than that, it has transported you to a realm of the senses, mysterious, erotic. You can't let go of it. You're thinking there has to be a way to capture it, to make it your own . . . to make it ours."

Her fingers caressed his face lightly and she took a step closer to him. She unbuttoned his jacket, pulled it from his shoulders, and tossed it carelessly to the floor. Now he could feel the softness of her breasts press against the linen of his shirt, and he caught his breath as her tiny hands slid to his back, pulling him even closer.

It was true that the euphoria of the music lingered in every nerve of his body, and Iris was a part of it, an essential component to his pleasure, because she shared and understood it.

"Iris . . ." His voice was hoarse. "You know that I have a wife. I must go home."

She pressed a fingertip to his lips to silence him, and when she spoke her voice was softer, more melodious than ever before.

"Aunt Elspeth is in the country. She thinks I asked my friend to stay with me, but I didn't. I don't have to go home. Not for hours . . . not for all night, if I choose."

Her nearness was intoxicating. Her scent filled his nostrils. She was tiny, delicate, and she made him feel taller, broader, stronger, wiser than he had ever felt. Before Iris came into his life he had never felt with a woman the magic that music brought to him, and even now he was unsure if his raging desire was in part the aftermath of the concert they had just left.

But here in his arms—and how had it happened that his arms were around her?—was a woman who loved music as much as he did, who understood it and him, who inhabited a world that no one else knew existed. They were an island society of two, adrift, removed from the realm of ordinary mortals. The mundane, the ordinary, the world of ships and cargoes, for them had no place in the scheme of things.

She stood on tiptoe and kissed his lips. Her mouth was soft, yielding, and a long sigh slipped from him. For a moment their kiss was tender, slow and cool as a summer breeze. Then all at once she became playful, withdrawing her mouth, then returning to nibble his lower lip.

Her fingers found the buttons of his shirt and unfastened them with astonishing speed. She shrugged her low-cut gown from her shoulders, and her delicate pink-tipped breasts spilled into his hands, feeling silken to his touch. Her arms encircled his neck and her kiss became teasing, lips opening like a rose, tongue darting.

Desire throbbed through his entire being. He had never known such arousal, such need. Blindly he sought to pull her closer, to feel every inch of her body pressed to his.

Somehow their clothes were on the floor in a tumbled heap and she stood naked before him wearing only the flowers in her hair, dark red carnations whose subtle fragrance combined with her own unique scent to inflame him still further.

She sank down onto the hearth rug, arms open to receive him and he dropped on his knees to worship her. In the flickering firelight, her body was miraculous perfection. She smiled at him, fondly, invitingly, and her small, soft hands sought his manhood and drew him into her moist warmth.

He heard himself gasp; then her hips moved beneath him in a tantalizing ballet that was beyond imagining, an intoxicating rhythm, a melody of drums and violins and pianoforte arpeggios that created chords such as no man had ever before heard.

When their twin stars exploded together in the cosmos and he began a deliciously languorous descent through the star-studded heavens, Stewart held her close and whispered, "Oh, my darling! My darling girl! I've never known such rapture! Thank you, thank you . . ."

She murmured lazily and nestled closer.

Still overwhelmed by her, he said shyly, "Iris . . . I love you."

"Yes. I know." She sank her sharp little teeth into the flesh of his chest and he jumped, startled.

Giggling, she said, "A love bite. I've put my mark on you, Stewart. Now you're mine forever. My slave. To do as I command. And I command you to kiss me—no, not on the mouth. I want you to kiss every inch of my body . . . starting *here.*"

As he bent his lips to her breast a disturbing thought flashed through his mind. He'd believed that virgins suffered pain and bleeding the first time; certainly he'd been told they exhibited some shame or, at the very least, reticence. But Iris showed none of these signs that she had just been deflowered. Was it possible he was not her first lover? The possibility was dismaying.

But his doubts were soon extinguished by rising desire. She laughed and whispered encouragement. "Ah! Yes . . . now andante, ooh! Wonderful, nice, yes—allegretto. Ah, oh! Now allegro, allegro!"

After a moment Iris murmured, "Darling, don't you think we might be more comfortable in bed?"

He carried her up the stairs. She was as light as a feather, warm and soft and pliant in his arms. And when they lay in his father's big four-poster bed Iris taught him all the ways a man and woman can give each other pleasure.

Time became meaningless, and he was shocked when the first silver streaks of dawn crept around the window curtains and found the tumbled array of the bed.

Iris slept in the curve of his arm, as lovely and ethereal as an angel. Her pale hair fell like a silvery cloud upon the pillow, and her full pink lips were parted in a childlike expression of wonderment. He marveled that one who looked as innocent as a child had last night transformed herself into a temptress with the carnal appetite of a courtesan.

In the cold light of dawn Stewart realized with a start that he was grateful he would not have to make an honest woman of her. How could a man trust such a wife? He felt an unexpected wave of tenderness for Alison, chastely at home in bed alone. Alison's present celibacy was testimony to her redemption. The old days and the old ways were behind her. Besides, she'd had to provide sexual favors in order to survive, a far different story from Iris's wanton flouting of the laws of God and nature.

All at once he was anxious to return home, to be there when Alison awoke. Without disturbing Iris, he slipped out of bed and quickly dressed. He left a note on his pillow, saying that he would return later to take her home in his carriage. Iris had told him she rarely arose before noon.

Still in the grip of guilt, he stopped on his way home to buy a large bouquet of fresh flowers from a street vendor for Alison. Then, seeing a man at work in one of the not-yet-open jeweler's shops, he pounded on the door and told the surprised man he wanted to buy a brooch. The one in the window, a beautiful ivory cameo encircled with tiny diamonds. Alison had taken to wearing rather severely cut gowns to the office, and the brooch would soften the high necklines.

Feeling somewhat relieved of his guilt, he urged the horse forward at a fast trot, thinking with pleased anticipation of Alison's reaction to the gifts lying on the carriage seat beside him.

Still, an argument with his conscience persisted. Had he been unfaithful? He and Alison had a business arrangement and a protective custody agreement, not a marriage; it had never been consummated. Since he had never slept with her, was it therefore possible to be physically unfaithful?

He was still trying to resolve that particular dilemma when he reached the stable where he kept his horse and carriage. Picking up the flowers and the small velvet case containing the brooch, he walked the short distance to his house.

The flowers were fragrant, and his sense of anticipation returned as he inhaled their scent. Alison would be delighted with his gifts, he was sure. He would place them at the foot of the stairs, so that when she got up she would see them right away. He would quickly bathe and change clothes and be waiting in the breakfast room. Since they now had a live-in housekeeper, he would have her prepare a special breakfast.

Turning his key in the front door as quietly as he could, he stepped into the hall.

Alison, clad in a flannel dressing gown, her hair straggling in unaccustomed untidiness about her shoulders, and her face haggard, paced around the hall. Behind her Mrs. Hughes stood holding Davey's hand. The little boy was in his pajamas and he seemed bewildered, looking from Mrs. Hughes to his mother.

The two women stared at Stewart, Mrs. Hughes in an accusing way, Alison's expression filled with agony.

"I'm sorry . . ." he began inadequately. He dropped the flowers and jewelry case on the hall table.

"Someone took Hope last night," Alison said, her voice sounding like tumbrils grinding down the road to doom. "They used a ladder to get into the nursery through the window. She was gone when I went to look at her about midnight."

"Good God! Have you sent for the police?"

Alison withdrew her hand from the pocket of her dressing gown and thrust a crumpled sheet of paper toward him.

Taking it from her, he read the note:

I am taking Hope Newton to her mother. She will be quite safe, so do not worry.

Bethany Newton, wife of Neil Newton (a pseudonym for Neil Fielding), escaped from the penal colony and, along with other absconders, is wanted for piracy. I am giving you this information so you will know that I am a bona fide representative of Bethany Newton, also so you will understand why Bethany herself cannot come for her daughter.

We are grateful to you for caring for Bethany's child and, when it is safe to do so, will write to tell you of Hope's progress.

A friend of Bethany Newton

31

BETHANY POINTED THE pistol at the clearing and held her breath. Beside her Teresa shook with fear. The desert scrub under which they crouched surely did not completely conceal them.

In a moment the Indians would reach the spot where they hid; they could hear their horses coming down the trail.

Her heart leapt into her throat as the first Indian dropped to the ground directly in front of the manzanita bush under which the two women hid. From where she lay, Bethany could see only his moccasins and leggings, bound with rawhide.

He stood motionless, only inches away, his horse behind him, and she knew he was aware of their presence. He called out something in his own language, which brought a second horse into the clearing.

We're lost, Bethany thought. She rolled over onto her side and looked into Teresa's frightened eyes. The girl crossed herself, expecting death. But Bethany could not raise the pistol to shoot Teresa. Her hands seemed to have turned to stone.

Even as she told herself that swift death at her hands was preferable to what would befall Teresa at the hands of the hostiles, another, more insistent voice clamored to be heard: *Where there's life there's hope. . . .*

In the periphery of her vision she caught a glimpse of another pair of feet swinging down from a horse, and these were clad in boots. At the same instant a familiar voice called, "Bethany? It's all right. It's Jack Cutler. You can come out."

Sobbing with relief, she scrambled out of the manzanita and flung herself into his arms.

He held her tightly, and when she raised her face to look at him, to make sure she was not imagining he had returned, he bent his head and kissed her lips with an exuberance that seemed inappropriate, making light of the dire peril she had been in so recently.

Still, she allowed the kiss to continue, needing to feel safe in his arms, and not at all repulsed by how nice his lips felt against hers. When at last she did pull away, he regarded her with amused blue eyes. "Why, my dear Mrs. Newton-Prentice, can it be that for once you're glad to see me?"

Ignoring him, she glanced fearfully at the Indian who stood a few feet away, regarding them.

"He's from the mission at San Juan Capistrano," Jack said. "Without his tracking abilities, I'm not sure I'd have found you." He grinned. "Until we got to the trail of clothing and hair combs and so on, that is, a few miles back."

A second Indian, little more than a boy, appeared behind them, leading several horses.

Jack extended his hand to Teresa and helped her to her feet. She murmured, "*Muchas gracias, señor.*"

Bethany said, "I thought you were on your way to New Orleans."

"We were. But the *Liberty* is now anchored in the bay near the del Castillo hacienda."

For a moment Jack's expression changed, giving a glimpse of the anxiety he'd experienced. "When we saw the burned *casa grande* . . . well, you can imagine what we thought. Fortunately we ran into three of the vaqueros who had accompanied you on your journey and learned you were safe but the horses had run off in a sandstorm."

"Thank God they're safe. But why didn't they return to us?"

"Apparently they had to steal the horses back from the Indians who'd taken them. From what I gather, this involved observing the Indian camp for a couple of days. And that brings up our urgent need to get back to the ship. That war party is still nearby."

"Knowing all this, why did you come alone? I mean, with just the two Indians?"

"Tom and Ned and Bourke came as far as the abandoned wagon. Once we picked up your trail we decided it would be best for them to keep an eye on the war party while I came after you. We found the body of your scout and buried him."

There were five horses, and Jack helped the two women to mount. "Where did you get the horses?" Bethany asked.

"Borrowed from the vaqueros. When they stole their own horses back from the Indians, they decided to take a few extra by way of retribution."

The relief at having the protection of the men and, no less, at not having to walk on blistered feet, caused Bethany to feel a strange sense of euphoria, although rationally she knew they were not yet out of danger.

They rode back to the abandoned wagon and found the others waiting in its shade. Tom jumped to his feet. "Thank God you're safe. Let's not waste any time getting started back to the ship. We saw dust clouds that looked as if they were kicked up by horsemen heading this way."

Bethany felt herself cringe at the sight of the burned fields when they reached the del Castillo rancho, and averted her eyes from the gaunt shell of the *casa grande,* wishing they did not have to pass this way but realizing it was the quickest route to the bay where the *Liberty* lay at anchor.

Jack maneuvered his horse closer to hers. "After we return their horses, the vaqueros will take Teresa to the mission to wait there for her parents. The fathers at the mission have already sent word to the Mexican army at the presidio that there are hostiles on the rampage, but it might take a couple of days for the soldiers to get here."

They were halfway across the burned fields when without warning a dozen horsemen materialized along a nearby ridge, with the sun at their backs. Arrows whistled through the air, and one vaquero cried out and fell. The horses reared and whinnied in fright.

For the next few minutes everything was confusion. Jack jumped to the ground, dragged Bethany from her horse, and flung her into a shallow gully. He yelled at the others to take cover. Teresa screamed hysterically.

The attackers thundered down the hillside toward them, their bloodcurdling yells causing icy fear to immobilize Bethany. She stared wide-eyed as the hostiles rode in a circle around the gully in which they lay.

After pulling rifles from their saddles, Jack and his men threw themselves to the ground, took careful aim and fired. One Indian fell heavily to the ground. The others rode in a circle at full gallop, and whenever the guns roared they slipped sideways from their saddles, leaving only a foot or a hand showing above the withers of their mounts so that the horses appeared to be riderless. When Jack's men had to stop to reload, the Indians swung upright again and sent a flock of arrows hurtling toward the gully.

A second vaquero was struck in the shoulder and fell back, gasping with pain. Bethany moved toward him, keeping as close to the ground as possible. Before she reached him, he had seized the arrow and pulled it from his flesh. Bethany tore a strip from the skirt of her cotton dress to stanch the flow of blood. She had discarded her petticoats at the start of the journey.

We are so few, she thought, as Jack fired again. But at least we have the advantage of the guns.

Time passed agonizingly slowly. They lay in the sun trap of the gully as the Indians circled, then withdrew. Somehow the pauses between the attacks were worse than the thunder of hooves and the fearsome yells. In the silences the specter of death or capture loomed, whereas during the attack they were all too busy to think, including Bethany and Teresa, who loaded the weapons and handed them to the men.

In one of the breaks between attacks Jack crawled over to Bethany and said, "As soon as it's dark we're going to make a run for the cliff. We left the longboat down on the beach. I want you and Teresa to remove your skirts."

"What?"

"You heard me. I don't want trailing skirts hampering you or catching on the chaparral. You'll have to run as fast as you can and then scramble down the cliff to the beach. When you get to the boat, pull it into the shallow water. If none of us come immediately, launch it and row to the ship."

"You're not going to send us by ourselves?"

"Ned will go with you. The rest of us will leave one at a time."

"Miguel said the Indians don't attack at night. Why can't we all leave together?"

"They may not attack at night, but I doubt they'll let us go either. We'll stay here to keep them busy. The sun is starting to go down. Tell Teresa to get rid of her skirt."

Bethany did so, and for once Teresa didn't argue. There was one final attack before the sun set, during which another vaquero died.

As soon as the light began to fade Bethany tore off her skirt and helped Teresa shed hers. They lay on the still warm ground in their pantalets and Bethany prayed as she had never prayed before. *Please God, let me live to see my child again.*

The Indians withdrew, and silence again claimed the hills. Jack whispered, "Are you ready?"

Bethany nodded, then laid her hand on his arm. "If anything happens to me, will you see that my daughter is cared for?"

For answer, he pulled her into his arms. "Nothing is going to happen to you if you do exactly as I say."

"Let go of me; the others are watching," Bethany whispered.

Ignoring the request, he went on, "Do you see the pine tree silhouetted at the top of the cliff—the one off by itself and bent almost to the ground? Run to it in as straight a line as you can. Don't stop for anything, no matter what you hear. The trail down to the beach starts just to the right of that tree."

"I'll tell Teresa. Will you let me go now?"

"Not yet. There's something else I want to say to you."

"Not now! Not here!" Bethany muttered.

"Why, my dear lady, what were you expecting? A marriage proposal?"

"No, of course not!" She squirmed in his arms, acutely aware of her dishabille.

"I merely wanted to tell you that there's no need to be afraid. We're going to live, you and I, at least long enough to enjoy the ultimate bonding of a man and a woman. I've waited too long and wanted you too much to be cheated out of that, Bethany."

Before she could respond, his mouth covered hers again in a kiss that she knew she would remember for the rest of her life. It left her breathless, yet strangely energized. Before she could speak he pushed her gently away. "It's time to go. Remember, don't stop no matter what you hear."

Ned crouched, staring out into the darkness, as the two women crawled up beside him. A vaquero waited also, holding the reins of three horses that had survived the attack.

When they were in position, the vaquero slapped the rumps of the horses, sending them galloping out toward the ridge where the Indians waited. A diversion, Bethany thought. They're hoping the Indians will go after the horses.

Ned said, "Now—run!"

They ran in single file and soon were out of breath. The long draining day of fear and tension, the lack of food and water, and the steep rise they had to climb all took their toll. Behind them a burst of gunfire shattered the night.

Remembering Jack's admonition, Bethany kept running toward the bent pine tree silhouetted against a starlit sky. She felt scrub brush tearing at her legs; her heart seemed to thunder against her ribs. An owl rose suddenly in front of them, and Bethany faltered, startled by the flapping wings.

"Don't stop!" Ned gave her a push. For an older man, he didn't seem breathless despite the climb. Teresa pushed past her, running in desperate fear.

Then the pine tree was in front of them, and they were descending the cliff, slipping and sliding in their haste to reach the beach.

As they ran across the soft sand they could see the longboat lying on its side near the water's edge. Ned pushed it into the shallows, and the two women climbed aboard.

Now they were shielded by the cliff, and the only sound they could hear was the soft sighing of the ocean. But that gunfire they had heard surely indicated that the Indians had seen them trying to escape and the men had been forced to shoot. Had they managed to get out of the gully? Were they alive?

Catching her breath, Teresa grabbed Ned's hand as it held the boat to keep it from drifting away. "Go, quickly!" she cried. "Take us to the big boat."

"No, we must wait for the others," Bethany said.

"They are dead! *Muerto!* We will be, too, if we don't go now."

"Someone coming down the cliff," Ned said. "One . . . maybe two men."

Bethany strained to see into the shadows. Only two? *Which* two?

Several different emotions assailed her simultaneously. She could still feel the imprint of Jack's kiss on her lips and knew she wanted, passionately, for him to be alive. At the same time she tried to prepare herself for him to be dead.

Was it possible that she had grown to care for him? No, no, she mustn't let herself care deeply for any man again; it would be too painful when she lost him, as she had lost Neil. She told herself that what she felt for Jack Cutler was gratitude, and the understandable interest a woman felt in a man who pursued her so ardently. Despite herself, however, she prayed that he was safe and was one of the shadows now sprinting across the beach toward her.

ALISON TUCKED DAVEY into bed, kissed his soft cheek, and tiptoed from the room. On the landing she paused, listening.

Piano music drifted up from the drawing room. Stewart was playing a piece she had never heard before, one that brought tears to her eyes and caused an unbearable crushing sensation in her chest. The music seemed to come from a part of Stewart's spirit, perhaps even his soul, that she would never know or understand.

She was unsure why it saddened her so, because it was perhaps the most beautiful piece she had ever heard him play. But then she was often close to tears nowadays. Whenever she came across one of Hope's dolls or saw her empty cot, or when Davey asked plaintively, "Where's Hope? I want Hope!"

How she missed the little girl! What an empty place in her heart she had left behind, along with a daily nagging worry about how she was faring.

Although Alison ached with fatigue and longed to go to bed, she went back downstairs. Stewart spent so little of his time at home these days, and during his brief visits to the office there was no opportunity to talk of personal matters.

He looked up as she entered the room and gave her a vague smile, obviously lost in his music. The candelabrum on the grand piano was filled with tall tapers, their flickering glow producing the only light in the room, a light that was both intimate and, at the same time, distancing.

"Did you get Davey back to sleep?" Stewart asked.

"Yes. He was having bad dreams again." The nightmares had started after Hope disappeared. The little boy worried that he might vanish next, and Alison had to constantly reassure him.

Stewart said, "You sound tired. Why don't you go to bed?"

She leaned on the piano. He didn't stop playing, and the sweet strains of the music were almost more than she could bear. "What is that piece? Is it something you wrote?"

"Yes. It isn't finished. I'm still working on it."

"What do you call it?"

"I haven't decided yet."

"Stewart, have I done something to make you angry?"

He scribbled something on the handwritten sheet of music on the stand. "No, of course not. Why do you ask?"

"You seem so far away lately, even when you're here. And you're not here much, or at the office. Davey and I scarcely see you."

He looked down at the keyboard, his hands caressing the keys with a reverent touch. "My presence at the office seems unnecessary. Between you and that great hulking beast of a warehouse manager, Rudd, I'd say you're handling the ships and cargoes better than I ever could."

"Hagen Rudd is a good man. He's been a great help to us."

"I just wish you wouldn't be seen around town with him, Alison. It isn't proper."

"I need someone to drive the carriage and deal with the dockers for me, and you're never available."

"You aren't using him as a crimp, are you? I notice our ships sail with full crews suspiciously often."

"We pay the sailors a fair wage now, and a bonus if they get the cargo there on time. And we won't tolerate brutality from the mates. That's why we never lack crews. Have you given any more thought to creating more passenger space? It really makes sense, Stewart. England imports far more goods than she exports, and our ships go out half empty. We could fill them with emigrants."

"Let's discuss it at the office, shall we? You're breaking my train of thought about the music."

"Oh, goodness, far be it from me to interfere with your piano playing," Alison muttered. "Is that where you were all afternoon?"

He had the grace to look guilty. "I'm sponsoring a concert for young pianists; I told you about it. I even asked you to come to one of the rehearsals, but you refused."

"I don't have time for such things, Stewart." She didn't add, *And neither would you, if you'd do your fair share of the work of the company.* Even though the words were not uttered, they seemed to float in the air between them rather than what she longed to tell him.

She wanted to say "Come to me, Stewart. Hold me, comfort me. I need you. Someone broke into our house and stole our little girl away from us, and I don't know how to deal with the pain of it. I need you to help me through this, but you've become unapproachable."

"I did suggest we hire a manager," Stewart said, "but you wouldn't hear of it. You will insist on supervising everything yourself." He stopped playing and slammed the keyboard lid shut. "If we're going to start another argument, I'm going to bed. Do whatever you want with the ships. Refit them, scuttle them—I don't care."

"I used to be able to talk to you," she said quietly. "We used to be friends, at least. But ever since that night . . ."

Where had he been that night? When did she lose even that fragile friendship? It had surely started to erode before that terrible night, but she didn't know why, or what she'd done to cause the decay.

He started toward the door. "I warned you that I wouldn't tolerate any more postmortems about that night. Do you really think even if I'd been here I would have been able to prevent someone taking Hope? Don't you think I miss her, too? But she was never ours. We had only temporary custody of my brother's child. Good night, Alison."

"Stewart—"

"Yes?" He stopped and looked at her.

"This is no marriage at all," she whispered miserably.

"But it's the one we both agreed to."

"Will it . . . will it ever be a real marriage, Stewart?"

For a moment she thought he might turn and come back to her, take her in his arms and hold her and tell her yes, he wanted that as much as she did. But in the flickering candle glow she saw an expression claim his face that sounded the death knell of that hope. He wore the unmistakable mask of guilt. Bowing his head he murmured something about the lateness of the hour and that they should not say anything they might regret in the morning.

Then he went upstairs to bed, leaving her in the dying candlelight, with her tears, and the memory of his music.

Mary stood at the bedroom window watching Alison and Davey playing croquet on the lawn at Riverleigh. The lawns rolled smoothly toward the cliff top where gulls wheeled lazily in the late summer sunshine. The sea was calm today, a deep indigo against the paler sky.

Adrian, mercifully, was at last taking a nap. He'd been extremely difficult during lunch. Recently he had begun to hallucinate as a result of his dementia and today had jumped up in the middle of the meal and declared that "they" had tampered with his food again. Mary had calmed him by ordering the dishes removed and fresh ones served, then had tasted everything first herself.

At least, Mary reflected as she tiptoed out of his room and went downstairs, with Adrian's present state of mind she had not had to explain who Alison and Davey were; therefore they could visit Riverleigh as often as they pleased.

As she walked toward the gazebo where Stewart sat watching the game, Mary considered again the changes that had come over her husband's middle son of late. Stewart's newfound self-confidence, undoubtedly the result of his superb handling of the Fielding Shipping Company, seemed to be overlaid with the gloss of pleasurable guilt. He had the air of a man concealing a secret life. This seemed inconceivable, in view of the hours he surely spent working. Besides, a secret life usually meant another woman, which was completely out of character for Stewart, especially at a time when his wife was so grief-stricken at losing Hope. Still, Mary was aware that tragedy concerning a child often drove a couple apart, and she wondered if Alison had noticed the changes in her husband.

A footman had brought a tray of lemonade and Stewart, seeing her approach, poured a glass for her. She took a seat beside him.

"Is Father asleep?"

She nodded. "I'm sorry he was so disagreeable at lunch."

Stewart grimaced. "Disagreeable is hardly the word for it. You're a saint, Mary, to put up with him. He's getting worse, isn't he? Can nothing be done for him?"

"According to the doctor, no." Mary clapped her hands as Davey made a good shot and the little boy waved to her. "How is Alison, Stewart? I mean, how is she *really?* She's been such a brick, but I know she must be in agony beneath that calm facade."

Stewart avoided her gaze. He twirled his empty glass. "She misses Hope, of course. We both do; she was such a delightful little girl. We would be happier that Hope has been reunited with her mother if the circumstances were different."

Mary sighed. "I wish we knew where Bethany was, how she's living, whether or not she is able to provide properly for her daughter. I shudder to think of the company she might be keeping."

"Sometimes I wonder why the gods decided to rip our family apart in such a cruel fashion," Stewart said.

"The gods, Stewart? I believe we must place a great deal of the blame on your father. He sent Neil away, he brought charges against Bethany, refused to help her baby. And as for Tom . . ."

They were both silent for a moment. They now knew that Tom had joined the escaping convicts and that he, too, was a fugitive. They also knew that Neil had perished during the escape and that Bethany was aboard the ship taken by the absconders. Word of this had taken months to reach England. The information had been assembled from the accounts of the sailors who had been put into the longboats from the pirated ship, from one absconder who had foolishly returned to England recently and been caught, and from a doctor serving in the colony who had apparently gone through a form of marriage with Bethany before Neil's death.

The doctor, a certain Wilberforce Prentice, was apparently anxious to find Bethany and marry her legally, now she was a widow. He had written to Adrian from an address in Liverpool, and Mary had responded briefly that her husband was indisposed but that they had no idea where Bethany was now. When Hope was spirited away, Mary did wonder if the doctor was somehow involved, but her letter to him had been returned as undeliverable.

"Have you told Father about Neil?" Stewart asked.

"What would be the point? He wouldn't understand. He doesn't remember any of you, not even Tom. Like it or not, Stewart, you're now the head of the family." Mary leaned closer and placed her hand on his arm. "I know how terribly difficult it is sometimes to put duty before personal desires, Stewart. But in the long run, you will be happier if you do."

He looked at her sharply, and for an instant she wondered if he might confide in her the reason for his strange attitude lately, or even if he somehow sensed her own misery that duty kept her bound to Adrian when she longed to go to the man she loved.

But instead Stewart rose to his feet and said, "They've finished their game. I promised to take Davey down to the beach at low tide to search for shells. We shan't have too many more nice days before autumn arrives."

She watched him stride across the lawn. Was it her imagination, or was there a new spring in his step? He'd always been a handsome young man, but had tended to shrink inside himself, facing the world with a self-effacing air as though apologizing for being there. That had certainly disappeared. Amazingly enough, in addition to running the shipping company, he now found time for his music again. He was a patron of young musicians, active in supporting the symphony orchestra, and last night she'd heard him at the piano after everyone retired, playing a hauntingly beautiful piece that she thought might be one of his own compositions.

He spoke to Alison, who looked at him in a way that Mary understood very well. Alison loved her husband deeply. Did Stewart realize how much? He took the little boy's hand and they walked away together.

Alison made her way to the gazebo, and now Mary saw that

her expression had changed from the happy, loving look she had given Stewart to one that was tight, tense. However, as she climbed the wooden steps of the gazebo she forced a smile. "Lemonade? How nice. I should have brought Davey over for some, but he was so anxious to go to the beach. He loves to be with Stewart, and lately Stewart hasn't had much time for him."

"He must be frightfully busy with the company," Mary suggested gently and wondered at the strange expression that briefly crossed Alison's face.

"Mary, I know you haven't been doing any entertaining since Sir Adrian's illness, but I wondered . . . well, it would be a tremendous help to Stewart if we could have a garden party here at Riverleigh for our most important clients before summer ends. We can't invite some and not others without offending them, and our house just isn't large enough." She paused, giving Mary a self-conscious little smile.

"But, my dear, what would we do about Adrian? You saw how he was today at lunch. I can hardly protect your guests from his outbursts by locking him up in his own house."

"I thought about that. We could take him and his nurse to our house. I have a housekeeper and a maid to help. It would be a change of scene for Sir Adrian, and it would do you good to be relieved of caring for him for a day."

"Take him across the water? Oh, I don't know . . ."

"He wouldn't have to go on the ferry with other people. I can get a private boat to take him, and our carriage will meet them at the Pier Head."

Mary allowed herself to contemplate the prospect of a garden party. How lovely it would be to fill the grounds with guests. She could almost hear the conversation and laughter. She had been so lonely since Adrian's illness.

She smiled. "Yes, let's do it. I've been starved for company. Did you have a date in mind? What about your guest list? I probably know some of the people you want to invite. Are they all Fielding Shipping Company clients?"

Alison wore an enigmatic expression as she replied, "Yes, I expect you know most of them. But there are two ladies I want to invite whom you haven't met. One is a patroness of the arts named Miss Elspeth Fotheringhill, and the other is her niece, a concert pianist whose work Stewart admires. Her name is Miss Iris Holloway."

THE TWO SHADOWS crossing the beach drew closer to where Bethany, Teresa, and Ned waited with the longboat. Now they could distinguish that one man carried a third man over his shoulder.

Seconds later Bourke dropped Tom into the boat and Jack jumped in behind him. "Shove off—now," Jack ordered. "The others are dead."

Tom was unconscious. The shaft of an arrow protruded from his thigh, and a second one was embedded in his shoulder. As the boat skimmed the dark surface of the sea, headed toward the *Liberty,* Bethany cradled his head in her lap.

"He's unconscious from loss of blood," Jack said. "Tom was wounded just as you left. We'll have to get that arrow out of him quickly."

He braced his feet against the side of the boat, grasped the arrow in Tom's thigh and yanked it out. Bethany turned away, thinking of the raging infection that had killed Neil.

Bourke and Ned dipped the oars into the sea and rowed as fast as they could toward the tall outline of the ship while Jack tore off his shirt and used it to bind Tom's leg. He decided not to remove the second arrow until they were aboard the ship.

Bethany held her breath until they were all safely on deck, where Leona waited with the rest of the crew. They embraced silently. There would be time later to talk; for now there were wounds to be treated.

As the crew pulled up the anchor and set sail, Bethany gave one last glance at the dark silhouette of the shore and thought sadly of the ruins of the gracious del Castillo hacienda. Was Jack's prediction correct, that the era of the Spanish Californios had already passed?

The following day Teresa was put ashore to await her parents in the care of the fathers at the mission, and the *Liberty* began the long voyage around the Horn. Tom, who was young and strong, withstood Jack's clumsy probing for the arrowhead buried in his shoulder.

An Indian boy, who had been named by the padres Buen Juan, was found hiding in the hold after the *Liberty* was well at sea. He begged to accompany the gringos because, he said, the priests had beaten him regularly. This seemed to belie the name given him, Good John, but they decided to allow him to stay.

Buen Juan soon proved his worth when he rummaged among the vegetables and plants Tom had brought aboard the ship to help ward off scurvy and found one that he said would prevent infection of Tom's wounds when applied directly to the area and left without bandages. This proved to be true, and long before the ship had to battle the storms of the Strait of Magellan, Tom was back on his feet.

When at last the *Liberty* drew near her destination, Bethany's grief over Neil had diminished from a sharp pain to a dull ache, and she began to look forward to a future where she would be reunited with her daughter. She thought of the other voyages of her life and this, the third, she told herself with rising optimism, should surely bring better luck than the previous ones.

The *Liberty* was in need of repairs and dry-docking to scrape the barnacles from her hull. They also needed a place to live. Tom decided to take a chance and ask his father's shipping agent in New Orleans for advice on these matters.

Louisiana's humidity caused Tom's shoulder to ache, and he was not in the best of moods when he set out to find the agent handling his father's ships. The harbor master informed him that the Fielding Shipping Company was now the Ivers Shipping Company and had moved into larger offices on the banks of the Mississippi.

Tom paused to watch a steamboat pull away from the levee, colored steam rising, calliope shrieking, paddle wheel churning the muddy water. A long line of black men, muscles glistening in the hot sun, unloaded cotton from a barge for transshipment to a vessel no doubt bound for the cotton mills of Lancashire. There was a bustling air of excitement, commerce, a promise of discoveries to be made here, and at the same time a sense of history. This was the site of fierce battles between the British and Andrew Jackson, Jean Laffite, and their ragtag armies, fought gallantly but foolishly, since a peace treaty had already been signed. The city also bore the unmistakable imprint of old France on its balconied buildings and walled gardens.

What could have possessed his father to turn over the Caribbean ships to Tate Ivers? Tom wondered as he pushed open the door and went into a dimly lit office. The shutters on the windows were closed against the heat of the sun and a couple of clerks worked by lamplight. As his eyes became accustomed to the abrupt loss of bright daylight, he looked with astonishment at the man seated at a desk at the far end of the room.

Tate Ivers, wearing an equally startled expression, slowly rose to his feet. "Tom? Good God, can it really be you?"

They met halfway across the room and clasped hands; then Tate pulled him into a bear hug. "Thank God you're alive. We'd given you up for lost."

"What in the name of all that's holy are you doing here, Tate? You're the last man on earth I expected to see."

"A long story, lad. And I daresay you've a few tales of your own to tell." Tate glanced at his clerks, who had stopped working to observe the new arrival. "I have a house not far from here. Let's go there to talk."

That evening Tate's housekeeper, an extremely tall and regal looking mulatto woman named Saffron, prepared a sumptuous dinner for Tom, Jack, Bethany, and Leona.

After toasting their safe arrival with an excellent wine, Tate, who now knew the story of their voyages from the penal colony, raised his glass again. "To a new beginning, for all of you, unshackled by the mistakes of the past."

"Hear, hear," everyone murmured fervently.

"New names for all of you might be in order," Tate continued. "And I suggest you sail your ship into the Caribbean as soon as possible and sink her on a reef somewhere."

Tom looked dismayed. "But, Tate, I'd hoped we had changed her sufficiently to use her, at least for a little while longer. Then I planned to return her to her owners."

"You need papers for her, Tom. A registry. And as long as that ship exists, so does the chance that you'll be hanged for piracy. Not worth the risk. You've got to get rid of her."

Tom shrugged philosophically. "In that case, I may have to ask you for a job."

"No need, lad. I'm going to make you a full partner in Ivers

Shipping, and believe me, you'll earn your keep." He turned to Jack. "There's a place for you, too, if you want it."

Jack regarded him with a quizzical stare. "Frankly, sir, I've had enough of the sea and ships to last me a lifetime. But I'm curious as to why you're so ready to harbor fugitives."

"Tom was like my own son," Tate answered with a smile. "A constant nuisance, hanging around me in Liverpool, forever wanting to go on board the ships, asking incessant questions. Bethany here was Neil's wife, and that's reason enough for me to do everything I can for her. You, sir, and you, madam"—he bowed slightly in Leona's direction—"are unknown quantities. I hope neither of you will return to your old ways, but if you do, I will see to it that you do not drag Tom and Bethany down with you." He paused. "No matter what it takes."

Leona—resplendent in a jade silk gown made in Yerba Buena and intricately embroidered and trimmed with black lace, which matched a mantilla she wore in the Spanish style—raised her glass and said cheekily, "All the best to you, too, ducks."

"Mr. Ivers—" Bethany began.

"Please, you must call me Tate."

"Thank you. When Tom called on you earlier today, Tate, you said you had news from England that you would share with us."

Tate's brows knitted. "Could we have dinner first? I'd prefer to pass along family news just to you and Tom. No offense, Jack, Leona, but it's none of your business."

"We have no secrets," Tom began, but Bethany said softly, "I'd prefer to wait."

Saffron entered the room bearing an enormous platter that emitted a spicy and aromatic steam. It proved to be fish in a deliciously seasoned tomato sauce, and a far cry from the fish they'd eaten on the voyage.

Later they left Leona and Jack in the living room while they went outside into the walled garden. Tate said, "Tom, I very much regret having to tell you that your father is seriously ill and no longer in command of his faculties. Before he became completely incompetent he . . . and I decided to dissolve our partnership in the Fielding Shipping Company. I took the Caribbean and American coastal trade."

Tom was silent for a moment. "I'm sorry the old man is ill. But I learned things about him, and about his running of his ships, that destroyed all my illusions about him. And as for splitting up the ships between you, you were a fool, Tate. You gave him the lion's share."

"I didn't have much choice in the matter," Tate said dryly.

"Who is running the Fielding line now?"

"Stewart."

"Surely you're joking! He hated the very idea of it."

"Nevertheless, he's doing an excellent job. He's acquired new ships, and has a reputation for getting cargoes to their destinations intact and on time. Not only that, but sailors are queuing up to sign on his ships. He has no need of crimps, and woe betide any mate who lays a lash across a seaman's back."

Tom shook his head in silent amazement at this apparent transformation of his rather dreamy, artistically inclined brother.

"Mr. Ivers," Bethany said, unable to contain herself any longer, "do you know anything about my baby daughter?"

"Hope is alive and well, I'm sure," Tate said carefully. "Lady Fielding arranged for her to be taken from the parish home and cared for by a kind young woman who later married your brother Stewart, Tom."

"Stewart? *Married?* I can't believe it. He used to stammer and blush furiously if a girl even glanced in his direction," Tom exclaimed.

"Thank God my baby is safe." Bethany realized she had been holding her breath. "Hope, they called her? I like the name very much."

"Well . . . there's more. Lady Fielding wrote that someone had taken the child from Stewart and Alison . . . it would be several months ago . . . with the intention of bringing her to you."

"To me? But no one knows where I am. Tom did ask a seaman he knew to find out where my baby was, but—" She turned desperately to Tom.

"He wouldn't have taken her," Tom said. "He's a sailor living aboard a ship. How could he have cared for her? He'd have left her where she was and sent word to us. Do you know of anyone else? What about your brother?"

"Roland? Surely not! He's barely able to take care of himself, let alone a child. He never came to see me after I was arrested, and I doubt he's even aware of my child's existence. Oh, dear heaven, Tom, I must go to England at once—"

"I feel I should tell you," Tate interrupted, "that Mary—

Lady Fielding wrote to me that Stewart and Alison made many inquiries, trying to find out where Hope was taken, but to no avail."

"You can't return to England, Bethany," Tom said. "You know that."

"But I must! Someone has taken my baby—"

"If you will be patient while I teach Tom all he needs to know about the trading here," Tate put in, "I will return to England and try to find your daughter." He paused. "I had intended to go anyway, as soon as I found someone I could trust to take my place here."

STEWART PACED DISTRACTEDLY back and forth in the drawing room at Victoria Gardens and from time to time glanced at the piano, as though accusing it of being the cause of all his problems.

If only, *if only* . . . The most overused, futile words in the English language. If only he hadn't gone to the concert that night, if only he had not attended Iris's recital, if only he had not brought her here and made love to her.

He'd tried to break it off the day after little Hope disappeared. Despite his protestations to Alison, he felt an unbearable guilt that he had been with his mistress when the child was taken, leaving his wife to deal with the shock of discovery all alone.

After telling Iris what happened he had finished lamely, "I feel like a swine for not being there. I . . . I must never break my marriage vows again. I don't know what came over me. I do apologize to you—"

Iris had laughed and poked him viciously in the chest with a sharp fingernail. "Do shut up, darling, and try to be rational about this. You say the child is being returned to her real mother, so you must have expected that would happen one day. It's not as if the baby is yours or your wife's, is it? What you do with me, my dear, has nothing to do with marriage vows or anything else. Together we enter a realm of the senses that ordinary mortals cannot begin to comprehend. We are two spirits above and apart from the common herd. Besides, I have some wonderful news: Aunt Elspeth has arranged for me to give my first public recital in a few weeks, and . . ."

Her green eyes sparkled, her dimples deepened, and she ran her little pink tongue teasingly over her lower lip, prolonging the anticipation. "Darling, one of the pieces I want to play is 'Wildflowers.' "

Stewart had wavered and been lost.

Alison never asked where he had been the night Hope vanished, but she had erected an invisible wall about her grief that shut him out, even when he tried to comfort her. After a while he gave up, but as soon as he withdrew from her, she began to berate him for leaving them unprotected. Since there was nothing he could say in his own defense, he responded by spending more and more time away from her, usually with Iris.

He met Aunt Elspeth, a vinegary spinster with piercing green eyes, a glorious profusion of pure silver hair, and a love of music and musicians that caused most of her acquaintances to overlook her acerbic tongue. Elspeth Fotheringhill lost no time in recruiting Stewart's aid in the form of generous financial support for both the symphony orchestra and the coterie of struggling young musicians for whom she arranged recitals and sought sponsors.

Elspeth behaved toward Stewart in a manner that suggested she accepted him as a rich would-be composer, dabbling in writing as a respite from his business activities, interested only in her niece's musical talent. But he had a feeling that Aunt Elspeth vicariously enjoyed the attention of the hordes of suitors, himself included, who flocked around Iris. She encouraged them and basked in the reflected glory of her niece's beauty and talent.

As he waited for Iris to arrive at the town house in Victoria Gardens on the sultry afternoon following her recital, Stewart seriously contemplated stowing away on one of his own ships in order to escape the ordeal to come. But he simply had to end his affair with Iris once and for all. He could not allow her to talk him out of it or to beguile him into making love to her again. She was a temptation, a weakness of the flesh that he had to overcome. He would never be free of guilt ever again, but at least he could live decently from now on.

He heard her key in the front door; then the vestibule door opened and closed. He waited for her to call out to him, but she didn't. After a moment he opened the drawing room door and looked out. She wasn't in the hall. Sometimes she liked to slip upstairs and change out of her street clothes. Often she brought a valise containing a filmy nightgown or sheer robe. Once she had come downstairs naked except for the ever-present flowers in her hair and a little silver chain about her ankle holding a tinkling bell. Attempting to put that memory out of his mind, he wondered if he should call to her to please keep her clothes on, but that seemed presumptuous. He went back into the drawing room to wait.

The morning newspaper lay on top of the piano and he picked it up and read the brief account of Iris's recital again. Her performance was acclaimed as surprisingly mature and professional for one so young, but the most lavish praise was reserved for a new composition she had introduced, titled "Wildflowers." The composer's name had not been revealed, and there was speculation that perhaps Iris Holloway had written it herself and, fearing it would not be well received, had presented it anonymously. The mystery of the identity of the composer, the newspaper stated, enhanced the enchantment of the piece.

Dropping the paper, Stewart picked up a decanter and poured two glasses of wine. Iris should be coming downstairs at any minute and always wanted one the moment she arrived.

He had just finished pouring the drinks when the door opened and the last voice on earth he expected to hear spoke. "Why, Stewart, I didn't know you were here," Alison said.

The blood rushed to his face; his hands shook as he put down the decanter and turned to look at his wife, knowing his expression must be a ghastly mask of guilt and confusion. "Oh . . . uh, Alison. What are you doing here?"

She smiled easily and walked into the room. "I came to pick up some of Hope's infant gowns and matinee jackets that I left here when we moved out. They were up in the attic. I thought someday her mother might like to have them. What about you? What brings you here?"

He stood with his back to the table holding the two telltale glasses so that they were concealed from her view. She walked to the sofa in the window alcove and sat down, then peeled off her gloves and removed her hat pins.

Oh, God, she was going to stay! What if Iris arrived . . .

"I decided to open the house again," he said unnecessarily, since it was obvious that all dust sheets had been removed and the house had recently been cleaned. There were also several crystal vases filled with fresh flowers. He always brought a large bouquet; it was something the flower-loving Iris expected. "I felt the house should . . . that is to say, it seemed a waste . . ." his voice trailed away.

Alison exclaimed, "Ah, of course! Why didn't I guess? No one ever uses the place anymore, so you're planning to sell it. That's why you've had it cleaned. What a good idea!"

Letting out his breath slowly, he said, "Yes, it did occur to me that our house is convenient enough to the office, so we don't really need this one, too. Father will certainly never use it again."

"Have you selected an estate agent to show it to prospective buyers?"

"Not yet. I . . . I was going to discuss it with you this evening, Alison."

"Yes, of course. And you've already talked to Mary?"

"Well . . . she always hated this place, and I should think you would, too. Mrs. Creel's evil touch seems to be everywhere."

Her glance swept the room. "I'd say you've pretty well eradicated Mrs. Creel's presence. I don't ever remember her buying such lovely flowers and, goodness, so many of them!"

His fingers itched to loosen his collar, but he stood rigidly erect, feeling perspiration form in clammy pools on his body. Alison's expression seemed to be devoid of guile or sarcasm. He swallowed an uncomfortable lump in his throat.

Alison said, "I must have had a premonition, mustn't I? I just suddenly got an urge to come and pick up my mementos."

The bay windows of the room were open to catch the late afternoon breeze, and from outside came the ringing of the bell on a baker's wagon as it moved slowly along the street, its driver hawking bread and pies. A sparrow landed on the windowsill and chirped cheerfully. The clock on the mantel struck the hour, and the Westminster chimes seemed to take an age to finish their melody. A frantic little voice at the forefront of Stewart's mind kept warning him that Iris would arrive at any second.

He cleared his throat. "How did you get over here? Did Rudd bring you?"

"Yes. He's waiting outside in the carriage. Could we drop you somewhere?"

"No, no, I'm sure you have better things to do." He hesitated, then with what he decided might be a stroke of inspiration, added, "Now that the house is ready to show, I thought I might interview some estate agents. I can take a hansom."

"I'll go with you," she said promptly, re-pinning her hat. "You know how you are when it comes to dealing with tradesmen. We must be sure you get a fair price for the house. We should find out what other similar properties have sold for before we enter into any agreement."

Casting about desperately for a way to get her to leave without him and unable to think of one, he waited until she was on her feet and moving toward the door before he left the table and wineglasses to follow her.

At the door Alison paused and looked back and he held his breath. How on earth could he explain those two glasses of wine?

But she merely commented, "The cleaning woman needs to clean out the grate. How odd. I was sure it was emptied when Mrs. Creel moved out, and there's been no one here to light a fire since."

He made no comment, and she led the way through the vestibule to the front door. As he turned the key in the lock he surreptitiously glanced up and down the street. Their carriage, with the hulking figure of Hagen Rudd in the driver's seat, waited at the curb.

Stewart placed his hand under Alison's elbow as they descended the steps and he was about to help her into the carriage when his blood froze. A hansom was rolling toward the house, and since the driver sat in an elevated seat behind the cab, Stewart could clearly see its passenger. It was Iris, lovely in a flower-sprigged summer frock. As usual she had flouted convention by not wearing a bonnet, her hair being elaborately decorated with fresh rosebuds, violets, and velvet ribbons.

In the minutes it took for the hansom to reach them Stewart died a thousand deaths. What would Iris say? What would Alison do?

His wife was now seated in the carriage and looking at him expectantly, waiting for him to climb in beside her. Rudd had raised the reins ready to snap them, and he, too, waited. Stewart gave a sickly smile.

The hansom drew abreast of them, and he looked imploringly into Iris's glittering green eyes. She raised one perfectly arched eyebrow but gave no other acknowledgment that she was aware of him as the cab, without slowing down, continued on its way.

Stewart's relief was so great he collapsed awkwardly into the carriage. He was almost sure that Hagen Rudd gave him a contemptuous look before they moved away, but then, Rudd glowered at everyone but Alison.

Before the day ended, Stewart was taken aback to find himself in the position of having sold the house in Victoria Gardens. The first estate agent they called on was looking for a house in the neighborhood for himself and promptly made them a generous offer. At Alison's urging, Stewart concluded the sale on the spot.

He was still reeling from this development when the final blow of the day fell. After dinner Alison told him that all the arrangements were now complete for the garden party at Riverleigh and the invitations had already gone out.

"Would you like to look over the guest list," she asked as she poured his after-dinner liqueur, "in case I've overlooked someone we should invite?"

Scanning the list distractedly, he came to a sudden halt when he reached the names of Miss Elspeth Fotheringhill and Miss Iris Holloway. The blood drummed in his ears and he didn't look up at Alison as he remarked, in what he hoped was an offhand tone, "I understood we were just having our business clients and their wives? I see you've asked Miss Fotheringhill and Miss Holloway."

Alison smiled benignly. "Yes, I thought you'd like to have a couple of your musical friends, to put you at ease, you know. Perhaps we could even persuade Miss Holloway to play the piano for your guests. She might even play that piece you wrote, 'Wildflowers,' as she did at her recital."

35

HOPE FIELDING HAD extraordinary language skills for a three-year-old and for this Will Prentice was grateful, since after she had exhausted herself crying for Davey and "Alison" and "Uncle Stew-Stew," Will was able to explain to her that they had merely been taking care of her but now she was with her real father and soon they would be reunited with her real mother.

"Am I a princess?" Hope asked, drying her eyes. "Mrs.

Hughes read me a story about a princess. She got tooken away by a wicked stepmother when she was a little baby."

"Well, yes, you certainly are a princess to me."

The child had refused to eat for the first few days and Will became alarmed that she would starve to death, but the explanation that he was really her father seemed to satisfy her, especially when he pointed out that she had never called Alison "Mother" and that Stewart was her uncle. Didn't that prove he was telling the truth?

"Davey called Alison 'Mummy,' " Hope said, "but she told me I must call her Alison."

"There you are, then," Will said.

"Alison *not* a wicked stepmother," Hope said firmly.

"There are good stepmothers, too," he pointed out. "But no one will ever love you as much as your real mother."

He had lost no time in getting the little girl out of Liverpool. He took her into North Wales to a tiny village within sight of Snowdon and rented a cottage from a Welsh-speaking landlady notable mainly for her complete lack of interest in her tenants.

As soon as the child accepted him and he could be sure she would not make a scene in public, he would be able to continue his search for Bethany.

He had given a great deal of thought to where she might be. The ship the absconders had taken had been bound for the Sandwich Islands. Without a navigator to plot a different course, the erstwhile sailors still might have been able to follow the charts to this destination, especially since it was now known that Tom Fielding, who had some knowledge of seamanship, was aboard. There were many islands in the group where a longboat might slip ashore unnoticed. The men would then have sunk the ship to hide the evidence of their piracy.

Will Prentice concentrated on winning the trust of Bethany's child while he made plans to sail for the Sandwich Islands. Ships' doctors were always in demand, and he had no doubt he would be able to persuade a master to allow his "little daughter" to accompany him.

Never having dealt with a young child, and fearing she might tell that she had been taken from her bed in the middle of the night by a stranger if he hired a woman to look after her, he treated Hope like a miniature adult. He offered her the same food he ate and allowed her to go to bed when she chose. He answered her questions as honestly as he could but soon found that she lost interest if his responses were too detailed.

"Is my mother pretty?" she asked one day as he helped her button her shoes.

"Yes, very. You look a lot like her." Even as he said it his heart turned over. The child had her mother's honey-gold hair and luminous gray eyes, the same delicate features and beguiling smile. She had a habit of tilting her head slightly when confronted by a situation she didn't understand, and he recalled Bethany did the same thing.

"Why did she go away and leave me?"

"She couldn't help herself. Someone accused her of a crime, and she was sent somewhere where she couldn't take you."

"Prison?"

"No, but something like it."

The little girl's eyes clouded. "My mother is bad?"

"No, absolutely not! She wasn't guilty . . . she didn't do the bad thing they said she did."

Despite his best efforts, the little girl cried almost every night for her lost family. She missed Davey especially. From bits and pieces of information Will obtained it seemed that Alison and Stewart Fielding were gone much of the time, leaving the children in the care of a nanny.

In desperation, Will began to read bedtime stories to the child to calm her, and this seemed to help. After a couple of weeks he discarded the fairy tales and began to make up stories about a beautiful island where a lovely lady lived among the flowers, and she was very sad because her little daughter was on the far side of the world.

With Hope curled up in the crook of his arm, Will went on, "So the little girl's father set off on a noble quest to find their lost child and bring her back to her mother's loving arms. They sailed on a big ship, with white sails flapping in the wind and the blue sea slapping against the hull, rocking the little girl to sleep every night . . ."

Looking down, he saw that Hope's eyes were closed. Curling golden lashes lay against petal-soft cheeks, and a single curl had strayed across her brow. A small hand lay trustingly on his chest, relaxed, vulnerable.

Without warning, thoughts of his own daughter invaded Will Prentice's mind, and he felt his first real pang of guilt, unsure if it had its origins in his abandonment of Emma, or if he regretted having taken Hope from the only family she had ever known.

Perplexed by emotions he had never felt before, he stroked the curl gently back from Hope's forehead and whispered, "I'll take care of you, little one, I swear it before God. Somehow we'll find your mother, and I'll see that you both live happily ever after, just like in the stories."

A month after he took Hope, Will applied for and was given a position as ship's doctor aboard a passenger vessel sailing for South America. From there he would find a ship bound around the Horn for the Sandwich Islands. His young daughter, listed on the manifest as Emma Hope Prentice, accompanied him.

STEWART AROSE ON the day of the garden party with a sense of impending doom. Plans for the affair had now expanded to include an evening of music and dancing. He and Alison had arrived at Riverleigh the previous day so that Alison might help Mary with some of the last-minute details.

Standing at his bedroom window as the dawn broke, Stewart searched the sky anxiously, hoping to see storm clouds, which might deter some of the guests from journeying across the river for that most dismal of affairs, an outdoor party moved inside. But the sky was clear and the onshore breeze already warm. A perfect day for an execution, he thought gloomily.

He had begged and pleaded with Iris not to accept Alison's invitation, but Iris, already furious with him for selling the Victoria Gardens house and thereby depriving them of a private place to meet, shrugged and replied, "Apart from the fact that I shall *relish* the opportunity to meet your wife, Aunt Elspeth is absolutely delighted at the thought of going to Riverleigh to meet Lady Fielding, who is well known for her charitable contributions."

Last night Stewart had had nightmares wherein Auntie and Iris and Alison were all chasing him around the rose garden brandishing gardening shears.

A soft tap on his bedroom door announced the arrival of his

valet with warm water for his morning ablutions, and Stewart dragged himself over to the marble-topped washstand and prepared to face the coming ordeal.

Alison and Mary were already out in the garden directing the setting up of tables, deck chairs, a canopy to cover the refreshment table. Footmen and maids hurried back and forth, while gardeners and grooms were busy stringing paper lanterns from the trees and concealing oil lanterns to illuminate the fountain and the great stone urns trailing a profusion of late summer blooms.

A wooden pavilion had been set up, open on three sides to the lawns, and this, too, would be lit by hidden lamps. A buffet lunch table would be set up here; then, this evening after the musicians arrived, the wooden floor would be used for dancing. The croquet court had been manicured and one area of the lawn had been prepared for a game of bowls.

Satisfied that all was proceeding according to plan, the two hostesses returned to the house to supervise the arrangements for dinner, which would be served in the main dining room.

Mary ordered the frowning butler to cover the long banquet table with a fine Brussels lace overcloth of gold, so that the undercloth gleamed through the lace. Gold-plated cutlery would be used, along with the finest china and crystal.

The butler's mouth opened in outraged disbelief. "But the master ordered all of those things packed away, and he's never told me to get them out."

"I'm telling you now," Mary said pleasantly. "Please do so at once and without argument." She stared him down and after he departed she turned to Alison.

"I've never dared use any of those things before. They were all put into storage after Adrian's first wife died, and he wouldn't let me bring them out." She paused. "You know, I've always felt like an intruder at Riverleigh . . . at least, until just now. Goodness, I don't know what's come over me!"

"I think it's about time you enjoyed all those nice things," Alison commented. "God knows, you've earned the right."

"How did Adrian behave on the journey to your house?" Mary asked anxiously. "I did worry about how a . . . a one-legged man would handle him."

"I hardly ever notice that Hagen Rudd is missing a leg anymore. He can do everything a two-legged man does. Sir Adrian was no trouble at all; in fact, Mr. Rudd felt your husband enjoyed the boat ride."

Mary sighed. "It's such a relief to have Adrian out of the house that I feel guilty."

"Don't be. Sometimes men don't know what's best for them, and we have to make their decisions for them," Alison replied. "We can't let them muck up their lives and ours, can we?"

The irritation in her tone caused Mary to look at her in surprise. Alison, who had always been so unfailingly cheerful, had lately shown flashes of anger and impatience that in anyone else might have been unattractive, but in Alison were somehow exciting. Perhaps because Mary had no doubt that whatever the cause of her annoyance, she would deal with it. Mary constantly discovered new facets to the personality of this young woman, who had had none of the advantages of birth, class, or education, indeed had been born into the lower working class and had married into it, yet had quickly adapted to a way of life she surely had never even glimpsed before marrying Stewart. Alison seemed somehow stronger, more determined, and more adaptable than any of them.

She had even weathered the terrible blow of losing little Hope, whom she had adored. A hint of sadness lurked in her eyes, which previously Mary had attributed to the loss of the child, but now Alison's remark about men piqued Mary's curiosity. "I hope you aren't speaking from personal experience, Alison. I mean, Stewart *is* a good husband, isn't he?"

Alison gave her a wan smile. "Yes, of course. I didn't mean . . . Well, you see, I came from a houseful of brothers, and I deal with men all the time. I suppose I get a bit impatient with them when they act like little boys." She bit her lip. "I'm not referring to Sir Adrian's illness, but . . . well, they all behave like fools at times, don't they?"

Mary made a mental note to try to learn more about what was obviously troubling Alison. Despite her denial Mary felt that it must have something to do with Stewart. But for now there was simply too much to attend to.

Catching sight of a footman carrying a chair, she called to him, "Don't take that outside until this evening. We'll use the deck chairs and garden benches this afternoon. After dinner we'll need more comfortable chairs on two sides of the pavilion."

"I'm going to the kitchen," Alison said. "There's something I need to do."

A few minutes later the cook was surprised when Stewart's wife drew her aside and asked for a small pot of honey, which she took with her up to her room and transferred to another pot. She added a little perfume to the honey before replacing the lid.

An hour before the first guests were due to arrive, at Mary's insistence Alison forced herself to lie on her bed in a darkened room, with pads of cotton wool soaked in witch hazel over her eyes. But after a few minutes of squirming restlessly she got up and opened the curtains. Daytime naps had always seemed to her like lying down to die, and she hated the sluggish awakening afterward.

Frowning, she fingered the muslin dress she would wear this afternoon before changing for dinner. Her evening gown was a lovely emerald satin, and she was well satisfied that the seamstress had created a masterpiece. But the muslin afternoon gown seemed too frivolous, too youthful and giddy by far. It was of palest lavender, with flounces of *broderie anglaise* and tiny rose-colored ribbon bows scattered randomly about the full skirt.

Mrs. Hughes, the only woman who knew of Alison's business activities, had selected the pattern and the muslin, and urged her to have the dress made.

"Oh, do dress like a young girl again, Alison, just for one afternoon, for your husband. He sees you in those dreary navy blues and charcoals and blacks every day. Why, you don't even wear that pretty brooch he bought you."

"The brooch he brought the night Hope was kidnapped," Alison had pointed out quietly, *to salve his guilt.* But she had given in and ordered the muslin gown.

Now, however, Alison was filled with doubts about the suitability of the dress. She'd have to wear it, of course, since it was all she had brought with her to Riverleigh other than the evening gown and a couple of simple cotton day dresses.

She had never been comfortable having a maid help her dress, so decided to start getting ready early. As she donned the muslin gown, she felt her spirits lift. It *was* very becoming, the delicate color seemed to make her complexion glow and contrasted strikingly with her chestnut hair, which she wore in her usual smooth coil at the nape of her neck. She put on a *broderie anglaise* sunbonnet tied with the same color ribbons as the bows on her dress.

Opening her dresser drawer, she withdrew a folded newspaper clipping about Iris Holloway's debut recital at the concert hall and studied again the passages she had underlined: "Miss Holloway always wears fresh flowers in her hair, which is fashioned in an intricate arrangement of curls and waves. She scorns wearing bonnets or hats of any kind under any circumstances, and indeed her crowning glory, which is as fair as moonlight, should always be on view. She is certainly not a young lady who bows to convention in these matters. A delicate beauty—tiny, fine-boned—she is rarely seen in any color other than white in the evening."

The last thing Alison did before going down to await the arrival of the guests was to slip the small pot of perfumed honey into a pocket concealed in the flounced skirt of her dress.

The grounds of Riverleigh seemed to burst into life as carriages arrived and guests began to stroll across lawns and linger in the shade of the trees to converse. The women wore light summer gowns and carried parasols that along with their bonnets protected their complexions from the unaccustomedly warm sunshine. Alison and Mary relied only on their bonnets, since they needed their hands free to greet their guests.

As she mingled with the guests, often meeting wives of businessmen for the first time, Alison kept glancing toward the circle of carriages on the gravel drive, watching for the arrival of the one she most wanted to see.

A prickly sense of foreboding warned her when Miss Iris Holloway and her aunt approached, although she was not looking in their direction at the time.

They were the last guests to arrive, long after the receiving line had left the terrace, and they stood at the top of the steps like divas awaiting the acclaim of an audience.

Alison murmured to Mary, "I'll go to them. You stay with our other guests."

Holding her head high, Alison walked up the steps. Stewart had materialized out of nowhere and was bending over to kiss Miss Fotheringhill's wrist. Iris stood at her aunt's side watching Stewart with a decidedly proprietary air. Alison had a quick impression of a petite, exquisite young woman with vivacious features, a mischievous smile, and a rather boldly direct gaze. She wore a white gown, cut far too low for day wear, which was embroidered all over with white daisies. She carried a tiny white lace parasol. White rosebuds, lilies, and daisies decorated her hair, which had been coaxed into an elaborate coiffure of tumbling ringlets and sweeping waves with liberal amounts of pomade that added to the glossy sheen. Alison noted that when an errant breeze whispered across the terrace, not one hair on Iris's head moved.

Stewart, wearing a sickly grin that appeared to be pasted on his face, introduced them.

"I've been dying to meet you," Iris said, placing a tiny lace-gloved hand into Alison's firm grip. "Stewart has told me so much about you." Her cat's eyes danced with merriment. She was clearly enjoying the situation.

"Oh? He told me nothing at all about you," Alison answered. "Except that you play the piano, of course. Perhaps you'll play for our guests later on."

"I'd love to play for *you,*" Iris said, her eyes fixed on Stewart. Turning to Alison she added, "Your dress is lovely. Do you think that color will ever come back into fashion?"

Aunt Elspeth said quickly, "I'm so looking forward to meeting Lady Fielding."

"Yes, it's a pity you arrived too late to be received by her. She's busy with her other guests just now," Alison said, hoping her Scotland Road accent had not returned, as it did when she was tense. "But you'll meet her later on. I'll have a footman take your evening gowns and bags up to one of the bedrooms. All the maids are busy, so I'll take you to the powder room myself. I'm sure you'll want to freshen up a bit."

Stewart promptly offered his arm to Iris, but Alison said sharply, "Miss Holloway will want to come with us, dear. They've had a long journey."

Leading the way into the house, Alison was only vaguely aware of the chatter of Aunt Elspeth, most of which concerned her niece's musical talent and her eager anticipation of meeting Lady Mary Fielding and obtaining her sponsorship of one or more of her musical protégés.

As they reached the ground floor powder room and Aunt Elspeth disappeared into the cubicle containing the commode, Alison said, "Your flower headdress is lovely, Miss Holloway, but I see that several strands of your hair have escaped in the back."

"Oh, pooh!" Iris exclaimed, annoyed. "My pomade is in my bag. Would you have the footman bring it down?"

"Oh, I'm sure I have some here somewhere, let me take care of it for you," Alison said, pretending to rummage in a drawer.

Standing behind Iris to coax her hair into place, Alison looked at the reflection in the mirror of a perfect oval face. Now that they were alone, those delicate features seemed to have taken on a sharper, craftier expression. Iris's green eyes regarded her disdainfully. "You know how to dress hair? Oh, yes, of course, I recall Stewart told me you weren't used to having a maid do it for you. You really seem to handle all this"—she gestured with graceful hands, indicating her surroundings—"very well, considering."

When Alison didn't respond, Iris bubbled on, "And you certainly don't look quite as old as I expected, from what I've heard about you from Stewart. I mean, it doesn't sound as though you're much fun to be with. Whoops! I didn't mean that the way it sounded."

Keeping her eyes locked on Iris's malicious stare, Alison surreptitiously pulled several curls free from the intricate flower arrangement.

Iris continued in a slightly louder voice, as though her listener were deaf, "Yes, you're not nearly as old as I thought you'd be. Although if you'd like a bit of advice, your dress *is* a bit young for you. One does have to beware of looking like mutton dressed as lamb, doesn't one?"

Alison merely smiled and dipped the comb into the little pot in her hand, applying the contents lavishly to several strands of gossamer-fine hair. "There, that seems to have taken care of it."

Aunt Elspeth reappeared and Alison ushered them both quickly outside, explaining that she must not neglect her other guests. She led them onto the lawn and presented them to Mary, then said, "Ah, here's my husband. Stewart, would you introduce the ladies to our other guests?"

The trio walked away, Iris slipping her arm through Stewart's and lowering her parasol so that the sunlight gilded her hair. She gazed adoringly up at Stewart, leaned closer, and murmured something that made him laugh.

Iris giggled and reached up with one hand to tweak his ear.

Mary watched in amazement, then turned indignantly to Alison. "What a brazen little minx! She's actually flirting with Stewart in full view of everyone—including you. What possessed you to invite her . . ." Her voice trailed away as she saw the expression on Alison's face.

She squeezed Alison's hand sympathetically. "I'm sorry. I

had no idea. I wondered why Stewart had been so jumpy since he arrived. But why bring her here?"

"I wanted to meet her," Alison replied. "I wish she weren't quite so pretty. She reminds me of a little filigree butterfly."

"Does Stewart know that you know?"

"I don't think so."

"Are you going to confront him?"

"No. I'm going to deal with her."

Mary glanced in Stewart and Iris's direction. Aunt Elspeth had drifted off by herself, leaving the two of them alone. They stood close together, deep in conversation.

Alison watched, too, more openly.

Iris raised her hand and batted at a fly or some other insect buzzing about her head. A moment later Stewart swatted the air near her face. Suddenly Iris ducked and stabbed with her parasol at some airborne menace. Stewart clapped his hand to drive off the attacker.

Alison gave a small satisfied smile. "Shall we circulate among our other guests? It looks as if little Miss Holloway is being taken care of."

Before she finished speaking, Iris ran with undignified haste from the spot where she stood, flailing her parasol about her head like a weapon. Stewart followed.

Alison walked over to the nearest knot of guests and engaged them in conversation and Mary, still wearing a puzzled expression, followed.

The afternoon grew even warmer; the breeze dropped. Lunch was served from the buffet table set up on the pavilion, and the plates were carried by footmen to small tables scattered about the lawn. Alison sat with their most important shipper and his wife.

In the periphery of her vision she saw Iris, a cloud of flies and gnats creating a black halo around her pale silvery hair. She was perched awkwardly on the edge of a chair at an otherwise unoccupied table. She had closed her parasol, which merely trapped the buzzing horde, and now used it to try to swat the insects away. A moment later Aunt Elspeth joined her niece. The other guests, who were choosing tables randomly, avoided going near her.

Long before any of the other guests finished eating, Iris was again on the move, walking distractedly about the grounds accompanied by her rapidly growing flock of insects, which now included several large bluebottles. She would break into a terrified run whenever a wasp or a bee joined their ranks.

Stewart, locked in conversation with a Lancashire mill owner who imported vast quantities of cotton from America aboard Fielding ships, could only sit and watch in fascinated dismay Iris's frantic ballet.

Alison overheard one guest ask another, "Why is that young woman dashing about like a mad thing? One would think she had Saint Vitus' dance!"

Several tables away Mary looked up and caught Alison's eye. She smiled conspiratorially and Alison wondered if she had guessed what had happened.

After the meal ended, most of the ladies decided to go indoors to rest, as Alison had anticipated, leaving the men to play bowls and croquet, to converse with one another, or to doze in deck chairs in the shade.

Iris fled toward the house and Stewart rose to his feet, but before he could follow, Alison was at his side. "Now is the time to talk about our plans for the new ships and tell about our new ports of call."

She slipped her arm through his in much the same way Iris had done earlier and drew him determinedly over to a group of men sitting in the gazebo.

For the next couple of hours Alison did not leave Stewart's side. She accompanied him from one group to another, and if he faltered when someone asked a question pertaining to the shipping company, she gently prompted him: "Why, you remember, dear, you said that you were going to . . ." or, "Stewart dear, didn't you tell me that . . ."

Eventually Mary sought them out. "Alison, you haven't had a minute's rest. Do go inside and put your feet up for half an hour at least. You'll be exhausted if you keep up like this."

"I'm all right, Mary," Alison replied. "Everything is going so well. Don't worry, I'll go inside in plenty of time to change for dinner."

Mary looked at Stewart. "Your little pianist friend's behavior is rather peculiar, isn't it? Is she somewhat eccentric?"

He colored. "Not usually. There seem to be an excessive number of insects about today. Because of the heat, I expect. She hates insects."

"Odd how they seem to bother her more than anyone else," Mary said, flashing a wicked smile at Alison.

"No doubt all those flowers in her hair are attracting them," Alison said coolly. "Perhaps she should have worn a bonnet like the rest of us."

"I noticed her hair is plastered with pomade," Mary said. "Especially in the back. A number of flies were actually sticking to it." She bit her lip, as if to keep from laughing, and moved on.

Stewart avoided meeting Alison's eye. "Perhaps Mary is right. You should rest before dinner."

"I don't like to rest in the middle of the day. It's such a waste of time. Sleeping your life away, my mother used to say. I like to feel I've accomplished something."

"You've certainly accomplished something today. We're going to have more cargoes and passengers than we can handle. One of the shipping agents floored me when he said he had buyers for our first cargo of tea from China. I didn't even know we had entered the China tea trade."

Alison knitted her brows thoughtfully. "When that decision was made you were probably helping Miss Holloway with her concert arrangements."

He had grown very pale. She added, "Speaking of whom, I'd better go and see if I can pick some gnats off her. Funny how insects gather about spoiled and rotten things, isn't it?"

She walked away before he had time to respond.

The house was quiet when she entered, and she went upstairs. Tiptoeing past the closed doors where the ladies rested, she paused by the one assigned to Iris and her aunt. She could hear muffled conversation, frantic whispers and little exclamations.

Alison tapped lightly on the door and opened it. "I'd like a word with you in private, Miss Holloway—" She broke off at the sight of Iris.

She sat dejectedly at a dressing table wearing only her chemise. Her pale hair was soaking wet, straggling limply about her shoulders. Flowers and ribbons were scattered around her on the floor. Aunt Elspeth hovered behind her with a towel and hairbrush.

Catching sight of Alison, Iris spun around on the dresser stool, her face livid. "You did this to me! You put something sticky in my hair and we had to use so much soap to get it out I'll never be able to do anything with it. Damn you! How dare you?"

Alison closed the door behind her. "How dare I? Why, my

dear Miss Holloway, I'd think that you of all people wouldn't have to ask that question. You're certainly daring, aren't you, now? You dared to chase my husband. You dared to come here and flaunt yourself. Did you think I asked you to come today so I could give you my blessing? Why, anybody with an ounce of sense would have known I intended to warn you to leave my husband alone."

Green eyes glittered maliciously. "You have no class at all, do you? I'd heard you were a common upstart from the worst slums of Liverpool. I see it's true."

Alison shrugged. "Of course it's true. That's why you'd do well to stay away from my husband. Upper-class ladies close their eyes to their husbands' little dalliances, don't they? Women of my class don't. They claw the eyes out of any tart who comes between them and their men."

Aunt Elspeth nervously dabbed her niece's head with the towel. "I don't think this is a proper conversation between a hostess and a guest."

"No," Alison said, "but it's a proper conversation between a wife and a slut."

"Oh!" Iris jumped to her feet. "Get out! Get out of this room."

"I can't wait to leave. It smells like a bawdy house in here. Why don't you go, too, before the ladies wake up? And don't forget what I said. Stay away from my husband or I'll make your life miserable. A few flies and wasps will be nothing compared to what I'll do if I catch you near him again."

Alison made her way to her own room. She closed the door and leaned against it, breathing rapidly. It had taken all of her willpower to keep from smacking Iris's vain little face.

Taking off her bonnet, Alison dropped it on the bed. Her emerald satin evening gown hung from the wardrobe door, shimmering in the late afternoon sunshine. The light from the lanterns tonight would also gild the shining satin, and the shadowed trees and shrubbery would be a deeper echo of the color, so that she would harmonize with the garden. When the dancing began, the draped backdrop of the pavilion would set off her gown. She had ordered the single wall of the pavilion draped in stark white. If Iris Holloway appeared in her white gown, with her near-white hair and lily-pale complexion, she would disappear into the background.

A soft knock on her door preceded the appearance of Lady Fielding, who was accompanied by her personal maid. "Alison,

I brought Johnson to help you with your gown and your hair. You have such lovely waves and your hair is so glossy and thick, you really shouldn't pull it back into that unbecoming bun."

Remembering how thin and limp and colorless Iris's hair had looked without its pomade and ribbons and flowers—there'd even been padding beneath the curls, Alison had noticed—she did think it was a good idea to flaunt her own luxuriant locks.

Mary returned an hour later and, seeing Alison standing self-consciously before a full-length mirror, clapped her hands in delight. "You look beautiful! Oh, Alison—Stewart is going to fall in love with you all over again."

But he had never been in love with her, Alison thought. Still, she did feel beautiful. The dress emphasized her womanly curves and small waist. She was not tiny and delicate like Iris, but with her hair falling loose in soft waves and her shoulders rising creamy and smooth above the ruched bodice of the gown, she presented a completely different picture from her workaday self. Would Stewart notice?

Mary was holding a velvet case and now she opened it. "I brought something for you to wear tonight." She held up an emerald pendant with matching earrings.

Alison gasped at the sheer magic of the glittering gems. "Oh, I couldn't! I'd be afraid of breaking them."

"You won't break them. Besides, they're a gift from your husband. They belonged to Stewart's mother."

"Why didn't he give them to me himself, then?"

"I think he's afraid to face you just now. He wanted me to present the jewelry to you as a gift from me, but I felt you should know the truth. Let's at least try them on, shall we?" She fastened the clasp of the pendant as Alison slipped on the earrings.

They both stared at her reflection in the mirror. Alison said slowly, "Why . . . I look like a highborn lady."

Mary wrapped her arms around Alison and held her for a moment. When she drew away her eyes had misted slightly. "I'm not sure when I began to love you like a daughter, Alison . . ."

Alison felt her own eyes fill with tears. "What are we crying about?" she asked, trying to smile. "This is one of the happiest moments of my life. Even though my husband has a mistress and God help me when she tells him what I did to her this afternoon—"

"Goodness! I almost forgot to tell you," Mary exclaimed. "They're gone. Iris and Elspeth left just after I brought Johnson up to you. They said Iris wasn't feeling well. Her head was all wrapped up in a scarf—" She bit her lip to stop a chuckle.

"Does Stewart know? He . . . didn't go with them, did he?"

"He's waiting for you downstairs," Mary assured her. "And, by the way, so are all the other guests. As soon as you're ready, I'll have dinner served. Now, you wait a few minutes after I leave. I want you to make an entrance. Come down the staircase slowly, Alison, and be sure to smile as though you haven't a care in the world."

Easier said than done, Alison thought as she stood at the top of the stairs a few minutes later.

Below in the hall the guests were standing in small groups waiting for the dinner gong. Stewart stood at the foot of the staircase, and as she came down he looked up and saw her. Her heart hammered at the expression on his face. He looked both proud and contrite, but something else lurking in his eyes caused Alison to take in a swift breath. Was it possible—oh, let it be so—that what she saw in her husband's eyes was the beginning of desire?

"I've never seen you look lovelier," he said when she reached him. "You're really quite dazzling."

"Oh, it's just the dress and the jewels," Alison replied, pleased by the compliment but so unaccustomed to receiving praise of any kind from him that she was inexplicably embarrassed. Stewart's jaw moved slightly, almost as if she had struck him.

She said awkwardly, "Thank you for letting me wear your mother's jewels."

"Mary told you, then?"

"Yes. I feel honored. But I'd have liked it better if you'd given them to me yourself."

"I was afraid they'd go the way of the cameo brooch I bought for you."

She looked away, fearing where the conversation might lead. She didn't want to talk about anything that had occurred prior to this one magical moment. It was almost like meeting for the first time.

The dinner gong sounded, and she slipped her arm through Stewart's. "Shall we go in?"

Neither of them mentioned Iris or her abrupt departure. When the meal ended and the guests drifted outside again, to a fairyland of lanterns and music and a still-warm evening, Stewart remained attentively at her side.

He danced with Alison whenever he could pry her away from the other men. For a blissful couple of hours they were carefree; the burdens of responsibility, loss, and estrangement were forgotten. Alison felt young and pretty. She laughed and danced, and although it was not in her nature to act flirtatious, she hoped that Stewart could read the invitation in her eyes.

Long after the last guest had departed Alison waited alone in her room, wishing passionately that he would come to her. She was still waiting, and wondering where the magic had gone, when the dawn broke the following day.

37

THE HUMID HEAT of New Orleans seemed to have drained all of Bethany's energy, and she put down her pen and leaned back in her chair. Picking up a closely written sheet of paper, she studied it with a slight frown of concentration.

Voices in the downstairs hall drifted up to her and she glanced at the clock on the desk with a start. Had she really spent the entire afternoon writing? No wonder her fingers were numb and her shoulders ached.

She went to the door of the room she used as both a bedroom and a study and stepped out onto the landing. Tom and Tate had returned from their world of ships and cargoes, and Saffron, looking like an Egyptian queen, took their hats and murmured in a voice that reminded Bethany of liquid velvet that cold drinks were waiting in the drawing room, and yes, Miss Bethany was at home.

Bethany wondered if Tate ever noticed the slight change in Saffron's tone, a slight tearing of the velvet, that occurred whenever she mentioned their female guest. It was a good thing Leona had decided not to accept Tate's hospitality, Bethany reflected, since Leona would certainly have noticed the housekeeper's disapproval and commented on it in something less than a ladylike manner.

Leona and Jack had been fascinated by the paddle wheelers traveling up and down the Mississippi, and they were now sailing up the river to Natchez. They had both attempted to persuade Bethany to accompany them, but Tom had declared, "Bethany is my sister-in-law and therefore I will take care of her. I like you very much, Jack, but you're no fit companion for a lady. Bethany and I will stay here in New Orleans with Tate."

Tate had agreed with him and offered his hospitality, along with Saffron's services.

As for Bethany, she wanted to remain in New Orleans to urge Tate to hurry to England and send word back about her daughter. Besides, heaven only knew where Black Jack Cutler might wander.

But after he left she began to realize how much a part of her life Jack had become. Sometimes, late at night when sleep eluded her, Bethany thought about Jack, wished he were less of a rogue and vagabond, and missed him.

She went down to the drawing room and asked the question with which she greeted the men every evening. "Is Tom ready to take over yet, Tate? Will you leave for England soon?"

They both smiled indulgently and gave their usual answer. "Soon. Be patient."

Saffron brought a tray containing a cool drink and offered it to her, and as Bethany took it she saw again the flicker of resentment in the housekeeper's amber eyes.

"Thank you," she said, wondering why she had the feeling that Saffron would have preferred to give her hemlock.

"And did you spend the day writing in your journal again, Bethany?" Tate asked.

She nodded.

"I can see why you and Neil were drawn together," Tate added. "He was always scribbling something, even as a small boy. Tom here, on the other hand, was like a caged tiger if he was kept indoors for more than five minutes at a time."

"Bethany, I do worry a little about that diary of yours," Tom put in. "I hope it doesn't begin before our arrival in New Orleans."

"As a matter of fact, it begins with my arrival at the hulks in Portsmouth, just before I boarded the *Peregrine* and sailed to the penal colony. It also describes in detail the horrors endured by female convicts en route, at the hands of the settlers, and in the infamous female factory."

Consternation was reflected in the expression of both men.

"Tom's right," Tate said. "It wouldn't do for such a damning piece of evidence to fall into the wrong hands."

Bethany thought of Saffron's resentful glances and decided to keep her desk locked from now on. Aloud she said, "But I want the world to know of the shameful conditions in the penal colony, especially for the women."

"And how do you propose to publish such an account?" Tate inquired gently.

"Well . . . I wondered if you could take it back to England with you—that's why I've been working on it so hard—and give it to an editor friend of Neil's. He'd know what to do with it."

Tom looked aghast and Tate said carefully, "But we can't risk your identity being revealed. The nations of the world have worked diligently to erase piracy from the high seas. You will not be safe from the long arm of British law, even here, if it is revealed that you were among those who took the ship."

"I thought my story might be published anonymously. Perhaps it could be serialized in a magazine or newspaper in the same way Mr. Dickens's stories are."

Tom sat bolt upright and pounded the arm of his chair with his hand. "That's it!"

"What is?" Tate asked, blinking as dust motes rose from the site of the blow to form a golden pathway toward a sunlit window.

"Bethany can convert her diary into a fiction—a story—and present it as such. She could still inform her readers of the horrible situation in the penal colony, but she can disguise the identities of all of us—herself especially."

"I don't know," Tate said doubtfully. "It would still be risky."

"Not if she includes enough fictional episodes, preferably as dramatic as those of Dickens, so that her readers will accept the whole as a well-researched novel rather than a firsthand account of life in the colony. Most important, she could use a nom de plume."

Bethany said slowly, "Reading has always been my greatest pleasure. I've often thought I'd like to write children's stories. In fact, when I was aboard the transport ship and later, in Australia, I worried so much about how I would tell my daughter what had happened to me that I invented a character to tell the story for me. I thought when we were reunited it might be a way to explain why I had to leave her behind."

"There you are, then," Tom said. "No need to send your story to England, either. There are publishers here."

Saffron glided noiselessly into the room again. "Dinner is ready, sir."

Jack Cutler appeared abruptly one morning when Bethany was struggling with the decision as to how much of the sexual degradation of the female convicts she could hint at in her story and still remain within the boundaries of good taste.

Jack came marching up the stairs, followed by a protesting Saffron, and pounded on Bethany's door.

"Ahoy the bedroom! Stand by for boarding!"

A moment later he stood on the threshold, resplendent in a new linen suit and ruffled shirt, a straw hat in his hand.

Saffron's voice floated over his shoulder. "Ah done told him not to come up heah. It ain't proper."

Seated at her desk, Bethany said, "Saffron is quite right, Jack. Why don't you go downstairs and I'll join you in a moment?"

"Don't have a moment. Just stopped in to let you know I'm back in New Orleans. Leona's back, too. I expect she'll be calling on you. Give my regards to Tom and Tate and tell them I'll be in touch."

He gave a sweeping bow and was gone.

Bethany blinked, feeling as though a whirlwind had passed through.

Leona appeared late that afternoon, bursting with news to impart. She, too, was opulently gowned in the latest fashion. Her hair, now grown out to her former luxurious mane, was topped by a bonnet that was little more than a frothy confection of feathers and veils. The old-gold gown and her tawny hair, along with her sinuous manner of moving, made her look more than ever like a sleek lioness.

The two women went into the walled garden to talk.

"You look wonderful," Bethany said. "Doesn't the humidity bother you?"

"I think I'm getting used to it. Do you like the dress? And what about my bonnet? Saucy, isn't it?"

"It is indeed. I noticed Jack was sporting new clothes, too. Did you both find a pot of gold at the end of the river?"

"No, ducky, *on* the river! You know, Jack wasn't thrilled that I elected to travel on the same riverboat as him, and if it hadn't been for the gaming tables, I doubt we'd have seen much of each other. We both like a game of chance, but I must say I'm luckier at cards than he is. That's probably why I'm so unlucky in love. Not that he has much luck in that department either."

Bethany looked puzzled and Leona continued, "Those riverboats, lovey, are floating gambling dens. I won enough to buy myself a nice wardrobe before we ever reached Natchez. Jack didn't do so badly either."

"Oh, I see."

"Now let me tell you the really exciting news. See, we met a young fellow named Louis LaFleur in one of the poker games. God, he's the luckiest player I've ever seen. He had an extraordinary run of luck, and in this one game there was just Louis and a businessman left. The businessman was so determined to win back all he'd lost that he wagered a gaming house he owned here in New Orleans, just tossed the deed right on the table."

Bethany, who had no interest in card games, wondered where the conversation was leading, but nodded politely.

"Louis is a rather frail lad," Leona went on, "and the businessman was furious at losing. He had this great hulking brute with him—a bodyguard, I think—who pulled out a knife. Jack stepped in and took it away from him. Then he suggested that the captain pull over to the levee, and Jack escorted both of them off the boat at gunpoint. Needless to say, Louis was grateful. In fact he followed Jack around, and more than once when Louis's good luck got a bit too much for somebody, Jack had to save his hide. To cut a long story short, it turns out that Louis is the only son of a very rich plantation owner upriver. He doesn't need his winnings; he just loves to gamble. On the way back to New Orleans he told Jack he was afraid he wouldn't live to enjoy his own gaming house—unless he had a partner to run it for him."

"He offered Jack a partnership in a gaming house?"

Leona nodded. "I had a good laugh, I can tell you. The very idea of a former highwayman being given free rein with all that money wafting around! It's like putting a fox in with the chickens. Anyway, this gaming house turns out to be a private club, one of the fanciest here in New Orleans. Besides the gambling rooms, there's a dining room and a French chef, musicians playing every night, and"—Leona paused for effect—"a little theater where they put on dramatic readings and even an occasional play!"

"Oh, Leona, how wonderful! A place for you to be an actress again. And a partnership for Jack!"

"Whoa! Not so fast. Black Jack isn't going to be a partner. He told Louis he wasn't interested and to hire himself a bodyguard. He suggested Bourke, and Bourke jumped at the chance."

Bethany privately decided it was just as well that Leona and Jack wouldn't be thrown together at the club, since they clashed constantly. Aboard the ship everyone had gone to great lengths to keep them apart.

"But wouldn't you know, Black Jack managed to make himself even more of a hero in Louis's eyes," Leona went on. "When he arrived back in New Orleans the businessman who owned the club reneged; he refused to turn the club over to Louis. He'd signed over the deed, but when Louis went to take possession, the swine said the club wasn't really his, that he'd just sort of taken it over from a previous owner, so he wasn't empowered to sign over the deed."

Leona paused. "Now here's the interesting part. Our Black Jack Cutler, former highwayman and God knows what else, he comes up with a *legal* way for Louis to get his club."

"But how?"

"Something called adverse possession, I think. It means if somebody uses a piece of property long enough it becomes his. He said American law is based on English common law, and it applies in England so probably would apply here, too."

"Was he right?"

"Well, Louis has his club," Leona announced triumphantly.

"I wonder how Jack learned so much about the law?" Bethany mused.

"Probably from being on the wrong side of it for so long!" Leona's merry laugh rang out.

She leaned forward. "Will you do something for me, Beth? Get Jack to find out when Louis is going to put on a play at the club, especially when they're starting casting. I *think* Louis likes me, but I *know* he hero-worships Jack. Maybe Jack could sing my praises a bit, say he saw me on the stage in London. He'll do it if you ask him."

"I'll ask Jack to come to tea. I've missed that rascal anyway."

"Don't let him know that," Leona cautioned. "He'll carry you off to his cave if you do."

* * *

Jack arrived promptly at four, as Bethany had requested, and she served tea in Tate's walled garden, at a small wrought-iron table in the shade of a magnolia tree.

"You look particularly fetching today, Mrs. Newton-Fielding," Jack remarked.

"I wish you would go back to calling me Bethany. I always feel I'm being chastised when you address me like that."

"Just trying to behave in a gentlemanly manner. Isn't that one of my main failings? That I'm not enough of a gentleman?"

Ignoring the sarcasm, Bethany continued, "Besides, I don't use the name Newton any longer, as you very well know. We all agreed to change our names."

They had all taken new surnames, but decided a slip of the tongue would be inevitable with first names and so had kept their own. Bethany used her grandmother's maiden name, which was Phillips. Tate suggested that Tom might like to become his nephew, Tom Ivers. Leona had already tried on and discarded several stage names. Jack, refusing to be serious, called himself Jack Spratt.

"Oh, forgive my error, madam. I meant, Mrs. Phillips," Jack said.

"Please, Jack. Let's not get into that kind of a discussion today. I thought we'd left all of that behind us." She didn't add, *when you saved my life in California,* but she felt that a turning point in their relationship had been reached soon after that. He'd been kinder, less mocking.

He sipped tea from an almost transparent china cup, his little finger elegantly cocked in a parody of social grace. "Forgive my cynical male perspective, but in view of the formal invitation to tea and the obvious pains you have taken with your appearance—your hair, by the way, is like a golden halo—I must infer that you want something of me."

Flustered, she said, "Could I not simply want to visit with a friend?"

"I've told you many times, I am not your friend, nor do I wish to be. My interest in you has more to do with lust than with friendship."

Bethany picked up the teapot to refill her cup, mainly so she wouldn't have to look at him, and decided to ignore the taunt by steering the conversation in another direction. "Leona told me about your new friend Louis LaFleur and his club. She said the place has a stage and plays are performed there."

"And Leona can already smell the greasepaint and hear the applause, I take it?"

"Would you put in a good word for her with Louis LaFleur?"

He laughed shortly. "I doubt she needs me to achieve her ends. Louis is mesmerized by her. I hope it's a case of puppy love and will pass."

"You don't like Leona, do you? Why?"

He studied the waxy perfection of a magnolia blossom with a frown of concentration, as though seeing one for the first time. "I can take her or leave her. But I don't think she's a fit companion for a young blue-blood like Louis, who by the way is at least ten years younger than she is. Nor, for that matter, is she a suitable friend for you. She's not of your class and you might pick up some of her bad habits."

"Jack! How can you say such a thing? How cruel of you!"

"Realistic, Bethany, not cruel. Her past speaks for itself. She was a thief in England and a whore in Australia."

"She did what she had to do in Australia to survive. How dare you condemn her for that! Besides, you were a thief, too. A highwayman, as I recall, one with a reputation for seducing ladies. Why do we never refer to a man of low morals in the same disparaging way as a woman? It isn't fair!"

"If you think I'm going to debate the double standard with you, you're wasting your breath."

Feeling she was rapidly losing control of the direction the conversation was taking, Bethany said quickly, "But you will use your influence with Louis on her behalf, in regard to acting again?"

"Of course." He frowned slightly, patted his mouth with his napkin, then pulled out a handsome gold pocket watch and checked the time.

Puzzled by his offhand manner, which was close to being rude, Bethany said, "You seem . . . so different."

He gave her a sidelong glance that was both quizzical and mocking. "Not gazing at you like a lovesick swain, you mean?"

Bethany flushed. "There's no need to mock me. I just meant that . . . on the long voyage around the Horn you were kind and thoughtful, I felt you were a true friend."

"Didn't I just tell you I don't want to be your friend?"

Perplexed by the hard edge to his tone, she bit her lip. "Why are you so angry? What have I done?"

"Nothing, unless you count inviting me here today simply to

ask a favor for Leona. Not very flattering. I hoped you'd missed me while I was away."

There seemed little point in admitting that she had missed him. She said defensively, "I didn't know it was a cardinal sin to ask a favor of a friend."

"There you go again with that friendship nonsense. Let me give you the facts of life, Bethany. You were quite right that I tried my damnedest to thaw out that casing of ice you've got around your heart. I thought, given enough time, you might feel for me at least something of what I feel for you. But months at sea didn't do it, more months in California, and still more months after coming to New Orleans didn't do it. So I give up. It's that simple. I'm sick and tired of competing with a dead man—a saint."

Unable to bear the harsh tone and the distant look in his blue eyes, Bethany jumped to her feet and walked away from the table.

She heard his footsteps on the flagged path, and a moment later he stood beside her. "You've got to put the past behind you, Bethany. Let him go. You're a young woman; you've a lot more living—and loving—to do. But you can't do either if you insist on burying yourself along with your dead husband. A ghost can't keep you warm at night."

"Please, don't! I asked you to come here so we could talk about Leona, not Neil."

He caught her wrist and pulled her roughly toward him. She was crushed against his chest, and there was nothing gentle about the way he caught the hair at the back of her head with one hand and pulled her head back so that he could kiss her. His mouth was hard, hungry in a way that left no doubt where he wanted the kiss to lead. She struggled weakly, but felt herself yielding before his superior masculine strength. When he released her she could only sag, breathless, against him.

She wasn't sure what she expected him to say when he looked down at her, but she wasn't prepared for his actual words, which were, simply, "Good-bye, Bethany."

38

WHEN ALISON'S CARRIAGE stopped in front of the warehouse on the Goree Piazza, Hagen Rudd was checking the shipping marks on several packing cases as they were loaded into a wagon for delivery to the docks.

He frowned. "You didn't tell me you wanted me to drive you today. What are you thinking of, driving the carriage yourself? You'll be talked about."

"More than I am already, you mean?" Alison asked as he helped her down to the cobbled street. She looked at the packing cases, which were marked with an inverted triangle over the initials T.B. "These must be the Thomas and Baines tools bound for China. Will we have a full cargo? I hate to send a ship out half empty, even if it does come back full of tea."

"Never mind that," Rudd growled. "Why are you driving the carriage yourself?"

"Why should I pretend I need a man to drive it when I can handle a carriage as well as you?"

He gave an exasperated sigh. "That isn't the point, even if it was true, which it isn't. If the horses bolted you wouldn't be able to hold them and I would."

The man loading the packing cases onto the wagon was staring at her, and Rudd said, "You—get on with your work and stop gaping." He turned to Alison. "You'd better come into the office."

They went inside and walked along a narrow aisle between stacks of boxes and crates to the tiny room he used as an office. She had become so accustomed to the clicking of his peg leg striking the floor that sometimes it was a shock to look down and see it. Almost as if to make up for the missing leg, the rest of his body was stronger, more agile than that of any man she'd ever known. Nothing stopped him, nothing daunted him. He worked twice as long and three times as hard as anyone else, and more important than any of his other attributes, Alison trusted him completely.

His office was neat and well organized. Several pieces of scrimshaw were attached to the walls, and although Alison had never questioned Rudd about them she was sure he had carved them himself. The remarkably detailed full-rigged ships carved into bits of whalebone and ivory showed great patience and, she thought, a deep and abiding love of the sea and ships.

Alison and Hagen Rudd had understood each other from the start. Neither of them wanted to remember their past; both lived in the present and kept a watchful eye on the future. They worked as a team, without much need to talk about what they did, or about any other aspect of their lives. Rudd, although respectful, didn't hesitate to do things his way if he felt it was more efficient than hers, and she had learned to look the other way rather than question him, since he was too good a man to lose.

Lately she had found herself asking his opinion on various matters pertaining to the business as a whole, not just the warehousing of cargoes. His knowledge of the shipping trade was far more extensive than he had indicated when she hired him, a bonus for which she was too grateful to examine too closely.

His obvious concern about her driving the carriage today surprised her, and she wasn't sure how to react to it. He had never before expressed such a strong concern about her personal welfare.

Pulling out a chair for her, he said, "You're getting a bit too cocksure for your own good, Mrs. Fielding. Some big bruiser sees you all by yourself he's going to pull you out of that carriage and take you down a peg or two. I've had to put more than one man in his place for making remarks about you waltzing around the docks. In the men's minds only women who aren't ladies do what you do."

"Oh, for heaven's sake, Mr. Rudd! You know very well that I'm running the company. No ships sail, no cargoes move, unless I say so."

He was silent, regarding her with the same ferocious expression she had seen him bestow on a worker who displeased him.

For a moment she stared back at him and it seemed to her that a silent battle was being waged in the space between them.

At length he said gruffly, "It's your safety I'm worried about. You're as clever and as canny in business as any man, but you haven't a man's strength. You need protecting. And while I'm talking out of turn, I'll come right out and ask you why that husband of yours lets you do what you do."

"Damn you, you mind your tongue," Alison snapped. "I'm not going to discuss my husband with you, or with any other man."

Rudd glared at her for a long minute; then something like comprehension dawned in his eyes and his expression softened. "Ah. So that's it."

"What do you mean by that?"

"Nothing." He picked up a bulky document from his desk. "Here's the manifest of the *Sea Dancer.* I expect that's what you came to see?"

She tossed it back onto the desk. "I asked what you meant by that remark."

"Look, it's none of my business. But if you want a man to take care of you the way a woman should be taken care of, well . . . don't be a better man than he is. Men are prideful creatures. They want a woman to look up to them, make them feel important. Maybe your husband doesn't feel important to you."

"I love my husband! I love him more than I love life—" She stopped, aghast that she had voiced the declaration aloud, to anyone. But the words had been torn from her heart, and Hagen Rudd knew it. He stared at her in a way that troubled her, and she wondered how she could have been such an idiot as to let their discussion become so personal.

"Your husband is a fool," Rudd said quietly. "The biggest fool I've ever known. Come on. I'll take you back."

"Stay where you are," Alison said. "I'll take myself back. I don't need you or anybody else."

Jumping to her feet, she stormed out of the warehouse. Outside, the tang of brine in the air seemed sharper than usual. Clouds scudded over the river and a strong breeze swayed the masts and the furled canvas of the ships lined up along the miles of docks. The Goree Piazza was a bustle of activity. Wagons loaded with crates and cases bound for distant lands rattled over the cobblestones, men's voices bellowed orders, ragged boys darted about at play or bent on some mischief, a few limbless beggars squatted against the warehouse walls. There were no women in sight. It was too early for the ladies of the night to be abroad.

Huge iron rings were still attached to the brick walls along the Goree, where once black slaves had been chained, awaiting transshipment to America. As she hurried past those ugly symbols of the trade in human misery now outlawed in England,

Alison made a mental note to have the rings removed from the Fielding warehouse.

Alison guided the carriage horses through the traffic, Hagen Rudd's words hammering at her brain. Surely she could not have alienated Stewart by relieving him of work he hated? Still, the fact remained that before she went to work in the company they had at least been good friends and companions, if not lovers. Would romantic love have come in time, if she'd just let well enough alone? Now they were uneasy with each other, not quite adversaries, but almost. That one evening at Riverleigh when they'd danced and laughed together after the garden party now seemed like a half-remembered dream. Although Stewart had spent more time at home since then and Alison was reasonably sure that he was not seeing Iris Holloway, he was even more withdrawn, spending hours at the piano, working on a composition that was disturbingly melancholy.

She suddenly realized that she had been so distracted upon leaving the warehouse that instead of turning the carriage around and going back toward the Fielding Company offices near the Pier Head, she was now going in the opposite direction. There were fewer people about, and several men catcalled and leered as she went by. She had never used the whip on the horses, but now she picked it up and cracked it in the air over their backs, turning at the next corner in order to double back the way she had come.

The minute she entered the alley she realized her mistake. A blank brick wall faced her, and the alley was too narrow to turn in. She would have to get down and try to coax the horses into backing the carriage out.

She was no sooner down on the ground than two men appeared out of nowhere. Before she could cry out, a brawny arm went around her neck and she felt herself dragged back against a barrel chest. A big hand closed painfully around her breast.

The second man loomed in front of her, roughly dressed, reeking of ale. He laughed and licked his lips, making obscene sucking noises. "Go on, give it to 'er! Asking for it, she is."

Alison struggled wildly, then bent over and sank her teeth into the arm imprisoning her throat. The man behind her yelped with pain and jerked his arm away, but the second man promptly moved in. His hand snaked out and caught the front of her jacket, and the buttons gave way as he yanked on it.

She made a fist and punched his nose, then brought up her

knee, but before she connected with his groin he twisted away, one hand clutching his nose. The other man knocked her bonnet from her head and seized her hair, pulling her off balance. She crashed heavily to the ground, and instantly one of the men was on top of her.

" 'Old her flamin' hands out of me way," he shouted to the other man, who grasped her wrists and pulled her arms above her head. She struggled and kicked but could not dislodge the man who knelt over her, systematically tearing off her clothes.

Feeling the grip on one wrist slacken, she managed to pull one hand free and raked her fingernails down the cheek of the man on top of her. In response, he slammed his fist into her face, sending stars dancing in front of her eyes. Muttering about teaching her a lesson, he bent and savagely bit her breast, then grabbed her hair and smashed her head back against the pavement.

His face blurred and she felt consciousness slipping away. Desperately she arched her body and screamed, fighting to cling to her rapidly fading senses. Hands, then a knee, went between her thighs, forcing them apart. She thought, Oh, God, help me!

Dimly she was aware of wheels grinding on cobbles, then a familiar clicking sound, and Hagen Rudd was upon her attackers like an avenging whirlwind.

With one hand he seized the man who was disrobing her and flung him back against the wall. There was a sickening thud as the man's head struck the rough bricks and he slid to the ground.

The second man attempted to kick Rudd's foot out from under him, but Hagen was too quick. Sidestepping as easily as a dancer, he swung his great fist to the man's jaw, dropping him with a single blow.

Close to fainting, Alison struggled to her knees and pulled herself up, clutching the side of the carriage for support. Through a red haze she saw one man crawling out of the alley on his hands and knees. The other was unconscious. On the street at the entrance to the alley stood the wagon, still loaded with Thomas & Baines packing cases, in which Rudd had followed her.

She pulled her torn clothes together as best she could as Rudd came to her, his craggy face creased with worry and rage. "Are you all right? Christ almighty, I should kill the bastards."

For a second she was afraid he might make good the threat,

as he turned toward the crawling man with a look of fury, but she caught his arm and said, "Let him go. You've more than taught him a lesson."

He touched her cheek with one finger. "You've a bad bruise, and I think you'll have a black eye tomorrow." He carefully avoided looking down at her seminaked body as he pulled off his jacket and wrapped it around her shoulders.

"If you say I told you so—" she began, her voice shaking.

"Come on, lass," he said gently. "Let's get you into the carriage and I'll take you home."

Mrs. Hughes had come to fill the hip bath with scalding water three times, but Alison was still reluctant to get out of the tub.

"Come on, dear. Let's get you into your nightgown and I'll bring you some nice warm milk," Mrs. Hughes said after Alison had been in the hot water so long that her skin had wrinkled. She took Alison firmly by the arm and helped her out of the tub, slipping a warm towel around her before discreetly withdrawing.

Alison rubbed herself vigorously, but could not rub away the imprint of those filthy hands on her body. At length she pulled her nightgown over her head and sat on the edge of the bed. She couldn't stop shaking.

Mrs. Hughes returned with a mug of warm milk, and Alison cupped her hands around it and inhaled the comforting aroma of grated nutmeg sprinkled in the sweetened milk. "Did Mr. Rudd leave?"

"Yes, he's gone. He was in the study with Mr. Fielding for a long time before he left."

Alison gave a long shuddering sigh.

Mrs. Hughes said, "Your husband would like to come up and talk to you. Shall I tell him it's all right?"

"No! I mean—just tell him I've gone to bed and I'll see him in the morning."

But even as she spoke there was a knock on her bedroom door.

Alison put down the mug and crawled under the covers, turning her back so that she faced the wall. She heard Stewart come into the room and say, "Would you excuse us please, Mrs. Hughes?"

The side of the bed creaked as he sat down. Alison kept her back turned to him. She felt his hand lightly touch her hair, and she screamed, "Don't touch me!"

"I'm sorry. I didn't know if you were asleep."

"I don't need any lectures from you, Stewart. Just go away and leave me alone."

"I wasn't going to lecture you. I wanted to comfort you. I'm sure you've learned a lesson today, and thank God nothing really serious happened to you."

Rolling over onto her back she looked at him and had the satisfaction of seeing him wince at the sight of her bruised face. "Nothing serious? I wasn't actually raped, you mean?"

"Don't think about it now. Try to put it out of your mind. Tomorrow I'll take you to Riverleigh and Mary will take care of you until you're feeling better."

"Oh? And who will take care of the business while I'm gone?"

He colored slightly. "It's my responsibility. I will. With Hagen Rudd's help. He and I had a long talk."

"About me?"

Stewart's handsome features were drawn into tight lines. "Actually more about me. Try to relax and go to sleep. Would you like me to brush your hair?"

Her scalp still hurt from the vicious way her assailants had pulled her hair, but she nodded, needing a tender touch, wanting so much for him to hold her close, to kiss her and tell her that he did not regard her as soiled because of what had happened.

Picking up her hairbrush, he drew it gently through a long strand of hair. Alison felt some of her tension dissipate. For the first time in ages she felt cared for, safe. She closed her eyes and instantly Iris's mocking countenance appeared.

Alison sat bolt upright and knocked the hairbrush out of Stewart's hand. It flew across the room and clattered to the floor.

"What—" he began.

"I won't share you, Stewart. Not any part of you. You're my husband, damn it, and every minute you spent with her was stolen from me."

He stared at her for a moment, and for the first time she saw a haggard look on his face and circles under his eyes that bespoke sleepless nights and worry. "This isn't the time to talk about it. You've just had a harrowing experience."

"Sod it, I *want* to talk about it now. I'm tired of pretending nothing happened. And while we're at it, I want to talk about how it was you could make love to her and not to me."

Stewart rose to his feet. He swallowed hard. "I want you to know that I haven't seen Iris since the garden party at Riverleigh. I . . . do beg your forgiveness, Alison. I'm truly sorry. I don't really know how it happened. It was as if she cast a spell."

"I don't want to hear about her!" Alison knew she was shrieking like a fishwife, but she couldn't stop. It was as if all the pent-up anger, not only at Stewart and Iris but also at the men who had attacked her, was bursting forth in a molten flood. "I want to talk about you, about the two of us, about when we're going to have a real marriage."

He said stiffly, "You're too upset for any rational discussion now. I'll leave you to rest."

Before he reached the bedroom door, Alison was out of bed and had slipped between him and the door. She flung out her arms to prevent him from leaving. "Oh, no, you don't. You're not going to turn your back on me tonight, Stewart."

Scarcely aware of her own actions, she reached up and seized his face between her hands, pulled him down toward her, and kissed him on the mouth. All the yearning and ardor she had been forced to suppress was in her seeking lips, in the way her arms slipped around his neck and clung to him. If he would make love to her, she knew that all the demons would be driven away, the loneliness of their loveless marriage, the memory of those men who had attacked her, the specter of Iris . . .

She could hear little whimpering sounds, and realized they were coming from her.

After a moment she realized, too, that he was not responding. He didn't try to disengage himself from her; he merely stood still, remote, unresponsive.

When at last she pulled away from him, he said in a small, tight voice, "I'll take you to Riverleigh tomorrow. You need a complete rest. Good night, Alison."

She stood aside to let him pass, avoiding looking into his eyes. She had never felt more humiliated or miserable in her entire life.

39

SIR ADRIAN FIELDING was on a rampage. He stormed about Riverleigh, bellowing at the top of his lungs, an incoherent babble that made no sense at all. Occasionally he would seize some object—a picture from the wall, a vase or ornament from a table—and hurl it down the stairs or through a window.

Mary followed him, pleading with him to please come and sit down and tell her what it was that had angered him.

"He's here, I tell you," Adrian shouted. "I saw him myself, glowering at me. He'll creep up on me and kill me if I don't find him."

"Who, dear?" Mary asked patiently.

He turned to her, empty eyes momentarily puzzled. "What? Why are you questioning me? I'm master here. This is my house. Ah, I know you! You're the one who was supposed to keep him out of the house. But you're not doing your job. Get out! You're dismissed."

Mary backed away from him, fearing he might strike her. A succession of nurses, all strapping young men, had come and gone. After a few days with Adrian, nothing would induce them to stay.

"Ah! There he is, the swine. I'll kill him," Adrian roared. He charged into her bedroom, picked up a poker from the fireplace, stumbled toward her dressing table, and smashed the mirror to pieces.

Mary watched until his rage had been spent and her precious mirror lay scattered in glittering shards.

His expression triumphant, Adrian turned to look at her. "You saw him? Arrogant bastard just glared at me, didn't speak. But I taught him a good lesson, didn't I? He won't be back. You can be sure of that." Satisfied that he had destroyed the stranger in the mirror, he collapsed onto her bed and a moment later he was asleep.

Mary closed the door and stood on the landing. She was trembling. A footman, who must have been hiding, crept shamefacedly out of the linen cupboard.

"Stay here," Mary said. "When Sir Adrian wakes up, take him back to his own room. Send a maid to remove the broken glass. Let me know the second Sir Adrian awakes."

The young man looked apprehensive, but said, "Yes, milady."

Mary went downstairs, thankful that Alison had taken her son for a walk on the beach and they had not been present for this latest outburst. Mary was deeply disturbed about what had happened to Alison, but felt that Riverleigh was hardly the safe haven Stewart seemed to believe it to be. Mary still didn't understand fully why Alison had been visiting the warehouse in the first place, let alone driving a carriage around the Liverpool docks by herself. Her poor bruised face made Mary want to weep. Since arriving the previous day Alison had not wanted to talk about her ordeal, so Mary had not pressed her for details.

Downstairs, she noticed that the day's post had arrived and lay on a silver tray on the hall table. With a start she remembered that she had not visited the post office for some time to pick up a letter from Tate. Had she, in fact, replied to his last letter? Her days were occupied with the turmoil of caring for Adrian, and there was never any time for her own pursuits. Besides, Tate continually pressed her to join him and asked why she felt she could not leave Adrian, who surely must have recovered from his wounds by now. How could she tell Tate that Adrian's doctors could offer no hope of a cure for his presenile dementia, but were quick to point out that physically Adrian was as strong as an ox and might live on for many years.

She went outside for a breath of fresh air and, halfway across the lawn toward the gazebo, saw Alison and Davey coming up the cliff path. The sea air was brisk with the approach of winter, and their faces were pink from the cold, further emphasizing Alison's purple-black bruises. They waved to her as they approached.

"Did you have a nice walk?" Mary asked.

"We saw lots of seaweed," Davey announced. "And a dead fish."

"How sad. What kind of a fish was it?"

"I think it was a whale. It was very big. We buried it and sang a hymn."

"It wasn't big enough to be a whale, Davey, more likely a

mackerel." Alison's eyes met Mary's over the top of the little boy's head. "Is everything all right?"

"Yes. Well, no. But . . ."

"You can run back to the house from here, Davey," Alison said. "I'll be along in a minute."

Mary added, "Ask Cook to give you a cup of chocolate. But no shortbread before dinner."

They watched the little boy run toward the house, and Alison said, "He loves it here. Thank you for having us."

"We mustn't leave him alone in the house for too long, Alison. Adrian is asleep, but I don't know for how long, and I can't count on the servants to watch him. Most of them are new anyway. I can't keep staff nowadays. But I did want to find out if there is anything I can do for you. I wasn't sure you'd want to talk in front of the boy. Does he know what happened to you?"

"Only that I had an accident."

"Alison, I don't want to upset you, but what on earth were you doing in that part of the city alone?"

"I was there," Alison said, a trace of bitterness in her voice, "taking care of business."

"You? But surely Stewart—"

"Mary, Stewart hates everything about the business. He spends very little time in the office and even less in the warehouse and at the docks."

"I wondered why he started off so badly, then rallied magnificently," Mary said slowly. She sat down on the bench encircling the wooden walls of the gazebo and pulled her cape closer to ward off the rising wind. "So that is why he turned to Iris Holloway."

"So you blame me for that?" Alison asked, her poor battered face indignant. "I had to help him with the work. Don't you understand? He just couldn't do it."

"Someone would have done it. You didn't have to. I'm not saying you drove him into Iris's arms, but you certainly made it easy for him, didn't you?"

"It's all water under the bridge anyway. I can't go back and undo any of it. Besides, I enjoy the work," she said defiantly.

Mary was silent, trying to understand, wondering what to say.

Alison said abruptly, "Stewart only married me to protect his brother's child. He . . . he's never been a real husband to me."

"Oh, my dear . . . I had no idea. How dreadful for you." Mary thought about the situation for a moment, everything now becoming very clear. Embarrassed by Alison's confession of an unconsummated marriage, Mary fumbled for something to say. "You know, Stewart was always shy, and he's still quite young and inexperienced with women. His life changed so suddenly, from carefree student to married man with children, responsibilities, and worst of all, the shipping company to deal with. I can quite see how Iris was able to seduce him. Not only did she share his love of music but she offered him a chance to *play.*"

Alison sighed. "Hagen Rudd told me to make Stewart feel more important, and you think I should play more. I'm thinking it's hopeless. He'll never care for me the way I care for him."

Before Mary could respond, a footman came running from the house and said breathlessly, "Sir Adrian is up, milady, and he's going from room to room, breaking all the mirrors."

Kneeling beside her bed that night, Mary prayed for strength and guidance. Her world had crumbled into confusion and terror, and it was futile to wait for a miracle to put matters right. She had to do something now.

When she arose the following morning she sent a message requesting her husband's doctor to visit her that evening, then sent word to Liverpool that she had to see Stewart right away.

She ordered a groom to bring the pony trap to the front door and drove it herself the short distance along a country lane to the village. At the post office she inquired if there were any letters for her in care of poste restante. There were two.

She sat outside and read them, heedless of the rain.

Tate's first letter was brief.

My dear,

I had a very unexpected visitor today. A young man who used to hang around the Liverpool office and the docks every chance he got. I'm sure you know who I mean and will be delighted to hear he did not, as we feared, drop off the edge of the earth. Yes, he's safe, well, and here in New Orleans. Alas, he is somewhat disillusioned about his father's business ethics, but after being shanghaied, that was to be expected.

Furthermore, he was accompanied by his sister-in-law, who is desperately anxious to be reunited with her child. Needless to say, there are some obstacles to be overcome for all concerned.

I have decided, therefore, that as soon as my "nephew," Tom Ivers, is able to take my place here, I will return to England.

Mary folded the letter. Tom was safe! What wonderful news. If only she could make Adrian understand that his favorite son was alive. It was also a relief to know that little Hope was undoubtedly on her way to her mother, since her abductor must have been Bethany's emissary. This would be good news indeed to both Stewart and Alison and perhaps ease them through the present crisis.

How strange, too, and how wonderful, that Tate was making plans to return just when she had decided to write and ask him to come home.

She tore open the second letter, which was dated a couple of weeks after the first: "My nephew Tom is much more knowledgeable about the shipping trade than I at first realized, and therefore I will be sailing to New York in two weeks, and from there will take the fastest packet to Liverpool."

Returning to Riverleigh as the rain began to fall heavily, she was confronted by a bedraggled figure lurching down the drive toward the gate house. Adrian wore a sodden smoking jacket over his nightshirt. His hair, which he refused to let anyone cut, was plastered damply to his unshaven face. His feet were bare and bleeding from the gravel.

She stopped the trap and called to him. "Adrian! Where are you going?"

He peered at her suspiciously, raindrops running down his nose. "Strangers have invaded my house. I'm going to fetch the constable. Must get them out. Can't handle them all myself. There are too many of them."

"Get into the trap, dear, and we'll go for help together."

He hesitated for a moment, then climbed in beside her. She jerked the reins to turn the horse, and went back down the lane.

"This isn't the police station," Adrian said, with one of his rare flashes of rationality, as she stopped beside a country house.

"No, dear. It's the doctor's house. I feel we should get a draft for you, to ward off a chill. It's so cold and wet today. Then we'll get the constable."

"Don't need a damned draft," Adrian grumbled, but she got out of the trap and tugged at his arm until he followed.

The doctor's housekeeper opened the door. "Oh, my goodness! Come in, Lady Fielding."

"If you would bring me some towels, and perhaps one of the doctor's dressing gowns," Mary murmured to her.

They were shown into a shabbily furnished sitting room where the doctor saw patients with minor ailments; the more seriously ill received house calls.

Minutes later the doctor, who was obviously preparing to leave on his rounds, appeared. "I did receive your message, Lady Fielding, and fully intended to call at Riverleigh this evening." He glanced, obviously embarrassed, at Sir Adrian.

The housekeeper returned with towels, a blanket, and a dressing gown. Mary said to the doctor, "If you will help me? And when my husband is dry and warm, perhaps a draft?" Behind Adrian's back she mouthed the words, *to put him to sleep.*

He nodded and went to a cabinet containing various bottles, mixed a stiff dose of laudanum, and handed it to Adrian. Mary held her breath, but Adrian took the glass without argument and drained it. The doctor said, "Perhaps you'll be more comfortable on the couch, Sir Adrian?"

By the time they had removed his wet nightshirt and wrapped him in the dressing gown and blanket, he was almost asleep. Mary whispered to the doctor, "We must talk."

They went to the doctor's study and he closed the door.

Mary said, "I didn't know what to do. I found him wandering outside in the rain."

"As I told you, Lady Fielding, this behavior can only become more pronounced. You have no alternative but to commit him. Have you discussed the matter with his son?"

"Not yet. I asked Stewart to come to Riverleigh today."

"Will he agree? We shall need two signatures. His and yours."

Mary twisted her gloves into a tight knot. "If there was a way to care for him at home, but I can't keep attendants; I can't even get servants to stay. My husband has become destructive, he breaks things." She told him about the menacing strangers Adrian saw in the mirrors.

The doctor nodded. "His dementia is advancing rapidly. His son surely sees that?"

"Stewart doesn't visit him very often nowadays. For one thing, his visits seem to agitate Adrian, and besides, he doesn't know who Stewart is. I've hesitated to tell him all that his father does, out of concern that Stewart might worry about . . . insanity in the family."

"My dear Lady Fielding, senile dementia can strike in the sanest families. It is not, we're certain, hereditary. It usually occurs late in life. At fifty-three your husband is one of the youngest victims I've encountered. We feel it has to do with the degeneration of the brain due to old age."

"But why do most old people remain in control of their faculties and, in fact, remain just as quick and capable as they ever were?"

The doctor spread his hands in a gesture that indicated he was at a loss. "Shall I prepare the commitment papers?"

"You said you knew of a private asylum?"

"Indeed I do, a gracious country home in Lancashire that caters only to well-to-do patients. Your husband will be comfortable and well cared for, so do put your mind at ease."

Stewart closed his eyes briefly in a prayer of thanks. "Oh, Mary, what wonderful news! Thank God! I always felt Tom was still alive, but to know for certain . . . When is he coming home?"

"I don't know. Tate's letter was brief. We'll learn more when he arrives. Stewart, there's something else we must discuss. It's your father. His condition worsens every day. I can't handle him any longer. The doctor knows of a private asylum."

Stewart felt himself grow pale. "You want to *commit* him?"

Mary bit her lip. "I don't know what else to do, Stewart. I've had a procession of attendants. Now the servants won't stay either. He terrifies them."

He turned to face the fireplace, where flames roared from a log, almost but not quite drowning out the moaning of the wind in the chimney. "Have you talked to Alison about this?"

"No, of course not! I haven't spoken to anyone but the doctor. I feel this has to be our decision—yours and mine. Why would you ask if I'd spoken to your wife?"

"Because Alison always seems to know best what to do. If you don't mind, I'd like to talk to her before I make a decision."

"Do whatever you feel you must. But, Stewart, surely Alison is in a rather delicate emotional state herself just now. After all, she was brutally attacked only two days ago, and this came hard on the heels of . . . other problems she's facing."

He looked away, obviously embarrassed that his stepmother knew of his infidelity. "Where is she?"

"She went up to put Davey to bed and dress for dinner. She should be almost ready."

"I think I'll go up to her."

Watching as he hurried from the room, Mary willed Alison not to step in and relieve him of one more burden. Why couldn't she see that her very strength was the wedge that drove them apart?

They came down to dinner together a short time later, and Mary thought, not for the first time, what an ill-matched couple they were. It was more than the physical differences between them. Stewart's somewhat languid good looks and dreamy eyes, his rather slender height and vaguely weary air, and, not least, his impeccable Oxford accent, were in sharp contrast to Alison's sturdy glow of health and energy, her direct gaze, and the matter-of-fact speech that despite her efforts didn't quite conceal her origins. Mary had overheard the butler whisper to the cook that the two of them were like a racehorse and a plow horse that somebody had forced into the same harness and they'd never get in step. Mary was inclined to agree. Her upbringing had instilled in her the belief that breeding could not be discounted, that it was as true of humankind as it was in the animal world. She loved Alison like a daughter, but would have wished for her a man of her own class, temperament, and strength of will. Alison pined for a man who would never be able to make her happy.

"Will Father be joining us?" Stewart asked.

"I've sent a tray up to his room," Mary answered. "Sometimes he'll stay up there quietly. He may do so this evening, because he had a rather exhausting day."

"Other times he comes bursting into the dining room," Alison put in. "And then no one can eat in peace."

An uncomfortable silence ensued, broken when Mary suggested they take their places at the table. She wondered what had transpired between Stewart and Alison and longed to ask if they had made a decision about committing Adrian. But they would not be able to speak in private until the meal ended, for servants would come and go and the butler would stand attentively by the sideboard to be on hand for any requests.

Alison's bruises were less noticeable this evening, thanks to the dim lighting and a heavy layer of face powder, but the swelling around her eye was still pathetically evident. She tilted her chin at a defiant angle that tore at Mary's heart, reminding her of a wounded child determined not to show its pain.

Ignoring the hovering butler, Alison said, "Stewart told me what you want to do, Mary. He's very upset about it."

Disconcerted that she would speak in front of the servants,

Mary murmured, "You know how difficult the situation is. If there were any other way . . ."

"There is," Alison said. "We'll take Sir Adrian back to Liverpool with us. We'll take care of him."

Dropping her napkin in surprise, Mary exclaimed, "You can't be serious! If we can't care for him here at Riverleigh, then how can you possibly—"

"The nurses you hired," Alison said, "I think they were expecting to take care of some feeble old man who'd had a stroke or something. I'll find somebody who can handle him."

"We want to do this, Mary," Stewart put in.

"I can't possibly allow it! You have a child in the house, and the business to take care of. It's quite out of the question to burden yourselves with an invalid, too. Besides, he's my responsibility." Mary suddenly remembered the butler, standing immobile behind her. She turned and said, "You may leave us. We'll ring if we need something."

"Let us at least give it a try," Alison said gently. "If we can't manage, Stewart will sign the commitment papers."

Mary could offer no argument to this, but a deep sense of foreboding gripped her.

40

SHORTLY AFTER TATE Ivers departed for England, Leona stopped by one morning to ask if Bethany would invite her and a friend to dinner.

"I'd love to, but I'll have to get Tom to ask Saffron if she'd mind if we had guests," Bethany responded cautiously. "Since Tate left, she ignores anything I say to her, and I don't dare go into her kitchen to prepare a meal myself."

"For pity's sake, Bethany, why not? She's just his housekeeper."

"And I'm his guest. I couldn't be so presumptuous."

"Thank God I wasn't brought up to be a gentlewoman," Leona said. "It's a real millstone around your neck."

"Tell me, who is the friend you want us to meet?"

Leona winked. "The one and only Mr. Louis LaFleur."

"Ah! I've been looking forward to meeting him. His club has become the most fashionable place in New Orleans, I hear."

"You should come and see for yourself."

"I'm not ready for that kind of thing yet. I'm still in mourning. Besides, I have no one to take me."

"What about Black Jack?"

"I haven't seen him since you came back from the riverboat trip. I don't even know where he's living or what he's doing."

"And I haven't been to see you, either, have I? I'm sorry, duckie, but Louis has been rushing me off my feet. It didn't occur to me that you might be lonely. I was sure Jack would be hanging around you boasting about his newfound respectability."

"Jack? Respectable? Tell me more!"

"Well, it began with him making sure Louis got proper title to the club. Then it turned out that there were some other legal problems, and Jack straightened those out, too. Then a couple of Louis's friends asked him for help, and before you know it, word spread among the club's patrons and several of them asked for Jack's advice on legal matters. He seems to know an awful lot about property rights and deeds and contracts and so on. So much so that Louis's father got one of the law firms in town to hire him."

"I can't believe it!" Bethany exclaimed. "Black Jack the *highwayman*?"

"One and the same." Leona chuckled. "I've got to run. Got a fitting for a gown. Let me know about bringing Louis to dinner. I want to show him that I've got a real lady for a friend."

To Bethany's surprise, Saffron seemed pleased when Tom told her that the owner of the club, renamed the Rake's Retreat, was coming to dinner. However, her light gold eyes became opaque when she learned Leona would be accompanying Mr. Louis LaFleur. Then Tom further surprised Bethany by suggesting he invite Jack also, as he wanted to ask his opinion about maritime insurance.

"Leona told me he's practicing law," Bethany said. "How on earth is he getting away with that?"

Tom looked at her strangely. "You should get Jack to tell you more about his life in England."

There was little likelihood she would get a chance to do so, Bethany thought.

On the night of the dinner party Saffron set an elegant table, and the cooking aromas drifting from the kitchen were appetizing.

Bethany had not seen Jack since their last encounter when he'd bidden her good-bye, and she was happy but apprehensive about seeing him again. She had missed him more severely than she could have imagined, but would have preferred for him to come to see her rather than Tom.

She selected and discarded several gowns the night of the dinner party, settling at last on a plain periwinkle-blue taffeta.

Leona swept into the house in a magnificent pale lemon-colored gown, her hair decorated with ostrich plumes and glittering rhinestones. She towered over the diminutive Louis, whose delicate features and softly curling hair made him look like a schoolboy. Little wonder men who lost to him in games of chance became enraged. But despite his boyish appearance and short stature, Bethany noted that Louis had the eyes of a buccaneer.

Jack arrived almost an hour late and made no excuses. By that time the others had consumed several glasses of wine and were being entertained by Leona's impersonation of a well-known actress who spoke with a slight lisp.

Jack's eyes went directly to Bethany, and she felt like a butterfly pinned down for a collector's appraisal. She lowered her own eyes, undone by his penetrating stare.

Over the chorus of greetings Louis's rather high-pitched drawl made itself heard. "Ah, at last! My dear friend and protector! One grows nervous when you are not near, *mon frère.*"

Leona ran her hand insinuatingly up Louis's arm. "Why, duckie, you know I'll always take care of you." The gesture was not lost on Jack, who glanced from one to the other and shook his head slightly, as though not believing what he saw.

Tom asked, "What will you have to drink, Jack?"

Ignoring the question, Jack said, "I didn't realize this was to be a dinner party. I thought you wanted to talk maritime business."

There was an awkward silence, broken when Louis drawled, "One of my spies informed me that you were burning the midnight oil in the law library, Jack. Is that why we haven't seen you at the club?"

"Isn't Bourke taking care of you? I should think he'd be more than a match for any rowdies. I've seen him handle half a dozen drunken sailors without even breathing heavily."

"Oh, *mon ami,* Bourke is fearsomely efficient. But I miss your company."

There was tension in the room. Bethany felt it and was uneasy. Jack had clearly come only because Tom asked him, and she wasn't sure if Jack's rather brusque manner was directed at her, at Louis or Leona, or perhaps at all of them.

Tom remarked, "Tate should be arriving in England any day. I wonder what my father will say when he learns I'm now part of the Ivers Shipping Company."

"You should have written to him, Tom," Bethany said. "He must have been terribly worried about you."

"You care about my father's feelings?" Tom asked incredulously. "After what he did to you and Neil?"

"I know the agony of having a beloved child snatched out of one's life. I sympathize with your father in that shared ordeal, despite everything else."

"Tom was shanghaied by his father's own men," Leona explained to Louis.

At that point Saffron came to announce that dinner was ready, and they went into the dining room. Bethany noticed that Jack had not joined in the conversation before dinner, and throughout the meal he remained unusually silent.

"You're very quiet tonight, Jack," Tom remarked.

Jack said shortly, "Why exactly did you want me to come, Tom? Is there a business matter you want to discuss or not?"

"Well, sometime before you leave I'd like you to have a quick look at a new clause in our insurance policy, but I hoped we could all spend a sociable evening together first. We haven't seen much of you since we came to New Orleans, I just thought . . ." Tom's voice trailed away before Jack's icy blue stare.

Bethany saw that Jack's gaze had flickered, almost imperceptibly, in the direction of Leona and Louis. She knew that he had never really cared for Leona, and Louis *was* terribly young, but why was Jack so upset at seeing them together?

"Perhaps Leona and I should leave you gentlemen to your brandy and cigars?" Bethany suggested, alarmed by the growing tension in the air.

"No, don't go," Louis said immediately. "I have an announcement to make."

Leona said doubtfully, "Maybe tonight's not the time, Louis."

"But, *ma chérie,* all of your closest friends are present. It is the best possible time." He emphasized the word "friends," staring hard at Jack.

Louis rose, glass in hand, "A toast! To my bride-to-be, the lovely Leona."

"Oh, what wonderful news!" Bethany exclaimed, aware that hers was the only congratulatory voice. She raised her glass, and a few seconds later Tom hesitantly followed suit, although he wore an astonished expression. No one turned to look at Jack, who made no move to pick up his glass.

Louis, his buccaneer's eyes suddenly as cold as flint, repeated in a deceptively soft voice, "To my bride-to-be, Jack. Leona and I, we are to be married."

Jack swiveled slowly in his chair to look at Louis. "You young fool. Why didn't you simply give her a part in your next production? That's all she really wanted."

"Jack! How can you be so rude!" Bethany exclaimed.

"Here," Leona cried angrily, "you arrogant bastard. Louis and me, what we do, it's no skin off your nose."

"You're old enough to be his mother. You're using him; you don't give a damn about him. And how much of your past have you told him? Does he know about Lieutenant Ruben?"

"Good God, Jack, watch your tongue," Tom said, aghast.

"Ah, Jeannot," Louis said in a deathly calm voice, using the French equivalent of Jack's name. "I cannot believe you of all people would insult my fiancée."

He stood up, drawing himself up to his full height; he was several inches shorter than Jack. "Apologize at once and give us your blessing; then we will forget this unfortunate incident."

"Look, Louis, a sore loser with a knife up his sleeve is less of a threat to you than marriage to this woman. I can save you from one, but not from the other. Still, I'll be damned if I'll give you my blessing."

Louis was deathly pale. "Then you leave me no choice but to call you out."

Jack stared at him for a moment, then gave a short laugh. "If you think I'm going to kill you because you have rotten taste in women, you're mad."

Bethany gasped. Louis, suddenly very pale, slapped Jack's cheek, a stinging blow that snapped his head backward. Louis muttered again, "Do you not understand what I am saying? I am challenging you to a duel. I intend to defend my lady's honor. My seconds will meet yours to make the arrangements."

Jack stood up. "And I'm telling you to go to hell." He strode from the room, calling to Saffron to bring his hat.

Bethany embraced Leona briefly. "I do wish you and Louis much happiness . . . but please excuse me. I must go after Jack and try to talk to him. This situation is intolerable."

She caught up with Jack halfway down the block and, breathless, said, "Please—I must talk to you."

He stopped, looked down at her for a moment, then signaled a passing cab and instructed the driver to take them slowly toward the river.

Sitting next to him in the shadowed closeness of the cab, Bethany felt as though she were confined with an angry tiger, but paradoxically at the same time she was curiously excited by the masculine power he exuded. She couldn't help but wonder what it would be like if he were to sweep her into his arms, ignore her protests, and . . .

Shocked by her own imagination, Bethany said quickly, "Jack, I can't believe—"

"Before you take me to task for what I said about your friend, I think you should know a couple of indisputable facts. First, Louis is the only son of a wealthy plantation owner. He comes from a background of old money and lineage that's linked to the French aristocracy. He's barely twenty years old."

"I don't want to talk about Louis. How could you have been so cruel to Leona? You of all people have no right to fling her past in her face."

"Her *past?*" he asked derisively. "What about her present? Louis is only one of half a dozen men she's dangling on a string. You know as well as I do that her only interest in a boy of that age is the fact that he can get her into the theater company performing at his club. I can't believe she managed to hoodwink Louis into proposing to her. I knew he was young and foolish, but I didn't realize he was blind, too."

Bethany privately felt that Leona and Louis were an ill-matched couple, but said, "She'll give up the others when they're married, you'll see. She's just so full of life and fun—"

"She'll never change, Bethany. If you have any influence over her, persuade her not to marry Louis. He's a boy in the throes of first love. If he marries her and she continues along the primrose path, we'll have all the makings of a first-class tragedy."

"Louis challenged you to a duel. What will you do?"

"Talk him out of it, if I can. Let's hope he'll see reason when he cools down."

"Jack . . . would you put your arms around me and hold me for a moment? I feel frightened. How did everything reach boiling point so quickly, without warning?"

His arm went around her shoulders instantly, and she nestled closer. He said softly, "Sometimes I forget how unworldly you are. Try to understand my concern for Louis. Leona will destroy him. His family will cut him off, and he . . . well you saw how quick he was to call me out, and he considers me his friend. If he finds out about her other suitors—who, by the way, have been showering her with costly gifts—he's bound to issue other challenges, and sooner or later one of them will kill him."

"I must believe that she'll give up the others and be faithful to him," Bethany said.

"Back in England Leona was an occasional actress but mostly she was what is politely referred to as a courtesan. She accepted gifts from men, including living expenses. That's exactly what she's been doing since arriving in New Orleans. Your loyalty to your friend is admirable, but leopards don't change their spots."

"You did. You're no longer a highwayman, are you?"

He made no response, but kept his arm around her as the cab rolled slowly along the narrow streets.

"Sometimes I worry about my little daughter," Bethany said. "I want her with me, yet I have nothing to offer her. If Tate finds her for me . . . oh, he must find her, but how can I take care of her? I can't live indefinitely on Tom and Tate's charity. You see, I'm trying to explain to you that although I don't condone Leona's way of life, I do understand how she was forced into it."

"Are you telling me you'd do the same thing in order to support yourself and your daughter?" Jack asked wryly.

"No! Of course not!"

"Don't ruffle your feathers. I was about to point out that for you there is an alternative—that is, if you could bring yourself to accommodate the carnal appetite of only one man."

"What do you mean?"

He reached up and tapped the back of the driver's seat. "Let us out by the river. We'll walk along the levee, and you can follow."

When they had left the cab and strolled some distance ahead

of it, Jack said, "I am now gainfully employed. I also have my share of the profits we made from trading up and down the West Coast. I invested the money profitably, and my assets are growing at a decent rate. As a matter of fact, I didn't do as well with considerably more effort and risk in my former profession."

Bewildered by his self-mocking tone, Bethany remained silent, waiting for him to continue.

"I suppose what I'm trying to say is that, like it or not, respectability seems to have caught up with me. I'm financially secure. I'm looking at houses with a view to buying one. All I need to complete the picture is . . . a wife."

He stopped, took her hands in his, and added, "I've no intention of going down on one knee to ask you this, and please don't harbor any delusions. If I could have possessed you without benefit of matrimony, I probably would have. I'm aware you don't love me. But it occurs to me now that you might need me. Besides, as I said, in my newly acquired state of respectability, I do need a wife to run my household, ensure my position in society, and present me with heirs. Since I've desired you for so long and since you meet all of my requirements—beautiful, educated, chaste—I'm asking you to be my wife."

Stunned, Bethany tried to collect her wits as he went on, "Before you say anything, let me point out the advantages for you. Besides being assured of your own security, you'll have that home and family you want for your daughter."

"Jack, I hardly know what to say. The last time I saw you, you were so angry, bitter . . . and now this. What brought about such a change in your thinking?"

"What does it matter? I'm paying you the highest honor a man can bestow on a woman. I'm asking you to marry me. If you'll say yes, we can be established in our own home before Tate finds your daughter and brings her to you."

"I do . . . like you very much, Jack. I've missed you these past weeks."

"That's not an answer. I need a yes or a no. And by the way, there will be no elaborate ceremony. It will be legal, but quiet. I think it's best to keep quiet about who we are and where we came from."

Bethany felt a surge of excitement. Marriage to a man like Black Jack Cutler—while he was not the great love of her life, as Neil had been—would certainly not be boring. "There's just one thing," she said. "I have no intention of being known as Mrs. Jack Spratt."

He threw back his head and laughed. "I won only one bet with Louis. He suggested we turn up a card and if I won I'd receive a double fee for my services. If his card was higher, I'd work for nothing. It was one of the very few times he ever lost or, for that matter, that I ever won. Oddly enough, he turned over a jack and my card was a king. Ever since, I've been known as Jack King at the club. You'll be Mrs. King."

As he bent to kiss her, Bethany thought fleetingly that she had used a false name with Neil also and it hadn't mattered; they had been idyllically happy together. Perhaps this was a good omen.

Wrapped in Jack's arms on the moonlit levee, feeling the urgent demand of his lips on hers, Bethany had forgotten that Louis LaFleur's seconds would be coming the next day to arrange a duel.

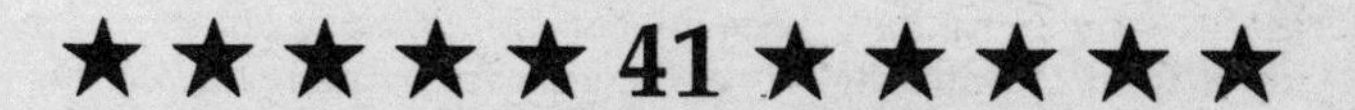

41

AT DUSK THE blowing of the conch shell and the lighting of the torches signaled the islanders that the feasting was about to begin. Coconut palms were silhouetted like slender ballerinas against the red glow of the setting sun, and the trade winds had diminished to mere zephyrs upon which wafted the heady fragrance of orchids, jasmine, and plumeria.

"Look," Will Prentice whispered in the ear of the little golden-haired girl who sat on the ground beside him.

Hope clapped her hands in excitement and swayed back and forth to the throbbing rhythm of the drums as the first dancers leapt into the clearing, twirling fiery torches perilously close to bare bronze flesh.

A long line of grass-skirted wahines, naked above the waist except for flower garlands, moved in behind the men. Leis of white ginger blossoms swung seductively, revealing firm young breasts, while bare feet, ankles encircled by flowers, moved soundlessly on the black sand of the volcanic beach.

"Watch the ladies' hands," Will said to the child. "They tell the story of the dance." He reflected silently that the swaying hips of the wahines were simultaneously telling a story as old as time. Little wonder the native rituals had shocked the missionaries.

"Won't they burn themselves?" Hope asked, not interested in the women, but wide-eyed with awe at the dexterity of the men with their torches.

"No. They practice for many hours. But you must never play with fire. You do understand?"

"Of course," Hope said, giving him a comical frown that indicated he surely should give her more credit than that for common sense.

Watching the dancers, Will murmured, "What a paradox these people are. A social contradiction. Compassionate barbarians. Illiterate yet intelligent. Fierce warriors who adorn themselves with flowers."

"Warriors with flowers," Hope repeated, giggling.

Will had fallen into the habit of addressing her as an adult, and sometimes she understood. Even when she didn't, Will enjoyed having someone to talk to who listened and accepted everything he said as gospel. Besides, she was so like Bethany, or as Bethany must have been in her childhood innocence. He never tired of watching Hope, the graceful way she moved, her exquisitely beautiful features, always animated, mischievous, curious.

On the long voyage to the Sandwich Islands, Will had grown to love Bethany's daughter dearly. In some mystical way she had re-created him. Before she came into his life he had treated the sick and the hurt in a dispassionate way, not feeling their pain or even truly viewing them as human beings. They were only the sum of their, usually damaged, parts. He had never felt unconditional love for another being, until he cared for Hope.

Now, too, the rest of the world regarded him differently. Ah, yes, Dr. Prentice is such a devoted father, caring for the little girl all by himself. Such a good man, he thinks only of the child. Will thought perhaps he even *looked* different. Less cadaverous, more alive. Above all, he had learned to be patient.

A chorus of sighs of anticipation whispered among the diners at the luau as the roast pig was lifted from the underground oven where it had been slowly roasting since before dawn. Lava rocks had been placed in the cavity of the pig, and the meat was so tender it fell into pieces as the ti leaves were peeled away.

"Want meat," Hope said firmly. "Don't want poi."

Will chuckled. He wasn't particularly fond of the bland native dish either. "You're a little carnivore. But you'll eat fruit and vegetables and fish tonight, too, not just pork."

"Carny, carny . . ." Hope repeated.

"Carnivore. A meat-eater."

"You, too!"

"Well, yes, that's true. Mmm, smells good, doesn't it?"

"Pololi au," Hope said, and he laughed. How quickly children picked up a foreign tongue.

"I'm hungry, too. Let's eat."

As the food was passed around and Hope fell upon hers, stuffing it into her mouth with her fingers as the islanders did, Will tried to ignore the nagging voice at the back of his mind that whispered it was time to move on.

There was no longer any doubt that the absconding convicts had set sail for some other destination. He had spent enough time in Lahaina talking to the crews of the whalers, and weeks in the settlement of Honolulu. Every missionary had been questioned. He had been taken by outrigger canoe to all of the islands known to have been visited by haoles, but the answers to his questions were always the same. Bethany and the others had not come here, he was certain. Where, then? The Marquesas? South America? North America? Or had they perished at sea? No, he must not think that.

He and Hope were living on the far side of the island of Oahu, away from the missionary settlements, because here the islanders had welcomed them, building a grass shack for them and sharing the bounty of the land and the sea. Caught in the siren spell of the islands, Will had let the days drift languorously by as he observed a way of life that was primitive, idyllic.

As the luau ended, he picked up Hope, already sated with food and fast asleep, and carried her to the shack. He placed her carefully on her bed of dried grasses and kissed her cheek. Then, although he fought briefly against the temptation, went outside and strolled through the scented dusk to a secluded grove where a waterfall cascaded down lava rocks into a clear pool.

As he knew she would be, Kamika waited for him there. She sat dangling her feet in the water, her hair a silken black curtain falling past her waist, a brilliant red hibiscus blossom tucked behind her right ear. A full moon had risen, bright as day. Her body glistened in the silver light, still wet from her swim.

For a moment he gazed at her, savoring her nakedness. In the settlements now under the stern influence of the missionaries the women were beginning to wear voluminous dresses, and the casual enjoyment of sex was fiercely discouraged. Shame was the first lesson taught by the clerics. But on this side of the island the playful pleasures of the flesh were a way of life. Kamika had come to him the very first evening, proud that she had learned his language from one of the sailors aboard a whaler. She liked haoles, she told him, and would be his woman.

When Will had tried to explain that he was a married man in search of his wife, Kamika expressed bafflement, unable to connect his remark to herself or to their pleasure in each other's bodies. She had leaned seductively close and removed her scant clothing, which the island women wore mainly as an adornment. He had never known a woman so innocently sensual. To Kamika lovemaking was as necessary as eating or breathing.

"I should resist you," Will said softly as he approached her now in the moonlight. "Yet I cannot. My love for my wife is a flame that I can never extinguish, yet when I am with you . . . desire overwhelms reason. I give in to a need for physical release, and although I feel guilty, I know that you do not. Adultery is not a *kapu* for you, as it is for me."

Kamika knitted her dusky brows, not understanding what he said and disturbed that it had something to do with *kapu.* "No *kapu,*" she said and, recognizing the hot look of lust in his sunken eyes, slipped from the rock and came to him, pulled open his shirt, carefully unbuttoned his britches, found his manhood, and encircled it with her lips.

After a moment he groaned and laid her back on the soft earth to plunge himself into her soft cocoon, rising and falling to the rhythm of the moon-commanded tides. At the moment he reached his zenith, as always only one name sprang to his lips. "Bethany," he said, "Ah, Bethany!"

Kamika sighed happily and squirmed like a contented kitten in his arms. She believed the word must be a haole expression of joy, since he always uttered it with such feeling.

Lying on his back with Kamika pressed close to his side, Will gazed at the star-pierced sky, inhaling the fragrance of the flowers, his body fanned by a warm breeze, and wondered how he would ever be able to tear himself away from this island paradise. With each passing day he fell ever deeper under its spell.

Hope was beginning to run wild like the island children. Her body was tanned by the sun, and she had learned to swim like a fish, even to ride the breakers beyond the reef. She had stopped asking when they would find her mother.

If they didn't leave soon, he knew they would remain here forever. Tomorrow, he promised himself, I'll make plans. Tomorrow, always tomorrow.

The following afternoon Will watched Hope playing with some of the island children on their favorite surfing beach, running fleet-footed over the shimmering white sand, her golden hair flying and her laughter floating on the warm trade winds. He saw now why those first days with her, when he had kept her cooped up alone with him in the Welsh cottage, had been so difficult. She was simply too gregarious, never truly happy unless she was surrounded by people. She loved the whole world.

Sometimes, when she turned her head suddenly, wearing an eager, inquisitive expression, or gazed adoringly at one of her special friends, he was reminded of Bethany and felt a stab of conscience. It was almost like reliving the mother's life through that of her child, sharing the wonder of each new experience, watching personality traits emerge that gave him an insight into the character of the woman he had loved but never understood. By observing the child in her formative years, Will began to realize the depths of Bethany's loneliness in the penal colony, isolated as she was from everyone but him. He recalled her attempts to make conversation, and his annoyance at the intrusion into the silence he so treasured. For him it was enough to see her moving quietly about his house, lying acquiescent in his arms at night. He needed no more, had not recognized that she did.

Once she'd tentatively asked if they could invite one or two of the marine officers to dinner. He'd been aghast. "I spend my days with them. Why should I want them intruding into my precious leisure time?"

She'd been lonely, of course, a feeling he'd never truly experienced or understood, until now. Strange that it had taken the child to open his eyes to the chasm between himself and Bethany, to make him realize that she would never have come to appreciate his love of solitude. Yet, even now, he was obsessed by her, by the memory of her beauty, her gentleness. He had lied to her about the death of her husband, had not told her that he had no intention of returning to England or that he intended to buy a sheep station and surround himself with the emptiness of the Outback.

Unable to find her after she absconded, he had kidnapped her daughter in the hope that she would be the lure to bring Bethany back into his life. He dared not dwell upon the wrongs he had inflicted on both the mother and the child, and sometimes he was haunted by fears of retribution. Yet he had charted a course he could not seem to abandon, despite its futility.

Logic told him that he needed a woman like Kamika for a wife, simple, uncomplicated, undemanding. Kamika was content merely to be there if he needed her, and take herself off to her own pursuits when he did not. In his blackest moments of despair Will told himself that his yearning for Bethany was a festering sore that would never heal and that he must excise it from his very being.

Then Hope would come running to find him and he'd sweep her into his arms and hold her, her gossamer hair blowing across his cheek, the sweetness of her childhood innocence purging his darkest despair, bringing the belief that somewhere, somehow, there would be a way for them to be together as a family, for Bethany to care for him because they both loved her daughter.

Hope was taking a nap, and Will had just returned from helping the islanders haul in the fishing nets when Kamika came to tell him that he had a visitor. A haole. She affected a stern frown, strutted pompously, and encircled her throat with a graceful hand, indicating a clerical collar.

Will hid his smile of amusement as he found himself facing a short, rotund man with sandy hair, a handlebar mustache, and a bad case of sunburn. He mopped beads of perspiration from his brow with an outsize handkerchief and seemed almost to be strangling on his clerical collar.

"Dr. Prentice? I am the Reverend Matthew Ellis. My parish is on the other side of the island. We recently built a chapel there."

"Come and sit in the shade, Mr. Ellis," Will said. "I'll get a drink for you. Coconut milk or passion fruit juice?"

"Thank you, that would be most kind. The juice, I think. I

came by outrigger and managed to lose my hat overboard. My face feels as though I'd fried it for several hours."

"I'll get you some salve that will take out the sting. But your skin is so fair, you really should try to hang on to your hat at all costs."

A short time later they sat in the shade of a banyan tree sipping juice and Will said, "You're American, aren't you?"

"Yes, sir, that I am. And you are English, I understand. My predecessor informed me that you came here in search of your wife, who was kidnapped by convicts escaping from the Australian penal colony?"

"That is so."

"But having established that the convicts did not come to the islands, you nevertheless chose to remain here."

"Mr. Ellis, what exactly is the point of this conversation?"

Before he could respond, Hope wandered out of the shack, rubbing the sleep from her eyes. She was completely naked. A moment later Kamika came running after her. She, too, was nude. Taking the little girl's hand, she called, "We go for swim before dinner."

As they strolled down the palm-lined pathway to the beach the missionary averted his eyes and cleared his throat. "That, my dear Dr. Prentice, is the reason I came to see you. Your daughter is turning into a little savage. I understand you are a devoted father, but, forgive me, you are going native and you are dragging the child along with you."

"If you came to ask how long I intend to stay here, I'll tell you it's none of your business," Will snapped. "I am not a churchgoer. I am not even sure, any longer, whether I believe in your God. He is too cruel a deity. Therefore I am not answerable to you or to any other missionary."

"Be that as it may, you still have a duty to your daughter. Every parent does. She should at least be exposed to the teachings, and the religion, of her own race. I don't mean to presume to tell you how to live *your* life, doctor, but please at least bring your daughter to Sunday school tomorrow afternoon. My wife conducts the class."

The missionary thanked him for his hospitality and left. Will was still sitting under the banyan tree thinking about their conversation when Kamika and Hope returned.

The following afternoon Hope was outraged when Will insisted on dressing her in one of the frocks she had worn on the voyage to the islands, complete with bonnet and pinafore and, horror of all horrors, stockings and shoes.

"They pinch my toes!" she wailed.

"We shall have to buy you some new ones. We'll go to Honolulu tomorrow. You've grown so much that you'll need new dresses, too."

"Not want dresses. Too hot."

They sailed around the island and Will handed the child over to the Reverend Ellis's wife, who was a short, rotund replica of her husband, but who had managed to keep from blistering her buttermilk complexion.

Will settled down to wait on a hard bench outside the chapel. When the class ended and children of all sizes and colors came streaming out, Will rose to his feet and Hope came flying into his arms. "Can we go home now? Can I take off my shoes? Can I, can I?"

At the same instant a bell in the chapel tower began to call the worshipers to the afternoon service and Mrs. Ellis bustled over to him and said, "We do hope you and your daughter will now join us in the chapel, Dr. Prentice."

"I think not, Mrs. Ellis. Good day to you."

"Dr. Prentice, before you go—I wonder if you are aware that there is a dire need for doctors here in the settlement?"

"I am not interested in treating the sailors who come ashore with boils and abscesses and injure one another in their brawls," Will answered shortly.

"And what about the islanders who are ill?"

"I've heard they are succumbing to diseases we contend with in childhood—measles, chicken pox—against which they apparently have no immunity and of which many are dying. Thus far, fortunately, these illnesses have not reached our side of the island, and I have no intention of carrying them there and exposing either my daughter or my island friends."

A group of island women arrived for the church service, and Will couldn't help but add, "Why do you insist they wear those ridiculous costumes? They are cumbersome and totally unnecessary in this benign climate."

Mrs. Ellis blushed a deep pink, and he took his leave, wondering if he had made a mistake in heeding the Reverend Ellis's plea that Hope be given a Christian education. Surely what the sailors and missionaries had wrought in these islands was an offense against God and nature.

Still, he continued to take the child to the chapel each Sunday, feeling that it would offset the fact that she ran wild the rest of the time. Besides, he reasoned, Bethany would have wished it.

Several weeks passed before he noticed that there were no longer any Chinese children among those attending Sunday school. This was strange, since there were many Christian Chinese on the island. They came on five-year contracts to work in the sugar plantations.

The missionary's wife had avoided Will since their first encounter, but he waited for her to come outside to greet the parishioners arriving for services. "Mrs. Ellis," he asked, "I notice that you no longer have Chinese children in your Sunday school. You did when Hope first started coming to classes. Nor are there any Chinese waiting to go into the chapel for the service. What happened to drive them away?"

The minister's wife looked at the ground. "We . . . we had to ask them not to come any longer." Her face was very pink as she added defensively, "None of the other churches allow them to attend services either."

"But why?"

"There is sickness among them," Mrs. Ellis muttered before retreating toward the chapel. "We're afraid of catching it. I thought you knew about it. You're a doctor, after all. Surely you of all people understand our fear."

The Reverend Ellis came to the door of the chapel to greet his parishioners. Will said to Hope, "Wait for me on the beach. I won't be a moment."

"Ah, Dr. Prentice, can we persuade you to attend services today?" the missionary asked, catching sight of him.

"I'm concerned that formerly there were Chinese children in Hope's Sunday school class, but now they are banned due to illness. What is this illness that you fear so much?"

The minister cleared his throat nervously. "I do assure you that none of the Chinese children who came to our class, at least as far as we know, have come down with the disease. I'm quite sure your little girl was not exposed."

"But what *is* it?" Will persisted. "Measles? Not smallpox?"

"The islanders call it *mai pake*—the Chinese disease. But we fear it might be a scourge that was well known in biblical times." The minister's pale, watery eyes darted about, and he lowered his voice, as if afraid that in speaking the name of the dread disease aloud he might bring the pestilence down upon his own head.

"We believe it might be . . . leprosy."

★★★★★ 42 ★★★★★

DAVEY PLAYED IN a corner of the office with a toy ship Hagen Rudd had carved for him, while Alison worked at the massive mahogany desk that had formerly been used by Sir Adrian Fielding.

She looked up as she heard the familiar clicking sound of Rudd's wooden leg on the floorboards in the outer office and his deep, rumbling voice announced, "I'll go in. She's expecting me."

Davey jumped to his feet as the door opened. "Mr. Rudd! Look, I've put the cargo in the hold, like you showed me."

"Good lad. What about the ballast? Ah, you've got it exactly right. Got to keep her on an even keel in those winter gales in the North Atlantic, haven't we?" He ruffled the boy's hair and pulled a chair in front of the desk in order to sit down.

"Take your ship out to the clerks' room, Davey, and play quietly while Mr. Rudd and I have a talk," Alison said.

"I didn't expect to see you here," Rudd said bluntly, the moment the boy disappeared. "I thought your husband would be back at the helm."

Alison fixed him with a level stare. "Stewart has a bad case of bronchitis."

Rudd made a sound that could have expressed anything up to and including derision. "That why the boy is here with you? I've heard he spends more time in the office than at home nowadays."

"No, Davey is here because there's no one to take care of him at home. Mrs. Hughes decided to go and live with her sister in Edinburgh, and my housekeeper left. I didn't want to leave Davey with just Sir Adrian's nurse."

"The old man is still with you, then?"

"Yes." Alison glanced toward the window, which was still glazed with an early morning frost that showed no sign of melting, and thought of the turmoil of her life. How had it come about that she was responsible for a shipping company, a desperately unhappy husband, a child, and a hopelessly senile man?

"Is O'Connor still looking after Sir Adrian?"

"Yes, he's very good with him. Won't stand for any nonsense, but he's patient, too." O'Connor, a young Irish immigrant with the strength of a bull elephant, had worked in the warehouse until Alison took him home to be Sir Adrian's attendant. When he protested that he knew nothing about taking care of sick people, Alison had responded, "Can you keep him clean, stop him from wandering away, and make sure he doesn't hurt himself or anyone else? That's all the nursing skill you'll need."

"Mr. Rudd," Alison went on, "the warehouse is running smooth as clockwork. You've got good men there now, and I think Bryce could take over as manager."

Rudd's expression, always eager in her presence, now creased with concern. "You're letting me go? What have I done to displease you?"

"Letting you go? Do you think I'm daft? Of course not. I'm promoting you. I want you to come and work here, as our chief shipping clerk. You'll have three clerks and two office boys under you. I'll show you the ropes myself."

He looked down at his peg leg. "Do you think that's a good idea? Oh, not that I couldn't do the job, but I'd have to meet your importers and exporters. How would they feel about dealing with a lump of shark bait like me?"

"With more cordiality than they dealt with a pushy female like me, I expect," Alison answered, grinning.

"You mean . . . you don't intend to stay on yourself?" For a split second disappointment registered on his weather-beaten face, but it was quickly replaced by a questioning look.

"Oh, I'll be here as often as necessary," Alison said. "But yes, I want you to take over for me. I don't want to put in so many hours. I'll stay in the background, keeping tabs on the accounts and provisioning the ships and so on."

Hagen Rudd relaxed visibly. He fished inside his coat pocket and pulled out a perfect miniature lighthouse carved from a piece of bleached driftwood. "I forgot to give this to Davey."

She took it from him and looked at it. "It's hard to believe those big hands of yours can carve something this tiny and detailed. You'll take the job, then?"

"Honored to."

"Good. I'll have a partition put up in one corner of the clerks' room, and you can use that area as your private office."

"A half-wall maybe? So I can keep track of who's coming and going and see that the clerks are getting the work done."

She nodded in agreement. Just having him near, Alison knew, would create a sense that all was well. She—and the business—would be in good hands. She didn't examine too closely all of her reasons for bringing Rudd into the office. Apart from the fact that he was capable of doing everything she did and more, she had often turned suddenly to find him watching her with a mixture of admiration and longing on his face. Hagen Rudd was aware of her as a woman, and that in itself, after Stewart's indifference, was salve to her wounded pride.

Stewart went into a paroxysm of coughing and couldn't stop. He clapped a handkerchief to his mouth with one hand and with the other clutched the back of a chair for support.

Iris waited impatiently for him to regain his composure. They were in her aunt Elspeth's fussily furnished parlor, a labyrinth of bric-a-brac, aspidistras, and antimacassar-clad chairs, dominated by a grand piano. When his coughing subsided, she said coldly, "A bit of a cough is no excuse, Stewart. Why, even if I'd been dying, I would have crawled on my hands and knees to see you."

"For God's sake, Iris," he said miserably, "I sent you a letter." He had written begging her not to contact him again, after several face-to-face attempts to break off the affair had ended with her ignoring his pleas and demanding that he make love to her. If he failed to keep a rendezvous, she bombarded him with letters and messages left everywhere he might be—his club, his tailor's, even his home. "I have to make you understand. We can't go on with this. I can't face Alison. I'm in a constant state of turmoil. I don't know where to turn."

"You could leave her," Iris suggested coolly.

He sank unsteadily onto the piano stool. This was the first time she had made the drastic suggestion. Iris the free spirit had vanished the day after Alison's public humiliation of her at the garden party. In her place there had appeared a sharp-tongued shrew who demanded rather than requested, threatened rather than cajoled. Stewart had become impotent with her, and this further infuriated her, although not enough to induce her to let him go.

"Well?" she demanded.

He cleared his throat. "You know a divorce is out of the question. There's never been one in my family, and I wouldn't bring that kind of stigma to the Fielding name. I would be ostracized, and so would you. We'd be persona non grata. My business would suffer, my family would be disgraced."

"Oh, to hell with your business and your family. Besides, we don't have to go through the muck of the divorce courts. You're an artist and so am I. We don't have to abide by bourgeois rules. If we lived together we would be regarded as Bohemian, exotic. Such an aura might even further our musical careers."

"You don't understand, Iris. I don't *have* a musical career. I have a shipping company to run and I rely upon my wife to help me with the business. She also cares for my father. How could I possibly leave her? Without her my whole world would collapse. But I could hardly expect her to continue her support if I were to leave her for you. The business would go to hell, and my father would have to go into an asylum. No one else can handle him, certainly not my stepmother, who is too gentle a soul to stand up to him. He doesn't dare cross Alison."

"I don't want to hear another word about Alison!" Iris declared. "Or what a paragon she is. If she's so wonderful, why hasn't she given you a child?"

He turned away quickly, trying to hide from her the one secret about his marriage he had never revealed.

She watched him, her mind quickly turning over possible reasons why this particular subject might cause him so much distress.

Moving closer, she slid her hand up his arm until it came to rest on his shoulder.

"Iris, please . . . I can't see you again."

"You do want a child of your own, don't you, Stewart?"

"Yes, of course, someday."

"Someday next summer perhaps?" She dimpled, suddenly sure of herself, and gave him a radiant smile.

He felt all of the color drain from his face, and all of the blood in his veins seemed to freeze. "You don't mean . . ."

"You're going to be a father, Stewart. We're going to have a child."

"But . . . you said . . ." His voice shook with desperation. "You said you hated children, that you'd never have any."

She shrugged. "One can't always escape the whims of Mother

Nature. I certainly didn't want to find myself enceinte, but there it is. So you see, you can never leave me now."

Aunt Elspeth entered the room carrying a tea tray. She wore a cunning expression that indicated she had probably been listening to their conversation outside the door. Giving Stewart an acerbic smile she said, "I think it might be a good idea to decide upon a course of action. First and foremost, my niece will require an allowance from you, starting immediately. There are also a number of debts we must settle—the seamstress, the wine merchant, and so on. I'm sure you will be very generous."

Two hours later Stewart stumbled out of the house, his mind reeling. Pulling his woolen muffler up over his mouth and nose to form a barrier against a bitingly cold wind, he felt his chest constrict. He thought gloomily that if his bronchitis became pneumonia perhaps he would die from it and that would be an end to his troubles. For one dizzying moment he thought about killing himself, but decided that would be too harsh a punishment for those he left behind, who certainly were not to blame for his ghastly mistakes.

He was surprised to find that Alison was home when he reached their house in Princes Park. She didn't normally leave the office until late in the evening.

"So there you are," she said as he came from the vestibule. "Why on earth did you go out in such weather? You'll catch your death."

He was chilled to the marrow, and his teeth chattered as he attempted to respond.

"Come on, off with your coat and in by the fire. I'll make you a hot toddy."

Moments later he was in his favorite chair, warm slippers on his feet, a blanket around his shoulders, and Alison was plunging a hot poker into a glass of rum. Davey was playing with his toy ship on the hearth rug, and the appetizing aroma of sizzling steak and onions drifted from the kitchen.

Absorbing all the scents and sounds of home, Stewart sipped his rum and wondered how he could have jeopardized all the comfort Alison provided for brief moments of sensual pleasure with Iris. Why had he not seen that Iris's demands would soon far exceed the pleasure she gave him?

Alison didn't ask where he'd been; she was more concerned with preventing him from catching a further chill. She had worked all day in the office, taken care of the boy, and come home to prepare dinner, all without help. In a few minutes O'Connor would bring his father downstairs, and they'd have dinner together. Alison treated the old man firmly but kindly, and he'd been less trouble lately. What a wonder she was, accepting every trial and tribulation life tossed at her. She deserved so much better than a rotter like him for a husband.

"Davey, run upstairs and tell Mr. O'Connor to bring Sir Adrian down now," Alison said. The boy hurried to obey.

Stewart said heavily, "I went to see Miss Holloway, to ask her not to send any more letters or messages to me."

Alison waited for him to continue, her expression composed.

"She . . . she told me she is going to have a child."

Her expression did not change. She appeared to be considering the announcement, rather than being shocked by it.

He cleared his throat. "Iris wants me to—"

"Never mind what she wants," Alison snapped. "What do *you* want, Stewart?"

"I want to disappear from the face of the earth, I'm so ashamed. Above all, I want to make it up to you, somehow . . . for all the heartache I've caused you."

She sank down onto the sheepskin hearth rug and absently picked up the sailing ship Davey had left there. The leaping flames illuminated her face, a strong, arresting face, open and honest, without artifice. The bruises from the assault were fading, but they still caused Stewart to wince inwardly, imagining what she had suffered. He felt a sudden overwhelming need to care for her, to protect her, not least from himself.

"I wish there were a way," he said slowly, "to erase all the mistakes I've made. But there isn't, is there?"

"Stewart, you do realize that we could have our marriage annulled, don't you? It's never been consummated. If you want to be free to marry her, just say the word."

"God, no!" he said vehemently. "I never want to see her again. But she and her aunt are insisting upon financial settlements. They have threatened to file a breach of promise suit unless I agree to leave you, which of course I have refused to do."

"*Did* you make her any promises?"

"No." He felt his cheeks flame. "But the . . . child she's carrying . . . I suppose there are implied promises. Her aunt Elspeth recited one legal threat after another."

"You just leave those two old maids to me," Alison said calmly.

* * *

A week later on a crisp clear winter morning Alison arrived at the home of Elspeth Fotheringhill and was shown into the parlor by Iris, who frowned at Alison and darted curious glances at the bulky portfolio she carried.

"You'd better fetch your aunt," Alison said.

"What are you doing here?" Iris demanded. "I only asked you in because I didn't want a scene at the front door for the neighbors to see." She patted her beribboned curls nervously, perhaps expecting a horde of voracious insects to descend upon her head.

Alison marched to the parlor door and called loudly, "Miss Fotheringhill, will you come in here please?"

Aunt Elspeth appeared almost immediately, sailing into the room like a galleon before the wind. "What do you want with us? We have nothing to say to you."

"Ah, but I've got quite a few things to say to you," Alison replied. She sat down, opened the portfolio, and withdrew a thick bundle of documents. The top sheet of paper was a list, and pointing to the first item with her forefinger, she said, "According to our solicitors, a breach of promise suit can be filed by a woman only if she has been promised marriage. Obviously a man who was already married cannot have made such a promise."

"My niece has been used and betrayed by your husband. Her reputation is ruined," Elspeth began, bristling. "She is with child. His child."

Identical pairs of green eyes, catlike and sinister, regarded Alison triumphantly.

Alison flipped through the thick pile of papers on her lap, although she did not read them, and she raked Iris's slender frame with a scathing glance. "Now, in regard to all this nonsense about you being with child. We both know that's the oldest ploy in the history of womankind, don't we? But if, in fact, you are pregnant— Oh, do excuse me for using that word. I forgot that you high-class ladies prefer less blunt allusions to the state of having a bun in the oven. . . . Anyway, if we hear any more lies about Stewart being the father, or about your plans to drag him into court, we'll just have to bring out our parade of witnesses— all of whom are gentlemen who will testify that they were having intercourse with you during the period when Stewart was seeing you. You've been a busy little bee with a number of musicians and musical directors, even a tradesman or two, haven't you, dear?"

The two spinsters exchanged startled glances. Iris clutched her throat, as though about to strangle. She turned desperately to her aunt. "She's been spying on me—"

"Shut up," Elspeth snapped in a very unladylike tone. "Stewart is too much of a gentleman to deny he's the father of your child."

Alison smiled serenely. "We all know there's no child, but for the sake of argument, let's suppose there is. Then let's suppose a certain gentleman was rendered incapable of fathering a child, due to a severe case of mumps in his late teens that went into his testicles. A doctor's affidavit to that effect, along with the fact that the gentleman's wife did not conceive during their marriage despite the fact that she had a child from her first marriage . . . Well, now, that would certainly be a bit of a problem to any woman claiming that the gentleman in question had fathered her child, wouldn't it?"

Two faces as pale as ghosts stared at her.

Alison added sadly, "I would have liked another child myself, if it had been possible . . ."

As her voice trailed away, Alison's finger moved to the next item on her list. "My solicitor further states that if I wish to I can file a suit against you. Let me see, now . . . it's called 'alienation of affections.' "

"You wouldn't dare!" Elspeth thundered. "You'd be held up to public ridicule."

"Well, no, as a matter of fact, I wouldn't. My solicitor says that in such cases sympathy is always with the wife." Alison lifted the stack of papers slightly, as though weighing their contents again. "He says we'd be able to use all these same witnesses to establish that you are well versed in seduction and in the alienation of affections."

"Aunt Elspeth!" Iris pleaded, her lip trembling.

Alison's finger moved determinedly to the next item on her list. "Ah, yes, I almost forgot Aunt Elspeth's part in our little drama . . . especially the financial demands made on my husband. My solicitor was torn between interpreting those demands as pandering—which means selling the sexual favors of her ward—or as blackmail."

The last word resonated in the sudden silence that fell. Elspeth Fotheringhill, Alison noted with satisfaction, now looked green around the gills.

After slipping the documents back into the portfolio, Alison rose to her feet. "You know what to expect if we see or hear from either of you again."

Stewart listened, in growing amazement, as Alison relayed all that had transpired. "*Mumps?* I was so young when I had mumps I don't even remember it." He chuckled. "How on earth did you come up with such an idea?"

"Mrs. Hughes told me it was the reason she and her husband never had children. See, I didn't exactly say it was you. I just said, let's suppose a certain gentleman . . ."

"But how did you manage to gather a list of her other paramours?"

"I didn't. Oh, I asked a few questions about her gentlemen friends at the last recital she gave, but the documents I carried in that portfolio were actually bills of lading. Only the list on top had anything to do with little Iris. And even that I made up. I didn't actually talk to our solicitor. But I did read a few newspaper accounts of court cases involving divorce suits, countersuits, the naming of corespondents, and suits for alienation of affections. As far as the breach of promise suit was concerned, I just used my common sense about how to deal with that."

He leaned back in his chair, shaking his head in disbelief. "You never cease to astonish me. I don't know what to say, I'm so grateful—"

"Stewart," Alison interrupted, "before you say another word, there's something else I want to tell you." She stared at him for a moment. "You're feeling better now, aren't you? Your cough doesn't sound as bad."

"Yes, thank you, much better. I shall be able to go into the office tomorrow."

"You'll find that Hagen Rudd is handling everything very smoothly. He's a lot better educated and more experienced in alongshore activities than he told us, you know. Between the two of you, you'll manage very well."

"I take it you've decided to give up going into the city? Oh, Alison, I can't tell you how relieved I am."

"Then there's the question of your father," she continued. "He seems to like O'Connor, who handles him very well. You could either keep them here or send them back to Riverleigh."

Stewart's expression changed from relief to one of apprehension. "You are ticking off the problems you've solved for me, almost as if—"

"Davey and I, we'll be leaving as soon as I've packed a few things."

Stewart's mouth dropped open. "Leaving, but—"

"I hope you can see your way clear to advance me a small sum to get started again. I believe I've earned it, Stewart, and I'll pay you back as soon as I'm on my feet. I know I won't be able to find a position doing the kind of work I did for the Fielding Company—unless I can somehow turn myself into a man—but I am going into business for myself, as a shipping agent. I certainly know all the right people, and since I'll just be acting as a go-between for the manufacturers and the shipowners, I won't need a lot of capital. Davey will start school after Christmas, so he won't need so much attention."

"You can have whatever you need; that goes without saying. But, Alison, please . . . I wish you would stay. I can't imagine you not being here when I come home."

His heart sank at the blank expression on her face. She listened but was unmoved. Casting about desperately for some way to convey to her how much he needed her, all he could do was to stammer, "Y-you know I'm very fond of Davey. I'd miss him, too. And Father is so much calmer when you're here . . ."

She looked at him with eyes that were no longer dulled with pain, but the resignation there was even harder for him to bear. She said quietly, "Our marriage was a mistake from the start, Stewart. We both know that. Let's not hold any postmortems or try to mend what's broken beyond repair. Let's just part with a bit of dignity, shall we?"

Stewart gripped the arms of his chair, feeling a paralysis of both mind and spirit, knowing he had to say something to keep her here, but unable to think of any words that would not sound like hollow promises.

Oh, God, what a fool he'd been, not to recognize what he had! When had he begun to love her with this aching sense of bonding, this need? Why had he never noticed that tender curve of her cheek? The clarity and depth of her eyes? The way her hair gleamed in the firelight, the appealing rise of her full breasts above her narrow waist? Why, as she was walking out of the room, out of his life, when it was too late, did he suddenly want her as a woman?

BETHANY DID NOT learn what transpired between Jack and Louis LaFleur's seconds, but Louis departed for his parents' plantation, taking Leona to meet them, and as far as Bethany knew, no date had been set for a duel.

Jack Cutler and Bethany Fielding, giving their names as Jonathan King and Bethany Phillips, were married on a sultry afternoon in New Orleans a week after he proposed, with only Tom and the wife of the justice of the peace as witnesses.

Bethany wore a simple muslin gown of palest blue and carried a small bouquet of mixed flowers. Jack wore a white suit—virginal white, he called it—that made his dark hair look blacker than ever.

Tom remarked, "You two make a very handsome couple. I feel as though I should be an assembly of several hundred to truly appreciate you. I still think Bethany's making a big mistake, and I'm not sure how you persuaded her to do this, but—"

Jack laughed. "You don't understand Tom, lad. Women are not nearly as afraid of holy matrimony as we are. It is a calling for them, their profession, their natural state of being. For us it is the most unnatural thing in the world."

"If you want to change your mind—" Bethany began, but Jack cut off her words with a kiss, despite Tom's presence, then swept her up into his arms and carried her out to the waiting carriage.

After the brief ceremony, the three of them had a festive dinner together in the restaurant of a fine old hotel near Jackson Square, where Jack and Bethany would spend their wedding night. The following day they would depart by riverboat for a leisurely cruise up the Mississippi, returning in time for the completion of a house Jack was having built on a secluded bayou just outside town.

Tom made a final toast and discreetly departed early, leaving Bethany facing her new husband and feeling suddenly shy.

Jack rose, extended his hand to her, and said, "Come on. Let's go up to our suite. I want you all to myself."

In their room Jack pulled her swiftly into his arms. She closed her eyes as he kissed her, and tried to conjure a vision of Neil. But Jack's kiss was not like Neil's gentle persuasion; it was a pulsing demand that she yield to him.

His hands went to the buttons on her basque and began to unfasten them with an expertise that no gentleman should have possessed. She tried to pull away and said, "I'll go into the dressing room."

"No, you won't. I'm going to undress you. There'll be no hiding in closets to undress in this marriage, my sweet, and no voluminous nightgowns."

Shocked, she clutched her gaping bodice to hold it together, but he removed her hands and continued relentlessly dealing with buttons and ties, petticoats, and even stays. By the time he'd finished, Bethany was scarlet with embarrassment, but at the same time strangely excited. It was almost as if she were witnessing the disrobing—and now Jack was swiftly dealing with his own clothes—rather than taking part in it, as if it were all happening to someone else and she was not responsible for the consequences.

When they were both naked, he picked her up and carried her to the bed. "Look at me," he demanded when she closed her eyes again. "I'm Black Jack Cutler, and I'm your husband. There'll be no ghosts sharing our bed this night."

"I don't know what you mean—"

"Oh, yes, you do."

His mouth covered hers again, and she felt the universe spinning out of control as a sweet lethargy claimed her limbs and the hot rush of almost-forgotten desire surged along her veins, tingling in nerve endings, making her skin feel exquisitely sensitive, receptive to his caresses, to his lips and tongue.

He was a practiced lover in a way that Neil had never been. But Neil was tender and loving, a distant voice protested. Neil cared about you, loved you, while Jack feels only lust.

But after a moment she was too lost in passion to think or to reason; she could only feel.

How did it happen that they reached the peak together? For an instant they hovered in that void between earth and sky where all of the secrets of creation seemed suddenly within easy grasp, then crashed over the edge and floated blissfully back to reality, locked in each other's arms.

As the steward was stowing their baggage in the cramped closet of their cabin aboard the paddle wheeler the following day, Bethany said, "Please leave the small valise out, steward. Perhaps it could go under the dressing table?"

Jack turned from the porthole and slipped a coin into the hand of the departing steward. He surveyed Bethany's valise curiously. "Do you have the family jewels in there?"

"It's my manuscript and notes."

"Good God. You brought it along on our *honeymoon?*"

She blushed and murmured, "I didn't want to leave it behind for fear Tate's housekeeper might find it."

Slipping his arms around her waist, he pulled her close to him. "But you asked the steward not to put it away. I'm warning you, Mrs. King, you won't have time to work on it because I have other pastimes for you to pursue." He kissed her lips lightly, then with rising passion.

She didn't think about Neil. She didn't think about anything beyond the thrill of Jack's body pressed to hers, his desire, which was like a flame, igniting a need in her that could not be denied.

Lying contentedly in his arms much later, listening to the wail of the calliope and the steady thumping of the paddle wheel as the steamboat pulled away from the levee, Bethany said, "You never gave me a chance to answer your question about my manuscript. I had the steward leave it out because I hope you'll read a little bit of it and see what you think."

Long past midnight Bethany awoke to find the lamp still lit in the cabin. Jack was sitting in the single chair, her valise open on his lap, a manuscript page in his hand.

Rolling to the edge of the bed, she said softly, "I didn't mean for you to deprive yourself of sleep."

He looked up with a start, as though surprised to find her there. "Bethany . . . this is very good. I didn't intend to read more than a few pages, but I couldn't seem to stop."

She sat up, pleased and wide awake. "Do you really think so? I kept in mind what Tom said about Mr. Dickens's writing. I noticed that as each episode of one of his novels was published in the paper he always ended with an exciting bit of action or some unanswered question, which compelled the reader to buy the paper the following week to see what happened. I attempted to do the same thing."

"You succeeded."

"You don't think any of us will be recognized, do you?" she asked anxiously.

"Your heroine is a combination of yourself and Leona, isn't she? I understand why you did that, but you might want to remove some of her more strident conversations. Will she kill the swinish lieutenant? If so, how will you handle her punishment? You can't let her get off scot-free. God-fearing readers wouldn't stand for it. An eye for an eye, you know . . ."

"I hadn't thought about that," Bethany admitted. "Perhaps she shouldn't kill him, even though it would be self-defense."

Jack put the page he was holding back into the valise and came to the bed. She moved aside to make room for him to sit down.

"Your hero may be a little too villainous, too." He grinned. "I recognized myself instantly, by the way."

"I thought he could redeem himself in some way," Bethany said more primly than she intended. "The rogue redeemed is always more interesting, at least in fiction, than the true-blue hero."

Jack rolled his eyes. "Phew! For a moment I was afraid you were planning some act of redemption for me. But tell me, why can't I find your sainted first husband in this epic?"

She looked away. "I don't know much about what happened to Neil in the penal colony."

His finger went under her chin and turned her face back toward him. There was a tightening of his jaw as he said, "Too difficult to write of deities, is that it?"

"Why do you harbor such resentment toward Neil? He's no longer here."

Jack's arms went around her and he held her in a fierce, painful grip. "But he's still in your mind. You think about him constantly. Do you think I don't know that when you lie in my arms you're pretending I'm him? I want all of you, Bethany, all your thoughts, all your wishes and desires. I don't want to share you, not even with a ghost."

She was silent. She could have told him that when he made love to her she was a part of only him, that his flesh fused with hers, his breath mingled with hers, that the life-force flowing from him filled her completely, answering all her needs, and that the feelings he created in her were too intense to allow any other image to intrude. But she held back. If she allowed Black Jack Cutler to possess her completely, would she lose him? For a man like him, wasn't the chase everything? Wouldn't his interest fade if she capitulated?

"It's very late, Jack," she said at last.

He sighed and released her. "Go to sleep. I want to read a little more of your manuscript." He paused. "On my last trip up the river I met a newspaperman in Vicksburg. I was wondering if we should give him a portion of your story and see what he thinks."

Alarmed, she exclaimed, "But it's not ready!"

"You wrote it to call attention to the plight of women in the penal colony, didn't you? Unless it's read, it's useless. You might as well have kept the thoughts in your head."

They left the manuscript in Vicksburg and spent their days and nights making love, dancing on deck, walking in the moonlight. Each minute was filled with newfound pleasures. Jack was a courtly and attentive husband, who caused the other women on board to sigh and resent their own men. On the surface they were the perfect couple, madly in love, completely engrossed in each other.

We're playacting, Bethany thought. It's a charade. We are acting the part of ecstatic honeymooners, but underneath we are still strangers.

When the steamboat returned to New Orleans it seemed that only hours had passed, yet they had been gone for several weeks, spending time in several of the gracious cities that lined the banks of the Mississippi.

Tom awaited them on the levee, and his expression was grave. "Louis and Leona were married on the riverboat before they reached his parents' plantation. His parents are outraged. Apparently they launched an extensive investigation into just who Leona is and where she came from. We could all be in trouble."

Jack swore under his breath.

Tom went on quickly, "There's more. He came to ask me when you'd be coming back and said you'd avoided the duel long enough."

Bethany clutched Jack's arm. "Oh, dear heaven!"

Tom said, "I hate to bring nothing but bad news, but . . . well, Bethany . . . there's even worse news from England."

* * *

Bethany was inconsolable. Nothing Jack did or said penetrated the veil of intense sadness that enclosed her. Her daughter was lost forever, and nothing else mattered to Bethany.

One evening Jack returned from the law offices to find that Bethany had spent the entire day in her room, not even bothering to dress. He disappeared for a while, returning with a tray of sandwiches and a pot of tea, which he set on a small table in the window alcove of their bedroom.

"I'm not hungry—" Bethany began.

"Well, I am. Come and sit with me. I hate to eat alone. Besides, it's time I told you my life story. You've been too polite to inquire and I've appreciated that, but as my wife, you're entitled to know."

He waited until she joined him, then poured her a cup of tea and placed a hefty ham sandwich in front of her, which she ignored.

"My father was a landowner, titled, wealthy, a firstborn son of a firstborn son," Jack began. "He owned tenant farms and various properties in London, but he left the running of the estate to a steward and had agents and solicitors to deal with everything else. He brought my older brother and me up to be about as useless as he was, except when it came to riding, fencing, and shooting, his favorite hobbies. Our lives were idyllic, a perfect blending of leisure and pleasure—that is, until my older brother, who was somewhat more headstrong than I"—Bethany rolled her eyes—"fell afoul of a certain duke's only son. There was a brief feud, culminating in a duel that left the duke's son dead. My father promptly shipped my brother off to foreign parts, and the duke, unable to exact revenge on my brother, set about the task of stripping our family of all we possessed, including our good name. The strain eventually killed my father, who suffered heart failure, and my mother pined away and joined him six months later. On his way back to England, my brother apparently fell overboard and drowned. I couldn't prove it was murder, but his death was highly suspicious.

"At the tender age of twenty-one I found myself without family, home, or assets. Not only that, but I had inherited my father's debts. False debts, I might add. I knew beyond a shadow of a doubt that he had not borrowed heavily against our land and other assets; yet everything we owned was mortgaged or in foreclosure. Our family solicitor could not explain this, other than to suggest a sudden and inexplicable urge to gamble on my father's part. My father *never* gambled. He loathed any activity that kept him indoors.

"I began to study all of the documents involved, to trace the deeds of title and so on through the legal process, and to learn exactly how a man's possessions could be stripped from him with the full sanction of the law. When I had exhausted the knowledge and resources of our family solicitor I went to London and combed the law libraries, questioning every solicitor and barrister who would listen. I worked as an office boy, a clerk; I served subpoenas, took depositions, copied legal documents, swept floors, spent all my free time in the assizes listening to trials. I was getting close to uncovering a conspiracy against my family when one night I was on my way back to the room I'd taken in Soho, and . . . I don't know what happened, except that I was hit over the head and came to my senses on a deserted highway outside London. I was wearing a mask; there was a pistol in my hand, a bundle of cash and jewels in my pocket. I was surrounded by policemen."

Bethany leaned forward, her own troubles temporarily forgotten. "Oh, how dreadful. You were arrested?"

He nodded. "Tried and convicted of highway robbery. Two passengers in a carriage traveling that night testified against me."

"You went to prison?"

"No. I managed to escape, out of the courtroom window, as a matter of fact. My budding law career was over; there was a price on my head. I decided if I was to be labeled a highwayman, then that's what I'd be."

Jack grinned. "During the next few years I met an interesting variety of people. I did attempt to relieve only the rich and powerful of their cash, but I must confess that any well-dressed fool who traveled the highways late at night might have heard my 'Stand and deliver.' At the same time word went out on the mysterious grapevine that exists among criminals that I had knowledge of the law. I even defended some of those very criminals in provincial courts, well away from London. I would don a beard and wig, affect a stooped gait and . . . well, you can imagine the rest."

Bethany realized she was absently nibbling her sandwich. "Is that how you were eventually caught?"

"No. I stopped a carriage one night, and there was only one

woman inside. I would have waved it on, but she fainted. I foolishly bent over her, to try to revive her, and the driver knocked me over the head. By then I was the notorious Black Jack Cutler, and they kept me in chains until the day I was put aboard the transport for the penal colony."

"Will Prentice told me that you were transported rather than hanged because the authorities feared if you were hanged you'd become a legend."

Jack affected an expression of mock dismay. "Damn. I thought I had become a legend anyway."

He stood up and walked around her, took her hand, and drew her to her feet. "Get dressed," he said softly. "I'm going to take you out for a carriage ride. You've spent too much time alone, brooding about your daughter, and I'm going to remedy that situation in future."

Bethany did as he asked. Somehow life was less of a burden when Jack was present. He never seemed to sink into the black moods of despair that plagued most men from time to time, nor did he allow those around him to cater to their own gloom. He was, in fact, a master at raising spirits. During the next few days Bethany found herself again caught up in a whirl of activity as Jack remained steadfastly at her side. When she protested he was neglecting his work, he shrugged and told her there was nothing that wouldn't keep. She learned from Tom that many of the people he helped were poor and oppressed and couldn't pay anyway, but like many other altruists, Jack had invested wisely, and the profits from those investments more than made up for the lack of income from his clients.

She was beginning to accept the news Tate Ivers had sent from England—although she still ached with longing to be reunited with her child despite the impossibility of that dream—when Tom came rushing over late one evening with disastrous news.

"I went home to get some papers I'd left behind. Saffron wasn't expecting me. I heard voices in the drawing room, and I was about to announce my presence when I overheard what was being said. I don't know who Saffron's visitor was, although I suspect he was sent by the LaFleur family. She was telling whoever it was that she'd heard us talking about the Australian penal colony and about a long sea voyage. She said she was certain that all four of us—Leona, Bethany, Jack, and I—were escaped convicts."

MARY'S HEART BEAT like that of a schoolgirl. She stared at herself in her dressing table mirror. Her eyes were bright, and her face was flushed, despite the winter chill that pervaded Riverleigh. He was here. He was waiting downstairs in the drawing room. Tate Ivers had arrived.

Drawing a deep breath, which did little to calm her, she draped a soft lamb's-wool shawl around her shoulders as she descended the stairs. The burgundy silk gown she had chosen to wear offered little protection from the damp chill, but it was the most becoming dress she owned and she wanted Tate to see her in it.

When she entered the room, he was standing with his back to the fire, and his face lit up at the sight of her. With two great strides he was at her side, and his arms went around her. He kissed her forehead, then her eyes, and finally her mouth. Drawing back, he gazed at her face, her hair, her throat and neck, examining every detail in the manner of a starving man who had suddenly found himself confronting a banquet.

"Mary, Mary . . . oh, my dear," he breathed. "How I've longed for this moment! How I've missed you."

"And I you, Tate," Mary replied shyly. "But please! We must be discreet. The servants—"

"Damn the servants. Why didn't you come to me?"

She was spared having to answer by a tap on the door, and a footman came into the room to attend to the fire. He seemed to take an age to open the copper coal scuttle and bank the already blazing fire.

Mary cleared her throat. "Did you have a good crossing?"

"We ran into a couple of winter squalls. Nothing serious."

As the servant departed, Tate took her hand and led her to a sofa, and they sat side by side, unable to take their eyes off each other. "The butler told me Adrian is not in residence, that he's staying with Stewart and his wife."

His unasked questions hovered between them for a second.

"I should have told you the truth about Adrian," Mary said. "At first we thought the pain of his injuries and the resulting infection was causing his confusion. He would forget things, accuse the servants and me of hiding various items from him, fly into a rage when he couldn't remember a name or a word. But then . . ." She explained briefly her husband's rapid degeneration and the doctors' grim prognosis.

When she finished, Tate said, "Stewart's wife must be a very understanding woman."

Mary placed her hand inside his, needing the comfort of his touch. "Tate, they're bringing Adrian home to Riverleigh in a few days." She bit her lip. "You see, Alison—Stewart's wife—has left him."

"Because of Adrian?"

"No. There were other problems. She did hire a very capable attendant, and he'll be coming, too." She felt tears prick the backs of her eyes. To have her beloved Tate so near, and yet to have to send him away again was too much to bear.

"What are you trying to tell me, Mary?" he asked gently. "That we can't be together? That you've decided Adrian needs you more than I do?"

"My duty . . ." she began.

He stroked her hand, brought it to his lips, and kissed it tenderly. "I would never try to force you to do anything against your will. I love you, Mary, more deeply and devotedly than you will ever know. My only concern is your happiness."

She sighed. "Oh, Tate. I feel so guilty . . ."

"You have nothing to feel guilty about. Mary, I must be here with you when Adrian arrives. I need to see for myself just how dependent he is on you."

"It's not so much that he's dependent on me. After all, he's been staying with Stewart and Alison. But how can I, his wife, think about my own happiness at such a time? Now, before I find myself drowning in tears of regret, please tell me about Tom and Bethany. Was she delighted to be reunited with her little girl? We wondered who had come for her. I hope you don't mind, but I've asked Alison to come and meet you. She was so shattered when little Hope disappeared, and it will be such a comfort to hear all about her new life."

"I wish I could give you both good news about the child," Tate answered grimly. "However, not only have they not been reunited, but Bethany never sent anyone to collect her daughter. She has no idea who took the child."

Mary's breath caught in her throat. "But there was no ransom demand. Who—"

"I will begin an immediate investigation. Mary, it seems that you and I must try to reweave all the broken threads in the Fielding tapestry."

A fierce winter storm howled in from the Irish Sea on the afternoon of the day Sean O'Connor was to take Sir Adrian back to Riverleigh, and Sean reflected gloomily that the weather was a fitting accompaniment to all of the other problems he faced in preparing for the journey.

Immediately after Alison and Davey moved out, Sir Adrian had caught a cold and then developed bronchitis, and so the trip to Riverleigh had been delayed. It was O'Connor's opinion that Sir Adrian's ensuing decline was the result of missing Alison and the boy. "Where is the woman who makes my dinner?" he kept asking. "The food is bad when she's not here. . . . Where is the little boy? I liked to watch him playing with his ships."

Getting him bathed and dressed became a major battle. Whenever Stewart tried to talk to him, he flew into a rage and smashed several pieces of furniture. Alison and the child had had a calming influence on Sir Adrian, whereas Stewart seemed to have the opposite effect. On the rare occasions when the old man had thrown fits while Alison was in residence, she had chastised him as she would a child, even smacked his hand once when he reached for a vase to smash. Sir Adrian had never again tried to break anything in her presence. Sean O'Connor hoped that Lady Mary Fielding would be able to deal as effectively with his charge, if he could ever get the old sod across the river.

Stewart had arranged for a boat to take them across to Birkenhead, thereby avoiding the public ferry, and from Birkenhead they would travel by hired coach. But Sean was uneasy at the prospect of taking his charge away from home in his present state of agitation.

The son, Sean observed, seemed almost as lost as his father. Stewart crept about with a long face, his gaze unfocused, and he'd lost his appetite completely. He left for his shipping company early and returned late. Alison had found a woman to come in and do the housework and prepare dinner, as long as she didn't have to live in, but the entire household had lost its hub when Alison departed.

"Sure and it's not happy I am about taking your father over the water on such a day, not all by meself," he told Stewart that morning.

"I'd go with you, but my presence seems to agitate him even more," Stewart said. "And you know how he is with strangers."

"P'r'aps if we could get your wife to talk to him?"

"Excellent idea. On my way to the office, I'll stop by and ask her to come over."

Stewart was delighted to have an excuse to see Alison. The days without her had been desolate for him. He felt as though his right arm had been torn out by the roots. It seemed ironic that he should feel so devastated just when all his other problems appeared to have been solved. There had been no further communication from Iris or from her aunt. Indeed an article about her latest recital revealed that she had played a piano duet with a young musician with whom she was reportedly romantically involved. The Fielding line was also running smoothly under the guidance of Hagen Rudd. But Stewart felt unhappier than ever before.

Alison had rented a modest house on the outskirts of Princes Park, and Stewart arrived there just as she was preparing to leave.

"Stewart, is something wrong?" she asked as soon as she opened the door in response to his knock. "Is it your father?"

"May I come in for a moment?"

She nodded, holding the door wider. She didn't extend the invitation beyond the vestibule, although she closed the front door. "I'm in a bit of a hurry, Stewart."

"Father is balking at going back to Riverleigh. I wondered if you would go and talk to him." It wasn't strictly true; his father had no idea he was being taken home, but Stewart didn't know what else to say. "He becomes upset whenever he sees me. I think some part of his brain reminds him that I'm the one who stood by and let his favorite son get shanghaied. I do feel he should go home to Riverleigh, don't you?"

"It isn't my place to say, Stewart."

"He . . . he misses you and Davey."

"I'll go and see your father as soon as I've taken Davey to school." She opened the door again, letting in icy blasts of air.

He hesitated, wanting to ask if there was anything he could

say to persuade her to come back to him. But it was evident from her preoccupied expression that she had already dismissed him from her mind. He murmured a thank-you and stepped out into the rain.

"You go with O'Connor and behave yourself, you hear?" Alison said to Sir Adrian. "He's taking you over the water. You'll go on a boat. You like ships, remember?"

"Ship," Sir Adrian said. "The boy has a ship. Where is the boy?"

"He had to go to school. I'll bring him to see you after you get home. Come on, now. Let O'Connor put your overcoat on for you, and your muffler. It's cold and wet out."

"Going on a ship," Sir Adrian told Sean, who was buttoning up his overcoat.

"That you are, sir. Here y'are, then, let's get your hat on."

"Shall I go with you down to the docks, or will you be all right now?" Alison whispered to O'Connor.

"Sure and I'll manage now, I'm thinking."

"Who are you?" Sir Adrian demanded of him.

"O'Connor, sir. Sean O'Connor."

"You're not my son."

"No, sir, that I'm not."

"My son was sent to the penal colony in Australia. He went on a ship."

Alison looked at him sharply, but his flash of awareness had already faded. There had been other such moments. Occasionally Adrian would speak coherently of events that had occurred thirty years earlier, but would forget what had happened only minutes before. Several times he had mentioned his ships, but of late she thought the vessels he spoke of were Davey's toys.

She handed O'Connor a slip of paper. "This is where I live, in case you need me. I'll come to Riverleigh as soon as I can. I want to see Lady Fielding. Good luck."

After seeing them on their way, she had to travel out of the city to keep an appointment with the owner of a Lancashire cotton mill, arriving breathless and flushed because she was a few minutes late.

"So you are A. F. Banks?" the mill owner asked as she was shown into his office. "Is this some sort of joke?"

"No, it isn't. Forgive me for deliberately misleading you, but

I have found that most men won't talk to a shipping agent who is a woman."

"And what makes you think I will?"

"In the letter of introduction I sent you, I gave you a number of reasons why it would be to your advantage to deal with me. I'll get you the best freight rates and guaranteed arrival dates of all the raw cotton you import, and if you ship any of your goods overseas, I'll take care of your exports, too. I know how to handle customs and consular documents, and I can get you the best insurance coverage. I'll even arrange packing, warehousing, and hauling if you wish."

"Your letter was impressive and that's why you're here. But if I'd known A. F. Banks was a woman—"

"I can still deliver all I promised. At least hear me out."

She spent the next hour explaining how she had run the Fielding ships, dealt with the biggest mill owners and manufacturers in the north, and knew all of the other shipowners. Hadn't it been her task to beat the competition? She knew which ships sailed on time and which owners were lax in their maintenance.

When she finished speaking, the man gave her a sly look. "Ah, but you haven't mentioned your other qualifications. A woman as pretty as you must have other attributes a man would find attractive. Shall we find a nice quiet hotel and have lunch together and talk about it?"

She tried to swallow her anger. "Will you at least give me a chance to prove I can do the job? Let me handle one of your shipments—just one."

"Go and find yourself a husband and have babies, lass. It will give you something to do and knock all this nonsense out of your head. I would no more let a woman handle my cotton than I'd let a fool from Bedlam ship it for me."

Disconsolate, she traveled back to Liverpool. An icy wind was blowing, and the joints of her fingers burned, warning that she might be getting chilblains. She took off her gloves and rubbed her hands together to get the circulation going.

Most of the shippers had refused even to see her. Resorting to the subterfuge of signing her name "A. F. Banks" so that she could at least have a face-to-face talk with a prospective client had been her last resort. Even the men who knew she had practically single-handedly run the Fielding Shipping line refused to entrust their cargoes to a woman. She was a threat to the male bastion of maritime commerce. If they allowed her to breach it, what would stop other females from attempting to follow suit? The result would be the collapse of society.

Sean O'Connor was waiting for her in front of her house, pacing frantically back and forth, his face a study in desperation.

"What are you doing here?" Alison asked. "Where is Sir Adrian?"

"Oh, Mrs. Fielding! Oh, the saints preserve us! He . . . he started a fuss the minute he saw the ships down at the dock. Carrying on about getting the cargoes aboard and where were the bills of lading and such like. I'm thinking for a minute he was back to running his own ships again. Well, anyway, I left him standing on the quay not more than six feet away from me while I paid the coachman and got the bags. Lord, I didn't turn me back for more than a second—"

"Where is he now, O'Connor? What happened to him?"

O'Connor wrung his hands. "I'm not after knowin', and that's the truth. We searched all over the docks for him. Vanished into thin air, he did."

"You're sure he couldn't have fallen into the river?"

"No, no chance of that, thank the Lord. We'd have heard a splash or a shout, or one of the dockers or sailors would've seen it."

"Could he have slipped aboard one of the ships?"

"I asked every tar I could find, but nobody saw him. Lord, I only turned me back a second—"

"Have you told Mr. Stewart?"

O'Connor shook his head.

"You'd better get on over to his office and tell him, then." As he was about to turn away Alison called after him, "Were there any Fielding ships docked nearby?"

He thought for a moment. "Why, yes, there was one. A ship that your husband ordered to come up from Portsmouth for refitting. The *Peregrine* was tied up at Princes dock waiting to go to the yard. You don't think . . ."

The *Peregrine.* Alison knew the ship's grim history—first a slaver, then a convict transport; it was also the vessel on which Hope's mother had been transported to Australia. "I'll go and see while you go for Mr. Stewart."

He looked doubtful. "Maybe I'd best go to the *Peregrine* and you go fetch Mr. Stewart?"

"If Sir Adrian is aboard he's more likely to come with me than with Mr. Stewart."

When she reached the Pier Head the wind was so fierce she had to hold down her skirts with one hand and clutch her hat with the other as she crossed the open area beside the docks.

Since the *Peregrine* was preparing to go into dry dock, Alison knew only a skeleton crew would be aboard. She went up the gangway and had to go looking for a crewman. He looked at her in disbelief as she explained that Sir Adrian Fielding might have slipped aboard.

"Haven't seen him, Mrs. Fielding, but I'll fetch the first mate."

"Check the cabins and the galley on your way. I'll look in the wheelhouse."

The mate mustered the few sailors aboard to search the ship. They returned to report there was no trace of Sir Adrian.

"You sure he came aboard?" the mate asked, clearly thinking she was mad.

"They didn't search thoroughly enough," Alison said. "They were too quick."

"They searched the main decks. They didn't go below. He wouldn't have gone down there."

"Have them search below."

For an instant she thought the mate would refuse, but he ordered a hatch opened and sent two hands below. A minute later there were muffled shouts and a crashing sound.

A frightened face appeared at the hatch. "He's down there, sir. But we can't get near him. He climbed up on one of the convict racks, and he's got a belaying pin. Tried to bash me flamin' brains out with it.

Alison turned to the first mate. "I'll have to go down and talk to him."

Even before he brought the *Peregrine* up from Portsmouth, the mate had heard stories about Mrs. Stewart Fielding, most of which seemed too outrageous to be true, but looking into her determined gaze, he decided not to argue with her.

Minutes later she was descending into the cramped quarters that had housed the convicts on their long voyage to oblivion. The mate lit an oil lamp to illuminate the narrow ledges on which the convicts had slept.

Sir Adrian crouched on the top bunk, his head and shoulders hunched below the bulkhead. He was rhythmically pounding a belaying pin against the wooden rack. Several rat-chewed blankets were draped on the bunks, and Alison could hear scurrying sounds in the darkness beyond the yellow pool of light cast by the oil lantern. She tried to close her nostrils against the assault of the foul air trapped belowdecks.

Cautiously she moved along the narrow aisle between the racks and spoke softly. "It's me, Alison. I've come to take you home."

In the dim light, his eyes seemed to glow red, like those of an animal. He tossed the belaying pin from one hand to the other and looked at her without recognition.

"Come on, now, get down from there," Alison ordered.

He glared down at her. "This is my ship."

"Of course it is."

"I'm going for a sail."

"That's right. But not on this ship. This ship's not ready to sail yet. She's got to be refitted. Come on, now, get yourself down here. I'll take you to your ship."

She had reached the rack upon which he crouched, and she stood directly below him. "Come on now, Sir Adrian, you remember me." She was reaching up with her hand to try to touch him when he struck.

The belaying pin caught her a stinging blow to the side of her head and knocked her into the arms of the first mate. At the same instant the ship rose on a river swell as the tide changed. The oil lantern the mate was holding flew from his hand as he tried to catch Alison.

In Alison's last second of consciousness she saw the flame from the lamp lick at a rotting blanket dangling from the lower rack. Then everything exploded into a wall of fire.

★★★★★ 45 ★★★★★

SUNLIGHT SPARKLED ON the azure sea, and the trade winds blew a shower of white ginger blossoms around Will's head as he waited for the Sunday school class to end.

Several island women also waited for their children, and Will had been surreptitiously observing one of them.

He had seen her before, waiting for her son, but today he noticed for the first time that her features had changed, taking on a leonine look. She also had several angry red patches on her arms which appeared to be fresh burns, but even though she bumped her injured arm against the corner of the chapel, she did not appear to feel any pain.

The chapel door opened, and the children came streaming out. He felt a stab of fear as he saw Hope walking hand in hand with the son of the woman he had been watching.

"Hope, come here," he called sharply. The little girl looked startled at his tone, but obeyed instantly.

The missionary's wife ushered the last of her brood out into the bright sunshine and, seeing Will, called, "Good afternoon, Dr. Prentice. How are you today?"

"That boy's mother," he said, indicating the child who now ran to greet the woman with the burned arms, "do you know if she is under a doctor's care?"

"Oh, you mean for the burns? I believe she accidentally knocked over a cooking pot."

And felt no pain, so did not at first notice that her flesh was being seared, he thought.

"We'll see you next Sunday, then, Dr. Prentice."

"No," Will said abruptly. "We won't be coming next week. We are leaving the islands. Say good-bye to Mrs. Ellis, Hope."

The little girl dutifully hugged Mrs. Ellis and over her shoulder grinned at Will. Hope had always protested that she didn't like Sunday school, and Will had been considering withdrawing her from the class. He didn't care for the missionaries' approach to teaching religion to the children, which was the same as their teaching of the islanders, consisting mainly of threats of hellfire and damnation for their sins. Furthermore, everything the children did, it seemed, was a sin. But his decision to leave had nothing to do with religion.

"Are we really going away?" Hope asked as they walked down to the beach where an outrigger canoe waited to take them back to their own side of the island.

"Yes. It's time for us to leave. We must go in search of your mother."

"Will Kamika come with us?" Hope was very fond of Kamika.

"No. She will stay here." Breaking the news of their forthcoming departure to Kamika would be painful, but he no longer had any choice. He simply could not expose Hope to the dread disease that clearly had broken out of the Chinese immigrant community and was infecting the native islanders.

Kamika was working in her taro patch, hoeing the rich red earth, when they returned. She smiled and waved, pushing her long dark hair over one shoulder.

Deciding that there was no time like the present, he sent Hope to change out of her Sunday dress and walked over to the taro patch. "Kamika, I wish to sail to the island of Maui, as soon as you can arrange for a canoe to take us."

"You want go to the island of Pele, the fire goddess? But why?" Kamika asked.

"We must travel to Lahaina where I hope to find a big ship to take us away from the islands."

Kamika's dusky features registered disbelief, then dismay. "No! No, I cannot leave. My people here."

"Yes, I know," he said as gently as he could. "I do not expect you to come with us. But the child and I must leave."

"But you come back," Kamika said firmly.

"No. We will not come back."

She gazed at him forlornly. "I not want you to go."

"Kamika . . . you knew that sooner or later I would have to continue my search for my wife. I told you that, at the very beginning. I, too, am sad that we must part, but the child needs her mother and I need my wife. This . . . interlude with you has been one of the most serene and pleasant periods of my entire life, and I will always remember you and these islands."

Her eyes filled with tears, and the sight was almost more than he could bear. He took her in his arms and held her. It would be more of a wrench to leave her than he had ever contemplated. She accepted him so completely, in her eyes he was not the surgeon superintendent, a gaunt and melancholy figure of authority, as he had been to Bethany. Here he was simply a man, with the same wants and needs as any other man. He realized with a shock that Kamika had been his wife in every sense of the word, although he had never considered her to be. The lovely island girl had given him her complete loyalty and devotion, and he felt wretched at having to abandon her. But Hope's life was at stake. He had chosen to take responsibility for the child and had to put her before anyone else.

After a moment Kamika put on a brave face and said, "I go to Maui with you. Have more time together . . . just stay until you sail away."

He nodded in agreement, his heart heavy. Giving up Kamika was going to be the hardest thing he'd ever had to do.

All of Kamika's friends gathered on the beach for alohas. Leis were exchanged and the gods were called upon to watch over the travelers. Even the haole God was asked to bring them safely home, and Will did not have the heart to tell these gentle people that he and the child probably would never return.

But at the last minute Will hesitated, sniffing the wind. "Perhaps today is not a good time to start our journey. There's the smell of a squall in the air."

The owner of the outrigger shook his head firmly. "We go. All plans made. Bad *kapu* to turn back."

Hope had already clambered aboard the outrigger, and she called to them to hurry.

Will cast another glance at the purplish clouds smudging the horizon. Tropical squalls often whipped around the islands, but for the most part the sturdy islanders ignored them, unless the winds grew to hurricane force. Perhaps this one would veer off. He helped Kamika into the canoe and climbed in himself.

They had been at sea for only an hour or so when the dark clouds moved swiftly toward them and a heavy rain began to fall. The islanders, who were constantly in and out of the water, ignored the warm rain. They kept the canoe moving over increasing swells for a time, until a strong gust of wind caught them and they were hurtled across the foaming surface of the sea, propelled by unseen currents.

Will gathered Hope into his arms, protecting her from the wind and spray with his own body. Feeling the child shiver, he told her, "We'll be blown off course. The oarsmen won't fight the wind and currents now. But no need to worry; as soon as the squall passes, we'll sail on to Maui."

Gradually the swells diminished, and as capriciously as it had risen, the wind moved on. As the rain abated to a thin drizzle, an island loomed ahead.

Silence fell upon everyone aboard the canoe as they stared at a bleak peninsula backed by forbidding mountains visible through a veil of misty rain. Hope pressed herself closer to Will.

Staring at the gloomy land mass, Will was overwhelmed by a sense of foreboding. A great sadness seemed to hover over the deserted shore, which was lashed by a rough surf.

Kamika also crept closer to him, and she, too, seemed to be

mesmerized by the loneliness of the peninsula. "We not stop here," she whispered, as though afraid the sound of her voice might anger the sleeping gods. "It is called Kalaupapa. The place of no sunset."

Will could understand why. The peninsula was battered on three sides by stormy surf and on the south side was walled off by towering mountains that were surely too sheer for any but the most agile to climb. It was a place of complete isolation.

He felt an overpowering sense of relief when they were able to escape the pull of the current and resume their journey to the island of Maui.

In contrast to the stark barrenness of the deserted and gloomy peninsula of Kalaupapa, Maui was even more abundantly fertile than Oahu, where they had been living. They had been to Maui before, shortly after reaching the islands. The whaling port of Lahaina on the leeward side of the island had been their first stop in the Sandwich Islands, and they had stayed for a time, hoping to hear news of the convicts' ship.

Hope said, "Mrs. Ellis told us that God made the earth and it was all finished in seven days. But Kamika said Maui boiled up out of the sea, and in the beginning it was just a black cinder."

"What Kamika told you is true. All of these islands are volcanic and did indeed boil up out of the sea. But now the ancient lava flows are covered with trees and flowers, and sugarcane and pineapples have been planted. Still, if we were to go to the giant crater of Haleakala you would see the burned-out reminder of Maui's origins. The islanders call it the House of the Sun."

"Pele, the fire goddess, lost her battle with the goddess of the sea," Kamika put in sagely. "And the god Maui snared the sun's rays with ropes."

Will smiled conspiratorially at Hope. "Their legends have only some basis in fact."

When they were on the beach, Kamika took a lei of purple and white orchids from around her own neck and slipped it over Will's head. "Aloha, Will. Aloha, Hope. I not go to Lahaina with you. I stay here and you come back to me."

"Don't you remember?" Will asked patiently. "We shall sail away from Lahaina on a big haole ship."

"Maybe you not find ship?" she asked hopefully. "I wait."

He stared at her for a moment, knowing she would go on waiting forever. "No, Kamika. Do not wait. I do not want you to wait. You are no longer my woman. We are not coming back. Go back to your people on Oahu. The canoe is still here."

Tears ran down Kamika's cheeks. "You not want Kamika no more?"

He said heavily, "No. I do not want you anymore." He turned away, feeling sad and angry, although at whom he was unsure.

Quickly he took Hope's hand to lead her away, but the child pulled free and clung to Kamika's legs. "You made Kamika cry! Oh, Father!"

Kamika was too overcome to speak and merely disentangled Hope's arms and ran from them, her long black hair flying behind her, her feet noiselessly skimming the sand.

The bustling town of Lahaina was filled with sailors who had come ashore from what appeared to be hundreds of whaling vessels lying at anchor. Although the sun was not yet over the yardarm, many of the seamen were already drunk and roistering. Will stuck out his fist to knock a couple of them out of his path and kept Hope's hand firmly in his.

He scanned the passing faces for anyone he might recognize, but they were all unfamiliar to him. He made straight for the Pioneer Inn, where they had stayed when they first came to the islands. This evening, after Hope was asleep in bed, he would pay one of the women to keep an eye on her while he prowled the saloons in search of a skipper or a mate who spoke of sailing shortly.

Halfway across the street he was hailed by a familiar voice. "Dr. Prentice! My wife told me you were leaving the islands. Are you boarding a ship here in Lahaina?"

Turning, he found himself face to face with the Reverend Matthew Ellis. "Yes, as soon as we find one. What are you doing here?"

"We are having a meeting in the mission house to talk about the problem of sickness among the islanders. We hope to convince the authorities that something must be done to stop the spread of *mai pake.*"

"What did you have in mind?" Will inquired. "Having the lepers carry a Saint Lazarus rattle and cry 'unclean'?"

Ellis blanched visibly. Will wasn't sure why he found the missionary so irritating, but the sight of that clerical collar always had the same effect on him. Besides, he was not about to commiserate with a man who had locked healthy Christian Chinese out of his chapel and who seemed to believe that those afflicted should be punished in some way.

"If you will excuse us, I must get my daughter out of the sun," Will said. "Good day, sir."

That evening as Will sipped fruit juice in a waterfront tavern several sailors began a drunken brawl. Knives quickly appeared, and one seaman was badly slashed. After having the man placed on a table, Will stitched up his wounds.

The following morning he was summoned to a newly returned whaler to set the bones of a man whose boat had been capsized by a breaching whale.

Word of his surgical skill spread rapidly among the sailors, and a constant stream of patients found their way to the Pioneer Inn. He didn't discourage them, since he clung to the hope that one of them might have encountered the convicts' ship. He was also able to question the ships' officers as to possible ports of call where he might continue his search.

Several times he made arrangements to sail aboard a departing vessel, but at the last minute there were sailors mangled by sharks, accidentally harpooned, or crushed by their prey, the great whales. There were raging fevers and a variety of sores and boils.

Weeks drifted by and he knew he would have to set a deadline and keep it. He made arrangements to sail aboard an American vessel bound for Oregon.

Two days before the ship was due to leave he had a visitor. He was setting a broken arm when the Reverend Ellis arrived. He wore a worried frown.

Trying to hide his annoyance, Will said, "Why don't you wait for me in the saloon bar? I'll be down in a moment."

He took his time making the cast, hoping the missionary would grow tired of waiting and leave, but when he went to the bar, Ellis was still there.

"What can I do for you, Mr. Ellis?" Will asked, taking a chair at his table.

Ellis squinted at him nervously. "You don't approve of missionaries, do you, Doctor?"

"I don't approve of your attempting to force the islanders to abide by our rules for living."

"You might like to hear about some of the native practices we managed to eliminate?"

"I already know you've taught them it's a sin to expose their bodies, or to enjoy them."

"I was referring, my dear doctor, to the fact that before we came to the islands only perfect babies were allowed to live. Even a tiny birthmark was a sentence of death for an infant. And if any unfortunate subject of the king allowed his shadow to fall across the path of his monarch, he was put to death instantly. We won't even get into the matter of human sacrifices to the heathen gods."

Will was silent for a moment. "You came to tell me this?"

"No. I came to ask your help. You know about the Act to Prevent the Spread of Leprosy?"

"Yes, of course. I expect you clerics used your influence on the legislature to get it passed? The first lepers have already been sent to the island of Molokai, I hear. To the promontory of land called Kalaupapa. An ideal choice, since it is walled off from the rest of the island by mountains too sheer for the sick to scale. We saw the peninsula when we were blown off course on our way here. A fearfully lonely place."

The Reverend Ellis twisted an unlit cigar between his fingers. Will had not seen him smoke previously and wondered if, like many others, he believed smoking would protect him from various diseases. At length the missionary said, "The health board is empowered to enforce the segregation of the sick, which of course is the proper thing to do."

"I heard they rounded up about a hundred and forty lepers in the advanced stages of the disease and took them to Kalaupapa."

Ellis avoided his gaze. "Yes . . . the missionaries did accompany them in the boats, in order to give comfort. I went along myself once."

"Is it true the sick were simply tossed into the surf, which is always stormy there, and had to struggle ashore? I heard there were a few huts left by the former inhabitants, who were evacuated, but the lepers are expected to take care of their own needs? I trust these accounts of the situation are exaggerated."

"Well, rumors are flying, Dr. Prentice. But it's true the lepers were not accompanied by any doctors or able-bodied people to care for them."

"And who do you expect to volunteer to go with them? Any care-givers would be condemning themselves to death along with their patients."

The missionary sighed. "Some of the islanders have hidden their sick in order to escape the health board. I fear we will never contain the epidemic unless we can convince them that they must go into exile on Molokai."

"What did you expect? They know if they are sent away they will never see their loved ones again."

There was a moment of silence. The missionary cleared his throat. "Some of your islander friends—the people you and your daughter lived among—have come down with the disease."

Will felt a wave of sadness. "I'm sorry to hear that."

"I thought . . . if you would return, Dr. Prentice, just briefly, of course, and talk to them, explain to them that they must send their sick away, they might listen to you. You're a doctor . . ."

Will's first impulse, which was to refuse, was stifled by acute concern for Kamika. He should have shown her how to recognize the early signs of the disease and warned her to avoid using the bowls and cups of the sick. He drummed his fingers on the wooden tabletop, considering. "The problem must be severe, for you to have journeyed here to ask this of me."

The minister's pink cheeks turned cherry red. "Some of the sick came to the chapel for sanctuary. Naturally we had to turn them away."

"I intended to sail for Oregon in a couple of days," Will said. "However, I will postpone my voyage and return to Oahu with you. I will have to find someone to take care of my daughter. I don't want to take her back and expose her, because children are particularly vulnerable."

Ellis's breath left his body in a long sigh of relief. "We would be most grateful."

Will spent the following day tracking down the facts about conditions in the leper colony, so that he could at least tell his friends the truth. It was even worse than anyone had imagined.

A superintendent was authorized to climb down the steep cliff once a month, but this was all the supervision the lepers had. Once they arrived in that forbidding place the isolation and the disease seemed to affect their minds as well as their bodies, and they were running wild. They were reverting to the ancient ways because Western medicine men had failed them. They were calling on the old gods, and it was only a matter of time before the sacrifices began again. The corpses of those who had succumbed to the disease were simply thrown into the lake.

Worst of all, some of the most depraved of the men had

formed a settlement they called the Village of Fools, to which they took young girls and even children, who were there without the protection of their parents, for the most vile depravities of all.

Little wonder the islanders feared being sent to the colony. Will heard that one man had killed a sheriff who tried to take him in.

Will made arrangements to return to Oahu, then went to see the skipper of a merchantman, whose acquaintance he had made while treating several crewmen.

The two men walked on the deck while Hope sat on a coiled rope, patiently threading blossoms into a lei. Overhead the sky was a brilliant blue. The ocean murmured against the hull, and a soft breeze carried the fragrance of flowers and spices.

"I understand you will not be sailing for several weeks, Captain Telford," Will said. "Your ship needs some repairs?"

"That's true. I'm not overjoyed with the situation, Doctor, I can tell you. Oh, it's a paradise here, right enough, but when we heard about the leprosy . . . Well, I'm already several crewmen short; I can't afford to lose any more. I wonder if I could prevail upon you to look them over while you're here?"

"The disease doesn't come on that suddenly, Captain. You've been here for only a few days. There would be no visible symptoms yet. But do urge your crew to be careful of their onshore activities."

Telford looked at Hope. The sunlight formed a golden halo around her head as she bent over her task. "Your daughter is as pretty as a picture. I have a little girl of my own, at home in Boston."

"My daughter is the reason I came to see you. You see, I too worry about exposure to the disease. But I must go back to Oahu, to be a part of the island where the sickness is rampant. I cannot take her with me; it is far too risky. Yet I am reluctant to leave her ashore here also. I wonder if I might leave her with you. Just until I return. I know of an island woman who is healthy and she is willing to come and take care of the child. You'll find that Hope is very well behaved, and she spent months aboard a ship on our voyages, so she would not feel confined. Naturally, I would pay for this privilege."

The captain agreed, and the arrangements were made. Will called Hope to him and told her she was to stay on the ship until he returned.

"Where are you going?"

"To see Kamika and her people."

Hope was outraged. "I want to go, too!"

"No, you can't come. There is a bad illness among Kamika's people, and I don't want you to catch it. I shan't stay any longer than I have to, but I might be gone for a couple of weeks."

Her face crumpled, and he picked her up and held her. With a shock he realized they had not been parted since the moment he climbed into her room in Liverpool, wrapped her in a blanket, and carried her away with him.

Sobbing against his chest, the child clung to him. "Don't want you to go!"

"You must be a good girl for Captain Telford. I'll be back as soon as I can; then we're going to find your mother. I promise you. Your real mother, Hope. Remember all the stories I told you about her? Well, soon you'll see they're all true. She's a beautiful lady, and she will love you and care for you. Don't you want to be with her?"

Sniffing, Hope nodded her head, although she was less interested in a mother she had never seen than in being deprived, even temporarily, of the love and care of the man she called Father.

He gave her his handkerchief to wipe her eyes and added gently, "Sometimes we have to give up one thing in order to have something better. It's time for you to give up these islands and the people you've known here, so that you can be with your mother. As soon as I've been to see Kamika and her people, we'll be on our way."

Captain Telford held her as Will climbed into the longboat to return to shore. She had stopped crying but looked so woebegone that he had to force himself to wave to her once and then not look back again.

The islanders were burly of build, and some were almost seven feet tall. Will had always been impressed by their physique and never more so than on the day he sat on the beach watching them ride the big winter surf. Ordinary men, he decided, could scarcely have lifted the immense wooden boards they rode, let alone have pushed them out through the translucent tunnels of the breakers, then balanced on them for the wild ride to shore.

The surf riders were in position now, sitting astride their boards waiting for the exact moment the curling wave would pick up the boards and carry them toward the beach. There! They were up, the wave curling over their heads like the neck of a green glass bottle, making a sound like a steam engine, and traveling just as fast.

As the bronzed warriors aboard their board-chariots hurtled toward him, Will was saddened to see that their numbers were so depleted. Some of them had been forcibly dragged away and sent to Kalaupapa; others were in hiding.

Upon his arrival the previous day, he'd spoken at length to the headman, attempting to explain the importance of segregating the sick, but it was evident that *mai pake* had already made devastating inroads among the people who had been so healthy and carefree when he first encountered them.

Afterward he would recall sitting on the beach watching the surfers as he waited for Kamika to return from her morning swim in the lagoon. She'd been asleep when he arrived late the previous evening and had already gone swimming when he arose this morning, so he had not yet seen her.

Waiting for her, he savored the perfection of the day, the spice-laden trade winds, the impossible blue of the sky, the rhythmic breaking of the white-foamed waves beyond the reef, the magnificence of the islanders.

He saw Kamika coming from the lagoon, and at a distance she was as she had always been, young, strong, beautiful. Her black hair flew behind her as she recognized him and broke into a run.

An ungainly run, not at all her usual graceful stride. He stood up slowly, a drum beginning a dirge somewhere at the back of his brain. She was limping.

Squinting in the sunlight, he strained to see her face. Surely she could not have acquired the leonine look so soon? Ah, no, she was as lovely as ever. She flung herself into his arms, laughing and crying and saying his name over and over again.

He calmed her after a time and held her away from him. He had to force himself to look down at her feet.

One foot was black with burns. He dropped down on one knee to examine her foot more closely. The skin had blistered and broken open.

"I clumsy." Kamika laughed. "Didn't see boards over the *imo* and stumbled into the hot coals. Maybe we have roast Kamika with our pork at the luau, yes?"

"You did this . . . just this morning?"

"Yes. But it not hurt. I go for swim and make better."

Straightening up, Will took her into his arms again. For a long time he couldn't speak. He thought of the child waiting for him to return to her, and he thought of Bethany so long separated from her daughter, and even of the young woman in England from whom he had taken Hope. Oh, God, how ironic the child's name was!

"Kamika, the men from the health board will be coming today to look for people who have the *mai pake.*"

She shuddered. "Yes. But they not find. The sick ones have gone to hide. Oh, Will, I so happy you come back. But where is Hope?"

He drew her down onto the sand. "Listen to me, Kamika. We must take you away before the health-board man comes."

Her eyes widened with fright. "No! I not sick. I not have lion's face. I not have uglies on my body!"

She was referring to the mutilation of the disease, something he could not bear to imagine on the body of the lovely young girl, but which was inevitable.

Kissing her forehead, he murmured, "No, my dear, you are as pretty as ever. But you see, you have terrible burns on your foot, and yet you feel no pain. And even as we speak, I am pinching the flesh of your calf as hard as I can, and you do not feel it. And these are signs of the disease. I'm sorry, Kamika . . . but you have the *mai pake.* Would to God that it weren't so, or that I could cure it for you, but you know I cannot."

She pulled away from him, screaming, a piercing cry of despair that sliced directly into his heart.

In that moment it was as if a blinding light clarified his future path for him. He did not belong with Bethany and her child; he never had. Bethany did not love him and never would. And had he merely been trying to replace his own lost daughter with Hope? He had wronged them grievously. He had to let them go now, to live their lives unburdened by his obsessive presence. There was even a way for him to redeem himself.

He caught Kamika's hands in his and held them tightly. She had loved him with all the devotion of her simple being. Now he would love her equally. "I won't let them take you to Kalaupapa. You will never have to go to that terrible place, Kamika, I swear it. I will take you away and care for you myself."

"No, you cannot! Then you, too, would catch *mai pake.*"

"Not everyone catches the disease. I am a doctor; I know how to keep from getting it," Will lied. "Any day now we'll have a cure. We will take care of each other until then. We'll go far away, up into the mountains where no one will find us. But we must leave right away, before the health-board men come."

"But . . . your little girl?"

"Hope is not my child. I was merely entrusted with her care for a little while. I'll send a message to Captain Telford, asking him to take her back to Boston with him and from there send her to England. She has family there who will take care of her and perhaps find her mother."

Kamika laid her head on his chest and sighed happily. "I always know Will come back to me."

BETHANY STOOD IN front of a lovely home adorned with white wrought-iron balconies in the Garden District of New Orleans, reflecting on the change in Leona's fortune and her own since they first met on the convict transport. What a long time ago that seemed now, although it was not quite five years.

Forcing her mind to concentrate on the urgent matter at hand, she went through the gate into the garden. The front door was opened by a black maid, and when Bethany gave her name, the maid's face became wreathed in smiles. "Why, Miss Leona she tol' me she was hoping you'd call, and now here you come!"

She led the way to a drawing room so opulently and gaudily appointed that it surely represented Leona's taste rather than that of her husband.

While she awaited her friend, Bethany prowled about examining china figurines and alabaster statuary, handsome mirrors and Italian marble urns. The brocade-covered walls were of scarlet and gold, and white satin sofas lined the walls. Although Bethany had never seen the interior of a bordello, she had an uneasy feeling that the decor in Leona's house would not have been out of place in such an establishment.

Leona came into the room, dazzling in brilliant orange silk, and swept her into a perfumed hug. "Oh, it's so good to have you back, Bethany. I thought your honeymoon would never come to an end. I hope you don't mind that we didn't delay our wedding until you got back?" Leona winked. "I was afraid Louis's parents might put a stop to it if we didn't strike while the iron was hot. When he wanted me to go home with him I was in a panic that they'd talk him out of it, so we had the captain of the boat marry us."

She chattered on, apparently not noticing that Bethany was desperately anxious to speak. When at last she could get a word in, Bethany said, "We have a crisis on our hands, I'm afraid. Jack and Tom are discussing what to do." She glanced about anxiously. "Louis isn't here, is he?"

Leona shook her head. "He's at the club."

Bethany told her quickly of Tom overhearing Saffron betray them. A long shuddering sigh slipped from Leona, and she collapsed onto a satin sofa, patting the seat beside her for Bethany to join her. "Louis's family has had people scouring around everywhere trying to find something they can use to get our marriage annulled. God's teeth, I hate to give it all up."

"I suppose we'll have to leave, start again somewhere else. Jack sent me to fetch you so we can discuss what to do as whatever decision we make will affect you too. Bourke is waiting in the carriage for us."

Leona's eyes widened. "I'd have thought Jack would have left me to my fate. He didn't approve of my cradle-snatching."

Bethany decided not to mention that Louis had sent word that he still wanted to fight a duel with Jack. He would probably change his mind when he learned the truth about his wife's past. "We should go, Leona."

"What about my things?" Leona's golden eyes swept the room in panic.

"Jack said to just leave everything and go to our house for now. There's no extreme hurry, because Saffron's information will have to be taken up the river to the LaFleur plantation."

Leona put on her bonnet and told her maid she and Bethany were going shopping; then they both went outside and climbed into the carriage. Bourke immediately urged the horses forward at a fast trot. He had been one of the first escaping convicts to join Jack in the Australian bush, and his loyalty and reliability were beyond question. A great hulking brute of a man, he had made an excellent doorman at the Rake's Retreat, as his fearsome appearance belied his gentle disposition.

As they traveled along the quiet early morning streets of New Orleans Leona said, " 'Struth, why did it all have to get mucked up again? Just when we were nicely settled."

"I'm not nicely settled, Leona. I'd been thinking about going home, even before this happened. You see, Tate Ivers wrote to Tom, telling him that there's no clue as to what became of my daughter. She just disappeared. Tate told Tom that I shouldn't hold out any hope of ever seeing my child again, that after all this time, the police cannot help. They told him I wouldn't recognize her, because she was taken from me the day she was born, and now she's nearly five years old."

"I'm so sorry, Bethany. But don't give up yet. You never know what might happen." She paused. "Maybe you'll have a child with Jack. You are happy with him, aren't you? You two seem so right for each other. Everyone says what a handsome couple you make. Not like me and Louis."

When Bethany tried to demur, Leona said, "Oh, I know people laugh at us behind our backs. Him being so short and me so tall, and him so young and a gentleman . . . But you know, looks are deceiving. It's a funny thing, but I love the little hothead. I truly do. I'd do anything for him. And he feels the same about me. I never thought I'd ever feel like this for a man."

"Do you think we could trust Louis? Would he help us, perhaps even go away with you, if we told him the truth?"

"No," Leona said at once. "I don't want him to know about my past life." The worried lines of her face softened slightly. "He worships me, Beth. I feel like I was born the day I married Louis—as if everything that went before was wiped out . . ." She brushed her hand across her eyes. "But it wasn't, was it? We never really escape from our past."

Bethany squeezed her friend's hand. "If he loves you, he'll understand. He'll go away with you."

"No!" Leona said savagely. "I'd rather give him up than see the disgust in his eyes when he finds out what I really am. If he doesn't know, at least we'll part with happy memories."

Bourke stopped the carriage and came to help them down. Bethany glanced briefly at the profusion of flowers and blossoms in the front garden as they hurried inside. Why hadn't she taken the time to appreciate them before? What a human failing it was to take for granted that there would always be time for such things in the future. She would have to leave this house without ever really coming to know it.

Entering the house, they were surprised to hear piano music coming from the drawing room. Tom was seated at the keyboard, playing "Scarborough Fair." Jack lounged in a chair nearby, but as the two women entered the room he rose to his feet to kiss Bethany's cheek and nod to Leona.

Tom smiled and waved to them. "My mother insisted we all take piano lessons, but my brother Stewart was such a blasted genius that Neil and I never played if we could help it."

Bethany looked from Tom to Jack in amazement. "Have you both taken leave of your senses? How can you calmly sit playing the piano when at any moment we could all be arrested?"

"Sit down, ladies," Jack said. "We believe we've found a way out of our dilemma."

"Dilemma, is it?" Leona inquired. "All right for you to talk. I'm the one with the most to lose. You can all leave with no regrets."

"It may not be necessary for any of us to leave." The two women perched nervously on the edge of chairs, and he continued, "We confronted Saffron and found out that the man she was speaking to yesterday was a lawyer hired by the LaFleurs to find grounds for an annulment."

"Well, I could have told you that," Leona snapped.

"You've never met any of his family, have you?"

She looked sheepish. "No. Louis wanted to take me to the plantation, but I was afraid to go. Once I had the ring on my finger I persuaded him to come back to New Orleans."

Jack's icy blue glance flickered over her speculatively. "You claim to be an actress. It's time to test your skills. Persuade Louis to try to reconcile with his family, and ask him to take you to meet them."

"Not bloody likely! They'd tear me apart."

Ignoring her, he went on, "You'll have to tone down your appearance, dress less flamboyantly. Bethany will help you select some conservative clothes to wear. No jewels in the daytime, and for God's sake don't paint your face. No perfume beyond a few drops of toilet water on your handkerchief. Lower your voice when you speak; ladies don't shout. No matter what the LaFleurs say to you, restrain yourself, don't answer back, just listen. Be a little tearful; be humble if you have to. Convince them that you love your husband."

"I do love my husband," Leona declared indignantly. She had listened in open-mouthed disbelief to his instructions.

Bethany said, "Jack, isn't it a little late for all this? If Saffron told the LaFleurs' lawyer that we're escaped convicts, we're going to have to leave at once."

Jack turned toward her. "Saffron was mistaken. She confused a hypothetical discussion for actual fact. The snatches of conversation about the penal colony she overheard concerned recollections and research to be used in the story you, Bethany, were writing."

Tom added, "After all, I had sailed aboard a ship to Australia, and Tate Ivers was once a partner in a company that leased convict transport vessels. We'd told you terrible tales about the mistreatment of the women there, and that inspired you to write your *fictionalized* pieces."

"Isn't a certain newspaper editor at this very moment reading your manuscript?" Jack asked. "He'll confirm what we say. The LaFleurs and their lawyer would be laughingstocks if they were to pay any heed to the garbled accounts of a servant who'd listened to snatches of conversation about a novel in progress."

Leona clapped her hands in glee. "Oh, that's bloody marvelous."

Tom said, "We've got to get our stories straight about where we came from. Jack and I decided we should stick as close to the truth as possible. We'll say I was a shipowner who traded on the West Coast. Bethany was my brother's widow, traveling aboard the ship with him. Jack and Leona were travelers who fell in love with Alta California and lived for a time in Yerba Buena. Before that, of course, we all lived in England, where Leona was an actress and"—Tom paused to grin—"Jack was studying the law."

Bethany felt her tension ease. It all made sense.

"Leona, you have to get the LaFleurs to drop the investigation," Jack said. "If you love Louis, as you claim, then you'll see that his family accepts you. All of our futures depend on your acting skills. You can't disguise the fact that you're a lot older than Louis, but you can certainly appear considerably less world-weary."

She bristled. "World-weary?"

"You want a more blunt description?"

Bethany said hastily, "What will you do about the lawyer Saffron spoke to?"

"I'm going to see him right now," Jack replied. He glanced toward the doorway, where Bourke had hovered during the conversation. "You can go back to the club, Bourke. You still have a job there. You understand what we're going to do?"

Bourke nodded.

"Just do your job, keep your mouth shut, and don't answer any questions," Jack added.

"Aye, sir," Bourke responded. He had to lower his head to back out through the doorway.

Tom grinned. "If you'd told him to walk on his hands through Jackson Square shouting that you're a saint, he'd have done it. That man is devoted to you."

"And why not?" Bethany asked. "He owes his life to Jack."

Jack visited the offices of the LaFleurs' lawyer the next morning and easily convinced him of Saffron's misunderstanding about Bethany's novel. But before anyone could breathe a sigh of relief, Louis sent Jack an ultimatum. Either their duel would take place at dawn the following day, or Louis would seek him out and shoot him down like a dog on the street.

The message arrived just as Bethany and Jack were finishing dinner and she read it over his shoulder before Jack could stop her. "Leona doesn't know about this," Bethany said at once. "I'll go to her and she'll find a way to get Louis to withdraw the challenge."

Jack's face was set in tight, angry lines, and his eyes flashed blue fire. "I walked away from his challenge once. I can't do it again. He won't let me. He's a damned Frog, full of misplaced Frog pride, and he'll die trying to save face."

"And you're an arrogant Englishman," Bethany declared, "who thinks you're superior to everyone else on earth and indestructible, and you're just as likely to die trying to prove it."

"What do you suggest I do? Turn tail and run? Or wait for him to come after me when I'm least expecting it? We have to settle this, Bethany, one way or another."

"Louis just doesn't know what's been going on behind the scenes. Why, it's thanks to you that Leona is preparing to go and meet his family. Couldn't you apologize for what you said about her before they were married?"

"I've already tried that. He refused to accept the apology. He insists his honor is at stake, that everyone knows he challenged me to a duel and he can't back down."

"But don't you see? If you fight the duel, you'll both lose. No matter who lives or dies—"

He gripped her shoulders and shook her gently. "We've been over this ground, over and over again."

Their argument continued for most of the night.

Just before dawn he said heavily, "I've got to go. I'm already late. Go back to bed and I'll come and tell you when it's all over."

"If you walk out of that door," Bethany said quietly, "you will not find me here when you return."

His hands fell to his sides and his expression hardened still further. "What are you saying?"

"I am telling you that I cannot condone this madness. If you fight a duel with Louis, I will leave you. I will no longer be your wife."

She held her breath, knowing that an ultimatum might not have the result she desired, but she was desperate and she had exhausted every other argument.

Jack's jaw moved, his eyes narrowed, and she felt her heart sink into her shoes. He shrugged. "So be it. I enjoyed our brief union, Bethany. It was, as they say, better than nothing."

As he turned to leave she raised her hand to stop him, but he moved too quickly. The door slammed shut behind him, and she was left staring at it.

After a moment she turned away, ran to her room, and dressed quickly. Less than half an hour later she knocked on the door of the house owned by Tate Ivers, where Tom was staying.

Saffron opened the door, and for a moment the two women regarded each another in cautious silence. Then Saffron said, "He's still asleep."

"Wake him up," Bethany answered. "I must speak with him at once. It's extremely urgent."

The housekeeper walked up the stairs so slowly that Bethany was tempted to go behind her and give her a push.

Tom came down right away, his dark hair standing up in unruly spikes, his night's growth of beard making him seem even swarthier. "Bethany, what is it? Is something wrong?"

"You didn't know that Louis insisted upon dueling with Jack this morning?"

"Oh, God, those two reckless fools. They'll spoil everything. I'll go and try to stop them. Where are they meeting?"

She told him of the secluded bayou where the duel was to take place, out of sight of the law, since dueling was prohibited, and he ran back upstairs to dress.

After he left, an uneasy silence descended upon the house. There was no sign of Saffron, who had evidently gone back to bed to avoid facing her.

Bethany prowled restlessly for a time, then reached a decision. She scribbled a note for Tom, propped it on the mantelpiece, and went home.

She had just finished packing when Tom arrived. He was alone, his expression too grim for good news.

"Sit down, Bethany," he said.

Her mouth was dry, her heart thudded. She sat on the edge of the bed and whispered, "One of them is dead."

Tom crossed the room and sat beside her. He put his arm around her shoulder. "They were already in position when I got there. Leona was there, too, begging them not to do it. And give Jack his due, he did say to Louis, 'If yet another apology will end this stupidity, then you have it. Do you want me on my knees begging forgiveness?' but Louis said it was too late for that. Jack had insulted the woman he loved and he was going to die for it. Then Jack told him he was the one who would die. Hadn't Jack saved his miserable hide many times over? Hadn't he defended him from several angry poker partners? Wasn't Louis forgetting how they'd met?"

Bethany waited, trembling, as Tom caught his breath.

"The seconds positioned them back to back and even started counting the paces—one, two, three, four. One of Louis's seconds was holding Leona, keeping her back, and she was struggling to get free. Then suddenly she screamed at Louis that what Jack had told him was true. That she wasn't fit to be his wife, that she'd lived a disorderly life and even killed a man."

"Oh, no!"

"Louis went crazy. He was shouting something in French, I don't know what. He spun around and pointed his pistol at Jack, and I yelled a warning. Jack turned, too. Oh, God, I felt as if my feet were mired in a bog; I couldn't seem to move fast enough. Leona broke free and ran between them. Then Louis fired."

"Jack didn't fire?" As the full implication of this hit her, a cry of pain rose to her lips. "Was he shot? Is he badly hurt?"

Tom swallowed. "No, Jack's all right. Bethany . . . it's Leona. Louis's shot went right through her heart."

Bethany sat very still. Her mind was surprisingly clear. After moment Tom, apparently unable to bear her silence or her omposure, asked, "Are you all right? Did you hear me? Leona dead."

"Tom . . . I would like to leave for England immediately. Do ou know of any ships that might be leaving today?"

He looked blank. "England?"

"Yes. I've decided to go home. My daughter is somewhere England and I'm going to find her. I should have gone long go."

"But . . . what about Jack?"

"I'm sure Black Jack Cutler will be able to take care of himelf. He always has."

"Won't you at least wait and talk to him first?"

"No. We've already said good-bye, this morning before he ft. I never want to see him again. I want to leave as soon as can."

"You really mean it? You want to go back to England?"

"Yes. Right away."

He stood up and walked around the room for a moment. "We ould sail today for one of the eastern ports—New York or Philelphia—and get a transatlantic packet from there."

She looked up in surprise. "We?"

"If you're determined to go, I'll go with you."

"You don't have to do that, Tom."

"Actually, I've been thinking of going back myself, ever since ate wrote that my father is in such poor condition. To tell you e truth, I get very homesick for England sometimes."

"Tom, we will risk having to pay for our crimes."

He gave a crooked grin. "You're the most unlikely pirate I've er seen, Bethany. We'll have to be careful, but we'll have Tate ere to help us."

"Could we go right away? I'm all packed."

"You don't even want to talk to your husband?"

She shook her head. "We've already said all there is to say each other."

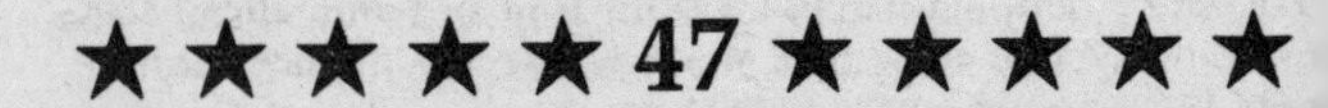

47

STEWART SAW THE flames as he and O'Connor approachec the docks and knew before they reached the ship that it was th *Peregrine* that was on fire.

He fought his way through the men on the docks who wer handing up buckets of water to try to douse the flames, which had started belowdecks and now roared out of a hatchway. Som of the rigging was ablaze, and the strong wind whipped the fir up the masts. It was clear there was little hope of saving the ship

Stewart prayed that Alison was not aboard, but knowing he determination . . . if she thought his father was on the *Peregrine* no one would have been able to talk her out of searching fo him.

At the top of the gangway a frightened crewman recognize him and stepped forward. "I'm sorry, sir. We didn't want to le her go below, but—"

Stewart felt an icy calm grip him. "Where is she? Who els is down there?"

"Your father—and the first mate is with her. They went dow into the old female convict quarters. None of them came bac up before we saw the smoke."

"Get me a blanket and soak it with water," Stewart ordered

"Mr. Fielding, sir, you can't go down there! Flames are pour ing out of the hatch closest to the female quarters. You'd hav to go down aft and work your way forward, and it's thick wit smoke, you'd never find them."

"Do as I say, man. Hurry. And fetch me a rope. Wet it down too." Stewart was already plunging his handkerchief into bucket of water. He tied it around his mouth and nose as h started toward the hatch.

The mate put a drenched blanket over his shoulders an handed him a coil of rope, which he tied to the hatch gratin before dropping down into the smoke-filled bowels of the ship

Playing out the rope as he went, he moved forward. As th smoke grew thicker he was forced to drop down on his knee ı the deck and crawl. The acrid bite of the smoke assaulted s lungs, and each breath he took seemed to sear his throat. is eyes stung unbearably, and he could see very little until at st a fearful red glow penetrated the billowing black cloud.

His heart sank. There was a solid wall of flame ahead that : would never be able to get through. He was too late. Still he ept forward, unable to turn back, wondering dimly if he might consumed by the flames himself.

He lay as close to the deck as he could, slithering, squirming, sping for breath, until his outstretched hand connected with mething that lay in his path.

Something very still. A prostrate body.

Groping with his hands he quickly determined it was a man ıd he wasn't breathing.

Grasping him about the shoulders in order to pull him back vay from the flames that roared even closer, Stewart realized ere was a second body under the first: The man had collapsed ı top of a woman.

Alison! Stewart hastily pushed the body of the mate away om her. He must have carried her this far before collapsing om inhaling the smoke.

Stewart wrapped the wet blanket around her and pulled it up er her face. He began to drag her back along the narrow companionway.

The smoke was now so thick he could see nothing. He folwed the rope he had laid down, but his progress was painfully ow. Beneath them the deck was hot, and he didn't dare conler that it might at any second burst into flame.

Oh, God, we're going to suffocate, he thought, feeling panic ralyze him. He lay still for a moment, fighting for breath, batng a fear so intense that he was sure it would destroy reason. aves of dizziness and nausea engulfed him, and each breath took seared his lungs.

Don't give up now, he told himself silently. If you lie here e flames will get you and Alison. Better the smoke than the e. You've come this far.

He began to inch forward again, dragging his wife with him. Then all at once he could see the stars overhead and shadowy ures reaching down for them. Alison was lifted up through e hatchway, and Stewart managed to hold on to his senses til he too lay on deck, feeling cool sweet night air seep into s tortured lungs.

* * *

Stewart stood beside the open grave as his father's remain
were lowered into the ground. No one was certain the charre
body was that of his father. It could just as easily have been th
first mate of the *Peregrine.* Stewart felt more regret than sorrow
*If only . . . if only I could have been the son you wanted m
to be. If only you could have loved me . . .*

Mary took the first handful of earth and dropped it on th
coffin. It rattled down with a finality that shocked Stewart ou
of an almost trancelike moment of introspection. He becam
aware of the cemetery, of gray headstones and winter-bare tree
etched starkly against a colorless sky, of the sad scent of ho
house lilies emanating from the wreaths and floral tributes.

The vicar's droning voice floated, words undigested, over hi
head. Stewart still felt weak from the ordeal of inhaling so muc
smoke, and his hands had been rubbed raw from dragging th
rope through the ship, but he was in the grip of a malady mor
debilitating than his physical discomforts. He drew a dee
breath, which caused him to cough, and surveyed the sma
group of mourners.

Tate Ivers stood close to Mary, his great bearlike fram
hunching over her protectively, and she seemed to draw strengt
from him. O'Connor was there and a few of Sir Adrian's busi
ness colleagues who remembered him from the old days. Su
prisingly, Mrs. Creel had come to the funeral. She stared dow
into the grave and shook her head, then looked around at th
others present as though expecting an explanation for this tur
of events.

The graveside service was brief. A memorial service had a
ready been held in the church. The mourners returned to th
carriages to go to Riverleigh.

Stewart whispered to Mary, "You won't mind if I don't g
with you? I loathe the almost partylike ritual of gathering at th
home of the deceased afterward for refreshments."

"Of course, you will want to go home to Alison," Mary sai
at once. "I'll explain your absence. Besides, there are very fe
mourners."

Tate shook hands with him. "You're a hero, Stewart. You
father would have been proud of you."

"I wasn't able to save him," Stewart said, wondering if every
one else noticed the hollow, empty ring to his voice.

"You saved Alison, and from what she told us, there was litt chance your father was still alive. Didn't she say the flames had fully engulfed the racks before the mate dragged her away?"

Mary laid her hand gently on Stewart's arm. "We are so proud of you, Stewart. You mustn't think about your father's passing. Tell yourself that, in a way, he had already left us long before the flames consumed the *Peregrine.*"

He watched as Tate helped his stepmother into the closed carriage and climbed in beside her. Just before the carriage moved away he saw Ivers take Mary's hand in his.

Stewart pulled up his collar against the frosty bite of the air and prepared to return to Liverpool. He needed to get back to the office and plunge into the world of commerce again. It was the only antidote he could devise to his continuing pain over losing Alison.

He had lost her; he accepted that. He had saved her from the flames, and she had expressed her gratitude for that, but she had not fallen into his arms and begged for a reconciliation. In fact, when he visited her in the hospital where they treated her burns—which, thank God, had not disfigured her face, but had singed her lovely hair and burned her hands and forearms—she had been more distant than ever. Her memory of those desperate moments aboard the doomed ship were vague. She recalled coming to her senses briefly as the first mate carried her through the fire, before losing consciousness again in the smoke.

She had refused to stay in the hospital for more than a day, insisting upon going home to Davey. Stewart hired a housekeeper and a nanny to take care of them, despite Alison's protests that she didn't need help.

"You don't need to worry about us anymore, Stewart," she said. "You've done enough—more than enough. You risked your own life to save mine and I'll be grateful to you always. But stop worrying about us now, please. You're making me feel helpless."

He gave a short, mirthless laugh. "Helpless? You, Alison? You're the last person on earth I'd describe as helpless. But, just to please me, keep the women I've hired until you're well again."

As Stewart walked around the deck of the ferry carrying him back to Liverpool, he was deeply troubled by his lack of true grief over his father's terrible death. In truth, he dwelt less upon that particular grief than upon the even more devastating loss of Alison. In some remote part of his mind he still wondered if there was anything he could have done to bring Alison back into his life.

Upon his arrival at the Fielding Shipping Company, Hagen Rudd followed him into his private office. "I didn't think you'd be coming in today, but since you're here, could I have a word with you?"

"Yes, of course. Please, have a seat." Stewart, like Alison, had found Rudd indispensable. In some ways he reminded Stewart of Tate Ivers, with the same quiet authority and aura of strength and dependability. Neither was a gentleman in the conventional sense of the word. Each man's knowledge and manners and attitudes came from common sense and life's experiences rather than from family background and education.

Hagen Rudd, like everyone else, had treated Stewart with a new respect since the fire aboard the *Peregrine.* He regarded Stewart silently for a moment, obviously hesitant to speak on some subject and then, at length, said, "I went to see Mrs. Fielding, your wife, this morning. I knew she wouldn't be well enough to go to the funeral and I thought perhaps . . . well, I went to see her."

"That was thoughtful of you, Mr. Rudd."

"I offered her my services, Mr. Fielding. I asked her if I could go to work for her."

Taken aback, Stewart murmured, "But I thought she had been unable to get a business started? In what capacity would you work for her?"

"We'd work together in the same way we worked together for you, Mr. Fielding. When she's well again, of course. She wants to be a shipping agent, and she'd be a good one. But she's a woman and no one will give her a chance." He paused, then added, "They'd deal with me, though."

Stewart turned away so that Rudd would not see his expression. With Hagen Rudd on her team there was no doubt Alison would be highly successful as a shipping agent. But Stewart didn't want her to be successful. If she was, he would never get her back.

"You'll be difficult to replace, Mr. Rudd, but of course I shan't stand in your way if you wish to leave."

"Thank you, sir. I wanted you to know in plenty of time."

In time for what? Stewart wondered. To find a replacement—for Rudd or for Alison?

* * *

Stewart and Mary were waiting in the library at Riverleigh for the arrival of Messrs. Langley and Crumbe, the family solicitors, for the reading of Sir Adrian's will, when Tate Ivers arrived.

"I've just received news from New Orleans," he said quickly, "that I want to share with you before the solicitors arrive."

They looked at him expectantly. He turned to Stewart. "Tom's coming home. He and Bethany are on their way."

Mary and Stewart both spoke at once. Tate raised his hand. "Before you get too excited—we have to consider the problems their arrival will precipitate. Remember, they are both still wanted for piracy."

Stewart, who had felt an overpowering sense of relief that Tom would be able to take over the company, felt himself sinking back into despair. "My God, piracy is a hanging offense! Why are they coming?"

"Bethany wants to find her child; she no longer cares about anything else. Apparently she's also had a tiff of some sort with her husband. And from what I gather, Tom wanted to see his father. It's too bad he didn't come before Sir Adrian died."

"Perhaps, for Tom's sake, it's just as well he didn't see Father as he'd become," Stewart commented.

"They're not using their real names, I hope?" Mary asked. "We must all be very careful that no one finds out they are coming."

"I've been giving the matter a great deal of thought," Tate answered. "Neither Tom nor Bethany was actually involved in the taking of the ship. Tom was aboard because he'd been shanghaied and merely chose to remain with the convicts. Bethany was there because her husband was aboard. Also Bethany had already received a pardon for her crime, although she didn't know it at the time. It was arranged by the man who went through a form of marriage with her, a surgeon superintendent named Prentice."

"What are you suggesting?" Stewart asked.

"I've been wondering if we could approach the owners of the vessel and put out some feelers as to whether they would accept restitution. None of the crew was harmed. We'd probably need to hire the best barrister in the country, just in case we need legal counsel on the piracy charges, and I'm sure we'll pay the owner far more than either the ship or the cargo was worth, but . . . well, what do you think?"

"I think we should do whatever we have to do to ensure their freedom," Stewart said.

"Oh, I agree," Mary murmured fervently.

Tate said, "You both realize that the costs involved might take a substantial bite out of your inheritance?"

"I'm sure Adrian left me very little," Mary said. "But whatever I have—"

Tate put his arm around her shoulders. "I'm going to take care of you, my dear, for the rest of your life. And I will also make a contribution to the cause, but I'm sure Adrian left the bulk of his estate to Stewart. After all, he's carried the full load all this time, so the decision has to be mainly his."

"My father told me he'd left the company to Tom and me equally, so half will go to Tom in any case. As for my share, I don't care if it takes every penny I have," Stewart said. "My brother's freedom is more important."

"Good. Good lad," Tate murmured. "Now we're ready to talk to the solicitors."

Stewart reflected, an hour later, that perhaps the conversation had been unnecessary, since apparently his father had made a new will, or had lied to him about its contents.

The last will and testament of Sir Adrian Fielding specified that all of his estate, the shipping company and various investments and holdings, Riverleigh, and all of his personal effects, were to go to his beloved son, Thomas Fielding. To Stewart he left the token sum of one guinea.

48

BETHANY STOOD ONCE again before the great mansion at Riverleigh. The home of the Fieldings appeared no less forbidding than it had that first time she saw it, and the memory of the night she had been caught retrieving Neil's ring was very much in her mind.

At her side Tom said, "Courage, Bethany. We're not behind bars yet. No constables waiting for our ship to dock, although I didn't much like the look of the customs officer, did you?"

Bethany attempted a smile. "You were really awful to him.

I've never seen you act so arrogant—you were almost a caricature of the imperious Englishman."

Tom grinned as they started up the terrace steps. "A man with a price on his head certainly wouldn't have called attention to himself in such a manner, would he?"

"Ah, now I see what you were doing," Bethany commented.

As he looked up at the stout walls of his home, Tom's expression became serious. "Old place hasn't changed much. Still looks like a fortress. It will seem strange without Father, though."

News of Sir Adrian's death, in the form of a letter from Tate, had awaited them when their ship docked. Tate had also explained that no one from the family would be meeting their ship, for obvious reasons.

"Tom, I'm so sorry you couldn't have seen him before he died."

A shadow crossed Tom's eyes. "From what Tate said, he wouldn't have known me, nor I him. God, what an awful end . . ."

She knew he was not speaking of his father's fiery death. She squeezed his arm sympathetically.

The front doors opened before they reached them, and they were immediately surrounded by people who must have been watching for their arrival.

A handsome young man stepped forward. He bore a slight resemblance to Tom but was not as robustly built and his features were more finely chiseled. He and Tom stared at each other for a long moment and then, their faces wreathed in smiles, caught each other in an exuberant embrace.

Bethany felt tears prick her eyes as the two brothers both began to speak simultaneously.

Stewart said, "I hope you understood why we didn't come to meet you? We didn't want anyone to wonder who you were or connect you to certain lawbreakers in the family. Tom, you devil, you always said you were going to be a pirate when you grew up! Let me look at you. Lord, did you grow more muscles? I can't believe you're really here at last."

Bethany felt a gentle hand on her arm and turned to look at Lady Mary Fielding. The years fell away and they were back in the court of the assizes, connected for one poignant moment by an unspoken plea for help for an innocent child. Bethany still remembered the comfort of Mary Fielding's compassionate gaze.

Mary opened her arms, and Bethany went into them. "Oh, my dear, I am so glad to see you safely home again. How I wish . . ." She didn't finish the wish, but Bethany knew she was thinking of her missing daughter.

Tate smiled at Bethany and said quickly, "Welcome home."

Tom shook hands with Tate. "Good to see you again." Turning to Bethany he said, "May I present my brother, Stewart?"

"Come on, everyone, let's not stand out here in the hall. We have refreshments waiting in the drawing room," Mary said. Despite her black mourning gown, she exuded a radiance that transformed her rather plain features. Bethany saw, too, that Tate never moved far from Mary's side, his eyes rarely strayed from her face, and the two of them seemed attached in some way, even though they did not touch.

The invisible thread connecting them made Bethany feel more alone than ever. How had it happened that in the few short weeks she had been Jack's wife she had become a part of a couple, so that now she found it difficult to function as an individual? But of course she knew the source of her present distress. It came from a need as old as womankind, the nesting urge, that all-encompassing urgency to provide for a child she carried.

On the voyage back to England, she had discovered she was carrying Jack's child, and was dismayed to realize how much she resented this. Wasn't it just like Black Jack to have the last laugh?

Bethany felt ill, far more so than when she had carried her daughter. She thought at first the sea voyage contributed to her constant nausea, but her condition had not improved since they landed. She was desperately tired all the time, her body ached with fatigue, and all of these physical symptoms were also, in her mind, entirely Jack's fault. Worst of all, there was no one for her to talk to, to share the burden. No husband, no close woman relative or friend. Oh, Leona, Leona . . .

"Was the voyage very trying, Bethany?" Mary asked solicitously. "Forgive me, my dear, but you are so pale, so thin."

The men were deep in their own conversation, and Bethany whispered to Mary, "I'm not feeling very well. Would it be possible for me to lie down?"

"Of course, come on. I'll take you up to your room. Alison is coming later, but if you aren't up to meeting her . . ."

"Oh, I'm longing to meet her. I shall be grateful to her, and to you, always, for caring for my baby." Feeling tears well again, Bethany added quickly, "I'll be all right if I can loosen my stays and rest for a little while."

Mary took her to a spacious bedroom and said she would send up a maid.

"No, please, I don't need anything." Bethany sat on the edge of the bed, feeling faint, wishing Mary would leave, but she was regarding her with great concern.

"Are you ill? Do you need a doctor?"

"I'm with child," Bethany answered, relieved to be able to tell someone.

Mary's smile of pleasure quickly faded as she noted Bethany's woebegone expression. "You don't sound too happy about it."

"My marriage is over."

"Oh, I'm so sorry. Does your husband know about the child?"

Bethany shook her head.

"You poor child. Life has not been kind to you, has it? First Neil and now . . . but surely if you and your husband loved each other when you married, you could repair the rift? Perhaps the baby would draw you back together?"

"I don't want it," Bethany said, close to tears. "I don't want Jack Cutler's child. I want my daughter back!"

Mary sat on the bed beside her and put her arms around her. "Of course you do. But you'll love this baby, too. You'll see."

When Alison arrived an hour later Bethany was composed, but Mary suggested the two young women should meet in private, and she would send Alison up to her.

Bethany rose to her feet as Alison entered the room and they regarded each other shyly, then hesitantly moved closer.

How much we have in common, Bethany thought. We have loved the same child, we have both endured hardships, we have both left our husbands and thereby invoked the wrath of society.

They clasped hands. "I don't know how to thank you . . ." Bethany began.

Alison said quickly, "I loved her so much. She's the sweetest, prettiest child you could ever imagine. So good, so clever. I can't believe anyone would harm her. I'm sure she's all right. Oh, God, Bethany, if I could put her into your arms, I would."

"I know, I know."

They looked at each other helplessly, each longing for the impossible to happen. But Tate had told both of them that too much time had gone by for the police even to attempt to trace the little girl. They had pointed out that very young children changed rapidly in appearance, and Hope would now bear little resemblance to the toddler who had been kidnapped. There were no clues, no witnesses, no way to start a search after all this time.

At length Bethany said, "Mary had a tea tray sent up. Let's sit down and talk. I understand we have a great deal in common."

Mary marveled at Tate's powers of persuasion, his persistence, his utter determination. He was, she decided, truly a man to admire and respect, as well as to love dearly. Within weeks of Tom and Bethany's arrival in England, Tate had set the wheels in motion for paying restitution to the owners of the vessel taken by the absconders from the penal colony, on condition that charges against Bethany and Tom be dropped.

On the day he brought the news to Riverleigh that this had been accomplished, Bethany surprised Mary by wistfully asking him, "I suppose it wouldn't be possible to have the charges against Jack Cutler dropped also?"

"You know that's out of the question," Tate answered. "Your circumstances, and Tom's, were quite different from Jack's."

"Why, Bethany," Tom said. "I thought you never wanted to see Black Jack again as long as you lived. Didn't you tell me you didn't care what became of him?"

Mary also glanced in Bethany's direction, but with less surprise. After spending time with the younger woman, Mary was convinced that, whether she realized it or not, Bethany loved Jack Cutler and missed him desperately. She had evidently acted in haste and was now repenting at leisure. Her situation was unlike the one that existed between Alison and Stewart, which Mary feared was irreparable. Alison and Hagen Rudd were jointly running the Banks and Rudd Shipping Agency very successfully, and Stewart had confessed to Mary that his attempts to see his wife alone had not been successful. She was always with Davey or with Hagen Rudd, and with Stewart she was polite but distant.

"Don't tell me you actually miss that rogue you married?" Tom continued.

Bethany had turned quite pink. "Please, Tom! Don't embarrass me."

"I had a letter from Jack," Tate put in conversationally, drawing attention away from her.

"How is he?" Tom asked.

"Still at large." Tate smiled and turned to Mary. "You'd have to know Black Jack to realize the significance of that." He addressed his next remarks to Bethany. "I'm being facetious. There were no repercussions, apparently, to the tragic death of Leona. It seems Louis's family was able to hush up the whole rotten business."

"The duel was all Louis's fault, not Jack's," Bethany said with so much spirit that the room seemed to resonate with it.

Tate's eyes met Mary's, and she knew they would have much to discuss in private.

Tate had moved into the house Mary had helped him renovate, which he had leased to tenants during his absence, and at his request Mary visited him there the following afternoon.

"We needed to get away from everyone, and especially away from Riverleigh," he said when she arrived.

"I sensed there was more to Jack Cutler's letter than you chose to reveal yesterday," Mary said as Tate solicitously pulled her chair closer to the fire and slipped a lap robe over her knees. The early spring weather remained very cold.

Tate's bushy brows knitted thoughtfully as he took the chair on the opposite side of the fireplace. There were a few silver streaks in his red hair now, and Mary had a sudden yearning to stroke his brow and run her fingers through his hair, to nestle close to him and lay her head against his chest. But, of course, none of this could happen until her mourning period for her husband was over.

He said, "Reading between the lines of his letters, I'd say Jack is pining for Bethany as much as she is for him. But what can one do with such stubborn and headstrong young people? How can one make them understand that love is more important than pride?"

"If there was a way to bring them together again, perhaps they would realize how much they love each other?"

"Jack can't come to England, and I doubt we'll be able to persuade her to go to New Orleans, so we're at an impasse. Besides, proximity isn't always the answer either, is it? Stewart and Alison move in the same shipping circles and must cross paths frequently, but their marriage is evidently over."

"I suggested to Stewart that perhaps he should court Alison. He never really did, you know."

"He might have to fight Hagen Rudd for her," Tate said wryly. "The man obviously adores her, although I doubt she's aware of it. I've never known a young woman like Alison before. When it comes to business, she has the mind of a man. Which brings me to why I really asked you to come here today, Mary. We must discuss the ships."

She looked at him expectantly. "I was wondering what will happen. With Tom inheriting the Fielding line as well as being your partner, it seems Stewart is left out in the cold. I feel sorry for him; he struggled so to keep things going. I can't understand why Adrian did such a thing. I suppose his mind was already starting to deteriorate when he made that last will."

"Tom intends to rectify that situation at once. He's decided to stay in Liverpool. He and Stewart will run the Fielding Company together."

"Oh, I'm so glad!"

"Mary . . . I would like to return to New Orleans very soon. There's obviously nothing to be done in regard to Bethany's daughter, and I can't neglect my own business indefinitely."

"I understand," Mary said with a heavy heart. "But I shall miss you dreadfully."

"Come with me," he said promptly. "I can't stand to wait a year or more until you feel you've satisfied society's demand for a mourning period. We can have the captain of the ship marry us on the voyage."

Mary didn't hesitate. "When can we leave?"

Tate was on his feet, sweeping her into his arms, kissing her mouth, laughing joyfully, promising to adore her forever, all at the same time.

A small blue glass dish containing two pale mauve hyacinths adorned Alison's desk in the cramped office she shared with Hagen Rudd near the Pier Head. After glancing at the hyacinths as she entered the room, she looked questioningly at Rudd.

As usual he was already at work by the time she arrived. They had an office boy to deliver and pick up shipping documents, but as yet could not afford to hire clerks, so handled all of the rest of the work themselves.

"Your husband sent them," he said, glaring malevolently at the hyacinths.

She made no comment as she took off her hat and gloves. A sealed envelope lay under the blue glass dish. Sliding the envelope out she opened it and read Stewart's note. "Please have dinner with me tonight. I must see you alone. I'll come to your office at six."

"He's like the rest of his class," Rudd said unexpectedly. "Can't stand the idea that he can't have every damned thing he wants."

Surprised, Alison stared at him. "Why, Mr. Rudd, I've never heard you speak so harshly of anyone, least of all Stewart. He only sent a couple of hyacinths. It's not a flogging offense."

"He wants you back, but he doesn't deserve you. He'll keep after you until you give in. You're a woman; you don't understand how a man's mind works. I know men. I know how they go after a woman they want, pursuing her, wearing her down . . ." He broke off, a dull flush spreading over his face.

Alison sat down at her desk, hoping he would not go on, but he continued, "Better for you to be with a man of your own background, your own class. Somebody who knows what it's like to be hungry and cold. Your husband never wanted for anything in his life. How can he appreciate a woman like you? We're alike, you and me, Alison—"

"Mr. Rudd," Alison interrupted firmly, "perhaps I'd better explain something to you. I'm married to Stewart Fielding and expect to remain so unless he decides otherwise. It doesn't matter to me, one way or the other. I'll never live with him again. I lost respect for him, you see, and I think maybe that's worse than losing love, because sometimes love can be rekindled, but respect . . . well, once it's gone, it's gone for good."

Rudd listened quietly, but she saw the unspoken questions in his expression. He was probably wondering how she could have lost respect for a man who had saved her life.

She was not about to explain, but just so he wouldn't misinterpret her intent, she added, "Besides, I don't think anyone can ever recapture their first real love. My first husband . . . well, I loved him with all the passion and purity of youth, and I can never be that young bride again."

"You're still young," Rudd said gruffly. "Perhaps someday you'll want to marry again."

"No, I don't think so, even if I was free, which I'm not. I'm going to make my own way in the world, Mr. Rudd. I'm going to make a life for my son and myself. With your help I'll make a success of this business, and I'll have no need of a husband."

He made no comment, but the look on his face needed no words. Alison felt sorry for him. She'd known the pain of unrequited love. She added quietly, "But, Mr. Rudd, I do have need of a friend."

"Then I'd like to apply for the position," he said.

She smiled. "So long as your friendship doesn't interfere with your business judgment."

"You're a hard woman, Mrs. Fielding," he said, but he grinned, and his eyes held hers for a long moment. They both knew they had a friend they could trust with their lives, and not many people could say the same.

Bethany felt a slight flutter just below her waist as she climbed into bed, and she pressed her hand to the spot wonderingly. She had quickened. The baby inside her had just made his presence felt.

She lay back on the cool linen pillow and felt a familiar sensation of peace, contentment, a sense that nature had everything under control. It was at once the most mystical, satisfying, calming, thrilling, humbling, uplifting emotion. She savored the moment, knowing instinctively that it marked the end of her ambivalence about this child.

The euphoria faded a little as sadness about her separation from her husband intruded. Oh, she needed Jack to be with her so that they could share this precious moment. She needed him, missed him, loved him . . .

Trying to harden her heart hadn't helped. Telling herself that he had elected to write to Tom and even to Tate, but not to her, had not helped ease her longing. She had irrevocably severed whatever tenuous bonds they had forged with each other. Jack Cutler clearly had no intention of forgiving her for leaving him, or she would have heard from him.

Neither Tate nor Tom discussed what was in the letters that came from New Orleans, and she had not asked, being unwilling to precipitate any discussions about her separation from her husband.

The baby moved again and she began to think about holding her child in her arms, imagining the love they would share. She was drifting off to sleep when the heavy draperies covering the bedroom window parted and a shadowy figure stepped into the room.

She was too startled to cry out. Besides, there was something familiar about the confident stride, the set of the shoulders, the tilt of the head. Surely she was dreaming?

But no, the side of the bed creaked as he sat down.

"Jack! What are you doing here? Oh, dear lord, they'll catch you and hang you—"

"Now, now, no wishful thinking. I'm sorry, my dear wife, but I have no intention of making you a widow a second time, so you might as well get used to the idea."

He tossed a folded newspaper onto the bed. "I came to deliver this."

"A paper? Are you mad? You risked your life to deliver a *paper?*"

He reached over and turned up the gas lamp on her bedside table, then opened the newspaper.

She glanced down at the headline: "Women in Chains, a Shocking Story of Females in the Australian Penal Colony. Episode 1."

Bethany stared at it. "This can't be my story."

Jack grinned. "Actually it is. They just didn't think your title would attract readers. They don't appear to have changed much else."

Although she was excited by the sight of her words in print, her husband's nearness was affecting her even more. Indeed her heart was beating madly. He was watching her closely, and not knowing what else to say, she murmured, "You could have just sent me a copy of the paper."

He shrugged. "I also brought your first payment for the story. The editor sent it to me, but you earned it, and I thought perhaps you could use it."

The baby stirred again, almost as if he knew his father was near. "Oh, Jack, I can't believe you came back to England. The risk . . . You'll hang if they catch you."

He was staring at her face. "You look different. Beautiful as ever, but . . . different."

She longed to creep into his arms, to feel his lips pressed to her hair. Every nerve in her body longed for his touch. She had to curl her hands into fists under the covers in order to keep from reaching for him. "Why did you really come, Jack?"

"To see you, of course. You've been my obsession, my only

need, from the moment I first saw you. Don't you know that by now? I love you with a passion that defies reason."

"You never told me before that you loved me," she whispered.

"Why else do you think I did all the things I did? For the fun of it? Ah, Bethany, Bethany . . ." He fished under the covers for her hand, pulled it free, and held it close to his heart. "I thought I was *showing* you that you are more important to me than anything else on earth, including my own hide."

"But you wouldn't listen to me when I begged you not to fight Louis, and Leona was killed—" Her voice broke.

"Louis wouldn't have let me back away. It had to be settled. You were already gone when I got back that day, spirited aboard some ship by Tom, I suppose. I never had a chance to tell you all that happened that morning."

"Tom told me what happened."

"Tom didn't know everything. He didn't know, for instance, that I *had* to keep my appointment with Louis that morning. In his message to me Louis included the chilling news that if I didn't appear at dawn, then Bourke had agreed to fight the duel in my place."

She thought of the gentle giant who had been with Jack from the earliest days of his escape into the Australian bush. Bourke's first loyalty had always been to Jack, even after he went to work as Louis's bouncer and bodyguard. Bourke would certainly have agreed to serve as a substitute to protect Jack's honor. He would not have been able to bear Louis calling Jack a coward.

Jack went on, "I pleaded with Louis again to call off the duel. I even offered to apologize publicly. I did that for your sake, Bethany. Do you think for a minute Black Jack the highwayman would have hesitated to kill him? But I left that Black Jack behind somewhere after I met you. Even before I went to meet Louis I'd decided not to kill him. If Leona hadn't flung herself between us I would have fired wild, not hitting him, and I doubt he would have hit me, but the requirements of the duel would have been met."

"Why didn't you tell me that, instead of storming off?"

"Because I wanted you to believe in me. I was angry because you didn't trust me not to kill Louis. I wanted you never to doubt that I would do the right thing. You'll never know how much I changed after I met you. I wanted you to see me as the man I'd become, not the man I'd been. I needed your faith in me."

"But Leona was *killed,*" Bethany said.
"She died in my arms," Jack said heavily. "Louis was like a
adman, ready to turn the pistol on himself. His seconds were
restling with him, trying to take the gun away from him. I held
r and she said to me, 'You saved my life, Black Jack, back
ere in the bush after I escaped from the female factory. Now
ve saved yours. I don't suppose I'll go to heaven for it, but
aybe I won't go to hell either.' "
"Oh, poor Leona . . . she was trying to save your life."
There was deep sadness in Jack's voice when he spoke again.
She and I never got along, as you well know. That makes her
crifice even harder to bear. But, Bethany, Leona wouldn't have
anted her death to separate us. While we were married, we
ere happy together, weren't we? You do care for me, just a
tle, don't you?"
All at once the tears she'd held at bay for so long erupted in
scalding flood. "Jack, I love you. I was afraid to tell you be-
use I feared you would lose interest in me. I thought you felt
ly lust."
He laughed softly and gathered her into his arms. "Of course
felt lust. I feel it now. But I feel much, much more."
Their lips met in a kiss that was filled with promise, but after
moment Bethany pulled away. "You shouldn't have come
ck to England! Oh, you'll be caught and hanged, and how will
tell our child that his father died on the end of a rope?"
Every muscle in Jack's body tensed. He placed his hands on
ther side of her head and held her, searching her face with an
tensity that startled her. "A child? Are you sure?"
She nodded, smiling. "Very sure."
"By the saints," he said slowly. "A little Black Jack. Is the
orld ready for one, do you think?"
Then tenderly, reverently, he drew her back into his arms and
eld her. And for Bethany everything was almost, but not quite,
erfect.

Tom offered one of the Fielding ships to take Tate, Mary,
ck, and Bethany back to New Orleans, with a master and a
rew they could trust. While the arrangements were being made,
ck stayed at Riverleigh.
Mary felt happy that Bethany and Jack had reconciled, al-
hough she anxiously counted the days before they left, fearing
e police would arrive at any moment to take him into custody.

She scanned the faces of the servants, wondering if any of them suspected that the guest who had appeared in their midst s mysteriously was a fugitive.

She also was aware that although Bethany had acquired measure of the serenity that often came over women who wer carrying a child, and she was clearly overjoyed to be reunite with her husband, there was still a veil of sadness in her eye Knowing its source, Mary hoped that the arrival of the new bab would help ease Bethany's pain over having lost her daughter

Only two days before they were due to sail, while the me were engaged in last-minute arrangements for sailing, Bethan took a walk through the grounds, enjoying the first hints c spring in the air.

She was halfway across the lawn when she saw Alison runnin toward her. There was frantic haste in her pace and besides, wh was she here in the middle of the morning when normally sh would be in her office?

Shading her eyes with her hand, Bethany watched Alison' approach, feeling icy terror creep along her veins. She must b bringing bad news, why else would she run so frantically? *Oh God, please don't snatch everything away from me again.* They'r coming for Jack. They're going to hang him . . .

"Bethany! Bethany!" Alison called breathlessly. She wave something over her head.

Bethany could only stand waiting, like a statue.

Panting, Alison skidded on the damp grass and thrust an en velope into her hand. "It's from America and it went to Stew art's house, addressed to Mrs. Fielding. He brought it to me Read it for yourself—I'm out of breath."

With shaking fingers Bethany unfolded the letter and bega to read:

Dear Mrs. Fielding,

My name is Wilberforce Prentice, and I took the child, Hope daughter of Bethany and Neil, from your home.

Hope is well, a beautiful little girl, just like her mother. have placed her in the care of Captain Telford of Boston, an he has promised to take her home with him and send this lette to you. I trust that since you cared for Hope as an infant, an since she is a Fielding, you will use every means within you power to reunite her with her mother, or otherwise provide for her, since I am no longer able to do so.

There is no need for me to go into my reasons for taking her away from you, nor shall I explain why I can no longer care for her. The reasons no longer have any meaning. I am sincerely sorry for the distress I caused by my actions.

If you find Bethany, tell her that I loved her and I loved her daughter, and that perhaps I have now found a way to make amends for my sins.

This letter will be accompanied by one from Captain Telford with whom you can make all necessary arrangements.

Forgive me, please, and if you can find it in your heart to allow Hope to speak of me occasionally, I would be most grateful. She knows how much I love her, and she understands why she will never see me again.

Very truly yours,

W. Prentice.

Bethany read it again, then slowly raised her eyes, which were brimming with tears, and looked at Alison, who was smiling and nodding. "Hope's all right! She's coming back to us."

Bethany was aware of birds singing in the newly budded trees, of the sharp tang of brine in the air. She looked toward the ocean and saw a ship, sails billowing in a strong breeze, leave the sanctuary of the river and head out to the open sea. Gulls wheeled over the cliffs, their raucous cries telling that winter was ending. She felt the press of the springy turf beneath her feet, and the playful movements of the child within her womb, and her spirits soared. She tried to speak, but no words would come.

The two women wrapped their arms about each other, each clinging to the one person on earth who completely understood her joy.